DOCTOR DOPE

Cosmos Goldstein called himself an ordinary dentist. The only difference was that he was better at his business than anyone else.

He had no debt. He had key members of the police in his pocket. He had computers at his command that could outwit anything the law could throw against him. Last year he had brought in nine hundred and eighty-eight aircraft, an average of nineteen each week, for a profit of three-point-forty-five billion dollars. And now at last he was about to achieve his greatest ambition: to make more money in a year than General Motors.

But what was good for Cosmos Goldstein wasn't good for America—as the toughest anti-drug squad in the country moved in against the man who had all the weapons and all the answers. . . .

"Robert Coram has been on the dope raids, followed the danger trail and knows the netherworld as only an insider can. Best of all, he's one hell of a writer. He combines a great story with riveting authenticity!"
—William Diehl, author of *Thai Horse*

NARCS II
DRUG WARRIORS

ROBERT CORAM

A SIGNET BOOK

NEW AMERICAN LIBRARY

A DIVISION OF PENGUIN BOOKS USA INC.

PUBLISHER'S NOTE

This book is a work of fiction. Names, characters, places, and incidents either are the product of the author's imagination or are used fictitiously, and any resemblance to actual persons, living or dead, events, or locales is entirely coincidental.

NAL BOOKS ARE AVAILABLE AT QUANTITY DISCOUNTS WHEN USED TO PROMOTE PRODUCTS OR SERVICES. FOR INFORMATION PLEASE WRITE TO PREMIUM MARKETING DIVISION, NEW AMERICAN LIBRARY, 1633 BROADWAY, NEW YORK, NEW YORK 10019.

SIGNET TRADEMARK REG. U.S. PAT. OFF. AND FOREIGN COUNTRIES
REGISTERED TRADEMARK—MARCA REGISTRADA
HECHO EN DRESDEN, TN

SIGNET, SIGNET CLASSIC, MENTOR, ONYX, PLUME, MERIDIAN and NAL BOOKS are published by New American Library, a division of Penguin Books USA Inc., 1633 Broadway, New York, New York 10019

First Printing, July, 1989

1 2 3 4 5 6 7 8 9

PRINTED IN THE UNITED STATES OF AMERICA

To the men and women in the Miami Air Branch of the U.S. Customs Service—brave professionals all.

Prologue

The sun-bronzed young couple snorted almost a quarter of a gram of cocaine before going for a nude swim in the warm shallow waters off Ramrod Key.

Afterward they held hands and laughed like children as they raced through the fine white sand toward a clump of palm trees that stood tall and straight in the quiet summer night. Then they were together, giggling, on a large red beach towel.

Beyond the trees a patch of sea oats stood motionless and stretched down to the point a half-mile away. The sea oats were clearly visible under a full moon that turned the ocean into an endless arc of hammered silver.

The boy noticed none of this. His eyes were on the girl.

She stretched out on the towel and wiggled her hips and dug her heels into the sand, a sea creature trying to become one with the land. The moon caused droplets of water on her body to sparkle as if she were lit by an inner fire.

The girl was aware of his worshipful gaze. Her hand reached for him and she giggled at his sharp gasp of pleasure. They kissed for long moments.

With a throaty giggle she threw her thigh across his body, rose to a sitting position, and maneuvered for a moment, her expression intense. Then she sighed in triumph, tossed her head back, and settled into a long slow rhythm. She smiled at the sky. The moonlight sparkled on her white teeth. The boy groaned, closed his eyes, and reached for her generous tight-skinned hips.

With no warning, no advance rumble of sound, the small single-engine aircraft roared over the young couple. It was below the tops of the palm trees, no more than twenty feet above the beach. The screaming propeller and the deep roar of the powerful engine caused the boy to half-open his eyes in bewilderment. He saw only the young woman, the perspiration of her straining body mingling with seawater and causing her to shine and glow in the moonlight. He smiled as he realized at a distant, almost subconscious level what had happened: a drug smuggler was inbound, traveling low and fast, and carrying maybe a load of nose candy. A fleeting cheer for the pilot crossed his mind before he again closed his eyes and surrendered to the magic being performed by the young woman.

Thirty seconds later the sizzling thunder of jet engines slashed across the soft evening. The second aircraft also was flying low. The two engines were throttled back so the aircraft could maintain position as it tracked straight and true behind the smuggler.

As the jet disappeared over the horizon to the north, its resonating roar echoed and reechoed and faded across the quiet night. And then the only sign of its passage was the oily vapor with the slightly burned odor that settled in its wake.

The young woman stopped moving and was staring, almost transfixed, over her shoulder to the north. The boy opened his eyes, sniffed the jet exhaust, and wrinkled his nose in disgust.

"What the hell was that?" he said.

1

Tension was growing aboard the small jet that sizzled up through the Florida keys at an extremely low altitude.

Mike Love, as PIC on the Cessna Citation, sat in the left seat of the darkened cockpit, long fingers light on the yoke. To his right was Dave, the copilot. On the starboard side, back toward the rear of the aircraft and hidden behind a bewilderingly complex panel of radar and FLIR controls, was J.T., the former Marine officer who was the AIO, the back-seater, the technician. Some back-seaters like to keep the sun shades open so they can see where they are, where they're going, and what's going on. Not J.T. The only world he was interested in was the world of the radar and the FLIR; the world of the red and white and green and amber lights before him. On the panel was a small window containing a set of numbers that changed back and forth between 00.0 and 00.5. The numbers told J.T. that the Citation was very low, somewhere between the surface of the ocean and fifty feet. But J.T. was not worried. Mike Love was the best pilot in the Air Branch; the ice man. Nothing rattled him. Mike, quiet and shy though he was, was king of the hard chargers; the pilot that the most aggressive copilots and back-seaters wanted to fly with, the pilot from whom one could learn the most about catching airborne drug smugglers.

With his left foot, the rangy back-seater pressed the intercom transmit button on the floor and asked, "Where you think he's going?"

9

Mike waited a moment. He never did anything in a hurry. He pressed the transmit button on the wheel and said, "Lauderdale."

"Think this guy is the Lauderdale Express?"

"Fits the profile. Single-engine. Arrives about eight P.M. Headed that direction."

During the past three months the Miami Air Branch had been hit hard by an invasion of single-engine aircraft. For a while the single-engine aircraft had been ignored. Cocaine was thought to be coming in on twins, often turbine-powered twins. The thinking was that there were too many twins loaded with coke to worry about some nickel-and-dime pilot in a single who probably was hauling ten pounds of pot out of the Bahamas. Then there were a few rumbles from Intelligence, little more than rumors, really, about a major cocaine-smuggling operation using single-engine aircraft. So the Air Branch had gone hunting. They scrambled on singles numerous times. Usually they never saw the aircraft. When they did detect and track it, the aircraft invariably broke away and disappeared, always over Fort Lauderdale. They simply disappeared. Now the members of the Air Branch were tense. They believed they were the best pilots in America and that their job was important, that they were keeping dope off the playgrounds and schoolyards of America. And they believed they could defeat any doper, anytime, anyplace. But the single-engine aircraft—they called them the Lauderdale Express—were beating them with embarrassing regularity.

"Whadda you think he's hauling?"

"Coke."

J.T. shook his head in bewilderment. A five-hundred-kilo load of cocaine had a street value of about fifty million dollars. Putting a load that valuable into a single-engine aircraft simply did not make sense.

"Intel was right," Mike said. "Guy in a single-engine, if he's really sharp, can give us more trouble than a turbine-powered twin, especially if he knows our radar and FLIR capabilities."

J.T. wearily rubbed his eyes. The aircraft had been on patrol, flying a racetrack pattern between the island of Providenciales in the Turks and Caicos Islands and the island of Great Inagua in the southern Bahamas, when the radar picked up a target climbing out of South Caicos. A radio check with C3I, the Command, Control, Communications, and Intelligence center in southwest Miami, known by the call sign "Slingshot," revealed that the aircraft was not on a flight plan. And he was showing no lights. He had to be a doper. No one else would be in such a hurry to go to Florida that he would fly a single-engine aircraft six hundred miles over open ocean at night.

Dave, the Citation's copilot, and J.T. were jubilant as they tracked the aircraft, but the only sign of emotion from Mike was when he clenched his jaw several times. Mike Love was a senior pilot in the Miami Air Branch; he was thirty-eight and had been chasing drug smugglers sixteen years. Those years had not caused him to become jaded. He had retained the eagerness and the intensity that he showed the first day on The Job, and he still took it as a personal affront each time he caught someone trying to smuggle a load of dope. In Mike Love's world, everything was black or white. People either were good—that is, they did not use drugs and they had no tolerance for those who did; or they were bad—they smuggled or used drugs. And those he saw as "bad" were exposed to his fearful Jungian shadow, the almost frightening predatory intensity he could bring to bear in his efforts to put them in jail.

The suspect aircraft turned to the northwest, crossed the lower Bahamas, then flew south of Andros. There, in an area referred to by Customs pilots as "the slot" because it represents a hole in radar coverage, the aircraft dropped to a few feet over the water.

The radio call came almost on cue. "Omaha Five Two. Slingshot."

Dave picked up the microphone. "Slingshot. Five Two. Go."

"Five Two, we no longer have radar contact with the target."

"We have him with both eyes," Dave said, referring to the radar and the FLIR. Sometimes a target passing through the slot would disappear for only ten or fifteen minutes. A sharp radar operator could use the last-known course and speed of a target and project where it might pop up into radar coverage. But radar was quirky and could be affected by everything from the weather to the heading of the aircraft. Sometimes the projections did not work, and once the aircraft disappeared in the slot, it was not reacquired.

The pilot crossed Dog Rocks at the northern edge of the Cay Sal Bank and held his course for the southern end of the Florida keys. Every move fit the profile of a doper. The circuitous route and the hazardous low-level flight would only be followed by a bad guy, a stone scammer, a righteous smuggler. This guy was dirty. And the Citation was the perfect high-tech tool to clean him up.

The unusually long nose of the heavily modified Cessna Citation is a not-so-subtle hint as to why the U.S. Customs Service calls the twin-engine jet a "sensor bird." The uninitiated, upon seeing the Pinocchio-like nose of the straight-winged blue-and-white aircraft, might think it almost comical. But those who know the aircraft and its capabilities would think it lethal. Inside the long snout is an impressive array of the latest electronic detection equipment available, including a model of the same Westinghouse radar used on F-16 fighters. The radar is powerful enough to locate a target one and one-half meters square—the approximate frontal area of a MiG-25—from a distance of forty miles. A Litton 72R inertial navigation system is integrated with the radar, as is a FLIR—a Forward-Looking Infra-Red detection system. The Texas Instruments FLIR is a magic piece of equipment that makes one believe in the wonders of technology. Its heat-seeking sensors are mounted in a turret on the belly of the aircraft and can transform thermal images, even at night or in stormy weather, into pictures on a television monitor. In addition to sensor equipment, the Citation's nose contains the black boxes for UHF, HF, VHF, and FM radios.

The Citation is a near-perfect platform for the electronics suite and a near-perfect aircraft for the demanding flight regimens called for in chasing drug smugglers. It has a dash speed of almost four hundred miles an hour, but then, once it catches a fleeing smuggler, speed brakes on each wing can be extended and—shuddering and trembling—the Citation quickly slows to the speed of the smuggler. With flaps and gear extended, the Citation, depending upon its fuel load, can slow to about one hundred miles an hour, slow enough to hold position behind even a single-engine smuggling aircraft. The Citation is America's front-line weapon in the long-running war on drugs. If the Citation can't detect and track an airborne drug smuggler, nothing can.

Tension continued to grow aboard the Citation. The intercom and radio transmissions became crisper. Dave and J.T. no longer joked. The atmosphere was all business.

Mike pressed the transmit button. "Dave, keep Slingshot updated. Confirm that BSO is on alert. And call Home Plate on company and make sure the 'Hawk crew has been given a heads-up."

Translated, Mike's instructions were for the copilot to make sure the radar operators at C3I knew what was going on, that the Broward Sheriff's Office knew a smuggler was headed in their direction, and that the Customs Blackhawk crew had been notified on the Customs FM radio.

Dave nodded. Everything was done. But Mike was a perfectionist. Dave looked out the window, looked at his chart, and asked, "Is that Big Pine Key?"

"Yes."

Dave opened a notebook and found the code name for Big Pine. He turned the radio transmitter switch to a preset UHF frequency.

"Slingshot. Omaha Five Two," he radioed. The alacrity with which Slingshot had told him the bogey had been lost in the slot indicated that a Customs specialist, not one of the Coast Guard guys, was working the radar. He was right. In the darkened interior of C3I, a sprawling but innocuous building located on the northeastern section of the old Navy blimp base in southwest Miami, a Customs officer was watching a radar screen that showed the Citation's discrete transponder code, the secret "spirit code," as it raced north through the Florida keys. Any Customs aircraft using the Omaha call sign was on a tactical mission; either it was trolling for a drug smuggler or it was in hot pursuit of a smuggler. When flying tactical, Customs aircraft were exempt from some FAA regulations. Under certain conditions, if cleared with FAA officials, Customs could fly below prescribed altitudes with no navigation or clearance lights, violate a TCA, fly in extremely close proximity to a suspect aircraft, and ignore speed restrictions in congested areas.

But FAA people grew anxious every time they looked at a radar screen and saw the distinctive transponder code of a Customs aircraft. Even if Customs was flying low over the open ocean, the FAA dweebs got their underwear in a wad. And tonight the Citation was headed straight for Miami's high-density airspace. The Citation's course would take it through the approach pattern being used by commercial jets landing at the Miami International Airport.

"Omaha Five Two, Slingshot," responded the Customs officer.

"Slingshot, we're approaching papa niner."

"Five Two. Slingshot. That's affirm. Radar shows you three nautical south of papa niner. Your target is one-point-two miles ahead."

Dave turned to Mike. "Cudjoe's up," he said.

Mike nodded. Miami radar did not reach this far south. But a radar balloon tethered at Cudjoe Key could, depending upon the altitude at which it was flying, provide radar coverage throughout the Florida keys. Most ground-based radar lose low-flying targets about twenty miles from the station when the targets fly under the "look-up" angle of the radar. The radar balloons have a "look-down" aspect designed to fill the holes in coverage that are a natural part of land-based radar. A second balloon, called the Cape, is at Patrick Air Force Base in central Florida; a third, Cariball, is tethered near Freeport in the Bahamas; and the fourth is in the Bahamas at the southern end of the Exumas. The balloons have the theoretical potential of tracking low-altitude targets for almost two hundred miles out to sea.

Drug smugglers are aware of the balloons' potential and a bit frightened of being detected by these high-flying radar platforms. Once when the balloon at Cudjoe broke its mooring cable, a smuggler came upon it and decided to wreak his own retribution. The helium-filled balloon had descended to near sea level during the cool of the night and was dragging its cable in the water. The gleeful smuggler tied the cable to the stern of his boat and slowly began making his way toward the Bahamas. The sun came up, heated and expanded the helium, and, before the smuggler was aware of what was going on, lifted his boat from the surface. A northeast breeze arose in midmorning and blew the balloon, and the dangling smuggler, back toward the Florida keys, where he was rescued by the Coast Guard.

"Omaha Five Two. Slingshot."

"Slingshot. Five Two. Go."

"Five Two, FAA advises exercise extreme caution approaching Miami area. Miami is in a push. Traffic landing to the west. You'll be mixing with heavy metal."

Before Dave could respond, Mike broke into the conversation. His voice was angry. "Slingshot, advise the FAA we'll be well below that traffic."

Mike had no patience with FAA nonsense when he was chasing a doper; not when four bad guys had eluded him in the past six days. The intercepts and the tracking in each case had been faultless, but when the dopers arrived over Fort Lauderdale they began performing abrupt and rapid changes in direction and then disappeared. Tonight's target would not escape. Mike would glue himself to the tail of the smuggler and, no matter what the guy did, stick with him.

The FAA supervisor who was the liaison between the Miami Air Route Traffic Control Center and C3I looked at the Customs radar operator in amazement. "Below the traffic. Is he in a boat or an airplane?"

The Customs specialist shrugged, leaned closer to the radar screen, and deadpanned, "He's leaving a wake."

The supervisor leaned over the screen. "His mode C must be inop. There's no altitude readout. It's showing nothing but zeros."

The supervisor pulled back and looked at the Customs radar operator. His eyes widened in amazement as he realized what was going on. "He's below fifty feet," he said incredulously. "Jesus Christ! You guys are out there with a seven-and-a-half-million-dollar aircraft and the pilot is so low over the water we can't get an altitude readout."

"And at night," the Customs officer added.

"Why?"

"That's where the bad guy is."

The supervisor whinnied in despair and walked away.

An hour and ten minutes later Mike Love straightened in the seat and wiped his palms on his khaki pants. Perhaps it was because of the humidity, perhaps because the tech rep had not tweaked the FLIR; whatever the reason, the FLIR picture was poor tonight. Mike had closed to within a quarter-mile of the target, but the picture still was hazy.

The Citation was abeam Miami and the FAA supervisor was hopping up and down in distress. The pilot of the unidentified aircraft had climbed several thousand feet in an attempt to hide among the hundreds of aircraft entering, leaving, and transiting the Miami TCA. There was no way to know his altitude. Close behind him, but staying under the TCA, was the Customs jet.

A Delta pilot carrying a full load of passengers aboard a 767 was on his final approach to the Miami airport when he saw the doper, lights out, silhouetted against the ocean. He called to complain but, in the middle of his transmission, paused. The Citation with its straight wings and distinctive nose was below him, hot on the tail of the first aircraft.

"Ah, Miami tower, we received no advisory on this single-engine aircraft that just crossed our flight path." He paused and then added in a voice dripping with sarcasm, "This is an international airport?"

The FAA supervisor heard the Delta transmission and scurried across the room. "Keep your guy under the TCA," he said sternly.

Mike was not concerned. The big jet was several thousand feet above him. The important thing was that Lauderdale was ahead and the bad guy was about to make his move. Mike had to be prepared. The Citation's radar covered a target only if it remained with a cone of one hundred and twenty degrees. With only a quarter-mile between the Citation and the target, the cone was narrow.

Mike looked at the small repeater screens in the cockpit. He grimaced and shook his head. "How's your picture back there?" he asked J.T.

"Not good. I'm going to manual." J.T. unslaved the FLIR from the radar, then carefully adjusted the gray scale. He switched from black hot to white hot and back again. Nothing worked. He rested his fingers atop the polished trackball that controlled the direction of the FLIR sensors. His eyes were locked on the fuzzy image of the single-engine aircraft on the screen. He tickled the trackball lightly, keeping the target in the middle of the screen.

Port Everglades was to the left, the four strobe-lighted stacks of Florida Power and Light clearly visible, when the smuggler suddenly made an abrupt ninety-degree turn to the west.

"He's approaching thirty degrees," J.T. warned. His voice had a slight edge as he notified Mike the suspect was approaching the edge of the radar's cone of coverage and entering an area from which he could easily break lock.

A number on the right side of the radar screen rapidly unwound from 2.5 to 2 and then through 1.5 to 1.

"Descending," J.T. warned, fingertips fast on the trackball. On the Citation's belly the FLIR pod turned so the sensors could continue to track the smuggler.

Mike turned and descended. At one thousand feet he punched in the autopilot. It would ensure he did not descend below a thousand feet. Aircraft turns could be controlled with a small dial, and Mike could watch for other aircraft.

Dave, his eyes roaming outside the cockpit, was talking constantly on the radio. Slingshot had given him a discrete UHF frequency to advise the tower at Fort Lauderdale's International Airport that he was transiting the airport control zone. He used the discrete UHF, rather than conventional VHF, to prevent the smuggler, who could have been monitoring the tower, from overhearing him. He was talking to Slingshot on "high fox," or high-frequency radio. And he was talking to Home Plate, the Air Branch, on an FM freq.

The smuggler flew west, tracking along the Seventeenth Street Causeway until it ended at Highway 1, then continuing west along State Road 84. At I-95, about three and a half miles after turning west, the target suddenly made another ninety-degree turn, this one to the north.

Mike cursed as he turned the heading dial. The bad guy had almost exceeded the limits of radar coverage. He had almost broken the radar lock.

"Descending. He's descending," J.T. warned, eyes on the screen, fingers flicking the trackball. He was in a high-stakes video game with a fifty-million-dollar load of cocaine for the winner.

The readout on the radar screen indicated the target was at five hundred feet, tracking north along I-95.

"I still got you, you son of a bitch," Mike muttered into his beard.

The silhouette of the target aircraft, a dark fleeting shadow, could be seen against the backdrop of automobile lights on I-95.

Mike, who was listening to the frenetic static-filled radio conversations, suddenly turned to Dave and shook his head. "Can you believe that shit?" he asked.

Slingshot had just told Dave that the Blackhawk helicopter on standby had scrambled on another target and would not be available to assist them.

"Ask them where the other 'Hawk is," Mike said.

"Alpha two," came the answer. Dave quickly flicked through his code book.

"Treasure Cay," he told Mike in disbelief. "I didn't know we had a deal going out there tonight."

"Son of a bitch," Mike muttered. But he didn't have time to wonder why the second Blackhawk was down in the Bahamas. The smuggler was approaching Executive Airport.

Again Dave had to use a discrete UHF frequency to advise the tower he was approaching their control zone at a low altitude.

"Unable that," responded the tower operator. "Traffic does not permit. And we're too busy to work you on uniform. Come up on victor." The tower operator wanted the Customs crew to switch from the discrete UHF frequency to a standard VHF frequency.

Mike flicked his finger at Dave, indicating he would handle the radio transmission. "Are you talking with the aircraft that just entered your control zone from the south? He's below pattern altitude."

The tower operator paused. "Negative," he said.

"That's my target. I'm coming through."

"I repeat. Negative on transit. Come up on victor."

Mike pressed the transmit button. His voice turned hard. "This is an Omaha aircraft. We represent the presidential task force on narcotics interdiction. Unless you want to explain to a Senate investigating committee why you prevented us from chasing a target and why you compromised a major investigation, you better clear out that traffic. And stay on uniform."

J.T.'s eyes widened. He leaned from behind his panel and looked toward the cockpit in amazement. Senate investigating committee?

After a thirty-second pause the chastened controller was back on the air. "Sir, if you proceed, it will be at pilot's discretion. And I'm contacting your agency for your name. Be advised, paperwork will be coming down regarding this incident."

Mike leaned over the microphone as if trying to get closer to the controller. His voice grated through clenched teeth. "Hang around. I'll come to the tower and give you my name. And I'll stick that paperwork where it belongs."

The smuggler prevented what could have been a continued exchange between Mike and the controller when he turned ninety degrees—again to the west—and tracked along Commercial Boulevard.

Mike turned the heading control dial. He glanced at the radar and the FLIR. The small single-engine aircraft remained in the middle of the picture.

Mike uttered a short choppy laugh. "Go ahead, slimeball, show me your best shot," he muttered toward the target.

"I don't like this," J.T. said. "We could lose him any minute."

Mike knew what J.T. meant. One of the problems with the radar, as F-16 pilots had discovered during Red Flag exercises when they chased small jets from the Aggressor Squadron, was that targets flying low over an expressway had a tendency to break lock suddenly. It had something to do with the harmonics effect of the doppler radar when its RF energy hit the chain-link fences along a road and caused the electronics equivalent of strobing. "Hold him tight on the FLIR," Mike said.

The smuggler reached the Florida Turnpike and

snapped to the right, flew north for about thirty seconds, and then abruptly pulled power and threw the small aircraft into a tight descending 180-degree turn. Now it was no more than a hundred feet above the Turnpike and traveling south at about eighty miles an hour. When the smuggler again reached Commercial Boulevard, he turned right and headed west, staying very low and holding his speed to about eighty.

Mike stayed with the smuggler during the first turn. But when the smuggler pulled power and reversed course, the aircraft jumped outside the radar's zone of coverage and broke lock. The radar went into its search mode and the screen suddenly was covered with dozens of targets. J.T. frantically flicked the trackball, trying to keep the doper on the FLIR, but the FLIR turret bounced against the stop before Mike could turn south. Now the target was lost on both radar and FLIR.

The sky over Fort Lauderdale, even with the radar on ten-mile range, was a veritable snowstorm of targets. J.T.'s eyes were intent on the screen and his fingers moved quickly and surely over the radar controls. His thumb moved the elevation of the radar antenna up and down, then fell into the hollow ringed button that controlled the acquisition symbols. His forefinger squeezed the trigger to lock a target on radar. He quickly rejected each target and moved to another as the radar symbology showed the speed and altitude of the new target bore no resemblance to the speed and altitude of the smuggler.

The Citation continued its smooth coordinated turns as Mike and Dave stared out of the cockpit, searching for the smuggler, while J.T. sought to reacquire him on radar.

After several minutes, J.T. sighed in defeat and said, "I lost him."

Mike continued the slow turns, sweeping back and forth through the darkness, senses finely tuned as he tried to think like a doper. What had the guy done? What would a doper do once he broke lock? Where would he go? What did the doper do after he made the sudden turn south?

"Where the hell could he go?" Mike said.

Dave shook his head, staring out the window for a dark shape, watching for a racing shadow as it crossed over a road or was silhouetted against a lighted area.

J.T. raised his head from the scope. Even in the surrealistic glow of the lights from the radar and FLIR controls, his disappointment was clear. He pressed the intercom transmit button with his left foot and spoke into the boom microphone against his mouth. "We lost him. He disappeared."

Mike looked out the window. He was flying south. To his left were the lights of Fort Lauderdale. To his right were a few lights and then the dark abyss of western Broward County; the Everglades. Where could the guy have gone?

"Keep looking?" he said.

J.T. shrugged. Being a back-seater is as much an art as it is a science. He knew, with the intuitive gut feeling that all good back-seaters have, that the smuggler had escaped.

"Mike, he's disappeared. We lost him."

Mike swung in wider circles, eyes roaming outside the cockpit and then back to the radar.

"Anything?" he asked over the radio.

J.T. again adjusted the radar controls. He flicked the azimuth scan switch from plus or minus ten to plus or minus thirty to plus or minus sixty. He moved the elevation control from a one-bar scan to a four-bar scan, and the range-control dial from ten miles up to eighty miles. He turned the mode switch through all the positions. Nothing. He shook his head. "He disappeared."

"An airplane can't just disappear."

"Mike, he's gone."

"Goddammit, not again." Mike looked out the window. "Not again."

2

Nick Brown, commander of the narcotics squad in the Broward County Sheriff's Office, sat in his new glass-enclosed office on the tenth floor of Trade Center South, the complex of office buildings at the southwest corner of the intersection formed by Cypress Creek Road and I-95 in Fort Lauderdale. The office, by police standards, was very posh. Blue-gray carpet covered the floor. The walls were white. Street narcs worked in a large, open bullpen, while sergeants and superior officers had private offices with windows and a view. This was the third office the narcs had occupied in the past eighteen months, and each move was into a building owned by a real-estate wheeler-dealer who was one of the sheriff's major campaign contributors.

Nick was the senior officer on the tenth floor but had the most Spartan office of all; even his sergeants had more memorabilia, plaques, flags, pictures, and maps on their walls. Nick's scarred and battered desk was bare except for a telephone and a small sign that said "So Many Colombians . . . So Little Time." A picture of his wife and two children was on the credenza. On the wall was a picture of Elmer, his pit bull, and several fuzzy pictures of a stern and stocky Nick Brown standing with smiling narcotics officers, all posing in front of various aircraft filled with marijuana and cocaine. But there was no picture of Nick posing with Don Johnson, star of the TV series *Miami Vice*.

Nick probably was the only supervisor of a narcotics squad within two hundred miles of Miami who did not have a picture on his wall of the long-haired blond actor. Johnson, who was as friendly toward cops as he was unfriendly toward the public, went out of his way to have photographs taken with local cops each time a sequence for his program was shot in a new location. It seemed at times as if every narc in south Florida, down to guys who were five minutes out of the academy, had photographs taken with Don Johnson. Then the cops thought they had to talk and dress and act like Johnson. They bought wardrobes of one hundred percent cotton; lots of colored T-shirts, white suits, and fruity shoes. They tousled their hair, bought cars they couldn't afford, dated local actresses, and began acting like caped crusaders. Nick called them "TV cops." Johnson had shot a half-dozen sequences in Lauderdale and Nick had never visited the set. He turned down every invitation because he thought Johnson was a bad influence on law enforcement in general and narcotics officers in particular.

Nick was bone-weary; working for Sheriff Hiram Turnipseed would sap the energy of a ferret. He leaned back in his creaky chair—it was a secretary's chair with no arms—propped his highly shined cowboy boots atop the desk, crossed his legs, then pulled slowly at his blond mustache as he stared at the smiling young man coming through the door.

Lance Cunningham wore scuffed boat shoes, faded cut-off jeans, and a T-shirt with a picture of a rampaging fire-breathing bull and the caption "Here's the Beef." Cunningham was Nick's star undercover agent, a man who had more ongoing undercover cases and more felony arrests than any other three agents combined.

Most young cops go through a bulletproof phase, a time when they consider themselves invincible. A few years' experience usually is enough to change that syndrome, to bring a measure of prudence into a cop's professional life. If outnumbered or outgunned, he does whatever it takes for him to live and fight another day. Not so with Lance. He would take on a buzz saw and laugh while he was doing it. He sought out high-stakes confrontations; he loved to go up against two or three guys at once, and he was not afraid of the devil himself. He *was* invincible. The bad guy had not been born who could outsmart him and the crook did not live who could beat him.

Nick shook his head as he remembered his most recent effort to point Lance toward a more responsible life-style. A month earlier he and his wife had taken the young undercover agent to church. Nick was an usher and his wife sang in the choir, so when they arrived, they simply pointed Lance toward a pew. Nick was assisting in taking up the collection when he heard a loud wheezing noise coming from the pew where Lance was sitting. He could hear it halfway across the church. Lance was sitting there bent over in the pew, shoulders heaving in emotion, a rasping noise coming from his mouth. People on either side of the agent were sidling down the pew to distance themselves from this person. Nick tried unsuccessfully to catch Lance's eye. Then, when Nick leaned over and nudged him with the collection plate, the agent broke into loud sobs. He reached down and took his backup pistol from the ankle holster and waved it about his head, causing not only people on the same pew but also those in surrounding pews to murmur in panic and scoot away. A rustle of alarm went through the congregation when Lance stood up, face contorted, head rolling about, and looked at Nick. He ignored Nick's warning stare and, in a breaking voice, said, "I've been touched by the power. I want to give up my life of crime. Will you help me?" He dropped his pistol in the collection plate and clutched Nick about the shoulders. Church members smiled in relief. The Almighty was at work. A wayward sheep, perhaps even a homicidal maniac, had been brought into the fold. Nick, aware of all the eyes on him, patted Lance on the shoulder, smiled nervously, and whispered, "I'm gonna kick your ass."

Lance was a rangy, almost slender guy, handsome, and stood a little under six feet. His closely cropped dark hair made him appear even younger than his twenty-eight years. He would have been just another handsome guy if it were not for his smile. People always noticed his pirate's smile; it was a maniacal go-to-hell smile permanently pasted across his tanned face. The smile was so broad that he constantly appeared on the verge of breaking into uncontrollable laughter. The smile, topped by a pair of dark eyes that danced and sparkled, caused people to wonder if he were only visiting earth temporarily. There was little that Lance took seriously. For instance, much of his time riding around Fort Lauderdale was spent looking for Central Cuban Dispatch—CCD, he called it. Lance believed that Fidel Castro was behind a plot to have old cars and trucks break down and snarl traffic on the streets of Fort Lauderdale. Each time he found a Hispanic driving a vehicle that had died on the street, he demanded to know the location of CCD; he thought it might be a warehouse somewhere near I-95.

When Lance bounced into Nick's office, he waved in excitement. He worshiped Nick. "Hey, *jefe*, you wanna try for the question of the week?" he asked. Without waiting for an answer, he continued, "I thought so. The question of the week is this: If you were on the equator making love to an Italian woman, where would you be?"

Lance stopped in front of Nick's desk and held his arms spread, palms up, grinning, waiting. Nick shrugged. He had not quite figured out how to deal with Lance's zany side. The young agent would not be ignored. If Nick reacted strongly, Lance would press even harder. Nick had more or less settled on a policy of simply letting Lance get it out of his system and to show as little reaction as possible.

"In equatorial guinea," Lance said triumphantly. He pointed his finger at Nick in mock sternness. "You didn't know the answer to the question of the week. No prize for you. No bubble gum today."

Nick nodded toward one of the straight-backed wooden chairs facing his desk. "Sit down."

Lance held up his hand. "Wait a minute. You get one more chance. What do eggs Benedict and blow-jobs have in common?"

"What?"

"You can't get either at home."

"Sit."

Lance plopped into the chair. But then, before Nick could say anything, Lance tilted his head and turned from left to right as he sniffed the air. He looked at Nick and leaned forward, sniffing rapidly and loudly.

"You're wearing that throw-me-down-and-fuck-me shaving lotion again," he said. He waggled a forefinger at Nick, shook his head, and rolled his eyes. He held his hand toward Nick, wrist limp, and said, "Ohhhh, you devil, you."

Nick flushed. Lance had finally gotten to him. "Shut up and listen," he ordered. Nick was not reticent in expressing his homophobia. It unnerved him to have Lance go into his mincing routine, especially in public, as he was wont to do.

"Act civilized," Nick said. "This person you're meeting doesn't know you're crazy as a Gadarene swine. Try to be professional. Listen to what she has to say. You got that?"

"Gadarene swine? I'm crazy as a Gadarene swine? What the fuck does that mean? I don't know what that means. If you said I was crazy as a shithouse rat, that I would understand. What's a Gadarene swine?"

Nick was losing his patience. His jaw clamped down hard and he stared up at Lance. Then Lance clutched his heart and rolled his eyes in mock anguish. "My leader thinks I need counseling."

"Your leader thinks you ain't seen the ball since kickoff."

"Okay, tell me her name again."

Nick looked over the pointed toes of his cowboy boots. "I told you," he said slowly. "Kimberly McBride. Our new senior intelligence analyst. Came from DEA.

Knows all that computer stuff. She's come up with some information that, if she's right, may result in the biggest case we've ever handled; bigger than the Bimini deal." He paused and then added, with only the slightest touch of irony, "That should please the sheriff."

But Lance did not hear. A shadow had flitted across his face when Nick mentioned Bimini. The Bimini investigation a year earlier had resulted in the savage mutilation of a young female undercover agent who was still undergoing psychiatric treatment and physical therapy.

"Boss, she won't be working the street, will she?" Lance was no longer smiling.

"Nope. She sticks with her computers and the telephone and papers."

"She ever been a street cop?" Like most cops, Lance was contemptuous of anyone in police work who was not a sworn law-enforcement officer, anyone who had not made felony arrests, anyone who had not known the adrenaline rush and the fear and sweat that are part of pulling a weapon and going up against law-breakers who had both superior numbers and superior firepower.

"I told you she came out of DEA. She's a federal agent who went through Quantico. She worked Intelligence in Miami before I hired her about a month ago."

"Another bull dyke," Lance mumbled. The ringing of the telephone interrupted the conversation. Nick stretched, trying to reach the phone without taking his feet off the desk. But his stomach and the muscularity of his arms and shoulders prevented him from having the reach. With a sigh, he lifted his boots and placed them on the floor, careful not to scuff them, then slid his chair closer to his desk.

"Yes," he said as he picked up the telephone. He pulled at his mustache.

"Send her in," he said. He glanced briefly at Lance, and his eyes, the cold impassive eyes of a longtime cop, warned the young officer. He looked up at the slender blonde woman who entered the office and closed the door. She carried a four-inch-thick manila folder in one hand and a cigarette in the other. Nick waved toward her and said, "Officer Cunningham, this is Officer McBride. You two will be working together."

"Kimberly McBride," the woman said. Her voice was soft. She placed the file on Nick's desk and stuck her hand toward Lance. He stood, shook hands, said, "Lance Cunningham," and sat down.

Kimberly McBride's glance lingered on Lance for a moment. She was puzzled. Every cop in south Florida had heard of Cunningham and his exploits. She had expected someone who stood about six-feet-six, weighed in at two hundred and fifty pounds, and had blood dripping from his fangs. But except for his maniacal grin, this guy seemed reasonably civilized.

Lance, in turn, as would any undercover cop whose life can depend upon a quick and accurate assessment of a stranger, unconsciously cataloged the woman: five-feet-seven, slender, maybe a hundred and ten pounds, brown eyes, short blond hair, something of the patrician about her. Unlike most female police officers, she did not wear trousers. She wore a tailored green suit. Nice legs. Around her neck were five necklaces, each having a different-colored stone and each hanging at a different level. The topmost stone—it appeared to be some sort of smoky quartz—was tight around her neck, almost like a choker, and the lowest stone, an amethyst, was barely above her waist. Her smile was neither cold nor coquettish; it was almost diffident; the smile of an insecure person who wants to be liked.

"How old are you?" Lance asked.

Nick shot him a warning glance. Kimberly's eyebrows rose in surprise. She took a drag off her cigarette, sat down, and said, "Thirty-two. Why?"

Lance shrugged. An older woman. She had more time on The Job than he did.

"Okay, let's do it," Nick said. "McBride, I want you to give Cunningham a quick overview of what you've found. You can brief him more fully later. Just bring him up to speed so we can make a decision here today."

Lance reached out and put his hand on Kimberly's left arm. "Don't use any big words. I'm a street cop," he said.

She smiled. "I'll keep that in mind."

"Do you have an ashtray?" she asked Nick.

"Somewhere," he mumbled, pulling open the bottom drawer of his desk. He rummaged around for a moment, then pulled out a large white ashtray upon which was written "Buccaneer Pointe—Bimini." He pushed it toward her, leaned back, and placed his boots atop the desk.

Lance stared at the ashtray as Kimberly opened the file folder. She took a deep drag from her cigarette, blew out the smoke, and on the next breath took another deep drag.

"When I was at DEA, a CI came to me with certain information," she began. "Eighteen months ago he was flying an aircraft that crashed on the Turnpike. Engine failure. The aircraft was carrying five hundred keys of cocaine. The pilot was convicted and served less than a year on a five-year sentence. He was released early because he had sustained serious injuries in the crash—compound fracture of one leg, cracked ribs, and a back injury that will plague him the rest of his life. It caused him excruciating pain and required frequent medical attention."

"There is a God," Lance interrupted.

Kimberly took a deep drag from her cigarette, blew out the smoke, and took another deep drag before continuing.

"The confidential informant believed that the person for whom he worked did not show the proper concern. He said his boss, a man named Cosmos Goldstein . . ." She glanced at Lance.

He shrugged. "Never heard of him."

She puffed on her cigarette. ". . . had provided a mediocre lawyer who came up with a mediocre defense, and who, contrary to what he had been told, would not pay for the ongoing medical expenses."

"My heart is breaking," Lance interrupted. "If he wanted to be around nice people, he should have gone into some other line of work. He deserves whatever he got."

Kimberly snuffed out her cigarette. She did not simply extinguish it; she pressed it down tightly and guided it around the large ashtray several times in one direction, and then in the other. She tamped it, flicked it, and again pressed down tightly and dragged it around the ashtray. She used the mangled butt to push the ashes into a pile in the middle of the ashtray, then reluctantly released it and immediately reached into her pocket, pulled out a pack of menthol lights, and fired up another.

Lance looked at her in astonishment. "Boss, you mind if I open the door? This smoke is getting to me."

"Sorry," Kimberly said. She puffed deeply as Lance walked to the door. He returned and moved his chair several feet farther away from her before he sat down.

"DEA never heard of Cosmos Goldstein, and my superiors there took somewhat the same position you took toward my CI. They figured he got what he deserved," Kimberly said. "But three weeks ago, right after I came here, he began giving me substantive information about Goldstein and his smuggling operation." She puffed on the cigarette. "I thought at the time it was because his animosity toward his former employer had overcome his fear. I was wrong. His fear had increased. He was doing it because he was afraid something might happen to him."

Lance's eyebrows rose in an unasked question.

"He died last week," Kimberly said. She paused. "He walked into a propeller." She looked out the window.

Lance's eyes widened. "That was your CI? Guys at the airport told me about that. Happened late one night."

Kimberly nodded. She was still looking out the window. "A pilot with four thousand hours of flying time walked into a propeller."

"That bothers you?"

Kimberly did not respond.

"You think he was thrown into the prop?"

She winced and again did not answer.

"Got any proof?"

"None whatsoever. But I find it hard to believe that a middle-aged guy with that much time in an aircraft would be so careless."

"Does this Goldstein guy live in Broward County?" Lance asked.

"Yes."

"Should be real easy to find. There can't be more than four hundred and ninety-eight Goldsteins in the Lauderdale phone book."

"This one's a dentist. Dr. Cosmos Goldstein."

"A Jewish doper dentist already." Lance laughed. "I don't believe this."

Kimberly pointed to her file. "The record shows that a Cosmos Goldstein of Fort Lauderdale was graduated from the Emory University School of Dentistry in Atlanta three years ago. Graduated with honors from the last class that went through before they closed the undergraduate part of the dental school. And, according to my CI, he began dealing coke when he was at Emory; supplied the entire campus. If you know Emory, that tells you he was a major dealer. The student body there is wealthy and spends a great deal of money on drugs. Goldstein says his goal in life is to make as much money in a year as General Motors makes in a year, and to do it before he is thirty."

"How old is he?" Lance asked.

"Twenty-eight," Kimberly said.

"Jesus, the same age I am, and he's trying to make more money than General Motors. This is my kind of guy. He must have a set of balls that won't fit in a washtub."

Nick sliced his eyes toward Lance. He rarely used profanity, and he never used profanity in the presence of a woman. "Go ahead, McBride," he said.

She nodded and continued. "Using information provided by the CI, information about Goldstein's corpo-
rate structure, and cross-checking that with the FAA
and various data banks, I've determined that Goldstein
owns, directly or through various shell companies, at
least five single-engine aircraft that he uses to smuggle
cocaine into Broward County."

"Single-engine?" Lance interrupted. The narcotics
squad had been alerted last night after Customs chased
a doper from down south to Broward County. The
bad guy beat Customs. Afterward, Lance's friend Mike
Love had called and said it was the fifth smuggler in
six days he had lost over Lauderdale. And all of the
smugglers were driving single-engine aircraft.

Kimberly puffed on her cigarette. Her eyes were
intense. She held up a finger. "Wait. I can identify
five. But I have reason to believe, and I'll know within
a few days, that the actual number may be twice that.
Perhaps even more."

Lance's eyebrows rose in mocking disbelief.

Kimberly paused. "You have to think in a strategic
sense. Don't dismiss him as penny-ante because he
uses single-engine aircraft. That's the beauty of what
he's doing." She puffed on her cigarette, then placed
it in the ashtray. In her intensity, she held out both
hands toward Lance. "Think about it. This guy is no
stereotypical doper; no long-haired, violence-prone crook
who happened to drift into smuggling because of the
money. He's bright, very bright; probably a nice guy. I
bet his neighbors love him."

"Yeah, sure they do. And they'll miss him when I
put his picture on a milk carton."

Kimberly was not deterred. "For the sake of argument, say he has ten aircraft. Two are down for maintenance at any given time. So he has eight flying. Each
carries about five hundred keys. My assumption is
that he works the aircraft pretty hard; airplanes don't
make money sitting on the ramp. But if each aircraft
flies only one load a week, and I'm quite sure it's
more, that's . . . what? four thousand keys a week?

About nine thousand pounds that this one individual is
bringing into Broward County."

Lance snorted. He knew the underbelly of Lauderdale better than any local, state, or federal narc. He
had informants from the street level to the penthouse
level. Lauderdale was his town; his turf. He had never
heard of a doper, a Jewish doper, for God's sake,
named Cosmos Goldstein. And he could not accept that
a guy he had never heard of was moving eight loads a
week into Broward County. The logistics of such a
smuggling operation would be massive. It would take
a genius to manage such an organization.

Nick pulled at his mustache and thought about what
Kimberly had said. In the narcotics world, truth always is stranger than fiction. He had seen and heard
and experienced things that Hollywood would have
dismissed as too bizarre or too implausible for a movie
script. Five years ago and he would have dismissed this
as a comic-book story; a fantasy. But then, he could
remember when fifty pounds of marijuana was a typical seizure and how cops laughed when they first heard
of thousand-pound loads. He could remember when
several ounces of cocaine was a typical seizure and a
kilo was a big deal. Now Broward narcs were regularly
knocking off thirty-thousand-pound loads of marijuana
and thousand-pound loads of cocaine. If an agent took
off a load of only a hundred keys of coke, the first
question was, "Where is the rest of the load?" It was a
given that another four hundred keys—almost nine
hundred pounds—had gone somewhere else. Now, perhaps once again the dopers were straining the limits of
credulity. Maybe there was a doper out there bringing
in as much coke as McBride said.

Lance leaned toward Kimberly. "How reliable is
your CI?" he demanded. He paused and corrected
himself: ". . . was your CI?"

Kimberly tapped the thick folder. "Everything I've
been able to check out, and it hasn't been that much,
was one hundred percent accurate. He knew what he
was talking about. The paper trail Goldstein is leaving
is very sketchy. He's smart and he's hidden behind

multiple layers of paperwork. I'm running up against lots of dead ends. But a group this size has to leave signs. I'll find them."

"Real estate?" Nick injected.

"The CI told me Goldstein owned several homes in western Broward County. And some commercial property. I'm looking. But most of his assets appear to be hidden in offshore banks. I'm developing an overview and then I'll come up with a strategic plan." She puffed on her cigarette and tapped the folder with an extended forefinger. "Computer printouts."

"Where does this guy work out of? Who are his suppliers? Where does he base his aircraft? There are not enough airports in Broward County to hide a couple of dozen working aircraft."

Kimberly smiled. "As I said, he's smart. He keeps the aircraft down on South Caicos in the Turks and Caicos Islands. That's about five hundred and fifty nautical miles southeast of here."

Lance rolled his eyes. He knew the location of the Turks and Caicos Islands.

"Some of his aircraft, the multi-engine aircraft, fly back and forth to Colombia and never come to the States," Kimberly continued. "All they do is bring cocaine and grass to South Caicos. The other part of the fleet, the single-engines, haul cocaine from South Caicos to Broward County."

She shrugged. "I don't know how he works it on this end. I haven't made any progress at all there. The CI would only talk about South Caicos." She paused and looked at the floor. "He was about to talk about this end when he . . . when he died."

"Okay, so for right now forget how he's moving tons of coke a week through Lauderdale," Lance said. "We have to go to his source. How can an operation that size exist on an island that small without the knowledge of the locals?

"It can't," Lance said, answering his own question. "If this Goldstein is doing half of what you say he's doing, he owns that island. Everybody there is dirty."

"Everyone?" Kimberly asked. She looked up and puffed on her cigarette.

"Everybody," Lance said emphatically. The intelligence analyst had just demonstrated her naiveté.

"Sounds worse than Bimini," Nick said. He nodded at Kimberly. "I understand what you say about this guy being different from most dopers. But I believe there is a potential for violence on this case. With this kind of money involved, they will kill you in a heartbeat. If the dopers dominate South Caicos, it's made them arrogant. They think they are above the law. They wouldn't hesitate to kill someone if for no other reason than they believe they can get away with it."

Lance shook his head in disagreement. "Boss, I just don't believe there's an operation moving that much coke through Lauderdale that we don't know about, an operation that some . . ." He paused.

"That some woman told you about," Kimberly finished. She tamped the cigarette in the ashtray and pushed it around in circles, not looking at Lance.

"Okay."

Kimberly smiled at Lance. She leaned closer, as if seeing his T-shirt for the first time. She nodded toward the emblem on his chest and said, "That's a lot of bull."

Lance's eyebrows shot up in surprise.

Nick smiled. Then he carefully placed his boots on the floor, clasped his hands, and leaned forward on his elbows. "Here's what we're going to do," he began. He looked at Kimberly. "I've got a lot of questions," he said. "But I don't have to see a burning bush to know that if there's any chance some bozo is moving that much cocaine through the county, then I'm going to take him down. Goldstein will become our top priority and I will allocate whatever manpower it takes to do the job."

He nodded his head in approval. "You did good work, McBride."

She nodded in appreciation, closed her folder, and lit up another cigarette. Nick turned toward Lance. "I want you to get a cash advance of five thousand dollars and go over to Naples and rent a single-engine aircraft."

"Rent?" Lance interrupted. "We got a hanger full of U/C aircraft out at Executive."

Nick held up his hand. "I know. But if this guy is half as smart as McBride says he is, he'll know they are publicly owned."

Lance nodded. Any doper who traced the ownership of an aircraft and found it was publicly owned—that is, registered to a government agency—would know it was owned by the police. Renting an aircraft in Naples, all the way across the state, would add additional smoke to cover his trail. He leaned forward in anticipation.

"You want me to fly to South Caicos?"

Nick shook his head. "I want us to fly to South Caicos, Cunningham." He emphasized the word "us." "I don't dislike even an island full of dopers enough to send you down there alone. We'll go down there U/C, spend a week, and find out what's going on."

Lance laughed. An undercover flight to South Caicos, even with his provincial, conservative, nondrinking, tight-assed boss, would be a lot of fun. He could spread his wings, maybe do a little street-level law enforcement. And he could mind-fuck the dopers until they didn't know what day it was.

Nick tapped the desk. "Before you get yourself all worked up, keep in mind that South Caicos is a foreign country. Remember the flap we got into over Bimini. We have no authority on South Caicos. We're not going down as police officers. We're civilians. We're on vacation. And all we're doing is gathering information, so leave your creds and your tin at home." He paused and gave Lance his hard look, the one that meant he was dead serious. "And we're playing by the rules. I won't have you going down there and pulling some of your stunts."

Lance started to speak, but stopped when Nick raised his hand, palm out, like a cop stopping a car. "Don't take a weapon. South Caicos is a British Crown Colony. They take a dim view of weapons."

"Do the dopers know that?" Lance asked. He paused. "How do you know so much about all this? You must have already cleared it with the sheriff for us to go into a foreign country." Lance laughed. "Boss, you're getting sly in your old age. You knew when you called me in here that we would be going to South Caicos."

Nick smiled and pulled at his mustache. "Open a case file," he said.

"Okay, and I'll come up with an operational name. But I think I'll be called 'The Ghost' on this one." Lance's smile broadened as he slowly rolled the words around in his mouth, savoring them. "I like that. The Ghost."

Kimberly bit her lips in anticipation. She looked at Nick. "You said you were going to gather information. That's my job. I think—"

Lance laughed.

Nick shook his head. "You can't go."

She stared at him for a moment, then picked up the folder and stood. "If you don't need me any longer, I'll return to my office."

"You understand why you can't go?" Nick asked.

Kimberly paused, fighting with herself. "I understand your thinking. But I want to add one other thing."

Nick nodded for her to continue.

She turned to Lance. "Goldstein represents a new kind of trafficker. He is the doper of the nineties. Low-key. Very much in the background. A brilliant guy with no criminal history. We shouldn't go into this like a bunch of cowboys." She talked fast to prevent Lance from interrupting. "We need first of all to gather intelligence; tactical and strategic intelligence. We need to pursue the case both in criminal and in civil avenues. We need to seek financial remedies. All of the old conventional methods, the surveillance and the shoe leather, are not that important in this sort of investigation. The objective here, the overall strategic plan, should be for us to work toward a conspiracy case. Perhaps we should even get DEA involved so they can work toward a RICO case or a CCE. I think this is big enough to get their attention."

"Let's see how it develops," Nick said calmly. "We may have to get the feds involved. South Caicos is a long way away. We may need Customs' aircraft and all that space-age stuff DEA has."

"This guy may be the doper of the nineties," Lance said, "but he's made at least one big-time mistake. He'll make more."

"What mistake?" Kimberly said. Her eyes widened. What had she overlooked?

Lance shrugged. "He's operating in Broward County. He's up against me." He smiled a beatific smile and palmed his hand against the sky. "And I am the wind. I am the thunder and the lightning. I am the one who will show this kosher doper the majesty of the law. I am—"

"I agree with the part about the wind," McBride interrupted. She turned and walked toward the door.

Lance looked over his shoulder at her departing figure. "I wasn't finished," he said in disappointment.

Nick was shaking his head. "I've got bad feelings about this one, Cunningham. We know zip about South Caicos except hearsay from a doper. And if half of what he told McBride is true, we could be stepping into a deep pile of crap."

Lance shrugged. "That woman smokes like a burning building," he said. "She's in awe of this Goldstein asshole, and if she uses the word 'strategic' one more time, I'm gonna throw up."

"She's smart. She came up with some good info." Nick paused. "What do you really think of her?"

Lance's expression grew serious. He appeared to be in deep thought. "Boss, you ever been in traffic behind an Alpha Romeo? One of those spiffy little sports cars with the tight, squeezed-in tail?"

"Yeah?"

"I think she's got an ass like an Alpha Romeo."

3

Page and Phillip, the young couple who had been on the beach at Ramrod Key the night the Citation roared over in pursuit of a smuggler, were racing north on the Florida Turnpike. They had been sailing on Biscayne Bay and were rushing to her home in Lauderdale Lakes, where she would change clothes; then they were going to a beach party. It was dusk. Page and Phillip were laughing; more from the cocaine they had sniffed than from the exuberance of youth. The top was down on Phillip's Toyota convertible and the wind ruffled their sun-streaked hair. Both were tanned and gleaming; they did not have a care in the world.

"Hand me a beer," Phillip said.

Page reached over the seat into the cooler, pulled out two bottles of beer, twisted off the tops with practiced skill, and handed one to Phillip.

At the intersection of I-595 and the Turnpike, she tilted her head and looked up at the maze of bridges and pillars and construction work. She giggled and her head lolled toward Phillip. "It's so spacey. It's from another world," she said.

Ahead of them three cars were traveling side by side at about sixty miles an hour. Phillip turned on his lights and flicked the high beams, but the car in the passing lane would not speed up. Phillip was impatient.

"Watch this," he said with a tight smile of anticipation.

Page laughed when he pressed the accelerator, darted across three lanes of traffic, and pulled onto the emergency lane along the edge of the road in order to pass the three line-abreast cars. She tilted back the beer.

The Toyota hit the parked flatbed truck at about seventy miles an hour. The truck was loaded with clusters of steel reinforcing bars. One cluster jammed neatly through the window of the car and impaled Phillip's head. He was jerked from the convertible and left dangling, a limp rag doll, from the re-bars. His arms hung loosely, his legs were bent at the knees, and for a moment his toes drew small circles in the blood pooling on the concrete.

The car traveled a few more feet before it jammed under the truck. A wrecker later extracted the twisted hulk of metal from under the truck and a rescue team used acetylene torches to cut the metal apart. Page's body was gently lifted out. The beer bottle had jammed into her mouth with such force that most of her teeth were gone. The top of the bottle had severed her spinal column and was protruding from the rear of her neck, a neat brown hole surrounded by a small aura of blood and unblemished suntanned skin.

Her beautiful eyes, even in death, were wide in horror. And where her mouth, the mouth so quick to giggle, had been, now was the dark jagged obscenity of a broken beer bottle.

When the county medical examiner filled out the appropriate paperwork, he listed the cause of death as a traffic accident. He did not conduct a blood test and therefore did not know about the high levels of cocaine in both bodies.

4

Cosmos Goldstein was a small wiry man, no more than five feet five inches tall and weighing a hundred and forty pounds. There was something faintly military about him; he was young and his black hair was closely cropped. His forearms and biceps were hard and ropy, and even sitting at the telephone in his home, he seemed at attention. His eyes, veiled and wary, missed nothing.

Goldstein hung up the white telephone, sighed, and stared out the window across the neatly clipped green lawn and the professionally arranged groups of bright tropical flowers. Beyond the yard was a pasture, and in the middle of the pasture was a barn. The pasture, measured on a bias from the southeast corner to the northwest corner, was twenty nine hundred feet. Goldstein had four homes on the westernmost edge of Sunshine Ranches, a subdivision in western Broward County. All were near undeveloped areas or expressways. He had another home on the Palm Beach County line just north of the east-west portion of the Sawgrass Expressway, one just west of Margate, and another near Tamarac. But this one was where he kept his computer and where he spent most of his time. It was where his mother called. And she called often.

Goldstein yawned. Conversations with his mother always left him feeling frustrated and angry. Those feelings, in turn, left him feeling guilty. His mother didn't understand. She simply didn't understand. She would never understand. She talked to him as if he were still a child: "Bubee" and "My kaddish," she called him. Always reminding him of how her husband, his father, God rest his soul, had struggled to save the money that sent Cosmos to college and then to dental school at Emory University. Emory's closing of the undergraduate dental school the year he was graduated was a sign from God, she said, of how Cosmos, the zelosen little Cosmos, had been destined to become a dentist. That's what God meant for him to do with his life. But now prospective patients were turned away; people she sent there were told her son was on an indefinite leave of absence. So what was he doing? How did he spend his time? She heard talk from her friends. Hints. They were all lies. Malicious, jealous lies. Little Cosmos would never do anything to embarrass his mother or to bring shame upon his people.

"You're right, Mama. Don't pay any attention to the talk. It's just talk."

"Bubee, Bubee. You're a dentist. Why aren't you in your office? What are you doing?"

"Investments, Mama. Investments. Just like Papa taught me. That's how I'm able to send you money and take care of you."

"So what's the name of the company? Are you the president? What do I tell people?"

"I work alone, Mama. My business is in my head. It's always been that way with us. I take a chance on myself. You and Papa taught me that."

"Oh, your papa. He never forgot how we had to leave Poland. Everything we owned in our pockets. All our friends the same. It's part of us."

She was right. It was part of all the Jews who had fled Poland, who had fled "the old country," whatever country in Europe that might have been. It was part of their collective unconscious always to be prepared to flee again, to have all their worldly assets as liquid as possible so they could, if the time ever again came, grab them and flee in the night. Because of their painful past, these were the Jews who rarely stood up to any sort of opposition. Even after the Six Day War, the war in which Israel looked down and discovered it had a monstrous set of balls, these were the Jews who tried to talk their way out of every confrontation; to appease, to mollify, to never make trouble.

Cosmos Goldstein had inherited part of that collective memory. Sure, he owned a few houses, but they all were for business purposes. Most of his assets, the half he did not give to those quiet and intense men who came every week, he kept liquid. If the time ever came, he could flee with only the clothes on his back. But he would still have the money in the overseas bank accounts. Millions upon untold millions.

Nathan and Irma Goldstein, like many Jews from the old country, were not quite sure how they wanted their son to be brought up. On the one hand, they instilled the Jewish heritage in him; on the other hand, they tried to separate him from that heritage. They were frightened and sometimes embarrassed about being Jewish. "Be a Jew at home and a person on the street," they told him. They were torn by their loyalty and love for their heritage and the desire for their son never to know the pain they had known. While many of their friends gave their children non-Jewish names in the hope it would help make them "a person on the street," Nathan and Irma could not name their son John or Ronald or Charles. Such obviously anglicized names would have caused them too much embarrassment. So they named him Cosmos, a Greek name, for the man whose boat they had ridden on after they fled south from Poland to the Mediterranean.

Cosmos Goldstein sometimes felt his heritage was pulling him apart. He did not know who he was. His mother wanted him to "be a person on the street" but yet she told him to stay away from shiksas and to date Jewish girls. She named him Cosmos, called him Bubee, and sent him among the goyim. Sometimes he hated being Jewish, an emotion that he ruefully realized made him a typical young Jew.

His heroes were Jewish, but they were men who caused amnesia among Jews who wanted to sanitize their past. Men such as Arnold "The Brain" Rothstein, who had virtually invented organized crime in America. For a few years after the turn of the century, until he was assassinated in 1928, he was the man who made millions in narcotics and in financing the criminal activities of others. Moses Annenberg, who, in the 1920's, used mobster and racketeering friends to achieve a virtual monopoly on supplying horse-racing information to bookies and publications that dealt with gambling. Out of this combination of horse racing and racketeering came one of America's great family fortunes; a fortune that, with the acquisition of numerous mainstream publications, enabled Moses Annenberg's son to become a U.S. ambassador and a friend of U.S. presidents. Meyer Lansky was another hero. Lansky was a man of incredible vision. He was one of the first to see the need to take profits from criminal activities and invest them in legitimate businesses such as hotels and real estate. But his greatest contribution was showing how to sanitize money by moving it through offshore bank accounts.

These were the heroes of Cosmos Goldstein, the men he sought not only to emulate but also to better. He revered their memory, and he wanted to use that memory as the foundation to reach higher. Sure, if he were caught, he would join Rothstein, Annenberg, and Lansky to become part of the Jewish amnesia. His family and friends would deny he was really Jewish. His name would be omitted from lists of prominent Jews.

Cosmos Goldstein smiled. One group—to a Jew the most important group of all—would never forget him. In the councils of power he would not only be remembered; he would be respected and praised. The quiet men would see to that.

Goldstein closed his eyes and mentally went over the numbers that made him so important to the quiet men.

Last year General Motors had had a profit of three-point-six billion dollars. Cosmos had brought in nine hundred and eighty-eight aircraft, an average of nineteen each week, for a profit of three-point-forty-five billion dollars. His goal this year was to bring in one thousand and ninety-two aircraft, an average of twenty-one loads per week, for a profit of three-point-eight billion dollars.

It worked this way. Most of the loads were five hundred kilos. He paid two thousand dollars a key for coke in Colombia. Five hundred kilos cost one million dollars. Security in Colombia and in the Turks and Caicos Islands, pilots, payoffs in south Florida, and money to buy new aircraft, cost another half-million per load. Thus, his average investment in each shipment was one and a half million. All he did was bring the cocaine to America. He was a broker, a wholesaler who resold the cocaine in Fort Lauderdale for ten thousand dollars a key or five million dollars a pop. His profit on each load was about three and a half million. It was quick and clean. Most of the activity was out of the country and therefore beyond the authority of U.S. officials. Smuggling cocaine across U.S. borders presented very little risk. With the help of his quiet friends, he had worked out a foolproof system. Except for the one aircraft lost almost two years ago when the pilot crashed, no aircraft of his had ever been seized.

Goldstein smiled. Neither the bumbling local narcs nor the federal agents had any idea who he was. And even if they heard what he was doing, they would not believe it. Cops never learned. Back in 1986 the Drug Enforcement Administration discovered a Mexican smuggler named Felix Gallardo was moving upwards of four tons of cocaine a month into the United States. They thought he was the biggest smuggler who ever walked, that nobody could do it better. But that was then and this was now. If an illiterate Mexican from the mountains of Sinaloa could move eight thousand pounds a month, a college-educated smuggler with the ambition of making more money than General Motors could move twenty, thirty, forty times that amount. Economies of scale. Logistics. Discounting for bulk purchases. A smooth-running, highly professional system. But most of all, intelligence. The quiet men provided him with the sort of intelligence that let him know every step the cops were taking, every technique they used, and every piece of technology to which they had access. He had computer disks that showed schematics and performance capability charts for the model of the F-16 radar that was installed in the Customs Citation. He knew the notch speeds of the radar. He knew the capabilities of the FLIR and under what conditions it performed poorly. He had a computer disk on which was a map of the primary roads in Broward County. It was this map that, when coupled with the capabilities of the F-16 radar and the FLIR, enabled him to devise a way for his aircraft to enter Broward County without fear of being forced down. Interdiction, for his aircraft, was not a consideration.

Goldstein looked out the window of his home and across the spacious lawn. Narcotics officers and newspaper reporters always painted people in his business as the lowest forms of life; benthic creatures beyond redemption, subhuman types. To cops, people in his business were scumbags and sleazeballs. But he was not of that ilk. Nor were any of the people with whom he dealt. He was a multimillionaire businessman, a genius in transportation and marketing who could teach those subjects in graduate-level business courses. He and his friends lived in the largest and most palatial homes in south Florida. They drove Mercedeses and Cadillacs and Porsches. They owned jet aircraft and yachts. They socialized with the top business and political leaders in the state. They gave small fortunes to charity; quietly, of course, so the newspapers never knew. But the people who counted, knew.

Goldstein was the living embodiment of the American dream, what every child of every émigré is told he can attain. Only in America could the son of emigrants seek to make more money than General Motors; and only in America could the son of emigrants, after less than ten years, be on the edge of achieving that goal.

Goldstein had bought more aircraft and now was averaging twenty-one loads of cocaine a week. That meant weekly profits upwards of seventy-three million dollars. Half he kept. Half he gave to his quiet friends. In cash. Every week. They would never forget him. And they would never let him be arrested.

He was invincible.

5

"Hey, *jefe*, here's the question of the week," Lance said as he opened the trunk of his black Lincoln—it was a car that had been confiscated from a group of smugglers—and tossed Nick's suitcase inside.

"Just drive. I don't want to hear it," Nick said as he turned and walked toward the door. "Drive slow. Don't give me your race-car routine."

Lance slid into the driver's seat. As usual he was dressed casually, and completely unlike the TV cops on the squad, all of whom looked as if they came from a Don Johnson cookie cutter. This morning Lance looked relatively normal. He was wearing khaki pants, boat shoes, and a T-shirt that said "Heaven Doesn't Want Me, and Hell Is Afraid I'll Take Over." Three heavy gold chains hung around his neck.

"You nervous about flying with the Ghost?" he asked Nick. "Hey, it's only about six hundred miles over some of the most shark-infested waters in the world; nothing to worry about."

"I'm not nervous; just thinking." Nick's cowboy boots glistened in the car's interior lights. His plaid shirt was cut in a western style. When he sat down, even the big gold belt buckle in the shape of a curved alligator was hard-pressed to prevent his stomach from flowing over the top of his blue polyester pants. Nick's height of five feet, six inches, combined with his broad shoulders and thick chest, made him appear over-weight. And it gave rise to his affectionate nickname of Fluf—an acronym for Fat Little Ugly Fucker. Nick would be forty in a month, a birthday that was causing him to engage in no small degree of reflection.

"I'm thinking too," Lance said. "I'm thinking it's good to get out early, to be on the road before Central Cuban Dispatch is operating."

"There's nobody here but us. It's not even daylight yet. You don't have to tell me Castro is behind a plot to block all the highways in America."

"Hey, when I get the Nobel Peace Prize for burning down CCD, you'll wish you had believed."

Lance wheeled out of the Trade Tower's basement, turned left onto Andrews Avenue, and then made a quick right onto the ramp that led to the southbound lane of I-95. He looked over his shoulder at the lights of cars bearing down on him in the predawn darkness, then quickly accelerated and moved into the traffic. "Long drive to Naples," he said. "What can we talk about?"

Nick rubbed his hand across his mouth. "Nothing. And I don't want any question of the week."

When Nick was with Lance and the two were not talking business, Nick tried to shift his mind into neutral. His star undercover narc had the attention span of a two-year-old. Lance could not abide silence. And his sense of humor, if it could be called that, bordered on the bizarre. There was that thoroughly unpleasant phase he had gone through when he not only recorded his bowel movements in a little book but also wanted to discuss them with everyone he met. He would call people at three A.M. to describe his latest bowel movement. Nick could never figure out if Lance stayed up nights figuring out how to add to his reputation as a whacker or if it all came naturally. It didn't matter. Being more than a little bit crazy was the prime ingredient of all good undercover narcs. And as long as Lance continued to be the best narc in the business, Nick could put up with him. Most of the time.

Lance turned right on Highway 84, the road he would follow across Florida to Naples. He looked at

Nick. "How about a strategic plan like the necklace
woman was talking about?"

"Necklace woman?"

"Yeah, your new intel analyst. Didn't you notice all
the necklaces she wore? Amethyst. Quartz. Five of
'em." He laughed. "I think she's half a quartz low."

"If wearing necklaces is her worst vice, I can live
with it," Nick said. He turned and looked pointedly at
Lance. "Some people have bigger problems. A lot
bigger."

"I got it. I know what we can talk about," Lance
said. He grinned, tilted his head, leaned toward Nick,
and began sniffing loudly.

Nick ignored him.

"Ohhhh, stud," Lance said. "You're wearing that
devilishly appealing shaving lotion again. I don't know
if I can keep my hands off you."

Nick glared. "Don't start that shit with me."

Lance laughed.

In the bright beams of their headlights, the tall
concrete pillars under construction for the bridges and
overpasses of Highway 595 were almost surrealistic.
Already the construction crews were gathering. If the
interchange and the construction of I-75 along the
route of State Road 84 were ever completed, it would
be an east-west freeway, the primary east-west route
between Naples and Fort Lauderdale, a straight road
across the width of the Florida peninsula right through
the Everglades and the Big Cypress Swamp.

"Be careful," Nick said. "They had a big wreck here
last week."

"Not to worry, *jefe*."

Nick became lost in his thoughts. He was apprehen-
sive about going to an island that, if Kimberly McBride's
sketchy information was correct, was dominated by
drug smugglers. If those smugglers had the faintest
suspicion, even a passing thought, that he and Lance
were cops, the two men from Fort Lauderdale would
never be seen again. And their deaths would not be
pleasant. Nick handled his apprehension by pulling

into himself, by becoming even quieter than usual. If Lance had any fear, which Nick doubted, he handled it by becoming even more talkative.

"Welllll," Lance said, drawing out the word. He was never reluctant to fill the vacuum of silence. "Since we are leaving the land of the free and the home of the brave for a week, I took advantage of my last night by spending a very fruitful evening on tooty patrol. Want to hear how I made out?"

"Nope."

"Hmmmmmmmmm." Lance pressed a button on the radio and began turning the dial, bouncing from station to station before settling on one station playing rock music.

Nick shook his head. Why would Cunningham listen to rock music? Why would anyone listen to rock music?

When he reached for the dial, Lance objected. "No, you'll put it on that Jesus station," he said. It was always easy to determine which vehicle from the car pool Nick had been driving because the radio always was tuned to WMCU, the radio station at Miami Christian College that broadcast sermons and religious music. It was not a format that appealed to the TV cops, several of whom had discussed registering an official complaint with the sheriff. They wondered if leaving the radio of a county-owned car tuned to a religious station violated the separation of church and state.

Such errant nonsense ended when Lance threatened to kick the ass of any agent who complained about Nick's choice of radio stations. To the TV cops, Lance was a legend; a fearful legend. They had studied his cases, particularly the Bimini investigation, when they were in the academy. They knew he would take on any two or three or four of them without a thought. This was the guy who, just for the hell of it, once swaggered into a truckers' bar wearing a Viking headdress—a round helmet topped by two long horns—from which flowed about three feet of mangy fur over his shoulders and back. He kicked open the door, looked around, and screamed, "Faggots! You're all faggots!" This got the attention of several truckers. They saw a guy with a strange light in his eyes and a weird smile on his face; a guy with spittle drooling from the corner of his mouth. He was not a big guy. Most of the truckers could have cleaned up the floor with him. But they sensed he was the sort of person who would have to be killed to be beaten. Anything else and he would keep coming back for more. It wasn't worth it. So when Lance again yelled, "Faggots! You're all faggots!", no one challenged him. The TV cops believed Lance was crazy. It was best to stay out of his way. So there was no more talk of complaining about Nick's choice of radio stations.

The TV cops didn't understand two things. First, they didn't understand how much Lance idolized Nick. Lance would rather have one "Atta boy" from Nick than to meet the President of the United States. Second, they did not know, as did Lance, the reason, or part of the reason, for Nick's religious nature. Nick's father, who had been a boat mechanic in Naples, was in church every time the doors opened. One Sunday after his parents returned from church and the family was having a leisurely meal, Nick—who was then in high school—was explaining again to his father why he had not gone to church that morning. But his father wasn't listening. "I want you to go to church," he kept saying. The argument grew heated. It ended when Nick's father had a stroke; right there at the table his speech suddenly became slurred, his eyes were rolling around, and finally, as Nick and his mother watched in horror, his head drooped in unconsciousness. Nick's father was revived at the hospital and it appeared he would recover with no permanent damage. Then, the morning he was to be released, there was another stroke, this time a massive one that sent him into a coma from which he never recovered. Nick's father died two days later and Nick blamed himself. If only he had attended church more often and sung louder and prayed more often and put a little more money in the collection plate, his father might still be alive. As

Nick grew older, he knew in an intellectual sense he had not been responsible. But the idea that he was to blame for his father's death was so deeply imprinted that he was never to escape. Now he went to church because he wanted to go. But there were times when he still heard his father's voice that day at the table. And often, particularly when he was alone, he would turn on his car radio to overpower the voice. Always he turned the radio to WMCU.

"I don't think it would hurt either one of us to listen to that station for a while," Nick said. "Considering where we're going."

"*Jefe*, you're in charge of Narcotics. You run the office. But you issued a directive that whoever is driving a county-owned car, boat, or aircraft is in charge of that vehicle and responsible for it. I'm driving so I'm in charge of this car. I like this station. I like rock music." Lance's smile and tone of voice held no sting.

Nick shook his head. He continued to stare ahead. He did not like rock music. After a moment he said, "Okay, Cunningham. You know I hate that stuff. You win. Turn off the radio and ask me the question of the week. Just keep the radio off."

Lance laughed and pressed the radio power switch. "Hey, you just made me a happy camper. Okay, here it is. Here's the question of the week. What does it mean if your mother and father fall into a swimming pool?" He looked at Nick in anticipation, sliced his eyes back toward the road, then again toward Nick.

Nick paused a long moment before he answered. "I don't know."

"It means the relative humidity is one hundred percent."

"You're not just a pervert; you're sick."

"Why, thank you," Lance said. He meant it.

6

It was not yet seven A.M. when the little Piper Arrow lifted off the runway at Naples and settled on an eastbound course. The aircraft crossed the Big Cypress Swamp and continued climbing to nine thousand, five hundred feet. Miami passed under the wing. Lance had flown single-engine aircraft into the Bahamas many times, but there was always a moment of apprehension as he crossed the coast and the horizon blurred into an endless expanse of water.

"We going nonstop?" Nick asked. He sat in the right seat, expressionless, sunglasses hiding his eyes.

Lance made a minute adjustment to the red-tipped knob that controlled the air-fuel mixture. "Could. We got long-range tanks. Just to be on the safe side, I'll stop at Rock Sound and top off."

Nick nodded in approval. "And check the weather again?" he said. Lance did not have an instrument ticket and Nick was concerned. Their options could narrow quickly if they were caught by weather in the remote stretches of the southern Bahamas.

The refueling took less than half an hour. Nick was dozing by the time the aircraft climbed back to altitude and headed toward South Caicos. Only a few scattered clouds could be seen—the usual cumulus buildups that start in the morning, often over land, and result in isolated late-afternoon thunderstorms. The air was hazy, and the midmorning sun was blistering hot through the windows of the Arrow. Lance turned on the automatic pilot. The aircraft droned south over Cat Island and then between Rum Cay and San Salvador, its heading and altitude unwavering. Samana Cay could not yet be seen. There was nothing in sight but the vast and dim reaches of the Atlantic. Lance glanced at his watch. Almost two hours before landing. He scanned the instruments. Everything in the green. He yawned and looked out the window. Nothing ahead but haze. Nothing below but the dull dark blue surface of the Atlantic.

"Space," Lance intoned. "The final frontier. This is the voyage of the starship Piper. Its four-hour mission to seek new worlds; to boldly go where no man has gone before."

Nick awakened and turned toward Lance. "What?"

"I forgot part of it. I left out a line and can't remember what it was. You a Trekky?"

"No, Baptist."

Lance laughed. "That might be the funniest thing you ever said."

"What?"

Then the radio, which had been silent since the departure from Rock Sound, suddenly blared forth. The drunken voice that cracked through the cockpit was loud and demanding. "Hello, hello, hello. Anybody out there? Somebody talk to me."

Lance jumped. Nick sat straight up, blinked his eyes, and looked around the cockpit. "Who is that?" he asked.

Lance quickly scanned the instruments. The sudden unexpected noise, coming while he was high over the ocean with no land in sight, was disconcerting. "Some asshole on the radio," he said.

"Hello, hello, hello. I need somebody to talk to," the voice demanded.

Lance looked at the comm window in the radio, checking the frequency. He was monitoring 118.4, the Miami frequency used by general-aviation aircraft flying between the U.S. and the Turks and Caicos Islands.

"Problem?" Nick asked.

Lance picked up the microphone. "Aircraft on one-one-eight-point-four, say your number."

The radio clicked and a loud happy laugh came over the air. "Why, hello there, good buddy. I'm glad somebody else's out here. It's lonesome as hell. Who are you and where are you?"

"I'm asking you the same thing," Lance said, his voice easy and light.

"Well, you can call me John. Or you can call me Earl. Or you can call me Sam," the voice drawled. "But my real name is . . . Ollie. This is Cessna one four Charlie Golf and I'm southbound over, well, hold on here and let me take a peek out the window."

There was a brief pause during which Nick and Lance looked at each other. in amazement. Lance's brow wrinkled. Something was gnawing at him and he couldn't put his finger on it. There was a subliminal tug from deep within his subconscious. He narrowed his eyes in concentration.

The voice returned. "I see some dirt down there that I think may be the Playa Cays. Hope so. I ain't seen Mayaguana, but it better be coming up soon."

"The guy's drunk," Nick said in amazement.

Lance pushed up the hundred-and-fifty-dollar Porsche sunglasses he wore when he was undercover and looked at the chart. He found the Playa Cays and spanned his fingers between them and his position. He keyed the mike and said, "Cessna one four Charlie Golf. This is Piper six niner Romeo. If you're over the Playa Cays, I'm about fifty or sixty miles on your six. Southbound in an Arrow."

"How about that? We both going south. I'm going to South Caicos. You headed in that direction, good buddy?" This guy Ollie talked as if he were on a CB radio rather than an aircraft radio. In addition, he asked a lot of questions. Nick and Lance again looked at each other. The naturally suspicious nature of cops suddenly emerged. Then they both realized no one could have known they would be at this point over the ocean at this time of morning. It was pure circumstance. It had to be.

"That's right." Lance laughed. "You a passenger or you driving?"

Loud laughter. "I better be driving. 'Cause if I ain't, nobody is. I was up all night drinking in Miami and I'd like to crawl in the back seat and pass out, but I better not do that. So keep talking, good buddy. Keep me awake."

"Okay, Charlie Golf, what you want to talk about?"

"Hell, I don't know. You said you're going to South Caicos. What hotel are you in?"

Again Lance and Nick looked at each other. Lance shrugged. "Well, we've never been down here before. But we were told the Admiral's Arms is the place to stay. That right?"

Wild laughter came over the radio. "You got that right. It's the only place. Who's we? You got your wife or girlfriend with you?"

Lance laughed. "No wife. No girlfriend. Just a . . . business associate."

The voice paused for a moment. "What're you doing on South Caicos? You guys divers?"

"Don't do much diving," Lance said carefully.

"Me either. Can't stand the sharks." The voice paused for a second. "Tourists don't usually come to South Caicos. You guys tourists?"

"Sort of," Lance said casually.

There was a long pause. Lance could hear static on the radio and realized Ollie was sitting somewhere in front of him with the transmit button of his microphone depressed. Lance could almost hear him thinking. Then Ollie came back. "Well, I'll show you the place. You guys keep me awake and I'll meet you in the hotel bar and take you on a guided tour."

Lance looked at Nick. Nick shrugged. Lance made a decision. He knew from the tone of the voice on the radio that the dynamics of the conversation had shifted. He did not know how or why, but he sensed that he and Nick had passed some sort of test; that the voice on the radio had made a decision in their favor. But who was the guy? And why was he going to South Caicos?

Lance keyed the mike. "Thanks, Charlie Golf. We'd appreciate that." He paused. "You still wide-awake? I'd hate to have to fish our guide out of the drink before we got there."

"I'm 'bout half there. You like conch fritters?"

"A lot," Lance said. "Good ones are hard to find."

A long groan of appreciation came over the radio, followed by the sound of smacking lips. "Admiral's Arms has the best I've ever seen. Little waitress named Pearl brings them around every afternoon about teatime—beer time for me—and passes them out. Well, she ain't all that little. She's got the biggest set of zonkers I ever saw. Your timing is just right. By the time we land and get to the hotel and have a couple of drinks, it will be conch-fritter time."

"They got Red Stripe down here?"

"Ooooohhhh, a beer lover like me. Yeah, they got Red Stripe and something called Red White and Blue. But look, if you're sitting out in the sun and Pearl comes up, leans over, and hands you a beer, it could be a bottle of cold piss and you wouldn't know the difference. The main thing is to drink a lot so you can see Pearl lean over."

"Sounds good."

"And it looks good."

For more than an hour the two men talked, inconsequential chatty talk. Lance determined that Ollie lived on South Caicos, where he had a job as a pilot; a comment that caused Nick to nod knowingly. "Guy's a doper," he said.

"You may be right, boss."

"Count on it. He's a doper." Nick looked at Lance in amazement. "We're not even there yet. We're almost at ten thousand feet, out in the middle of nowhere, and you find a doper to talk to."

"The Ghost has magical powers."

Nick snorted.

Lance grinned. He pointed a forefinger straight up. "Hey, maybe your friend is looking after me."

"Somebody is."

Suddenly Ollie was back on the air. He said he had to prepare for landing, that South Caicos was in sight, and he would be switching to the tower frequency.

"See you at the hotel," Lance said.

Loud laughter. "Look for the guy wrapping himself around a case of beer." More laughter. "Charlie Golf out."

"I think he's had enough beer," Nick mumbled.

But Lance didn't hear him. Suddenly something had registered. Now he knew what it was that had troubled him earlier. It was the aircraft number. Usually general-aviation aircraft have one letter at the end of a series of numbers. Two letters almost always signify, on a large aircraft, the initials of a corporation; or, on a small aircraft, the initials of the owner. It's the airborne version of a car's vanity tag. Charlie Golf was phonetic for CG. And CG were the initials of Cosmos Goldstein.

Lance grinned his pirate's grin and turned to Nick. "Boss, I think we've been talking to one of Cosmos Goldstein's pilots."

Nick looked at him, waiting.

"Charlie Golf. CG. Cosmos Goldstein."

Nick grunted. "Could be. Could be something else."

"Nope. My gut tells me that guy works for Goldstein. If Goldstein is so damn cocky he can put his initials on an aircraft, then he is not worried about getting caught."

"Pride goeth before a fall," Nick muttered.

"Hey, this will be large fun. We're going to have a goodly time on South Caicos." Lance rubbed his hands together with delight.

A few moments later the Piper Arrow crossed the northeastern tip of Providenciales, the long island across the northward crescent of the Turks and Caicos chain. Time to begin the descent. Below the aircraft stretched the shallow Caicos Bank, the source of lobsters that were frozen and shipped all over the world. The waters were white and green, signifying a depth of no more than ten feet. Numerous dark spots—coral heads—were visible. A few moments later, where the crescent of the islands curved back to the south, clearly visible against the pale water was South Caicos. Lance turned a few degrees and lined up so he could make a straight-in approach to runway one zero.

As Lance and Nick approached land, they noticed several dark shapes in the shallow water. Nick peered over the glare shield. "They look like airplanes," he said in amazement.

"Jesus. They are," Lance said. He pointed to the left. "There's a DC-3, a C-46, and that one's either a DC-4 or a DC-6. I never can tell them apart." Nick nodded. "I see one of those Cessna push-pull jobs and another DC-3."

The aircraft were clearly visible, the tails, wings, and most of the fuselages above the shallow water. All had apparently crashed while landing or taking off from South Caicos.

"Dopers," Nick said. "They either ran out of gas, or tried to land at night and screwed it up, or had some kind of problem on takeoff."

"There's another one—no, two—up ahead in the bushes. Off to the left of the runway," Lance said. He checked to make sure that the fuel switch was turned to the tank containing the most gasoline, the landing gear was down, the mixture was rich, and the propeller in low pitch.

"Piper six nine Romeo, your traffic is the Bonanza that just landed. You are cleared to land," came the voice of the tower operator. His speech was clipped, precise, and very British.

Lance checked the airspeed. "Seat belt on?" he asked Nick.

Nick gave him a thumbs-up.

"I think we're ready to land," Lance said. He wiggled his shoulders and flexed his fingers as he watched the Bonanza turn around and taxi off the runway. They were on short final. "Okay, boss. Last chance to back out."

"Put this thing on the ground."

Lance landed and let the aircraft roll. Then he turned

around on the runway, taxied back, and turned left onto the large apron. It was chockablock with aircraft.

Lance taxied slowly, carefully. To the right was a DC-6. Two men were standing under the wing talking to a man who had just stepped out of a taxi.

"Look at that," Lance said, nodding to the left. Two C-46's sat side by side. Both were painted a pale flat gray on the bottom and a dull black on the top. "Workers," Lance said. "With that paint job you can't see them against the sky. And anyone flying above them can't see them against the ground or water. You got any paper?"

Nick took a pen and a small notebook from his shirt pocket. He placed the notebook on his leg. "Call out the numbers and a brief description of those on your side," he said. "I'll get the ones on this side."

Lance taxied slowly, calling out color and type of each aircraft, followed by the tail number. Nick wrote rapidly. "This is gonna make McBride's computer light up like a Christmas tree," he said.

Almost all of the aircraft had mud-spattered wheels and tail surfaces, an indication they had been flying out of dirt strips. Many had pitted propellers, another sign of flying out of rough fields. The leading edges of the horizontal stabilizers were dented and scraped, marks left when propellers kicked up rocks during takeoff. Tail numbers on several clearly had been altered or covered with duct tape. Some had different numbers on each side of the tail.

"Most of these have only the pilot's seat," Nick said. He was writing rapidly.

"Got to have room for dope," Lance said. He nodded toward his left. "Look at the antennas. Most of these birds have HF radios. You don't need those unless you're doing some long over-water flights."

"A lot of them are modified. Look at the cargo door on that Bonanza," Nick said. "Off to the right. Just past the Seneca." Neither man pointed. They were taxiing toward the tower and knew that tower operators could be watching through binoculars.

Lance laughed. "I've never seen so many hatches over the cockpit. Add-ons. They don't come that way."

"Gotta be able to get out. You can't if the cabin is jammed with coke," Nick said.

"Look over here to my left. Ten o'clock," Lance said. Nick turned. A Piper Cherokee, its tail almost dragging the ramp and its nose pointed toward the sky, sat parked by itself. A slim man wearing khaki pants and a khaki shirt stood nearby.

"That may be the most overloaded thing I've ever seen," Nick said. "Look at the mud on the wheels. Take a look at the pilot, the guy in khakis. Wimpy-looking smuggler."

The two men were astounded. It seemed that almost every aircraft parked on the ramp had one or more signs of being used for smuggling. Did no one but smugglers use the airport at South Caicos?

Lance crossed the first parking apron and taxied onto the main ramp in front of the tower. To the right of the tower in the corner of the ramp were the fuel pumps. The propeller of the Bonanza that had landed ahead of them was winding down as a lineboy came forward with a gasoline hose. Ahead was the tower. Lance could see the sign for Dora's Restaurant in the terminal building. It was a carbon copy of dozens of other airport buildings in the Bahamas and the Caribbean: white, open windows and doors, and a general air of sun-blasted ennui. But it was also different. There were so many people about. It was early afternoon, generally a time of torpor and languor in these latitudes, but there must have been two dozen people on the ramp. And through the open windows of the restaurant could be seen another dozen or so. Were all these people smugglers? They couldn't be. Two men in uniform were strolling toward them, probably the local Customs and Immigration officers. They were carrying a folded black object. It appeared to be a large suitcase.

"South Caicos ground, Piper six niner Romeo. Where do you want us to put it?" Lance radioed.

"Piper six niner Romeo, turn right and park on the northwest corner of the ramp. Next to the brown Cessna two oh seven."

"Six niner Romeo," Lance said. "Can you send us a fuel truck?" He slowly added more power and taxied toward the corner.

"That's affirmative, sir. If you want a quick turn-around, taxi to the pumps. If not, we can have a truck there in a few minutes."

"We'll tie down and wait for the truck."

"Look at that," Nick said in amazement. "See the Bonanza being refueled. The yellow one. That's the aircraft that landed just ahead of us."

Lance glanced to his left. Through the windows of the Bonanza he could see that the cabin was jammed with green duffel bags.

"Cocaine," Lance whispered. "He's topping off his tanks for the run to Florida. Ummmmmh! I'd like to bust him," Lance grunted in anger and frustration. "We don't have an HF radio and I don't trust the telephones down here. We don't have any way to alert Customs."

"Unless he crashes, that load will make it through," Nick said.

"So will most of the others," Lance said. "We've got to figure out some way to get word to Customs when a bad guy takes off from here. They could figure out a window and pop him."

A given type aircraft flies at a known airspeed. By using that speed, and the distance from South Caicos to south Florida, a window—a probable arrival time—can be computed. The Customs Citation could be waiting to intercept the smuggler. The problem was notifying Customs.

"That could be a quick way for us to get caught," Nick said. "We might just have to let the loads go without doing anything except collecting tail numbers."

Lance was grim. "Boss, I don't know if I can do that." He pulled up near the Cessna 207. The rear door was open and a young man sat there in the shade, obviously waiting for the Customs and Immigration officers, who waved and smiled as they approached.

"I thought those guys were coming to see us. Guess they're seeing that guy," Nick said. He watched the officers, his face expressionless, as Lance turned off his strobe lights, radios, and navigation equipment. He pulled the fuel mixture and waited as the propeller sliced to a reluctant halt. He pulled four pages of aircraft numbers from his notebook, folded them, reached up under and behind the instrument panel, and carefully wedged them between two wires.

His eyes were drawn back to the two officers. "That's a fuel bladder," he said.

Lance looked up. The two uniformed officers had unfolded the black object and were showing it to the young man in the open door of the Cessna 207.

"The two oh seven is loaded," Lance said urgently. Because of the bright sun, almost directly overhead, he hadn't noticed. But the interior of the Cessna 207 was packed with dark green duffel bags. What Lance had earlier thought was shadow in the interior of the aircraft was duffel bags. Lance turned to Nick and laughed. "Boss, this place is a smuggler's wet dream. And we are here among 'em. I never saw so many smugglers in one place in my life. I hope we never arrested any of these assholes."

"Let's turn this thing around. We may need to get out of here in a hurry," Nick said. He opened the door, unhooked his seat belt, then reached up and curved his hand over the top of the door and pulled himself out of the seat. "My ass is tired," he grunted. It had been a long flight. Nick stepped onto the wing, followed closely by Lance.

As they stepped onto the ground and walked toward the tail of the aircraft, they nodded toward the two officials in uniform who were talking to the man at the rear door of the Cessna 207. The officers ignored them.

They pressed down on the horizontal stabilizer enough

to lighten the load on the nose wheel, then pushed sideways, spinning the little Piper around so it could be backed into the parking space near the 207.

"They're arguing over a price for the fuel bladder," Nick whispered.

"Yeah, I heard," Lance said in disbelief. "The two cops are selling that doper a bladder. He thinks it's too expensive."

As Nick and Lance walked toward the nose of the Piper, they heard the young man say his fuel bladder had ruptured on the flight from down south. A lock on one of the duffel bags had pressed against the bladder and rubbed a small hole in it. The two officers nodded in sympathy. They could afford to be patient. The pilot had to have a bladder and they had the only one available. He would pay their price.

Lance and Nick pushed against the leading edges of the wings, guiding the Arrow into its parking space. Lance tied the aircraft down as Nick unloaded their luggage and locked the door.

Lance stood up when he saw a heavyset man in rumpled clothing marching across the ramp, eyes fixed on them. He noticed that when the two officers standing a few feet away saw the man, they stopped talking and waited, almost deferentially, as he approached. The man was big, about six-feet-two, and weighed well over two hundred pounds. A full beard, black and bristly, covered his face.

The man stalked up to Lance and Nick. He put his hands on his hips and stared at them. He looked over their shoulders at the little Piper they had flown. Then, after a long moment, he spoke. "How much did you have to pay to rent that Arrow back in Naples?"

7

Kimberly McBride backed out of her garage, reached up and pressed the button on the door-closer that was snapped to the sun visor, then continued to the street. She waited a moment until the garage door closed, then pressed the accelerator on the three-year-old Ford sedan and drove slowly away. Twice she looked over her shoulder toward her home. Ever since she had been divorced, she felt guilty about leaving her son at home with a sitter. The sitter was a college student, a girl who went to evening classes and then to her job as a cocktail waitress over on the beach. She usually was getting up as Kimberly was leaving the house. She spent much of the day studying. If there were a conflict in the sitter's schedule, the neighbors, the retired couple next door, were always willing to keep Jonathan for several hours. She had an ideal situation but still she worried. That, too, was part of the legacy of her divorce from Pete. She had met Pete not long after she graduated from college and joined DEA. They both were going through the academy. She was one of four women in the class of fifteen and was not interested in romance. She wanted to begin her career. But Pete made her laugh. He was so funny. They began having drinks and dinner. She graduated first in the class and he was second. He said it didn't bother him. Then both had been assigned to Miami. He was in an enforcement group while she worked in intelligence. They married soon afterward and bought a home in Davie, a suburb of Fort Lauderdale about a half-hour up the expressway from the Miami DEA office. Jonathan had come along two years later and life was sweet and wonderful, just the way she always thought it would be once she was married.

One of the things she enjoyed most about Pete was his love of flowers. Strange in a man, especially a macho young DEA agent. But after they bought a house, Pete spent most of his weekends in the flower garden. And in the spring, or what passed for spring in south Florida, he always planted new flowers, fertilized and weeded them, and rejoiced like a small boy when they began blooming. He even sat Jonathan on the grass beside him and showed him how to dig in the dirt with his little spade and rake. Jonathan was Daddy's little helper. The flower garden became a metaphor for their marriage. The rich lush growth and the bright colors symbolized the beauty and the joy of their time together. At some subliminal level she realized this and she nurtured the metaphor as Pete nurtured the garden; she bought fertilizer and tools and always looked forward to early March, when her husband began anew in the garden. She would stand in the kitchen window and watch Pete, with Jonathan beside him, and there were times when she thought her heart would break from sheer happiness.

Then came Pete's big career break; his first important case. Pete and a female agent went undercover in a cocaine case up in Jacksonville and things changed. Their family changed. During the next six months she saw her husband only twice. Once was at Thanksgiving, when he came home for two days. He was nervous and angry and critical. She thought it was because of the tension of undercover work. She did not realize the depths of his anger until the incident with Boswell, her cat.

While her husband had been out of town, she had begun letting her big yellow cat sleep in the house. On that night, of all nights, Boswell found the bread crumbs she had placed in a large pan where they could dry out and be used in the turkey dressing. Boswell urinated in the bread crumbs. The next morning Pete was having coffee when she pulled the crumbs from the pantry and realized, first from the moisture of the crumbs and then from the odor, what had happened. Pete picked Bos up by the tail and flung him into the bushes. It broke Bos's tail. Sometimes, even today, Bos occasionally would squeal when he sat a certain way and hurt his tail. After throwing the cat out of the house, Pete threw his coffee cup against the wall and stalked out. He did not come home for Thanksgiving dinner.

Then there were the sudden silences when she approached a group of her husband's friends at work. And she noticed how when Pete's name came up, his friends could not look her in the eye.

He did not come home for Christmas or New Year's. One of his friends in the enforcement group called and said the undercover case was being wrapped up and he would be out of the country for several weeks.

Her husband came home in March. He still was edgy and angry and critical. He found fault with everything she did, and he was unusually harsh with Jonathan. In the past, ignoring the kidding of fellow agents, they had gone to lunch together once or twice each week. But now when she wanted to go to lunch, he was too busy. He seemed uneasy when they met in the halls. And he began going to work early and staying late. They never rode to work together as they had before. And then, when he did not pull out his gardening tools and plow the soil and plant new flowers, she knew. There was someone else. The overgrown weed-jammed flower garden continued as a metaphor for their marriage, for her pain and confusion.

When she confronted him, Pete did not deny he was having an affair. He and the female agent had become involved during the Jacksonville case. They spent Christmas together in Nassau. Pete said it was Kimberly's fault; that she was not a good mother, that she was too interested in her work, too interested in clothes, and too ambitious. He said she ignored the house and ignored Jonathan. She knew none of that was true, but nevertheless it hurt and scarred her deeply. She came to believe that if he said it, and if he believed it enough to want a divorce, then it must be true. After all, she had picked this man from all others to be her husband. He was someone special. He knew more and felt more than other men. If he said she was a bad person, then she must be a bad person. Why else would he have wandered from such a happy home? She must be incompetent. She must be a poor mother. Even today, a year after the divorce, she found herself wanting to prove to him that she was a good person, that she was competent, that she was a wonderful mother. It angered her. She had done nothing wrong. He was the one who had committed adultery, who had walked out, who had wanted a divorce. Yet he blamed her. In an effort to move ahead with her life, she had tried several things. There had been the Forum, once called est, and the biggest crock of sophistic nonsense she had ever encountered. Now she studied books on crystals and wore crystals and carried crystals in her purse. She knew the power attributed to them was as nonexistent as the benefits attributed to the Forum. At least in her case. Where else could she turn? Sometimes she felt as if her life were a runaway, out-of-control garbage truck. Every turn she made seemed to scatter embarrassing parts of her life over someone else's lawn. Every gust of wind blew private and personal parts of her into public view. Behind her was nothing but garbage.

She was half-embarrassed that she sought solace in such things as the Forum and crystals. She had been an honor graduate of Penn State University. She knew better. And she knew the diffidence and insecurity she felt were not justified. Sometimes, when she heard herself talking to Lance, she was appalled. She was as diffident as some green kid right out of college. And she had more law-enforcement training and background than he did.

It was that deep sense of insecurity that caused her to go to work so early these past few weeks. She awakened Jonathan every morning before she left, hugged him and kissed him and told him she loved him. And then she told him to go back to sleep. She felt guilty about her son. Maybe that son of a bitch Pete was right; maybe she was a poor mother. But she needed the money for her and Jonathan; she had to work. Thank God she had held Pete's feet to the fire on the house. Not only did she keep the house, Pete was making the payments. And he was giving her money for Jonathan. Nevertheless, Broward County paid about half of what she had formerly made with DEA. It was tough.

The big difference in the house these days was the flower garden, or what had been the flower garden. It was overrun with weeds. The heavy rains and hot sun of south Florida caused weeds and bushes to grow in such abundance, they squeezed out most of the flowers. Occasionally she saw the gleaming yellow blossom of a golden trumpet, a fragile amaryllis, or a small delicate blue and pink lantana, and she would weep. She could not help it. Strange that a sight that once had brought her such great joy now caused an almost unbearable anguish. Today the sight of flowers caused her such pain that she would not have even a potted plant in her house or office.

Work was the sovereign panacea for Kimberly McBride. She would be on the telephone for hours today, calling intelligence officers throughout south Florida. That was one thing she had learned at DEA: an intelligence analyst is no better than her sources. She had cultivated other analysts in other jurisdictions and had often called to pass information to them. She stayed in touch. They were her friends, part of the close-knit brotherhood. Usually they talked about George Bush. That was a favorite topic among narcotics experts. And it seemed as if every day, the president gave them something else to add to their lore of Bush stories. Bush was a former director of the CIA and former head of the South Florida Task Force. The latter, since the early 1980's, had been the nation's premier agency in the long-running war on drugs. When Bush was vice-president and head of the task force, he constantly exaggerated the significance of drug seizures and the impact of the task force. The best measure of Bush's task force's impact on the south Florida drug scene, and the reason cops referred to the task force as "The Bush League," was that when he took over, cocaine was selling for fifty-five thousand dollars a kilo in Miami. Today it was so plentiful the price had dropped to about ten thousand a kilo.

Now Bush was president; the same bozo who, during the presidential campaign, said interdiction alone could solve America's drug problem. The consensus among law-enforcement people was that Bush was a weenie, a preppy weenie. The boy tried hard, but if the truth be known, he simply couldn't find his ass with both hands and a flashlight.

Now Kimberly would talk to her contacts about something else. She would call her friends in the intelligence networks throughout Florida. One of them, somewhere, would know someone who worked or who had worked for Cosmos Goldstein. She would seek that person out. He would know others who had worked for Goldstein. And each of them in turn would know others. Somewhere along the line, one would flip and talk to her of Goldstein's operation. When trying to find a smuggler to flip, one should always start with boozers and skirt-chasers. They are vulnerable. But even more vulnerable are pilots. Pilots are the weak link in any smuggling organization. They know lots of people on both ends of the pipeline. They do not have a bandit mentality, and they imagine themselves as professionals; men above the dirt and grime. They are reasonably bright; they have to be in order to get an instrument ticket. They have a romantic perception of themselves and they have egos only slightly smaller than Rhode Island. If you can flip a pilot, you can get lots of information. Give them a big bite of a reality sandwich; talk to them about the jail sentences they are looking at; if they are young, tell them of the homosexual rapes they might experience in the slammer, and sooner or later you are looking at someone who wants to be your friend, someone who will tell all he knows and all you ever wanted to know, someone who will rat on his mother. Reality sandwiches, if properly administered, are wonderful for inducing a change of attitude.

Kimberly would call Lance. He would know of a doper pilot. Somebody would flip. Somebody always flipped.

8

Lance and Nick stared up at the big man. They were painfully aware of the two officers and the smuggler standing behind them, listening, watching. Nick wiped his mouth and casually glanced over his shoulder. He expected somebody to pull a weapon any second.

Lance's smile widened. "Great. How'd you know we're from Naples? We met?"

Then the big man laughed, a loud booming laugh that Lance and Nick instantly recognized.

"The expression on your faces. You guys look like you got caught eating shit." He held his arms wide. "I'm one four Charlie Golf. It's me: Ollie," he said. "We got a book up in the tower that tells who owns every aircraft in the U.S. Somebody new comes in, we check 'em out. I decided to hang around and give you guys a ride to the hotel. I was in the tower when you called. How about a ride to the Admiral's Arms? Beer is on me."

"Hey, guy, we appreciate it," Lance said. He heard Nick's sigh of relief as he reached out to shake hands with Ollie. "I'm Lance and this is Nick."

The two men had decided to use their real rather than fictitious undercover names. That way they would not have to worry about making a mistake; and besides, Lance knew from long experience that smugglers use only first names. To ask someone his last name, or if the name he used is his real name, is a breach of the unwritten code. It simply is not done.

"Good to meet you," Nick said.

Ollie looked at the men standing beside the 207. "Grab your bags. I want to speak to those guys," he said. He walked toward the 207, right hand held up in a wave.

As Lance reached to pick up his suitcase, he whispered to Nick, "Hey, boss. You crap in your knickers?"

Nick shrugged. "Not much to that guy. You notice his shoes?"

Lance sneaked a quick look at Ollie's shoes: a tired pair of loafers; scuffed, unshined, and run-down at the heels. Looking at someone's shoes was Nick's way of getting an instant reading on the person. He might glance at his shirt or tie or suit. But none of that mattered if his shoes were run-down or, most heinous of all, unshined. Nick believed it signified a grave character defect. A pair of well-kept shoes signified that one had control of his life, that he possessed discipline and self-control.

"They might be his mother's shoes," Lance said.

Moments later Lance and Nick sat in a red station wagon with Ollie. Lance sat in the front seat while Nick sat in the back with the luggage.

"One quick stop and we're outta here," Ollie said. He drove rapidly across the ramp toward the runway, then veered toward the DC-6, where two men stood under the wing talking with a taxi driver. Ollie rolled to a stop. The two men looked at him expectantly. "I talked to the Doctor," Ollie said. "He knows about the late departure, so don't worry. The battery should be here in less than an hour. As soon as you install it, get on down south. Call me on HF when you take off from down there and I'll have a crew here to off-load you."

The two men nodded. Ollie wheeled and drove rapidly across the ramp.

"Tower doesn't care about people driving around the ramp?" Lance asked.

"Tower, schmower. As much business as I bring them, I could park a camper on the ramp and they would direct the aircraft around me."

"You mentioned the Doctor back there. Somebody sick?"

Ollie laughed. "No, that's the guy I work for. He owns this island. The island and everybody on it. I'm his pilot. Chief pilot."

"Sounds like you're a good man to know."

Ollie laughed. He was still half-drunk. "You already know me." He turned left away from the airport and drove at high speed down the long sloping hill that led from the airport into Cockburn Harbour, the village on the south end of the island. He swerved around numerous holes in the road, sometimes driving on the road and sometimes off the road. To the left were the salinas that once had provided enormous amounts of salt to the world. The salinas were large flat open areas onto which seawater had been drained. As the hot sun evaporated the water, sheets of salt remained. The salt had been packed into sailing vessels and shipped around the globe. But the industry had withered away several decades ago.

The streets of Cockburn Harbour are narrow and filled with holes. There is little difference between the paved and the unpaved.

Ollie waved to the right. "One dock is over there, East Harbour, and another one is down on the south end near the hotel."

The station wagon slowed and turned right up a slight incline onto a circular driveway. Ollie waved. "Here we are. The Admiral's Arms. Best-known hotel in the least-known bunch of islands south of Miami."

The driveway leading into the hotel is lined with a profusion of color: the startling yellow flowers of the golden trumpet, the deep purple of bougainvillea, the dark red of numerous poinsettias, and tall branches of white oleander that wave gently in the breeze. But noticeable even over the soft smell of all the flowers is the overpowering, almost cloying sweetness of the reddish-orange frangipani—one of the most beautiful, and most poisonous, of Caribbean trees.

Behind the abundance of color is the hotel; a dull,

drab building. About it is a vague, almost indefinable air of benign neglect. A young person would describe the hotel as funky; an older person would think it decrepit and seedy. It is more than the need for maintenance or for paint that comes to every Caribbean building if ignored more than a few weeks. It is the sort of building where one unconsciously looks for mildew. And when one brushes up against a door or table or chair, one unconsciously looks at his clothes to see what sort of heinous stain is there. Four steps lead into the hotel. The floor of the entrance is covered with a dark red tile. To the left is a large open room where the only furniture is two battered sofas and the only wall decoration a shredded dart board surrounded by a three-foot circle of pockmarks. To the right of the entrance and up another step is the bar, a dim dark cave of old wood that reeks of stale beer. On the wall at the rear, like primitive ritualized cave paintings, are dozens, perhaps hundreds, of aircraft numbers. When a pilot stays at the Admiral's Arms, he can muddle through a box filled with white stick-on letters and numbers, pick out the appropriate series, and paste them on the wall—proof positive that he has been to South Caicos. The smugglers, and they comprise by far the majority of the pilots, paste up their numbers, secure in the belief that they will never be seen by a cop. On the left, as one enters the bar, are six stools. A patron can sit on one of these, prop his elbows on the carved and initialed bar, and look from the darkness into the blinding sunlight and see the swimming pool and, beyond, a harbor that once sheltered pirate vessels.

If one continues through the bar, he enters a great open dining room containing bare floors, bare tables, and plastic-covered chairs. An expensive television set— the gift of a smuggler who did not like to read and who grew tired of sitting around the pool—is propped atop a table in the corner. The only condition to the gift was that it be on twenty-four hours a day. And so it is, bringing all day and all night the bizarre wonders

of south Florida to the even more bizarre world of
South Caicos. A few tables against the wall are small
enough for two or four people. But most of the room
is taken up by two large tables, each of which can
accommodate more than a dozen people. Guests at
the hotel are divided into two groups: divers and smugglers. The divers congregate at one of the large tables
and the smugglers at the other. The two groups are
easy to identify. Divers are sunburned with sun-streaked
hair, wear casual clothes, and spend much of their
time trying to figure out how to operate the huge
watches they wear. Their conversation is loud, ani-
mated, and revolves around the fish or plant life they
saw on the latest dive. This group rarely has more
than a couple of drinks and, unless a night dive is
planned, usually goes to bed early. Smugglers, on the
other hand, usually wear creased jeans, lizard-skin
cowboy boots, large gold belt buckles, expensive de-
signer shirts, and sunglasses. They are soft-spoken and
a bit wary. Most of them spend a lot of time in the
bar. A diver and a smuggler might nod in passing;
they might even exchange pleasantries. But with the
occasional exception of a young female diver who likes
to live dangerously, they avoid each other.

A wing of guest rooms stretches off to either side of
the bar. The smugglers usually are in one wing, the
divers in the other. On both sides the rooms are
spartan. Each has a bare light bulb in the ceiling,
hooks on the wall for clothes, and a single straight-
backed wooden chair.

Ollie escorted Lance and Nick into the hotel. They
dropped their bags in the entrance as Ollie called
loudly for the manager.

The manager, a man of about forty, was at the
doorway of the bar talking to a tanned man in white
shorts. The manager made little effort to hide his ire
at what he thought was rudeness on Ollie's part. "One
moment," he said, using the tone one adopts in talking to an obstreperous child.

"I only just got off my boat," the man was saying to

the manager. Judging by his accent, he was British. "Just there at your dock. And this little blighter, he couldn't have been more than ten years old, comes up and asks me to buy some coke." His indignant voice rose an octave. " 'How about some coke, mon,' " he mimicked. "I'm telling you the lad needs guidance," he said.

Four men at the bar, smugglers by their attire, nodded and grinned. "Most certainly," one of them said.

"David, these are my friends. Take care of them," Ollie said.

The manager nodded in apology to the yachtsman and turned toward Lance and Nick. "How long are you staying?" he asked. Lance and Nick noticed the veiled hostility in his eyes.

"Maybe a week," Nick said.

"The rate is a hundred dollars a person per day. That includes three meals. Pay me in advance for three days. If you stay longer, pay for another three days." The manager held out his hand.

"Do we register?" Nick asked.

Ollie interrupted. "Not if you're with me. Just give the guy his money and I'll take you to your room."

Lance pulled a thick roll of expense money from his pants and peeled off six one-hundred-dollar bills. The manager took the bills, said, "You're in number six," and walked away.

Ollie smiled and motioned for Lance and Nick to follow him. "David's an A.K. He's uptight about those of us in The Business," he said over his shoulder as he turned left and walked down the narrow stone walkway. "He likes the divers. The Doctor is thinking about buying this place and not letting anyone but people in The Business stay here."

Ollie stopped before a louvered door with a rusty "6" nailed on it. He pushed the door open and walked in. "Don't worry about your things being in an unlocked room. None of the rooms have keys and nobody's ever had any problems."

He motioned toward the two single beds. "Throw your stuff down and let's go to the bar. I'm buying."

From the corner of his eye Nick noticed an almost imperceptible shake of Lance's head. "Give us a few minutes," he said. "I want to walk around, get all the kinks out. It was a long flight."

Ollie laughed. "Beer will get rid of that. Okay. Won't take you long to see this place. When you go out, turn right, walk along the water for about two blocks, turn left, and find your way back. Nothing to it. I'll wait for you in the bar."

Lance grinned. "Will Pearl be there?"

"She always is," Ollie said. He ambled away, humming some tuneless ditty.

Lance looked around the small dingy room. "This looks like where the people at Central Cuban Dispatch live. What a fucking dump." He looked up at the ceiling, then around the room. "Joe Shit the Ragman wouldn't stay in this place." He looked at Nick. "If Elvis is hiding out, this would be the perfect place."

Five minutes later Lance and Nick were standing at the edge of the water. Conch shells littered the coral-edged beach. Offshore a dozen boats were anchored. Several hundred yards away was a chain of small islands stretching to the south. Nick looked over his shoulder. No one was nearby.

"Cunningham, you ever seen a place like this?"

Lance picked up a queen conch shell and examined it. Near the top was a small hole where someone had cracked it with a hatchet, then reached inside with a knife to sever the foot of the conch from the shell. "Not even Bimini. I wouldn't have believed a place like this could exist. The bad guys own this place."

Nick nodded. "Those officers at the airport were bent."

Lance laughed. "Since they were selling a fuel bladder to a crook, I'm inclined to agree with you."

"What'd you think of Ollie?"

Lance shrugged. "I think he's a good ole boy with one hell of a big job; the daddy rabbit of this island. He said he works for the Doctor. That's gotta be Goldstein."

Nick nodded in agreement.

Lance continued. "We stick with him, we're home-free. He thinks we're down here to check out the joint, maybe do a little smuggling. I say let him run interference for us."

"We got to be careful. These guys will take us for a one-way boat ride if they even think we're cops."

Lance shrugged. The trouble with working with Fluf was that he was so conservative. He went strictly by the rules. He sat around and watched and listened and plodded along like some old man. He never did anything that, if revealed in court, would compromise the investigation. For him, that worked fine. Nick had never had a case tossed out because of an illegal search and seizure, a bad arrest, an illegal wire tap, or any other questionable procedure in the arcane and recondite areas where high-priced defense lawyers like to roam. Fluf plodded along, depending on certitude and rectitude and patience and tenacity. He personally had investigated more than four hundred cases. Those cases, once he finished them, were locked down tight. Every corner was sealed. Every window and door was shut. And everyone involved was convicted. He had never lost a case in court. Nick was living proof that a tortoise could outrace a hare.

Lance had a different philosophy. He liked to kick ass, to burn down stash houses filled with millions of dollars' worth of drugs, as he had done on Bimini. He liked to walk on the edge, to mix and mingle with the dopers, to hang out at the bar and match them drink for drink, and then, after they were passed out, to search their luggage or to use one of his special keys to search their aircraft. He would hide under a window listening to their conversation and knowing, if he were caught, he would be killed. He liked to mind-fuck the dopers. His pirate's grin and the weird light in his eyes endeared him to smugglers. They thought he lived up to their image of what smugglers should be like. And even older, experienced smugglers found themselves talking freely to Lance. They wanted him to respect them. Lance enjoyed getting close to smugglers, earning their trust and confidence. But most of all he enjoyed that moment after they were arrested when they marched into court and saw him sitting at the table with the state's attorney. In that magic moment, when Lance smiled and waved from across the courtroom, they knew they were going to jail. Every one of them, every single one, always said the same thing: "I knew you were a cop." Sure they did. That's why they committed criminal acts in his presence.

But he couldn't catch all the dopers. There had been two Lauderdale dopers who, after a long investigation, Lance realized would never be brought to trial. They were too well-insulated, too far removed from the action. Their pilots and humpers and drivers and accountants and security guards would be arrested. But the big guys would walk. They would continue to smuggle, continue to spread marijuana and crack and cocaine and whatever else in the pharmacological lexicon people wanted throughout Broward County and throughout America. They would sell cocaine to children and thereby plant the seeds that could result in a harvest of destruction for an entire generation, a harvest that might not be realized for ten or twenty years. Children not yet in their teens would learn better living through chemistry before their parents could teach them better living through other resources, and all because a couple of smugglers were smarter than the cops. So, on two occasions, multimillionaire smugglers simply disappeared. Lance kidnapped them, trussed them in heavy cables, put them in his boat, and carried them out to the Gulf Stream, where he stopped, cut off the engines, and drifted under the torrid sun. "Here's the deal," he told each. "For you there is no Miranda, no lenient judge, no light sentence, no time off for good behavior, and no parole. In other words, you ain't got no civil rights. You've been responsible for at least a dozen deaths. What goes around, comes around. I'm giving you the same chance you gave the people you killed—none." Then he tossed them overboard. Investigations had later begun. Case files were opened. And there were token expressions of concern and of a continuing investigation when the press made inquiries. But the case files were soon shoved to the back of a drawer and forgotten.

Lance started to respond to Nick's comment about dopers taking them for a one-way boat ride, when he noticed a small boy with a big grin approaching. "Hi," he said.

"Hey, mon," the boy responded, white teeth flashing in his dark face. "You want to buy some kayludes?"

"Some what?" Nick growled.

"Ludes, mon, kayludes. They cheap."

Nick was horrified. "No, we don't want any fucking kayludes. Get your ass home where you belong."

The boy stared at Nick in surprise, then backed up and looked at Lance. "Hey, mon, why you bring your father with you to the island?"

Lance laughed. The boy scampered away when Nick took a step toward him.

"Nick, you're surrounded by the philistines. You ready to go back to the hotel?"

Nick scratched his chin, squinted, and looked across the dazzling green waters at Dove Cay, across Big Cut, and toward Long Cay. "Yeah."

A block north, Nick slowed to admire the serene beauty of the Anglican church of St. George the Martyr. It was a small sandy-colored church placed in a grove of enormous casuarina trees. Sunlight filtered through the trees and bathed the church in an otherworldly orange glow. The omnipresent easterly breeze rustled through the trees and caused them to sigh and whisper like overheard remnants of prayer. The roof and the shutters of the church were painted a deep burgundy and provided a striking but harmonious contrast. There was something about the church that caused one to wonder if it had been picked up from another place, a place of love and serenity and grace, and moved as a leavening agent to that part of South Caicos most favored by drug smugglers, a few doors from the Admiral's Arms and a few paces from the dock.

As Nick paused in reverence, a teenage boy detached himself from the shade of a casuarina tree and sauntered forward. He was smiling as he held out a hand toward Nick. In his hand was a small envelope across which was written in large bold type: "And he sacrificed and burned incense in the high places, and on the hills, and under every green tree." Under the quotation were the words "II Kings 16:4" and "St. George the Martyr." Nick recognized it as a church collection envelope, and, thinking the boy was soliciting a donation, reached for his pocket. "A dime bag, mon," the boy said.

Nick paused. "A what?" He grabbed the envelope. It was full and soft. He opened the envelope. The sweet, pungent odor of marijuana lifted to his nostrils in the warm afternoon sun. His eyes widened and his mustache almost quivered in anger. He tossed the envelope to the boy and said, "Get your ass away from me." The boy looked at him in bewilderment, then smirked and strolled back to the shade of the casuarina tree.

Nick caught up with Lance. "Cunningham, that little asshole was peddling dope in a church collection envelope." Nick rubbed his hand across his mouth. He looked around the village as if expecting lightning to strike or the Huns and Visigoths to appear any moment. His eyes were troubled. "What sort of place is this?"

9

When Lance saw Pearl coming toward the table, he leaned over, banged his forehead on the table, and began warbling, "Waaaaahhhhh. Waaaaaahhhh. Waaaaahhhh. Testosterone alert. Testosterone alert."

Pearl was a slender young woman who appeared to be about twenty-five, though it was difficult to know for sure because she had the tight luminescent skin that some women of the islands, if they are fortunate, are blessed with. Pearl had bright eyes, a shy smile that exposed perfect white teeth, and a walk that was somewhere between a gliding sashay and an indolent saunter. Her feet were bare and she wore a pale gray one-piece cotton dress that had been washed until it was soft and clinging. Pearl had enormous breasts and, unlike most of the God-struck women in these religion-haunted islands, she wore no bra. As is the case with many slender women who have large breasts, she did not sway or bounce when she walked or turned or stopped. If there was any movement at all under the gray dress, it was a tremor of pride.

Lance looked up, whimpered, and again banged his forehead on the table. "Waaaaahhhhh. Testosterone alert. Testosterone alert."

Ollie was shaking with laughter. But Nick was not amused. "What's the matter with you?" he growled.

Lance looked up and watched Pearl as she stopped to pick a bougainvillea blossom. "You ever been driving down the highway, pull out to pass someone, and

suddenly realize you are head-to-head with a Winne-
bago?"

Nick nodded.

"Happened to me," Ollie laughed.

"Okay, you ever been driving down the highway
and pulled out to find you were head-to-head with two
Winnebagos?"

Ollie shook his head. "Now, that's never happened."

Lance moved his head toward Pearl, who was again
ambling in their direction, the bougainvillea blossom
in her hair. "Now it has," he said.

"You gentlemens want more beer, maybe some more
conch fritters?" Pearl asked in a voice that had both
the crisp pronunciation of the British and the singsong
lilt of the islands. She held her forefinger in the
corner of her mouth and looked out over the ocean as
she talked. Although her feet were rooted, she shyly
turned her shoulder back and forth in the almost diffident manner of a teenager.

"Not for me," Nick said. He had been nursing a
beer for several hours.

"We'll have a couple more," Lance said. He reached
for Ollie's empty bottle and placed it with his, waiting
for Pearl to lean over and pick them up. She did. One
at a time. And each time the boat-necked opening of
her dress sprang open.

Pearl stood. She traced a finger slowly through the
beads of perspiration on her shoulder and neck and
down into the opening of her dress, then back up to
her neck.

"What about fritters?"

Ollie shook his head. "We've had four orders. No
more. We're about to eat dinner."

Conch fritters are easy to prepare, but difficult to
prepare well. At the Admiral's Inn they are done to
perfection. Fresh conch is chopped and hammered
until it is tender, a major miracle in itself. Then the
conch is mixed with meal, herbs, and finely chopped
onions before being pressed into lumps about the size
of a lemon and dropped into boiling oil. The crisp

fritters, almost too hot to hold, are dipped into a bowl of spicy cocktail sauce, eaten, and chased with beer.

Pearl glided back toward the dining room. At the steps leading up toward the bar, she turned and glanced over her shoulder at Lance and smiled.

"Waaaaaaaahhhh. Waaaaaahhhhhhhh. Oh, shit. I'm suffering from DSB. I got to do something."

"What's DSB?" Ollie asked.

Nick held up his hand, palm out. "You don't want to know," he said.

"Deadly semen buildup," Lance said seriously. "I begin suffering if I go more than a day without tooty."

Ollie threw his head back and howled. "Meshuggener." The jovial pilot, who had been about half-drunk when he landed, had, as the afternoon wore on, become even more jovial. He and Nick, two men of about the same age, had gotten along, but it was Lance who Ollie more or less adopted. He saw in Lance what he imagined he had been fifteen years earlier.

It was after an hour or so of drinking that Ollie leaned forward and adopted a confidential tone. "Look, I know what you guys are down here for," he said. "You're checking the place out. You want to do something. Maybe I can help." Ollie's smile was broad and friendly. But his eyes were alert. And in his eyes, buried deep, was a hint of coldness and cruelty. Ollie would do what he had to do.

Neither Nick nor Lance responded. Ollie looked first at one and then the other. "Maybe you want to haul a cargo through that needs security. You need to know the procedures; who do you talk to to set it up, who do you pay, how much, that sort of thing. Am I right?"

Nick stared at his long-warm bottle of beer. Lance grinned and shrugged.

"Look, we understand each other. Okay. You don't have to say anything. I appreciate that. Some people come down here and talk too much." Ollie took a long drink of beer and smacked his lips in appreciation.

"Well, you guys came to the right place. And because you helped me on the flight down, I'm going to help you."

So all afternoon Ollie talked of himself, of South Caicos, and of his group in The Business, the group headed by the Doctor. Ollie was from Jacksonville. He had flown a helicopter in Vietnam. Part of his job was ferrying what he called "bigwigs" from the airport to the U.S. embassy to the presidential palace. "That was all they saw of the Nam," Ollie said. "Then they went back home and later I would read newspaper stories where they told how great the war was going, how we were winning the war. I'm a saint compared to those assholes. I don't lie. I don't hurt people. I don't kill people." He took another long drink of beer and said defiantly, "I am what I am and I do what I do."

Ollie looked across the stone seawall at the postcard view of the green and blue waters. He waved his arm expansively. "I've flown it all and I've flown it from everywhere," he said. "And this is the best. The heat can't touch us here. We can do what we want to whoever we want. This is paradise."

Lance and Nick said little. Ollie was in an expansive mood, so they sat back and let him talk. Nick thought there was a defiant little-boy air about Ollie. When Ollie told how his wife had divorced him because of his smuggling, and how he had not seen his daughter, an only child, for nine years, he became sad and wistful. Nick finally decided Ollie was one of life's losers, one of the perpetual misfits running about the earth seeking to justify his criminality. He also decided Ollie reminded him of Sheriff Turnipseed. Both seemed to have a mean streak. With the sheriff it was much closer to the surface. Ollie, like many fat people, buried his meanness under laughter and joviality. Nick believed that meanness is almost always an inherent part of the psychological makeup of fat people. They are not, as popular lore has it, jolly and fun-loving and compassionate. They are mean and petty and vicious right to the marrow of their bones. Nick would be very careful around Ollie.

The big bearded man drained a beer bottle. "I've smuggled everything from Sara Lee cakes to blue jeans," he said. "Once I crashed a DC-4 off the north coast of Cuba. I was carrying a load of blue jeans and I thought I had lost not only my aircraft but my entire investment."

"So what'd you do?" Lance prompted.

"I sold the jeans as preshrunk and made twice as much money as I would have ordinarily."

Ollie laughed and motioned for Pearl to bring another beer. "This is a crazy business," he said. "But of all the places I've ever been, this is the best."

Pearl stood close to Lance when she brought the beer. She nodded at Ollie, then looked down and flashed her shy smile at Lance.

Ollie saw a boy standing in the shade near the bar and motioned for him to come to the table. It was the boy Nick had seen earlier selling marijuana.

"Gimme a dime bag," Ollie said, handing the boy a folded greenback. The boy glanced warily at Nick as he passed Ollie the white envelope. He shuffled nervously as he looked at Nick's hard eyes. "You look like the heat to me," he said defiantly.

Lance threw his head back and laughed.

"And you look like a little smart-ass to me," Nick said.

The boy turned and walked away.

"You fellows want any of this good smoke?" Ollie said, carefully rolling a cigarette.

"I sell that shit. I don't smoke it. Especially not when I'm working," Nick said.

Ollie nodded agreeably. "Look, bubela, I can live with that. The Doctor tells me the same thing. He gets pissed because I like to smoke a little. Then he gives me a kiss and everything is okay." Ollie licked the edges of the joint, lit it, and inhaled deeply. "Best smoke, best blow in the world right here on South Caicos. It's here and it's cheap. If I have too much during the day, I just swallow one those little ole Rohr seven one fours before I go to bed and I sleep like a baby. Ready to get up and fly tomorrow. Either that or start all over with the beer."

Nick was glad he was sitting across the table from Ollie. The east wind was blowing smoke from the joint away from him. Occasionally Lance laughed his maniacal laugh, grabbed Ollie by the elbow, and said, "I am a happy camper."

Each time Lance said this, Ollie would go into gales of laughter and say, "Camper, schmamper."

The afternoon was well advanced when Lance held up his beer bottle, looked at Ollie, and said, "I propose a toast."

"Toast away," Ollie said, holding his bottle aloft.

Lance paused, grinned, and said, "May the skin of your ass never cover the head of a banjo."

"I'll drink to that," Ollie said. He drained his beer bottle and motioned for Pearl.

Ollie paused, giggled, and paused again. "Look. You guys want to hear something funny?"

"Lay it on us," Lance said.

"You know who made it so easy for us? You know who made it so easy for guys in The Business to work out of here?"

"Who?" Lance said.

"Missionaries. It was the fucking missionaries. Tight-ass Baptist missionaries. They still come down here. One was out at the airport when you landed. Nose of his Piper almost straight up in the air. It was loaded with Bibles and a motor scooter. They started I don't know how long ago. They built all the little dirt strips around the islands. They built a strip up on West Caicos; the island's deserted and makes a great alternate for us. They built strips on Provo, North Caicos, Parrot Cay, Pine Cay, Middle Caicos, Grand Turk, and Salt Cay, not to mention several others not on the charts, plus a few of the old dried-up salinas that we can use with single-engine aircraft."

"What abut the cops?" Nick said.

Ollie shrugged. Then he said very slowly, "We own

every cop, every Immigration officer, every Customs officer, and everyone who works in the tower. They all work for the Doctor. Since he doesn't come down much, and since I'm his man in the islands, they all work for me."

"What about cops on the other islands?"

Ollie looked at Nick. "Look, I'm telling you they are not a problem. Ahh, once in a while, some heat will come over from Grand Turk and seize an aircraft." He laughed. "They're afraid to spend the night. As soon as they leave, we steal the airplane back and fly it away."

Ollie turned up a beer bottle and drained it in great gulps. He motioned for Pearl. "The only people who ever have trouble on South Caicos are the guys who come through and don't want to pay. If you pay the guy in the tower, pay the Customs and Immigration people, pay the cops, you won't have any problems. You'll have to fork over ten grand to bring a load through in the daytime. If the tower knows you're coming, and knows you want a quick turnaround, they can have you on your way in less than fifteen minutes. But don't try to come through without paying. It causes problems for everybody. And you're open game for pirates."

"Pirates?" Nick asked.

"Yeah, some of the locals don't think they're making enough out of The Business. Getting greedy. They won't fuck with my people. But if somebody tries to sneak a load through by working only with the gas truck, the guy who drives the truck alerts the pirates. Smart-ass lands. Pirates come out of the bushes shooting. Smart-ass dies."

Lance and Nick nodded.

"Pigs get fat. Hogs get slaughtered. It's that simple," Ollie said. "Speaking of the heat, you guys should worry about the heat back home, not down here."

"What do you mean?" Nick asked.

"I've heard of a guy in Fort Lauderdale, his name is Brown, who is supposed to be some kind of one-man task force. Hear he's tough. Straight. Won't take money and won't cut you any slack."

"And his name's Brown?" Nick asked.

"Yeah, Nick Brown. Ever hear of him?"

Lance and Nick instinctively crossed their legs in order to quickly reach for their ankles, where each usually kept a pistol hidden. They realized their pistols were back in Fort Lauderdale. Was this guy playing with them? Lance looked at Nick, his peripheral vision checking to see if anyone were approaching Nick from the rear. Nick did the same for Lance.

Lance leaned forward. "Hey, I've heard of the guy. Heard he's a real asshole," he said. "He's nothing to worry about. The guy you need to worry about is one of his agents. I hear he is unshirted hell. I forget the name. Somebody told me he carries the old guy."

It was the "old-guy" part that got to Nick. He glared at Lance.

Ollie shook his head. "Never heard about anyone who works for him; they're all gofers. Guy to worry about is Brown." He waggled a finger, looked owlish, and said in almost a pedantic fashion, "Believe me. I know whereof I speak."

"We're across the state from there, but we sometimes get to Lauderdale," Nick said. "You know what this guy looks like?"

"No, just his reputation."

"You don't worry about him when you go up that way?"

"I don't worry about anything when my men haul their shit north. We got a foolproof system. If Customs intercepts us, we beat them. They've never busted one of our aircraft; intercepted a few, but never busted one. And when it's time to put the shit on the ground, we got a system that the heat can't touch. The Doctor is a smart little son of a bitch."

"You gonna tell us about it?" Nick ventured.

Again Ollie waggled a finger. This time he did not look owlish; his eyes were hard and clear. The two cops realized that even though Ollie was drunk, he was not a sloppy drunk who talked too much. "You two ever go to work for me, I'll tell you. Until then, figure out your own system."

Ollie smiled. "I will tell you one thing about the Doctor. He's nobody to fuck with. You know what he does when you go to work for him as a pilot?" He looked at Lance and Nick. Then he answered his own question. "He takes out an insurance policy on you. A million-fucking-dollar insurance policy. And you know who's the beneficiary?" Again he looked from Lance to Nick. And again he answered his own question. "You got it. He is. You go to work for the Doctor and you suddenly got a million dollars' worth of insurance on your life. And you know if you fuck up, if you drop a dime on the Doctor, if you decide to get out of The Business, there's a damn good chance he's going to collect."

Ollie turned up his beer and took a long gulping swallow. He wiped his mouth. "Happened to a guy the other day. The Doctor thought one of his pilots was talking to the cops. That poor son of a bitch had an accident; walked right into a propeller."

Then Ollie, in one of his sudden mood shifts, changed the subject. "Look, let's eat. You guys hungry? They got the best turtle steak here you'll ever eat. You can't get turtle in the States."

Lance pushed back his chair and stood up. "Sounds good to me."

"It's time. It's time," Ollie said, rubbing his stomach.

Pearl, who was standing nearby in the shade of a bougainvillea tree, sashayed over to the table. As Nick and Ollie walked toward the dining room, Lance lingered to talk with her. They whispered for a moment and then he walked away.

Ollie sat at the head of the smugglers' table with Lance on one side and Nick on the other. The men who came to the table smiled and spoke to Ollie. They either worked for him or were smugglers who had gone through him to bring their loads through South Caicos. The men were deferential toward Lance and

Nick, two new guys who obviously were friends of Ollie. Conversation at the table revolved around the esoterica of drug smuggling.

Ollie pointed to a young man, he appeared to be in his late teens, sitting down the table. "I've seen some crazy sons of bitches in this business," he said. "But that kid is the craziest."

The young man looked at Ollie and grinned in appreciation.

"Look, you know what he did?" Ollie asked. "He came down here in an eighteen-foot day sailer. Six hundred miles. Down through the Bahamas and a lot of open water in a fucking toy boat." He motioned at the young man. "Tell them the rest of it," he said.

"I wrote 'L-O-Y-C' on the transom," the young man said, as if that explained it all. "When people in the Bahamas asked me what it meant, I told them the Las Olas Yacht Club. They treat you better if you belong to a yacht club."

"Las Olas Yacht Club?" Nick asked.

"Name of a street in Lauderdale," the young man said. "The boat belongs to my girlfriend. She thought I was taking it to Bimini. She doesn't know I'm down here."

"Or that you'll be carrying a few hundred pounds of coke when you go back," Ollie finished.

"That's right."

Nick glanced casually at the young man. He would remember the face. He would have the marine unit of the narcotics squad track down the sailboat and put a beeper on it. He had the PC. Then, if this little wise guy left the country again, he would get popped when he returned.

Through most of dinner, Lance kept glancing toward a tanned blonde sitting at the table of divers. She was a tiny woman with an impish face and the tight muscular body of an acrobat. She wore a pink halter top, white shorts, and boat shoes. Her hair was tied up in a ponytail. She saw Lance staring at her and, for a while, ignored him. Then she smiled, and he knew, by the reckless expression in her eyes, that she thought he was a smuggler; that she wanted to be close to danger; that she wanted to have an experience she could go back home and talk about.

"Why you making goo-goo eyes at the blonde?" Nick asked. "Can't you keep your pants zipped? I thought you and Pearl were buddies?"

"We are. She's waiting for me in her room. I'm going there as soon as I finish dinner." Lance grinned. "Can I borrow some of your throw-me-down-and-fuck-me shaving lotion?"

Nick did not answer.

"Hey, guy. We got a big-time testosterone alert going on here."

Ollie looked at Lance with respect. "You're the first guy I know who's been there, and God knows, enough have tried."

"She said her boyfriend was at the airport tonight. He work for you?"

"Sometimes. A humper. Unloads aircraft. I've got a six due in with about eight tons of grass. It has to be broken down into smaller loads for single-engine aircraft. He'll be out there until midmorning tomorrow."

"Then I'll have plenty of time."

Nick was not pleased that Lance was going to the room of a woman involved with a doper. He wanted Lance in their room where they could quietly rehash the events of the day as Nick took notes in his small meticulous handwriting. The notes were dated; a time was written on them; then they were hidden, stashed away in a fold in the bottom of the drapes that hung over the windows in his room. The notes would stand up in court. And they would be devastating. Nick wanted to talk to Lance. He was worried. All of this was too easy. Everything was falling into their laps. Nick had a feeling of impending disaster.

Ollie slapped Lance on the back in almost fatherly pride and said, "I'm glad you guys are here. You're alrightniks. We're going to have fun the next few days. Tomorrow I'll take you out to the tower and introduce you to those guys. That's enough work for one day. Then we can get started on the beer."

Nick stood up and rubbed his stomach. "It's been a long day. I'm going to bed."

"It's been a long day. I'm going to Pearl's room," Lance said.

"It's been a long day. I'm going to the bar," Ollie said. He stood up, pushed the chair back, rubbed his big belly, and walked toward the bar singing "Mamas, don't let your babies grow up to be pilots."

The men at the smugglers' table had heard the song before. They laughed. The people at the divers' table did not know whether they should laugh or whether they should pretend they hadn't heard. They looked uncomfortable. All except the blonde wearing pink. She laughed. She waved at Lance as he walked away.

Pearl was in the staff quarters, the last two or three rooms on the west wing of guest rooms. There was no light showing through the window when Lance knocked softly at the door. He thought he heard a whisper from inside. He pushed and the door slowly opened. He entered and out of habit stepped quickly to the side before he shut the door behind him and stood quietly, waiting for his eyes to adjust to the darkness. Then he saw her. She lay on the bed, her slender body a dark shadow against the white sheets. Bars of light from the louvered door fell across her upper body, making stripes across her stomach, her breasts, and her face. She smiled and held out her arms, wiggling her fingers, motioning him toward her.

He quickly stepped from his clothes and draped them across a chair. And then he put one knee on the bed and leaned over, kissing her and rubbing his chest against her breasts. She reached up and seized the long muscles that ran along the sides of his chest, groaned, and pulled him closer. He kissed her breasts, then the long flat planes of her stomach. He would have continued but she reached down and put her hand under his chin and pulled him toward her.

"No, don't kiss me there," she whispered urgently.

Lance had forgotten. Women in the Bahamas and the Caribbean are uncomfortable with oral sex. He had rarely known an island woman who liked to play or to experiment or do anything other than have sex in the missionary position. But that was okay. Because while sex in the islands is unimaginative, it is of added vigor. When it comes to plain old garden-variety industrial-strength fucking, island women are hard to beat. And so it was with Pearl. Once Lance moved atop her and then into her, she sighed, drew up her legs until her feet were planted beside Lance's hips, bared her teeth in a feral grin, again gripped his ropy latissimus muscles, squeezed, and began thrusting her hips. She met him more than halfway and—with each thrust—grunted in intensity. Perspiration glistened on her body, causing her to have the appearance of polished ebony. Perspiration pooled on her stomach and caused loud splats as their bodies came together.

Then they were still, arms and legs entwined, bodies stuck together in salty sweat and glistening musk.

It was five A.M. when Lance moved from the bed and dressed. Pearl was sprawled across the rumpled bed. Lance laughed softly. "God damn, this room smells like the monkey cage at the zoo."

Pearl looked at him with a quizzical expression.

"I love it," Lance added. He sat on the bed and gently caressed Pearl's breasts.

"Thank you."

"For what?"

"For being gentle when you touch me."

"Here?"

"Yes." Pearl was embarrassed. She put her forefinger into her mouth and turned to face the wall. "My boyfriend hurts me."

She turned to Lance and smiled ruefully. "He will be back tonight."

"What about during the day?"

"I'm off for two days and I will be with him." Her voice was soft. She shrugged and Lance noticed that her breasts barely trembled. "I must. He will be here after you are gone." She smiled shyly. "But after I return to work, maybe he will again have to go to the airport."

"I hope so," Lance said. "Roll over and go to sleep." He kissed her, then stood up and walked toward the door.

Behind him was a soft giggle. "I can't," she said.

He paused. "Can't what?"

"Roll over and go to sleep." She cupped her breasts. "Not with these."

Lance shook his head in awe. He sighed. "Well, just go to sleep." He waved and was gone.

Thirty seconds later he was opening the door to the room he and Nick shared. "Hey, you awake?" he whispered.

"Quiet," Nick growled.

"Hey, boss. I just had a head-on collision with two Winnebagos."

10

Jennifer Nichols began smoking cigarettes in the seventh grade. She was thirteen, the age at which the largest percentage of children begin smoking; and, also like many children who begin smoking early, she soon graduated to other drugs. This is not unusual. Nicotine is what drug counselors call a "gateway drug," and there is a documented relationship between smoking and "hard" drugs.

By the time Jennifer was in the tenth grade she had tried grass, uppers, downers, PCP, LSD, prescription drugs, and cocaine. Cocaine was the best; not as terrifying in its effects as some of the others, and offering a transcendently sweet euphoria that caused her to forget, for a while, what her life had become.

Jennifer's parents, like most parents, had no idea she was using drugs. They would not have believed it had someone had the temerity to tell them their daughter was a druggy. To them, Jennifer was going through a phase; she was experiencing the tumult all children know in the turbulent passage from childhood to adulthood.

Jennifer had no trouble raising money to buy cocaine. She was young and attractive. Tourists in Fort Lauderdale were all too willing to pay for her favors; quick sex in a hotel room while the guy's wife was on the beach, or a blow-job while driving down Highway 1. There were a few regulars, local men whom she saw once or twice a month. The one who paid best was the undertaker who liked to dress her in black hose, black shoes, black underwear, and a black dress. He would have her lie down in a bronze casket placed in a room where there were several bodies for viewing by the families. Then he would come in wearing his black clothes and he would fuck her in the bronze casket while soft funereal music played over the loudspeakers.

Jennifer became pregnant twice and each time had an abortion.

Then, one day on the beach, Jennifer met a young man, a student at Dade Junior College. He was innocent enough and good enough and so filled with hope for the future that he made Jennifer want to regain her humanity.

She told her parents part of her story. To tell them all would have been to break their hearts. They paid for her to enter a drug rehabilitation program up in St. Petersburg. A place called Straight.

The night before she was to leave, she made love to the young man she had met on the beach, the young man who now was such an important part of her life. It was their first time. When she realized she was pregnant, she told the counselors at Straight, and she stood up and told the other kids at Straight. She and the young man, who now visited her on the weekends when her parents drove up from Fort Lauderdale, planned to be married.

Jennifer was one of the lucky ones. She had the desire and the motivation to take charge of her life, to leave cocaine behind. She had discovered what many people twice her age do not know: that one secret of happiness is not doing things that cause guilt. When she left Straight she was clean, and she knew she would stay clean.

She and the young man were married on a warm winter day when the air was crisp and clean and one could see forever. Then their child was born, a little girl who had its mother's eyes and its father's smile.

It was only a matter of hours before the doctor realized something was wrong with the newborn child.

Something terribly wrong. It broke into spells of gleaming perspiration. It was irritable. There were severe behavior swings from hyperexcitability to a comalike sleep. Rigid muscles. Tremors. Seizures.

The baby was a cocaine addict; there had been enough cocaine in Jennifer's blood for her child to become addicted in the womb. The little girl died during a grand mal seizure.

Jennifer went home the next morning. She was dressing for her daughter's funeral when, without a word, she walked out the back door, hurried two blocks to the canal, and crawled over the railing. She fell, tumbling and weeping, into the dark waters.

Two days later her body, or what was left of her body after the crabs had finished, was found tangled in the roots of a mangrove thicket.

11

Cosmos Goldstein rolled his shoulders to relax the tension that had accumulated from two hours of leaning over a computer screen, bent forward, and pressed one of the keys on the right side of the keyboard. It was amazing. When his two silent friends had come by the previous day to pick up their weekly load of money, one handed him a diskette and smiled.

Goldstein smiled in awe as he stared at the amber figures on the black computer screen. Where did his quiet friends get this stuff? How did they do it? There had been the diskette with all the technical information and graphics on the capabilities of the F-16 radar; then the one showing how the FLIR operated and its capabilities. The words "TOP SECRET" were stamped across the top of almost every screen-load of data. This one was equally fascinating. It detailed exactly how a U.S. Customs apprehension team worked. The apprehension teams were aboard the Blackhawk helicopters, but occasionally, if the runway were long enough, the 'Hawk too far behind, and the dopers about to get away, a sensor bird would land and the copilot and back-seater became the apprehension team. Techniques were basically the same.

What Goldstein did not understand was why the Citation was always used to intercept his single-engine aircraft. The single-engine aircraft inevitably lost the sophisticated high-tech sensor bird. Customs had not yet figured out that the Blackhawk was the aircraft smugglers feared most. Smugglers knew that, contrary to what Customs said, it was possible to beat the balloons. If a pilot had the chutzpah to get down in the wave clutter, down at about fifty feet, he could usually avoid detection. He might show up as an intermittent target, but it would take a sharp radar operator to detect and predict his track. He knew Coast Guard radar operators did not have the skills to do this, but that a few Customs guys could. Goldstein's single-engine aircraft came in low enough to avoid detection by the balloons. There was always the rare chance of a cold hit by a trolling sensor bird. Rare, because Goldstein had a former FAA air-traffic controller in a house near Homestead Air Force Base. The controller called South Caicos or any en-route smugglers every time a Citation or Blackhawk took off. Many times, when a load was inbound, Goldstein's air-traffic controller had called the Air Branch, either on a VHF radio or on the telephone, and given them a bogus sighting of a low inbound aircraft, an airdrop in progress, or a crashed aircraft. Many times, Goldstein's controller had simply suckered the Blackhawk out of position.

Goldstein was as frightened of the Blackhawk as he was of anything. It was the one aircraft used by Customs that gave its crew the capability of discovering his secret.

Most smugglers brought cocaine into Florida aboard commercial airliners or in container loads of freight aboard cargo boats. Big turbine-powered twin-engine aircraft brought in large loads. These three were what Customs and the Drug Enforcement Administration looked for—airliners, container freight, and big twins. Until recently they had ignored single-engine aircraft as nickel-and-dime stuff not worth their while. The thinking was, why use men and equipment to take down an amateur in a single who might be hauling fifty keys max, when those same men and equipment could be used to take down a twin with eight hundred keys or a load of container freight with a thousand keys?

Goldstein took advantage of that thinking. He had his singles come in during the late afternoon or early evening when there was a flood of traffic from the Bahamas. He particularly liked Sunday afternoon, when dozens, maybe hundreds, of general-aviation aircraft were returning from the islands. Sometimes his pilots attached the heads of mannequins to the aircraft seats so, if they were intercepted, it would appear they had two or three passengers aboard. Duffel bags of cocaine were jammed in the aisles or between and under the seats. Even on the seats. But never above the edge of the windows so they could be seen from the outside. And then there were the procedures he had devised for his pilots to break radar lock if they were intercepted by Customs, procedures that always worked. They had to work. They were founded on the certain knowledge of what the F-16 radar could and could not do. First, the pilot of an intercepted aircraft headed for the deck, no more than several hundred feet of altitude, and flew north or south along one of Fort Lauderdale's heavily traveled expressways. If the pilot slowed to a speed under one hundred knots, he was below the notch at which the radar could detect him. Therefore the radar broke lock and went into an automatic-search mode. If the radar operator was sharp enough to lower the notch, then the radar could not distinguish between expressway traffic and the target airplane. In addition, fences along the expressway caused a strobing effect on the RF beams from the doppler radar. Finally, the high-density-traffic areas around Fort Lauderdale showed up on radar as numerous blips. The screen was covered with dozens of possibilities. In the meantime, the pilot had been banking and yanking, making the abrupt 180-degree changes in direction of which a single-engine aircraft is capable, and moving beyond the sensor bird's immediate area. When he figured his aircraft was lost in the expressway clutter, the doper pilot made a ninety-degree turn to the west, flew a few moments, and landed on a short field. The landing strips in reality were pastures adjacent to Goldstein's homes in western Broward County. Perfect for single-engine aircraft.

Goldstein again smiled in admiration of his quiet friends as he pressed the return key, each time bringing up a new color graphic of Customs' apprehension procedures. Most of the graphics were designed with a twin-engine smuggler's aircraft in mind.

The four members of the bust team were fearsome apparitions. The diagram showed that each wore black fatigues, the same sort worn by SWAT teams. Their trousers were bloused into black boots. Each wore a pistol, usually a nine-millimeter with the fourteen-bullet clip. Each carried an automatic rifle, usually the CAR-15. Because of the sandstorm kicked up by the Blackhawk's powerful rotors, team members wore tinted goggles. They had radios strapped to their hips and each had a "pigtail" running to the earphones over his head.

Goldstein wondered idly at what point in the bust the apprehension team unplugged their earphones from the helicopter's radio jacks and plugged them into the FM radios they wore on their hips, the ones tuned to Customs' house freq.

The Blackhawk was fast enough to intercept and hold position with most single-engine aircraft and with a lot of twins. During practice intercepts, Customs had discovered that if the 'Hawk pilot got too close to the target, particularly if flying in the traditional behind-and-above mode, its sound could be heard over the noise of the doper's aircraft. So now the 'Hawk flew behind and below. Once one has heard the unique noise of the 'Hawk, it is a sound easily recognized and is rarely confused with another helicopter.

Usually the 'Hawk maneuvers to stay out of sight until the doper lands. Then the 'Hawk pounces. It comes out of nowhere and approaches over the top of the doper so the downwash from the rotors, a 150-mph-plus downwash strong enough to hold upwards of nineteen thousand pounds in the air, will cause the drug-laden aircraft to rock and roll and twist and shudder as if it is about to flip inverted. This causes first a bewilderment, then fear, then—when the distinctively shaped 'Hawk is visible—a moment of abject terror. The 'Hawk lands in front of the doper; how close depends upon how invincible the Customs pilot feels that day, but always close enough that he is eyeball-to-eyeball with the doper. The doper sees a solid black helicopter with a thin trim line of gold paint and, on the nose, the words "Coke Buster." In that instant the doper usually wishes he had gone into some other line of work.

Sometimes, even before the 'Hawk has settled firmly onto the ground, the apprehension team is out and running—two men out each side, all rushing straight off the helicopter's nose so they won't be decapitated by the rotors. The team leader usually stands in front of the chopper with an automatic rifle pointed at the doper pilot. His men fan out off each wing tip. They point weapons at the pilot and copilot as the fourth man runs behind the smugglers' aircraft and opens the door.

According to the documentation Goldstein studied, the decision to have a Customs officer open the door of the smugglers' aircraft was a difficult one. Some Customs officials wanted to wait until the smugglers opened the door. It was felt that if Customs took the initiative, the smugglers might start shooting.

But the basic idea is to take control of a highly volatile situation as quickly as possible. So it was decided that an interdiction officer should open the door. Then, while standing under the belly of the aircraft, he does a "quick peek"; his head bobs up and he looks down the length of the aircraft toward the cockpit. It is very fast, a snakelike up and down, too fast for anyone inside to take aim and pop off a round. Then the officer moves forward and looks toward the tail to make sure no one is hiding to the rear of the aircraft.

In the meantime, other members of the apprehension team are seeking to convince the pilot and copilot to cut the engines and put their hands in sight. The first thirty seconds are crucial. If a pilot is going to rabbit, that's when he will do it. Several have elected to do so. With visions of big-time jail sentences dancing in their heads, they ram the throttles forward and try to run.

Dopers have rammed the 'Hawk in the past. Now the 'Hawk pilot keeps his power up; he is prepared for an immediate launch. A five-million-dollar helicopter is too valuable to risk crunching on a doper's aircraft. Preparing to flee is very difficult for 'Hawk pilots. They are predators. And, like most predators, they are aggressive, committed, dedicated. It must be emphasized to them, over and over, that their job is to put the apprehension team in position to neutralize the doper aircraft. They are not to play with the 'Hawk as if it were a bumper car in a carnival.

If the doper pilot and copilot seem confused or unsure of what to do, one member of the apprehension team flips the ailerons of the aircraft, moving them briskly up and down. This causes the yoke in front of the doper crew to turn hard from left to right and back again. Or the team member on the tail of the aircraft flips the rudders. This pushes the yoke into the stomach of the pilot and copilot and gets their attention.

A slashing movement across the throat by one of the team members is a universally understood aviation signal to cut the engines. Both hands clasped on top of the head indicates the crew members are to do the same. Except for the team leader standing in front of the helicopter, the members of the apprehension team are protected by the wing tips of a twin-engine aircraft, or by being out of sight in the rear. If either doper moves from his seat, he is thought to be seeking a weapon, and all members of the apprehension team consider it a hostile situation. Their weapons are cocked and safeties are off.

The copilot is brought out first, hands on his head. The team member under the aircraft passes him down the steps to the member who has come around from the left wing tip. He is quickly cuffed and searched and told to get a close look at the runway. If he is a bit slow in sprawling out facedown, he is assisted. Sometimes not gently. And he finds the surface of the runway is not nearly as smooth to his face as it is to the aircraft wheels.

Then the pilot is brought out and the procedure duplicated.

Goldstein moved on through the contents of the new diskette. Near the end was a section telling how relatively easy it was to secure a twin-engine aircraft. The design of the aircraft made it easy to do what an apprehension team does. Almost as an afterthought, there was a section detailing the procedure for taking control of a high-wing single-engine aircraft. It dismissed the chance of this ever happening. According to the disk, which appeared to be a copy of an official Customs training aid, smugglers, especially cocaine smugglers, rarely use single-engine aircraft. But in the rare chance that Customs ever had to deal with one, the apprehension team was cautioned that it was the most risky and danger-ridden apprehension of all. The members of the apprehension team have no wing to hide under; they are exposed, out in the open. And the pilot sees them clearly. He probably could shoot two Customs officers before anyone could respond.

Goldstein smiled whimsically as he turned off the computer, removed the diskette, and placed it into a drawer. All of this was academic. Customs had never busted one of his aircraft. They never would. Even if a sensor bird managed to stay with one of his aircraft and follow it to the landing site, the crew would never be able to bust the load. Goldstein knew the law and the rigid requirements Customs had to follow in order to make an arrest. His system meant that certain elements in those requirements would never be met. That is, unless the 'Hawk happened to be in the right position at the right time and the crew acted with lightning speed. But that combination of events was so statistically remote that it should not be considered.

The only other thing he had to fear was a government agent rolling one of his employees, turning an employee into a government snitch. He knew that ninety-nine percent of the time when a load is lost, a snitch is involved. It's common sense. The government rarely has the capability to get inside a group of smugglers and know when a load is coming in. So they cajole and threaten and promise and do whatever it takes to have someone inside the organization tell them everything. There are many ways to cover a snitch's involvement. One favorite used by the DEA was to let the load land, be off-loaded onto a truck, and then go down the expressway. Miles from the airport, when the dopers were beginning to feel confident, the truck's engine would suddenly die. It would stop running. A state trooper would just happen to be in the neighborhood. He would stop seconds later and order the driver to move the stalled vehicle off the expressway. "Move it now or I'm calling a wrecker," he usually said. The driver, panic-stricken at the thought of being caught with a load of coke, usually replied by saying he would go hire a wrecker. He would disappear, never looking back and usually grateful that he had escaped, while the cops would announce a fortuitous seizure. Actually, the truck's engine had been killed by a "knock-off switch" placed there by the DEA. Then there was the gambit used with motherships carrying drugs. The pickup boat would be waiting and all would be going well. Then, maybe a hundred miles or so before the mothership reached the off-load spot, it would be detected by a Coast Guard cutter that, the dopers thought, just happened to be in the area.

Goldstein knew all the tricks and legerdemain used by federal agencies to cover the involvement of a snitch. And he never hesitated to do what he had to do when he believed one of his employees had been flipped.

As Goldstein locked the door to the computer room, he nodded in approval. It was him against everything the U.S. government could throw at him, and he was winning. Winning to the tune of an average twenty-one aircraft per week. They did not even know he existed. If they did know, they would not accept it. They were incapable of believing that one man could do what he was doing. That was the way Goldstein liked it. This year he would reach his goal of making more money than General Motors.

He paused outside the door, rubbed his tight muscular stomach, and smiled a satisfied smile. His quiet friends assured him he was safe. The system he had devised ensured his aircraft would never be caught.

He was invincible.

12

The Miami Air Branch of U.S. Customs sits on a remote southwest corner of Homestead Air Force Base at the end of Runway Bravo—a decommissioned runway that runs northwest-southeast. To drive to the Air Branch from the west gate of the sprawling air-defense facility, one must move to the far-right traffic lane immediately upon entering the gate. Then, after crossing the railroad tracks and making a hard right turn past a half-dozen white buildings, the road begins a gentle curve to the left. At the stop sign, one must make a hard right to cross a drainage ditch and then another hard right on the road that leads to a hangar and a cluster of mobile homes that serve as offices. Except for the hangar, the largest structure is a building called the "five by" or the "bull pen." In the mid-1980's, when the long-running War on Drugs heated up and Congress began allocating large amounts of money to various federal agencies involved in narcotics, the number of pilots and crews at the Miami Air Branch mushroomed almost overnight from about two dozen to almost one hundred. To give the crews a place to do the never-ending paperwork that takes up their time when they are not flying, five mobile homes were patched together. Around the outer edge are small offices. But most of the space is taken up by the huge open area in the middle. It is filled with sofas and chairs which face two television sets against the wall.

Across a narrow parking area from the bull pen is the main office. A sign over the entrance says "Authorized Personnel Only," and coded push-button locks secure all doors. The same code—a five-one-three-four sequence—opens each door.

After entering the front door, crossing a hall, and passing through a small room that contains the bulletin board and a coffee machine, one enters the operations room—nerve center of the Air Branch. Along the rear wall, in front of an enormous wall map of South America, the Caribbean, Bahamas, and much of the United States, is a waist-high wooden divider. Behind the divider, two men answer telephones and monitor radio conversations of all Customs aircraft. Across the room are two plastic-covered boards, one of which is topped by the name of the command duty officer in charge of the shift, and a listing of the troops under his command. The second board lists the status of the Air Branch's "assets"—all the available aircraft. At the top of the board are the Air Branch's flagships—the Citations—followed by the CHET's, highly modified Piper Cheyennes known as Customs High Endurance Trackers. Then come the King Airs, Titans, and the other royalty of the fleet, the Blackhawk helicopters. Down at the bottom of the board is an aircraft listed as the "Gonad," which is the Air Branch's not-so-affectionate name for an Australian aircraft called the Nomad. This lumbering twin-turbine aircraft is extraordinarily expensive. Customs was ordered to buy the Nomad for evaluation as a marine-patrol aircraft. If it passes the evaluation, which it probably will, then more will be bought in an effort to help Australia with its balance of payments.

Mike Love stood before the board, studying it in detail. His name was listed alongside one of the Citations. If the Citation were launched, he would be the pilot.

On the wall to the left of the two men behind the wooden divider is a large board listing recent drug busts, where the busts took place, the lead agency involved, and the case officer on each. Behind this board is a small room containing the highly classified TECS system, a computer that gives the names and backgrounds of all known and suspected drug smugglers. The numbers of their aircraft, names of their associates, and many relevant and irrelevant details of their lives are listed. If a fixed-base operation at a one-pump fueling station on a small remote airstrip in north Florida is suspected of building auxiliary fuel tanks for smugglers, his name is in TECS. If the manager of a hotel in the Bahamas is known to cater to drug smugglers, his name and the names and backgrounds of his business partners are in TECS.

The operations center is something of a war room for the Air Branch. If a stranger could get into the highly sensitive room, the very nerve center of the U.S. Customs interdiction effort, he would think he had walked into a room of aging fraternity boys. Dress is casual—everything from rumpled flight suits to blue jeans and T-shirts. The dark blue boat shoes that are standard Customs issue are very much in evidence. Pilots, most of whom are in their middle thirties, have the erect posture, short hair, and bright intelligent eyes of men who served several hitches in the military. Laughter and pranks come easily to them. Their nicknames for each other range from the flattering to the cruel. Their banter is, at best, scatological, and their jokes range from jovial ethnic slurs to detailed descriptions of certain bodily functions. In short, there is something to offend everyone.

Most Customs pilots have the experience to get high-paying airline jobs. And occasionally one does leave for an airline. He is immediately considered a civilian, an outsider. He is looked upon as if he somehow got into Customs by mistake. Customs pilots are involved in a brand of aviation that is done nowhere else in the world. Outside of combat flying, there is nothing in aviation that even approaches what they do. And there is no place for those who are not one hundred percent committed to The Job. Some of the men are legends—old heads like Roger Woolard, who can take off in the Citation, zoom it to altitude, and get an hour or so more cruising time than the book says can be done. Woolard is famous not only for his flying skills but also for the dedication and aggressiveness that are hallmarks of a great Customs pilot. It is said, for instance, that once in the Bahamas when he found a smuggler about to take off for America with a load of drugs, he could not get Bahamian officials to respond in time to stop the load. So he bounced the wheels of the Blackhawk up and down on the wing of the smuggler's aircraft until the wing was too damaged for the smuggler to take off.

Another of the older pilots once was monitoring a load of dope inbound through the Bahamas. The doper pilot was a snitch who had told Customs when and where the load was coming through. But the guy flying in the right seat was a homicidal Colombian whose job it was to see that the load got to its destination. A way had to be found to allow the load to be taken down without putting suspicion on the snitch. The Customs pilot told the doper pilot, who was wearing earphones, to take off his headset, turn on the cabin speakers, and do everything he was told. Then, in a clipped authoritarian British accent, the Customs pilot, now in the persona of "Nassau control," vectored the doper pilot on a series of complicated courses before ordering him to land. The load was taken down and the Colombian never suspected what had happened.

Crews at the Air Branch are a loosey-goosey bunch. The loud conversations early one evening were typical. It was about the same time that Lance and Nick, six hundred miles south, were sitting down to eat turtle steaks with Ollie.

Pig Pen, who is never reluctant to tell people he is the best Blackhawk pilot at the Air Branch, leaned on the wooden divider puffing on a cigarette. His hair needed an oil change. He wore a flight suit that other pilots swore had never been washed. "I'm gonna have to quit eating," he said seriously. "Everything I eat turns to shit."

At the other end of the divider, Vicky and Corky, the two female radar operators, were telling a new back-seater about a recent chase in which the smuggler had crashed and burned. "I got on the radio," Vicky said, "and I told Slingshot the doper had crashed and that we had a crispy critter in the aircraft."

One of the new pilots had a telephone against his right ear and a finger pressed hard against his left ear. "I am not just interested in what you call cheap physical stuff," he said. "I want a meaningful relationship." He paused. "Something that will last at least several hours."

John, the muscular supervisor from C3I, heard Freddy, a dark-skinned Puerto Rican pilot known as "Papa Doc," talking about a bust near San Juan, where two dopers had shot at him. "Shot at you?" John said in mock disbelief. "I thought you Puerto Ricans only used knives."

A snippet of conversation floated from the computer room. "When I was at Gitmo I had all my laundry done so I could come home with clean clothes. They kept my underwear. There's some pervert walking around down there with my drawers on."

"The guy must not have seen the racing stripes," said another voice.

"You mean the skid marks?"

Members of the apprehension team came out of the armory carrying automatic weapons in one hand and clips of ammunition in the other.

Two back-seaters popped in from the ready room down the hall. "The Coast Guard launched a Falcon on the bad guy," one said. "I was watching the Coasties on radar when they did the intercept. It was like watching a monkey trying to fuck a football."

"Yeah," the other said. "The Coast Guard has done for law enforcement what panty hose did for finger fucking."

Moonbeam, a Citation pilot who seems determined

to prove anew each day that he exists in his own time and space continuum, told Larry, the command duty officer, of his recent court appearance. "I was on the stand," Moonbeam said earnestly. "The doper's lawyer asked me what were my personal feelings about drug smugglers. I asked him if he wanted me to be absolutely honest. He said yes, so I told him I thought smugglers ranked somewhere between baby rapers and barn burners. And you know what? The jury broke out in applause."

One of the new pilots was telling a skeptical old hand about a date he had had the previous evening. "She wasn't in the car five minutes and she had her hand on my bird," he said.

"What d'you mean, your bird?"

"You know." He pointed at his groin. "My bird."

"Why do you call it a bird?" The older pilot was annoyed.

"Because that's what it is. That's what I've always called it. My bird."

"Jesus H. Christ," exploded the pilot. "Call it your dick, your pecker, your cock, your crank, your schlong, your weenie, your whatever. But don't call it a goddamn bird."

The eyes of the new pilot widened in alarm. "No, no, no. I could never do that. It's my bird."

"Well, I hope your little birdy goes tweet, tweet, tweet," the older pilot said. He turned and walked out of the room in disgust.

Paul, a bearded hotshot of a 'Hawk pilot, was studying the operations board. One of the new pilots said to him, "I'm giving up bowling for sex."

"Yeah, why is that?"

"The balls are not as heavy and I don't have to change shoes."

John Boy, a former Marine pilot, slammed his open palm down on the divider and said, "Gentlemen"—he nodded toward Vicky and Corky—"and ladies, I propose a toast."

Boos and hisses. "Save it for the club this afternoon," Vicky said.

John Boy stood atop a chair, held aloft his cup of black coffee, and looked around the room with the lordly disdain manifested by psychopaths and former Marines. "Here's to two hundred and fourteen years of romping, stomping, hell, death, and destruction," he said. His voice grew louder and faster. "Highly dedicated, highly motivated, high-stepping, low-crawling, roguishly handsome, global soldiers of the sea. C-rat-fed, beer-cooled, lean, green, mean, fighting machine. Slop bucket full of balls"—he placed his right forefinger on the elbow of his extended left arm—"dick this long, enough hair on their ass to weave a horse blanket." He paused for breath, then shouted, "The Corps! Aaaaaaauuuuu."

"Marines are like bananas," was the laconic response of one of the ex-Air Force fighter pilots. "They're green and they die in bunches."

"Ignore John Boy," said another ex-Air Force fighter jock. "His medical has expired."

The chatter of the operations room came to a halt when Keith, a Citation copilot working behind the wooden divider, picked up the red telephone that is a direct link with C3I, listened a moment, hung up, and pressed a button that sounded the Klaxon. Throughout the complex of buildings could be heard the wailing sound: "ah-oooooo-ga . . . ah-oooooo-ga." Then Keith was on the public-address system: "Launch the Citation. Launch the Citation. This is a scramble. Launch the Citation."

Every person in the operations room froze for a second. The rowdy fraternity-house banter ended instantly, and the demeanor of pilots and crews became dead serious. The pilots and crews knew whose name was listed on the board to fly the Citation, but even so, every eye turned to the situation board, instinctively registering the name of the pilot and cataloging his abilities. Several heads nodded in approval when Mike Love's name was seen. Mike was a quiet, almost somber man, but when he strapped on an airplane and chased a doper, he became as aggressive as an amorous moose. And he had the same disregard for obstacles. Mike believed in neatness and order. In his closet at home all of his white shirts were hung together, followed by blue shirts, then striped shirts, then other colors, then his sport shirts. His sense of order so permeated his being that the money in his wallet not only was lined up in denominational order but also had all the dark green sides facing the same direction. Further, the portraits on the bills were all upright. Mike could thumb through his money and see the ones followed by the fives followed by the tens and then twenties. And the upright and unsmiling faces of Washington, Lincoln, Hamilton, and Jackson looked out, all in the proper sequence. If a bill was out of order or turned upside down, Mike felt as if he had been violated. His sense of order had been kicked awry. His world had been shaken. But nothing disturbed his sense of order so much as a drug smuggler trying to enter America. With Mike it was a black-and-white issue. A host of international treaties plus federal, state, and local laws made it an illegal act to import certain controlled substances into the United States. That was the law. Smugglers were breaking the law. They had to be caught and brought to justice. No exceptions. That was the way it was. And to detect a smuggler and then have that smuggler beat him not only upset the natural order but also made Mike angry. "Angry" is not strong enough. He became angry when he accidentally placed money in his wallet upside down. When a smuggler escaped, he became furious. He became cold and aggressive and relentless.

The pilots at the Air Branch were not worried about Mike. He was the best. He had a good copilot and the best back-seater at the Branch. It was a good crew. If a smuggler were out there, they would find and track him. Several people in the room looked at their watches. Six-fifteen. The smuggler should reach the coast about seven-thirty or eight P.M., roughly the time the single-engine aircraft that had been beating them regularly for several months had been coming through.

"The Lauderdale Express is running tonight," one of the pilots said. Several others nodded in agreement.

Larry Karson, the preppy command duty officer, looked at the status board, then turned to Pig Pen, who was listed as the Blackhawk pilot. Larry clapped his hands and pointed to Pig Pen. "Get ready to fly," he said. "Let's turn jet fuel into noise." He flicked his finger toward Big Ed, leader of the apprehension team. "Let's hit the heavens, guys." He turned and pointed to Keith. "Give BSO a heads-up. If this is the Lauderdale Express, the Broward guys need some notice."

Mike heard none of this. He was running at the first note of the Klaxon. He was through the coffee room, around the corner, past the rest room, and into the hangar when Keith finished his launch command. Already mechanics were standing in front of the Citation, waiting for the inertial navigation system to align so they could disconnect the auxiliary power unit. The Citation was "coned"—that is, it had a three-foot-tall orange plastic cone by the open crew door. The cone signified that the aircraft was cocked and locked—it had been pre-flighted and the INS was set for a five-minute alignment.

Mike climbed gently into the Citation. If the aircraft were bumped or jarred during the alignment process, it would take a full fifteen minutes for the INS to be realigned. Dave, the copilot, and J.T., the back-seater, stepped aboard. J.T. pulled up the steps and locked the door. He moved to his seat behind the radar and FLIR control panel.

Six minutes after the Klaxon sounded, Mike was taxiing at almost takeoff speed down Runway Bravo toward the active runway.

"I'd like to bring up sensor power," J.T. said.

Dave clicked the microphone switch twice, giving approval for J.T. to divert power to the radar and the FLIR.

Dave was on the radio. "Homestead ground, Omaha Five Two taxiing for takeoff."

"Roger, Five Two. Winds light and variable. Altimeter point-niner-five. Runway your option." The radio conversations were fast, crisp, and efficient.

The runway was fast approaching. "Switching to tower," Dave said.

He turned the VHF radio switch to 126.2. "Tower, Omaha Five Two will be ready at the intersection. Like a right turn."

"Five Two cleared for takeoff. Right turn eastbound approved."

As Mike came to where Runway Bravo crossed Runway 5, he tapped the brakes and slowed for the left turn onto the runway. He wanted to take the turn as fast as possible without throwing too great a side load on the Citation's landing gear. Three-quarters of the way through the turn, he slowly but surely and confidently pressed the two lollipop-shaped throttles all the way forward. The Citation surged and was off the ground and turning right toward Biscayne Bay before it was halfway down the runway.

Almost immediately came the voice of the controller. "Omaha Five Two, freq change approved."

Mike nodded in appreciation. The guy in the tower had anticipated their request. He was sharp. This was going to be a good chase. He sensed that the aircraft he was racing to intercept was the Lauderdale Express. And he was ready with a new technique. Tonight he was going to bag a doper and maybe five hundred keys of coke.

"Permission to turn on one and two," J.T. said over the intercom. The pilot or copilot had to know in advance when the number one and number two inverters were switched on because they caused an enormous drain on the electrical system. The yaw damper could be knocked off and sometimes the master warning light came on.

Dave clicked the microphone.

As the Citation gathered speed, Dave switched frequencies. "Slingshot, Omaha Five Two."

"Five Two, Slingshot. Go." The voice of the radar operator at C3I was crisp and confident. This had the markings of a good intercept, one of those rare times when everything is clicking, when all the systems are up and working, when all the parts of all the Customs network are combined in a marvelous synergy. On these rare occasions it is clear to a Customs pilot that he represents Truth, Justice, and the American Way; that the forces of the Almighty are aligned on his behalf.

"Slingshot, Five Two requesting bogey dope."

"Bogey bears zero one zero for one eight five. Intermittent target."

Mike smiled in anticipation. One of the balloons, either George Town or Cariball, had detected the bogey. The information was fed down a fiber optics cable from the balloon to the ground, and then, by data link, to C3I. An intermittent target meant the bad guy was down in the wave tops, in and out of the clutter. The guy had to be a doper. No back door, no circuitous route for this guy. He was bound straight for Fort Lauderdale.

The Lauderdale Express was running.

Dave leaned forward. "Understand zero one zero for one eight five."

"That's affirm."

"He's coming across at Nassau, trying to mix in with the other traffic," Mike said.

Dave looked at the compass, then at the sectional chart. A target ten degrees off the nose of the Citation and one hundred and eighty-five nautical miles away would—just as Mike said—be approaching Nassau from the south. Dave, like many of the young ex-military jet jocks now serving as copilots at the Branch, had gone to work feeling a bit patronizing toward the older pilots, particularly those who, like Mike, had learned to fly as general-aviation pilots rather than in the military. These pilots thought that if they could drive a military jet, no civilian pilot could teach them any-thing. But they quickly learned that chasing drug smug-glers is more demanding and more dangerous than flying military jets. In addition to the flying skills, one must think like a smuggler and anticipate what a smuggler might do under every set of circumstances. One has to be willing to snuggle up close enough to a smuggler in flight to count the rivets on the aircraft; one also must have the confidence and the skills to fly fifty feet over the ocean on a moonless night, and to track a smuggler at treetop level on the darkest night across the trackless wastes of the Everglades or the Big Cypress Swamp.

To new Customs pilots, the Florida keys, Bahamas, and the Turks and Caicos Islands were a confusing jumble of hundreds of islands, most of which looked more or less like all the others. But the older guys could fly down the Florida keys or over almost any island in the Bahamas and instantly know where they were, and where the runways—charted and uncharted— were located. They could, upon receiving bogey dope from Slingshot, almost immediately translate it into a precise location for the target.

Mike pressed harder against the throttles, pushing the Citation on up to its dash speed of almost four hundred miles an hour.

By now the radar and the FLIR had run through their built-in tests and were operational. As the air-craft leveled at thirteen thousand, five hundred feet, the radar was on a four-bar scan and blasting out prodigious amounts of energy, searching from the ground up to nineteen thousand feet and for eighty miles in front of the Citation. The "footprint" of the radar, the width of the cone of coverage at wave-top level, was wide enough that no smuggler could blast through at high speed and be undetected.

Omaha 52, a U.S. Customs sensor bird, was up and operational, all systems in the green.

Slingshot came back. "Omaha Five Two, target bears three five zero for eight eight miles."

Dave looked at the small repeater screen by his left knee. It had not yet picked up the target. "Roger. No joy," Dave said. He glanced at Mike in amazement. Mike, without being given vectors by Slingshot, had offset the target a few degrees, preparing to transition from the head-on approach to the target's six-o'clock position. He was doing this better than a military jock trained in air-defense intercepts.

About five minutes later came Slingshot. "Omaha Five Two, bogey bears three four five for three eight miles."

"No joy."

J.T. was leaning forward over the console, thumb resting lightly on the button that controlled the acquisition symbols, forefinger ready to squeeze the trigger. He should have the target any minute.

He waited. One second there was nothing and the next there was a green square in the middle of the upper screen. J.T. rapidly slid the acquisition symbols over the target and squeezed the trigger. Bingo. The green square changed to a diamond.

"We have a judy," J.T. said over the intercom. "Three five zero for two six miles. On the deck."

"Slingshot, Five Two," Dave radioed.

"Five Two, go."

"We have a judy."

Now control switched to the Citation. No longer would the crew receive bogey dope from Slingshot. It was up to J.T.'s wizardry and Mike's aggressiveness; it was now a combination of science and art, technology and intuition; a mixture of twentieth-century electronics and eighteenth-century entrail-stirring.

It was good against evil.

The target's altitude readout on the radar showed 00.0—still in the wave tops—and flying at almost two hundred miles an hour. It was a high-performance single-engine or a light twin. The closure rate between the two aircraft was almost six hundred miles an hour.

Mike glanced down at the small radar screen, reading the numbers, mentally working through infinitely complex calculations. For a daytime head-to-head intercept, a Customs pilot must exercise extreme care to stay out of what is called the "interceptor avoidance zone"—the two hundred and forty degrees of scanning area the doper has when he looks out of the cockpit. This area is five miles deep. The target must always be kept forty-five degrees off the left or right side of the nose. As the two aircraft meet, the Customs pilot, always keeping the bad guy forty-five degrees off the nose, begins turning until he is in trail.

Mike did not have to worry about the avoidance zone at night. His strobe and nav lights were off. Even so, he swung a few degrees to the south, increasing the làteral offset so he could more easily turn in behind the smuggler once they passed each other.

He watched the radar closely, cross-checking it with the FLIR, which now was slaved to the radar. When the radar showed the smuggler off the left side of the Citation's nose, Mike racked the Citation up on the left wing tip, reduced the power, and lost altitude rapidly as he fell in trail behind the target.

In the rear of the Citation, J.T. adjusted the FLIR from "black hot" to "white hot" and back again. Black hot seemed to provide the best picture. He checked the closure rate. A rule of thumb for an intercept was that if the bad guy was flying at a hundred and fifty knots or greater, the closure rate could be at a hundred and fifty knots until the Citation was one mile in trail. Then, pulling power to idle would enable the Citation to coast up on the target's tail without overshooting. J.T. nodded in approval. Mike, as usual, had the numbers bracketed. J.T. looked at the small dot in the middle of his radar screen. He leaned closer and touched the dot with the tip of a pen. He would never touch the screen with a finger; it left a greasy smudge that had to be cleaned with a special chemical. That was one thing J.T. hated about flying VIP's aboard the Citation. Invariably they touched the screen with their greasy fingers.

Before anyone else would have seen anything other than a blur on the screen, J.T. identified the target.

"Single-engine," he said. He leaned even closer. His eyes narrowed. "Looks like a Bonanza." J.T. moved his eyes to the altitude readout on the radar. "Still too low to ID."

"We're coming up on Bimini. He'll climb when he crosses the VOR," Mike said.

Moments later the Bonanza crossed Bimini and began a slow climb.

"How'd you know that?" Dave asked in amazement.

"If I were a doper, that's what I'd do. He's coming up to Miami radar coverage and he wants to look like everybody else. He might even file a flight plan."

"But Bimini is closed at night."

"Right. But sometimes there is outbound traffic. It's not that unusual."

Dave switched the VFR radio to the frequency of the Miami flight-service station. The Bonanza pilot was filing a VFR flight plan between Bimini and Fort Lauderdale International. After the FAA technician finished the read-back, the pilot said, "November nine four six Echo. That's correct."

"We got his number," Dave said. He reached for the microphone.

"That's not his number," Mike said. He looked at the radar. "The asshole has leveled off at forty-five hundred. Let's take a look."

With his left hand light on the wheel, his right hand ready on the throttles, and his eyes jumping back and forth between the FLIR picture and the closure rate on the radar, Mike began the most difficult task a Customs pilot faces: a night identification of a suspect aircraft.

He jockeyed the Citation throttles, slowly approaching the aircraft until he was below and directly astern the target.

"It's a Bonanza," Dave said in amazement. How had J.T. known that minutes earlier?

Mike watched the FLIR, seeing the target grow

larger and larger until it filled the screen. Then it
slowly disappeared off the top of the screen. Because
the FLIR is mounted on the belly of the Citation, it
has a blind spot directly ahead of and slightly above
the nose of the aircraft. The target was so close it was
in the FLIR's blind spot.

Mike looked up and saw a small red glow, the
exhaust stack of the Bonanza. Carefully, ever so carefully, making sure the Citation remained straight and
level as he snuggled up even closer, he moved in. Now
he could see a faint glow from inside the bogey's
cockpit. The doper either was looking at his charts or
confirming a radio frequency.

Mike slid out to the left. "Do it," he said.

Dave held the flashlight against the cockpit window,
aimed it carefully, and made sure the beam would not
hit the doper's cockpit. He cupped it with his hand to
keep the glare from hitting Mike's eyes, and then
switched it on. The tail of a yellow Bonanza was about
twenty feet away. "November three eight seven Charlie," he said. He turned off the light and wrote the
number on a pad.

"Slingshot, Five Two."

"Five Two, go."

"We have a number. Ready to copy?"

"Go."

"November three eight seven Charlie. Should be a
yellow Bonanza."

"Roger. Stand by one." Mike knew that somewhere
in C3I, a technician was entering the Bonanza tail
number into the TECS computer. He would know in
seconds if the aircraft was a known or suspected doper.

"The guy didn't see us," Mike said. "He doesn't
know we're on his tail. I'm going to try something new
tonight. I'm going to lay back about three miles."

"Five Two. Slingshot."

"Go."

"You have a hit. That aircraft is positive in the
system."

Mike broke in. "Would you make a hard copy of that info and fax it to the Branch?"

"Affirm."

Mike reduced power and pulled off to the side. Too many dopers had tossed bales of marijuana out of their aircraft in efforts to disable a Customs aircraft for Mike to hang in close when there was no need to do so. And there had been times when dopers shredded packages of cocaine and tossed them out the door, causing great clouds of cocaine dust and forcing Customs pilots to bank and yank to avoid ruining an engine by ingesting the highly alkaline material.

"He gave the FAA a phony number when he filed his flight plan," Dave said. He was surprised. In the orderly flying world of military aviation, filing a flight plan using phony aircraft numbers was unthinkable.

"Welcome to the NFL," Mike muttered, eyes on the radar. He adjusted the power to maintain position three miles behind the target.

About fifteen minutes later the Bonanza was approaching Fort Lauderdale International. Slingshot had coordinated the Citation's approach with the control tower at Lauderdale. Lauderdale was now aware that a smuggler, followed closely by a Customs aircraft, was approaching its control zone.

Then Slingshot was on the radio. "Be advised there are no assets to assist you. Seven Zero launched on another target and no longer is available."

"Fucking bastards. Stupid sons of bitches," Mike exploded. He picked up the mike. "We got to have a bust aircraft," he said. "Unless the target lands at a major airport, we can't land with him."

Slingshot came back. "We show him flight-planned to Lauderdale International. He's headed directly there. So we gave Home Plate the okay to launch Seven Zero on the other target. You are approved to land at International and handle the bust."

Mike shoved the mike back into the clasp and shook his head in disgust. He turned to Dave. "That asshole ain't landing here. That's the fucking Lauderdale Express. What's the matter with those idiots at Slingshot?"

"Target descending. Airspeed slowing," J.T. said, eyes on the radar. He looked at the FLIR. "He's dropped his gear."

"He's landing," Dave said. It appeared Mike was not infallible after all. Dave reached for his pistol and checked to see that the passageway to the door was clear. He and J.T. would handle the bust.

"Bullshit," Mike said. "He's not landing." The Lauderdale Express had beaten him too many times in recent weeks for him to believe the aircraft, an obvious doper, was landing at a major airport. "J.T., stand by," Mike said urgently. "He's going to break any second. Stay with him."

Dave looked at Mike in disbelief. The doper had his gear down and had slowed to a hundred knots.

"I got him," J.T. said. He was leaning over the console, eyes intent on the clearly visible target, using his fingertips on the trackball to keep the target centered on the FLIR screen.

The Bonanza crossed the beach, descended to eight hundred feet, and lined up for a right downwind at Fort Lauderdale International. Then suddenly the doper pilot sucked up his gear, added power, dropped to four hundred feet, and sliced across the takeoff end of the active runway.

Immediately the angry tower operator was on the radio. "Bonanza niner four six Echo, do immediate right two seventy and continue downwind."

No answer.

The tower operator asked a Bahamas Air pilot to abort his takeoff run.

"That's a zoo. We'll go around the south side and pick him up to the northwest," Mike said. There was a bitter taste in his mouth.

Dave, using a discrete UHF frequency, told the tower they were continuing westbound on the edge of the airport control zone.

"Roger. Good day," the controller said, glad to be rid of the Customs jet.

"Where is he, J.T.?" Mike asked urgently. "Don't lose him."

J.T. snorted in frustration. "I got about twenty targets on the screen. We got traffic everywhere."

By then the Bonanza pilot had slowed to eighty miles an hour and was traveling north up I-95 at an altitude of about one hundred feet. Some cars on the expressway were going faster than he was. The Citation's radar never picked him up again.

Eight minutes later the yellow Bonanza landed on a grass strip on the western edge of Fort Lauderdale. Five hundred kilos of cocaine were aboard.

13

"We can't go to the airport until after dark," Nick said. "It's on a hill, the surrounding countryside is flat, there's only one road, and whoever is in the tower can see everything that goes on in all directions."

"So. We can sit out there in the bushes. Practice some male-bonding stuff." Lance grinned and rolled his eyes.

The two men were sitting by the pool. Nick was wearing a bathing suit and had sunburned to a throbbing, pulsating red. He looked like a lobster. He was nursing a beer that had long ago grown warm. Lance, claiming the heat was causing him to be dehydrated, was on beer number eight. He was wearing cut-off jeans and a T-shirt that said "I Go Where the Oboe," an inscription that had caused Ollie no small degree of consternation. Ollie had lurched off to take a nap, saying he wanted to get in shape for some serious drinking that evening.

That morning, the jovial pilot had taken them to the airport and introduced them to Bertram, the chief controller, who said they should expect to pay ten thousand dollars in order to bring a load through the airport. He gave them his telephone number and told them to call two days before they came through with a load, and he provided them with radio frequencies to use when inbound. Nothing to it. No big deal, he said. It happened several dozen times a day on South Caicos. Go by the rules and you'd have no trouble. The main rule, he made clear, was that he be paid.

Now Lance and Nick were talking quietly at a table near the pool.

"You're right," Lance said. "It's okay. You can take a nap after dinner. Then, say about midnight, we can go sit on the airport. I rented a couple of bikes."

Nick glared at his partner. "I don't need a nap," he growled.

"But, boss, you got a birthday coming up. The big four oh. You can join the dinosaur club. Be thinking about social security."

Nick's eyes narrowed. "What will you be doing?"

"Me? When?" Lance said innocently.

"After dinner, when you think I should be taking a nap. What are you doing?"

"I'm increasing my vast reservoir of skills and therefore my value to you."

"What are you doing?"

"I'm going on a night dive."

"You what?"

"I'm going diving."

"Who with?"

"A diver."

"I didn't think you were going with the governor."

"I'm going with that little blonde. We talked at lunch." Lance laughed. "Her friends are horrified that she's going out alone with a killer dope smuggler." He pointed toward Dove Cay, a hundred yards offshore. "We're swimming off the beach. Her friends can keep an eye on her, and I'll be back in plenty of time for us to do our secret-squirrel stuff."

"Don't you have any morals at all?"

"No. But I do have standards."

"What are they?" Nick asked in disbelief.

"A woman has to have a heartbeat and an animal has to have a bath."

"That's more than I figured."

Lance leaned across the table. "Hey, boss, this is

good cover. Drinking. Raising hell. Ollie and his buddies don't have a clue that we're police officers. I'm doing this for the cause, to help keep America free."

Nick shook his head and looked across the water. "I'm worried about this deal. It could go bad any minute. Everything is so out in the open. I've been trying to figure out what kind of enforcement activity we can mount to close this place down once we get back. I don't have an answer." He gingerly touched his face. "On top of everything else, I'm sunburned and I've got to sit out in the boondocks all night."

"You'll be okay. We'll be okay. Hey, you're with the Ghost. I got it covered. You need to put aloe on your face. It's great for sunburn."

"Aloe?"

Lance pointed toward the flowerbed along the walkway. "It's everywhere."

He stood up, walked a few paces, and broke off a stalk from a large sprawling aloe plant and used his thumbnail to split open the pulpy green blade. "See that stuff oozing out? That's aloe. Spread it on your face and shoulders."

Nick wrinkled his nose. "It stinks."

"Doesn't matter. It'll get rid of the pain from the sunburn." Lance handed the stalk to Nick. "Break off several stalks and rub it all over your face and neck. I'm going to talk to my little blonde honey."

It was twilight when Lance and the tiny blonde stood near the dock on the south end of the island and strapped on their scuba tanks. Lance could not keep his eyes off the blonde. Emma was her name. She was a gymnastics instructor from Atlanta and her body was hard and tight and sinewy. Her pink bikini almost glowed against her tanned skin. Even in the gathering darkness the fine sun-bleached hair on her arms shone like a golden aura. The overwhelming impression Lance had in looking at her was roundness. Roundness and tightness. Her small breasts were round and tight; her body had the taut roundness of a balloon that has been slightly overinflated; her muscular buttocks were round and tight; her legs and calves were round and tight.

Lance looked at her, rolled his eyes skyward, laughed softly, and uttered a quiet, "Waaaaaahhhh. Waaaaaahhhh."

Emma looked up. "What?"

"Just talking to myself."

Emma spat into her face mask, rinsed it out, and slid it over her blonde hair. She smiled and waved the flashlight tied to her wrist. "You have good batteries?"

"My batteries are overcharged."

She wrinkled her impudent little round mouth into a moue. "I mean in your light."

Lance turned on his light. "Seems to be working."

"Ready?"

"Lead the way."

Emma smiled again, that reckless daring smile, and said, "Your first night dive is something special. This is going to be a real treat." Then, fins in her hands, she waded into the ocean. Nick followed, his eyes watching the hard muscles of her behind as they pushed her bikini into tight little round hills. When she was in water almost to her waist, she stopped and put on her fins, put the mouthpiece into her mouth, inhaled once to test it, then slid her mask over her eyes. She removed the mouthpiece and said, "Here we go."

"Right behind you."

Emma put the mouthpiece back in, turned, dived forward, and kicked, disappearing in a splash of white bubbles that glistened in the gathering darkness.

They had agreed to stay on the landward side of Dove Cay, in the relatively shallow water, and not go beyond the small island where "the wall" plunged to about seven thousand feet. The shallow waters had only a few reefs and there were no large areas of grass. They were swimming slowly, only a few feet above the sandy bottom, and their lights reflected off the sand and bathed them in a soft penumbra.

The only sound was the sibilant hiss of their regulators as they breathed. Several times Emma reached out to touch Lance's arm, to get his attention and point out shells or pieces of coral. Lance had two theories about women. One was that Monday night was the best night of the week to have a date, particularly if the woman was in her late twenties or so and beginning to hear the ticking of her biological clock and beginning to wonder if she might get married. Monday night was a lonely night for women. The weekend had just passed, and if the woman had not had a date, she probably had spent the weekend reading a novel or watching television. Chances were there was a lot of hugging and kissing and screwing in the novel or on the television programs, so the woman was horny. Yep, Monday night was the best night of the week for a date. The second part of Lance's theory concerned touching. He believed that if a woman reached out to touch a man on the arm or shoulder, as Emma had done when she wanted to point out something, it signified a certain willingness, a receptivity toward more touching. There was nothing cold or calculating about Lance's theory; he had developed it from observation over a period of years. He decided to reconfirm the second part of the theory, the part about touching.

The next time Emma stopped to look at a conch half-buried in the sand, Lance continued swimming; his right hand moved up her legs, lingered over her behind, then held her waist and rolled her over to face him. She turned the light and saw him take the regulator out of his mouth and motion for her to do the same. All he could see was her face and mask. Her eyes sparkled in the bright light as she took several deep breaths and then removed the regulator. Lance pulled her closer and her muscular legs locked around him as they settled to the sand. When they tried to kiss, their masks banged together and he could hear her making giggling noises as she pursed her lips tighter.

Lance tried again. If they both turned their heads at the proper angle, it was possible. Their rolling about stirred up a cloud of sand. Emma turned the light on her face so Lance could see, and held up a finger, motioning for him to follow. She turned and swam about twenty feet away to get out of the sandstorm they had created.

When Lance caught up, he pointed the light toward Emma and his eyes widened when he saw that she had removed her pink bikini and stuffed it inside the waist strap holding her scuba tank. He quickly took off his bathing suit and slid it under his belt.

The next ten minutes were a strobing kaleidoscope of the senses. Their ears were filled with the harsh rhythmic "whoosh" of their breathing as their regulators expelled large bubbles of air. They kissed, awkwardly turning so their masks would not collide. Their hands roamed over each other. Except for quick lightning flashes of light that roamed across their bodies, they could not see each other in the underwater darkness. Their flashlights dangled from wrist cords as they touched and fondled. And occasionally Lance glimpsed a strand of blond hair, a breast, or a muscular thigh. They were weightless in the underwater darkness, floating and drifting. Lance pulled the mouthpiece from his lips, seized Emma's hips, and effortlessly hoisted her, turning his head to the side so his lips could slide across her breasts, her stomach, and then lingered. He pulled his head back, put the regulator into his mouth, took several deep breaths, and moved toward her again. He removed the regulator from his mouth as he reached for Emma. Her legs moved high until they rested across his shoulders. Her salty taste was mixed with the salt of the dark sea. As he took another deep breath from the mouthpiece, he sensed Emma drifting downward, her legs sliding over his shoulders and then around his waist. As they came together Emma locked her hard acrobat's legs around Lance and they floated from the sandy bottom to the surface and back to the bottom, threshing up a small sandstorm on the bottom and roiling the surface as they broached, sometimes vertical, sometimes horizontal, and sometimes rolling over and over as Lance's fins kicked and fluttered in a feeble motion.

Then they were quiet, floating, not moving, Emma's legs still locked around Lance. After a while the pace of their breathing slowed. Emma reached down, found her light, and pointed it toward her face. She pulled the mouthpiece from her mouth, signifying she was running low on air. Lance nodded and they swam toward the beach. She did not bother to put on her pink bikini.

As they approached shallow water, Emma stopped and waited. She put her arms around Lance, turned her head to the side, and kissed him. He felt her legs lock around his left leg as they rolled over and over through the water. Then suddenly she was gone, a fish swimming rapidly toward the nearby beach. He paused, shook his head, and slowly swam after her.

Moments later he stood in waist-deep water, watching the pink of her bikini disappear over the small hill toward the hotel. And he realized why she had swum away so quickly. As they kissed, she had taken his bathing suit from where it was wedged in his scuba harness.

Nick threw his comb down in disgust and said, "What the . . . ?" when Lance, streaming water, carrying his rented scuba tank in front of him, jerked open the door and jumped inside. Lance was nude. He carried his bathing suit in his hand.

"She left it by the door," Lance explained.

Nick stared. "Who left what by the door?"

Lance placed the scuba tank, mask, and fins on the floor and waved his bathing suit as he strode toward the tiny bathroom. "My bathing suit. She left it by the door."

Nick turned and stared after Lance. "You walked through town bare-assed? By the church?"

Lance stuck his head out of the bathroom. "Hey, they sell dope by the church. What's a bare ass? Besides, I did something I've always wanted to do, something I've tried to do but never could. And it was wonderful."

"What?"

Lance's eyes were dancing. "I did it standing on my head."

Nick stared. "You did what?"

"You know. I did it. Standing on my head. Upside down. Feet in the air. How many people do you know who've done it standing on their head? None." Lance turned on the shower.

Nick raised his voice. "You're a sick puppy. I've said it before and I'll say it again. You're sick."

"I'm going to enter myself in the *Guinness Book of World Records*." Lance stuck his head around the shower curtain, panned his hand in an arc, looked up, and said, " 'First man to fuck standing on his head. Lance Cunningham.' "

"We gotta talk."

Lance was back under the shower. "So talk to me, sweetie."

Nick grimaced. "That aloe stuff you gave me. I can't get rid of the smell. You playing some kind of joke?"

"Didn't it work?"

"Yeah, it worked. But it stinks. It's real strong. I put it on my face and neck and that's all I smell. I smell like dog crap and I can't wash it off. I took three showers and I still smell like dog crap."

Lance laughed. "It does have a wee bit of an odor. But it works."

"No it doesn't. I'm walking around smelling like a pile of dog crap."

Lance stuck his head around the shower curtain. His face was streaming water. "But a pile of dog crap with no sunburn."

"Don't do me any more favors, Cunningham. And hurry up."

At dinner Lance wore a long-sleeved black T-shirt with a picture of a .357 Magnum under which was written "Gun Control Is Holding Your Weapon with Both Hands." It was a sentiment shared by many smugglers. One of the great ironies of the drug war is that, in many areas, cops and smugglers are philosophical blood brothers. Both groups are extremely patriotic, oppose gun control, support increased military spending, and, in general, are at the conservative end of the political spectrum.

Lance was the butt of numerous jokes from the smugglers' table. Several had seen him running through town on tiptoe, scuba tank held before him, glancing furtively in all directions. Another had seen the tiny blonde in the pink bikini drop a bathing suit by Lance's door. Ollie was in near-hysterics. He nodded at Lance's shirt and said, "I heard you came through the village holding your weapon in both hands." But Ollie had other reasons, good reasons, to be happy. In the last two days he had sent eight aircraft to Fort Lauderdale and, as usual, all had gotten through. If nothing happened, he could easily send twenty-one, maybe more, this week. "The Doctor is pleased," he told Lance. "Customs intercepted one aircraft, but the pilot made the feds look like idiots." He laughed. "What a system. What a system."

The divers, too, had heard the story of how Lance had raced through the village wearing nothing but a scuba tank. But their laughter was cautious. And they glanced frequently at Lance to see if he knew they were talking about him. Emma, however, was rather pleased with herself. Several times she glanced mockingly at Lance, smiled, and waved.

After dinner, as the smugglers ambled into the bar, Lance lingered at the table. Almost immediately Emma, eyes shining, was sitting next to him.

"Mad?" she asked.

"About what?"

"I didn't think you would be." She paused. "My

friends think I was crazy to do that. They thought you or some of your . . . some of the . . ." She paused and blushed. She had almost said "gangster buddies" or "the drug smugglers."

" 'Friends' is the word you're groping for."

Emma nodded. "They thought you or some of your friends might . . . might . . ."

"Huff and puff and blow your house down."

Emma paused. She reached out and put her hand on Lance's arm. "You're not what I expected from a . . ."

"From a smuggler. You're having trouble with the King's English tonight."

"Does that upset you? To be called a . . . smuggler?"

"That's what you think I am?"

"Well, isn't that what all the people at this table are?"

"Where did you hear that?"

"Everybody knows it."

"If I were, would you expect me to say so?"

Emma's eyes were wide. Lance looked down at her. She was like so many civilians who thought drug smugglers were romantic figures. Her life was so bereft of meaning, so devoid of substance, so lacking in fulfillment, that she had to reach out to a man she thought was a drug smuggler. Her experience with Lance—not with him as an individual, but with him as a drug smuggler—was the high point of her life. When she returned to Atlanta she would talk knowingly of drug smuggling on South Caicos, tell how daring it was to sit in a dining room with a group of smugglers about to go to Colombia or about to take a load of cocaine into Florida. And she could tell how she actually met one of the smugglers. It was all so neat; so terribly neat.

"What time do you get back from your morning dive?"

"I won't go. I'll be ready whenever you say."

Lance looked at his watch and nodded toward the bar. "I'm going to be busy with these guys for several hours. Business. Why don't I come to your room later?"

She smiled, shrugged a tan shoulder, and again squeezed his leg. "The door doesn't have a lock."

"It may be late."

"Wake me."

"Very late."

"Wake me."

"What room?"

"Eighteen."

"I'll be there."

14

"Here's the question of the week," Lance said. "How do you screw a fat woman?"

Nick did not respond.

"Roll her in flour and aim for the damp spot."

Nick sighed and looked down the runway. The two men were crouched under a small bush near the edge of the runway at the airport on South Caicos. They were near the junction of the taxiway and the runway, where they had a clear view of the tower, the ramp, and the runway. It was one A.M. and they had been waiting more than an hour.

"I'm thinking of starting a new business," Lance ventured.

After a moment, when Nick did not respond, he continued. "Yep, think I'll get into this cryogenic business I've been reading about. I got this idea where I can freeze people. Charge them five thousand dollars. Then I'll charge their estates about two thousand a month to keep them in a state of suspended animation. I'll manage all their assets for however many years they want to sleep. Say for the next twenty or thirty years." He looked at Nick. "What do you think?"

"I think you'll be dealing with your people."

"What d'you mean?"

"Your brain's been frozen for years."

Lance chuckled softly and looked down the runway in impatience. The night was warm, and in the lee of the hills to the east there was virtually no breeze. The moon was up, and in the pollution-free air the night was so clear and bright that trees cast dark shadows. Visibility was extraordinary; almost as good as during the day. White clouds could be seen ten miles off-shore. The night had the quality of the old western movies where night is depicted simply by turning down the camera's F stop a couple of clicks.

Nick and Lance wore long pants and long-sleeved shirts to protect themselves from squadrons of giant buzzing mosquitoes that filled the air.

"Of course I could start a rock band," Lance said.

Nick stared at him. "Can't you be quiet ten minutes? You're like a kid."

"Don't you want to know the name of it?"

"Name of what?"

"My rock band."

"What rock band?"

"The one I'm going to start."

Nick sighed. "So what's the name of the rock band you're going to start?"

Lance smiled. "Cold Smegma. Whatta you think?"

Nick shook his head and looked down the runway.

In a voice of disgust Lance asked, "What's that smell?"

Nick did not answer.

"Nick, what's that smell? It's awful. The worst stinking odor I've ever smelled."

"What smell?"

"That stinky dog-shit smell."

"I don't smell anything." Nick looked at Lance with narrowed eyes. "If you're talking about that aloe stuff, I took another shower."

"Boss, with that mixture of mosquito repellent and aloe, you smell like hammered shit."

"Don't I know it."

Lance took a small pair of binoculars from his shirt pocket, unfolded them, and placed them to his eyes as he looked first at the tower and then toward the southern sky. "If anybody's in the tower, I can't see them. And no aircraft." He brushed a mosquito from his face.

Nick pointed down the runway. "Go work your way down toward the other end of the runway. See if anybody's there. When you get back, if nothing's going on, we'll call it a night." Lance, who had visions of what was waiting for him in Emma's room, grinned. "I'm outta here," he said.

He bent over and scurried through the shadow of the bushes toward the end of the runway, where he made another sweep with his binoculars. He listened. Nothing. But his intuition, which had always served him well in undercover situations, was sending out nagging alarms. People were around. Something was about to happen. The very air had become charged. He was alert, listening, looking. The fact that he heard or saw nothing did not cause him to relax. Something was afoot. Then he saw the reflection of the moonlight off the window of a car approaching the airport. The car was showing no lights.

Lance was halfway down the runway when he paused. For a moment he thought he heard the distant hum of aircraft engines. He took another step. There it was again. Then it disappeared. Lance stood and placed the binoculars to his eyes.

Suddenly something cold and hard pressed into his neck. He had been jabbed with enough guns to know what it was. He froze.

"Awright, mon, who are you and why are you here?" came the lilting English accent. It was a local man.

"I'm looking for birds," Lance said. He wiggled the binoculars. Again he thought he heard the distant resonating of an aircraft engine.

After a pause came a snort of derision. "Birds? What sort of birds might you be looking for in the middle of the night? No birds fly at night, mon."

Lance was thinking rapidly. He could distinguish between a hummingbird and a buzzard, but that was about the extent of his knowledge of birds.

"A double-breasted dowager. Seen any?"

"A double-breasted dowager? Mon, I never heard of that bird," came another voice. There were at least two of them. He wondered if the second man were armed. He wished he had brought a weapon.

"What about the pink-rumped honeybun? I'd really like to see one of those."

"I think maybe I hit you with a rock stone, mon. Then you tell me what you are doing here on the airport with those little glasses." The second man had no sense of humor.

The sound of the airplane came again. Now it was a quiet steady sound. Why hadn't the two locals heard it? The sound would reach them any second. Who were they? He turned to face the two men, ignoring the gun pressing into his neck. He could not control the flicker of fear that crossed his eyes when he saw two men, both armed with automatic rifles, crouched in the moonlight. One of the men, the leader, he had seen in the bar at the Admiral's Inn. Ollie had pointed him out as the chief minister of the Turks and Caicos, the highest local official in the islands, second in power only to the British governor. "He's one of the pirates I told you about," Ollie confided. "Got his own little band of rip-off artists. Watch him. He's a sneaky bastard."

"Seen anybody from Central Cuban Dispatch?" Lance asked with a wide grin. "I think this might be their international headquarters."

"I know I hit you with a rock stone, mon," said the second pirate, the guy with no sense of humor. He hadn't even asked what the hell Central Cuban Dispatch was. Maybe he lived in south Florida. Maybe he knew about CCD.

Lance switched tactics. "I work with Ollie," he said angrily. "You assholes back off. I'm here to protect his interests." He nodded toward the sound of the aircraft. Now it was clear in the soft night. "That's the bird I was looking for. That bird flies at night." He nodded toward the automatic weapons pointed at his face. "I hope those guns are made of candy. Because if you don't point them somewhere else, I'm about to make you eat them."

Lance was following the cardinal rules of undercover work: never be put on the defensive, always
take the initiative, always take command of the
situation.

The two men slowly lowered their weapons. They
tensed and became visibly agitated when they heard
the aircraft. They looked at one another. "That is not
Ollie's airplane, mon. We know that," said the chief
minister. "We know that. The fellow flying it does not
work for Ollie. He is trying to bring an aircraft through
without paying."

Lance nodded patiently. "That's why I'm here. To
make sure no one who works for Ollie, or for the
Doctor, is dealing with this aircraft."

"How does Ollie know about this?" the chief minister asked, nervously fingering his weapon and looking
toward the rapidly approaching aircraft.

"Ollie and the Doctor knew about this aircraft before you did. They know everything that happens on
this island."

The sound of the aircraft was growing louder. It was
close, coming in fast and low, making a straight-in
approach. It would land and pass by within a few feet
of Lance and the two men.

"I do not work for Ollie," said the chief minister. "I
know him. And I know the Doctor. He called on me
the last time he was on the island. We have an understanding." There was an edge of fear in the man's
voice when he spoke of the Doctor.

Lance dropped his arms. The two men said nothing.
"I know that. And I know why you are here. Ollie
does not object." He nodded toward the aircraft; it
was a small twin-engine, clearly visible, about two
miles off the end of the runway. "People like this must
understand how we do business here. You do what
you have to do. And don't worry about Ollie."

Lance nodded and walked into the bushes, shoulders tight. The two men said nothing. Lance walked
slowly, wondering if he suddenly would feel the ham-
mer of bullets between his shoulder blades. It was the

middle of the night and he was on a runway where a doper was about to land. These guys were pirates. They were about to do a rip. They were nervous. Nick was too far away to help. Even if he were here, what could he do against two guys armed with automatic weapons? Lance continued to walk. He could feel the bright light of the moon and feel the warmth of the evening. He smelled the hundreds of small purple flowers that bloomed across the island. All of his senses were tingling. It was as if his nerve ends had suddenly been exposed. His heart was beating rapidly. Adrenaline was pumping. Sweat was pouring down his face, down his neck, and between his shoulder blades. But he did not wipe away the perspiration. Nor did he swing his hands at the mosquitoes buzzing about his head. He kept his hands by his sides, in plain sight of the pirates, and walked slowly.

Then he knew he was safe. He was far enough into the bushes that the two men could not see him. He glanced over his shoulder and ran to the right, dodging bushes and leaping clumps of turk's-head cactus. A moment later he stooped and scuttled rapidly, back toward the runway. The aircraft would land any second.

Then he heard the tiny squeak of tires. The aircraft was on the ground. He stopped and looked through his binoculars. An Aztec. He panned toward the edge of the runway where the two men had been. There they were, hidden behind a low bush, rifles at the ready.

As the aircraft drew near, the staccato rattle of automatic-rifle fire ripped the early morning apart. Lance saw tiny bursts of fire leaping from the barrels. The Aztec, its left tire shot out, veered toward the two men and came to a grinding, shuddering halt as the punctured tire chewed itself to pieces. Lance knew from how the aircraft veered and from how quickly the tire had self-destructed that the aircraft was heavily loaded.

Suddenly the door on the right of the Aztec popped open. A man was standing on the right wing, staying in the shelter of the aircraft's loaded cabin. Lance saw a head and a gun barrel poke over the fuselage and then there was a sweeping arc of small bursts of fire as a sustained rattle of gunfire ripped the night apart. The doper was methodically hosing down the bushes in a ninety-degree arc. It sounded like a MAC-10.

"Shit, shit, shit, shit," Lance muttered as he dropped to the ground. Bullets zipped and popped and whistled through the leaves overhead. One thudded into a cactus near his head. Lance tried to force his body deeper into the sand. The sharp point of a yucca plant jammed his ankle, but he hardly noticed.

Then the two pirates began firing. Bullets thunked into the loaded cabin. Now the doper had something specific to aim toward. He stuck his rifle over the fuselage and let loose a long burst. This guy had lots of ammunition.

The smuggler ducked. But he had moved too far forward and a dozen bullets passed through the cockpit window and caught him in the groin. He screamed and fell to the ground. The two pirates loosed another burst at his body. After waiting a moment to make sure he did not move, they slowly walked forward, weapons held at the ready.

Lance knew what would happen. The locals would off-load the dope, move it to a stash house, and later sell it to a smuggler.

Lance backed up, quietly moving away until he could no longer see the aircraft. Then he turned and ran toward Nick. Five minutes later he approached the corner of the taxiway where Nick was hiding. "Hey, boss, you there? It's me," he whispered.

"You okay?" came Nick's worried voice. "I heard gunfire."

Lance straightened up. His face was covered with sand and the knee of his pants was ripped. He glowed from heavy perspiration. His eyes were bright with excitement. But he sauntered toward Nick as if he were taking a stroll in the park. "Boss, today I fucked standing on my head and I've been shot at. It's been a great day."

"I heard the aircraft coming in and I thought I saw you talking to the pirates. What happened?"

"We had a little chat. I told them about my bird-watching and then went on my way."

"Bird-watching?" Nick exploded. "Aren't you ever serious about anything?"

"Boss, I'm serious as a heart attack. I told them—"

"Never mind," Nick interrupted. "Let's get out of here."

Ten minutes later the two men found their bicycles in the bushes near the road. As they prepared to mount, Lance sniffed. "Hey, boss," he said. "What is that smell? Smells like stale dog shit. That aloe or that throw-me-down-and-fuck-me shaving lotion?"

Nick didn't answer. He crawled atop the bike and began pedaling rapidly down the long winding road that dipped down the hill, passed the salinas, and came into town. Behind him was Lance, head tilted to the clear night sky, thinking of Emma's waiting body, and moaning, "Waaaaaahhh. Waaaaahhhhh. Waaaaaahhhh."

15

It was eight A.M. on the sixth day when Lance and Nick took off from South Caicos bound for Grand Turk. The tension of spending five days surrounded by smugglers, aware every second that being identified as cops would result in their deaths, prompted an emotional letdown and an adrenaline cutoff that caused even the usually ebullient Lance to be quiet and grumpy. The enormity of what they had discovered on South Caicos stunned them. Anywhere from two to five of the Doctor's cocaine-laden aircraft were leaving South Caicos each day bound for Fort Lauderdale. The standard load was five hundred keys—eleven hundred pounds of cocaine. Nick realized that McBride's earlier estimates of the Doctor's operation were conservative, far too conservative. Goldstein was bigger than Quintero, Fonseca, Gallardo, Ballesteros, Salcido, and Contreras, the biggest and best-known of the Mexican cocaine traffickers. And no one had ever heard of this guy. That was what was so amazing. He was probably the biggest cocaine trafficker in America, and no one knew of him. Extraordinary.

How could a big-time smuggler be so shadowy? What if McBride were right; what if this guy was the smuggler of the 1990's? What if there were more out there who were just as smart, just as big, just as shadowy?

In addition to the Doctor's aircraft and all the other aircraft loaded with cocaine, there were the boats that left several times a day bound for the western Bahamas, where their loads were broken down into smaller shipments and put aboard go-fast boats—the high-powered craft known to the public by the generic name of Cigarette boats—for the final dash into Broward County. Nick hoped the boats were not as successful as the aircraft. In the past five days, not one aircraft, not a single one, had been stopped. Ollie, no matter how drunk he became, would not divulge the Doctor's secret. It was obvious that single-engine aircraft were the heart of the plan. But how could any airplane, single-engine or multi-engine, avoid detection by the balloons? How could they elude the sensor birds with such consistent infallibility? What were they doing that caused Ollie to have no concern for U.S. Customs? Whatever the Doctor was doing, whatever technique he was using, it was the most successful ploy Nick and Lance had ever seen. Street-wise, tough-guy smugglers they knew and could deal with. But this guy was a technical wizard who stayed two or three steps ahead of them all the time.

Lance was ready to return to Lauderdale. He had the tail numbers of dozens of aircraft and boats he had seen loaded with cocaine. Kimberly could put those numbers in her computer and maybe break through convoluted multiple layers of ownership back to the Doctor. There were numerous names to check out. Most of them were only first names. But they could be matched with mug shots and pilots' records; they could be cross-checked with what various CI's might know. Lance was anxious to hit the bricks, to start working street sources, to use wire taps and pen registers on the Doctor's telephones, to put this man he now called Doctor Death under twenty-four-hour surveillance, to roust him on traffic charges and find an excuse to search his car, to impress upon this scuzzball the majesty of the law, to let Doctor Death know his days were numbered, that the Ghost was on his six. It didn't matter if Goldstein were smart enough to be a rocket scientist, sooner or later he would make a mistake. They all did. And when that time came, Lance would bust his chops.

"If all we had to do was chase dopers, we could go home and do all that," Nick said. "McBride was right about one thing. We have to think strategically. That means we have to go over and kiss the governor's ass. We can't do anything down here without his help."

For South Caicos to be squeezed dry, Nick knew the governor would have to give not only his approval but also his cooperation. After all, this was a corner of the British empire. Americans simply could not waltz in, start arresting people, confiscating aircraft, and seizing dope. He had to tell the governor what was taking place on South Caicos, get his reaction, and feel him out about allowing American lawmen to come to the island and put the big hurt on the Doctor's organization.

After taking off from Runway 10, Lance held the easterly runway heading as he climbed to twenty-five hundred feet. He crossed the north-south expanse of beach on South Caicos and was over the cobalt blue of the twenty-two-mile-wide Turks Island Passage, the seven-thousand-foot-plus-deep channel that separates the Turks Islands group from the Caicos Islands group, the two divisions of islands within the archipelago. The Turks Island Passage is the route used each year by migrating whales, and one can stand on the beaches of South Caicos or Grand Turk or Salt Cay and see the gamboling leviathans as they make their way south toward the shallow banks north of the Dominican Republic.

The Turks and Caicos Islands, an archipelago about one hundred miles across, consists of eight major islands and about forty smaller cays. If these islands are known to the outside world at all, it is usually among three groups of people: philatelists who collect the brightly colored souvenir stamps of birds and fish that are published in the islands, scuba divers who come here from all over the world to dive in waters where visibility usually exceeds two hundred feet, and drug smugglers who take advantage of the accident of geography that placed the islands halfway between Colombia and Florida.

The Caicos Islands, by far the larger of the two groups, begin in the north at West Caicos and stretch in a great arc through Providenciales, a dozen or so small cays, North Caicos, Middle Caicos, and South Caicos. In the Turks Islands are Grand Turk, Salt Cay, and a handful of small keys. Geologically, the islands are similar, a geographic, though not political, extension of the low, barren Bahamas ending at Mayaguana, a few miles to the north, and at Great Inagua, to the west. Islands within the Turks and Caicos archipelago also are alike in that most are surrounded by extensive coral reefs and numerous shipwrecks. The islands are almost as unspoiled today as when they were discovered five centuries ago.

All of this is not to say the islands are a homogeneous lot. Each retains its own character, its individuality. Each has its own separate story. West Caicos is uninhabited, brooding, mystical. Providenciales, or Provo, as it is called, is the cosmopolitan resort center of the islands, and its rapidly growing population, now about four thousand, makes it the most populated of all the islands; well on its way to becoming the Nassau of the Turks and Caicos Islands. Pine Cay, one of the tiny cays between Provo and North Caicos, is the location for the exclusive Meridian Club and the only island in the Turks and Caicos group that is a privately owned enclave for wealthy white people. North Caicos is something of a garden center for the islands, as it grows limes, papayas, sapodillas, oranges, and grapefruit. Middle or Grand Caicos is the largest island of all—forty-eight square miles—and one of the least-populated. Here one can find the ghostly sun-bleached decrepit remains of cotton plantations once owned by loyalists who fled Georgia and South Carolina during the American Revolution. The names of those loyalists remain today among the islanders who took the names of their former masters. The north shore of Middle Caicos, the Atlantic shore, is marked by limestone cliffs and some of the loveliest and loneliest beaches in the world. Then there is South Caicos, the fishing center of the islands. Some two hundred thousand pounds of conch and three-quarters of a million pounds of lobster are shipped from South Caicos each year. Not to mention the unknown tons of marijuana and cocaine. About twenty-two miles to the east is Grand Turk, the seat of government, with a British expatriate community of about two hundred, a number that brings the population to about thirty-eight hundred. Salt Cay, ten miles south of Grand Turk, is a tiny, quiet, and remote triangle of an island, the last island in the Turks and Caicos to discontinue the salt industry. The country is stitched together by Turks and Caicos National Airline, usually called TCNA, that has frequent daily flights among the islands.

A few minutes after reaching his crossing altitude of twenty-five hundred feet, Lance saw the hazy outline of Grand Turk. On the south end of the island, and lined up so he could make a straight-in approach, was the runway. To the left of the airport and along the blinding white beach on the west side of the island was Cockburn Town. Even though a few of the islands have towns—Cockburn Harbour on South Caicos, Cockburn Town on Grand Turk, Conch Bar on Middle Caicos, Balfour Town on Salt Cay, and a grouping of a half-dozen stores on Provo called Downtown—in reality most of these are more settlements or villages than towns, since they usually contain only a few hundred people. In each village the streets are quite narrow, usually unpaved, with brightly colored houses jammed hard against the edge of the road. Donkey-drawn carts clickety-clack down these yesteryear streets.

Nick was wearing a neatly pressed pair of jeans, sharply pressed western shirt, and gleaming cowboy boots. Lance had on his uniform: scuffed boat shoes, shorts, and a wrinkled green T-shirt with a picture of a fiery-eyed Ayatollah and the inscription "Kick the Shiite Out of Iran."

Nick did not approve. He narrowed his eyes as he

looked at Lance. "You ever think of dressing like a grown-up? I mean, we're going to see the governor."

Lance shrugged. "So he's governor of a bunch of bird-shit-covered sandbars that nobody but dopers ever heard of. Big whoop. I should have brought my tux."

"You could at least look neat."

"I'll let the gov touch my dick. If he's a typical Brit, that'll make him happy."

Nick sighed. "Well, at least you don't dress like a TV cop." Nick looked out the window. To the south he could see nothing but the blue-black water topped by an occasional touch of white as a wave broke. Talking of TV cops reminded him again that he was getting older, and how much his profession—the only job he ever wanted—was changing. Big-city cops, particularly in south Florida, no longer were cops. They were caricatures of cops. He could remember when being a narc was the same as being a prince; when being an undercover narc was the same as being a king, the professional elite of the sheriff's department. Undercover narcs made all the big cases. They were a tightly knit band of brothers who even had their own bar; they didn't drink with uniform guys. Now the U/C guys drank at the same bar with the harness bulls. It was as if they stopped being narcs when they were off duty. They put on their all-cotton Don Johnson outfits, pimp shoes, strapped on a Rolex, jumped into cars that cost four years' salary, and went out to play the role.

Even worse, they were a treacherous bunch of young bastards. Every one of the ferret-eyed little pricks was lying in wait for a fellow cop to bend a regulation, to violate a procedure, to take a shortcut in the arrest or processing of some dirtbag crook. They were all snitches; snitches against their own, their brothers. They wanted to climb up through the ranks on the broken backs of fellow cops rather than on the upright records of how many felony arrests they made. They had no sense of honor, no pride in being cops. To them it was not a calling, it was just a neat job. After all, a TV series had been made about what they did.

"Cunningham, I'm thinking about leaving."

"Me too. I'll be glad to get away from all these shit maggots and get back home."

"No, I mean leaving."

"Leaving what?"

"Leaving the BSO. Going back to Naples. Going home." Nick paused. When he spoke, his voice was so soft that Lance had to strain to hear him. "Things are not turning out like I expected. The sheriff's making me do things I don't want to do, things I believe are wrong. Too many of my men wear fag shoes and think they're Don Johnson."

Nick pulled at his mustache and mumbled, "That show probably will be in reruns for twenty years. Fuck up another generation of cops." He sighed. "I got a few acres just east of Naples. And Joe D'Alessandro, the state attorney over there, a good man, has offered me a job as his chief investigator. Wants me to hire a staff."

Lance was surprised. Nick believed in loyalty. Saying he was forced to do things he believed were wrong was the closest he had ever come to criticizing the sheriff. And it had never occurred to Lance that his boss might pack it up and move on.

"Hey, boss, you're just coming up on forty. It's menopause. Hang tough and push through. I'll get you some medicine for your cramps. I'll take you to the promised land."

Nick shook his head. "No. This may be my last case in Broward County." He looked at Lance. "Don't screw it up."

Lance laughed. "Hey, I'm a mean motor scooter and a bad go-getter."

Lance, anxious to break the black mood that had suddenly descended upon the cockpit, reached out and touched the radio, verified that he had entered 126.0 into the radio, then picked up the mike, called the tower, and was given permission to land. General-aviation aircraft were supposed to park on the south side of the runway, but Lance turned toward the commercial ramp on the north side. He taxied to the side of the ramp, turned around, and shut down the engine. As he and Nick crawled down the wing to the ground, blinking from the bright sunlight and wilting from an already-blistering day, an Immigration official sauntered up. Before he could deliver some officious pronouncement, Lance preempted him by saying, "We have a meeting with the governor. Where is his office?"

The Immigration official paused, then pointed toward the southwest. "Over there. About a mile."

"You got a cab?" Nick said.

"Go through the terminal. There should be one at the door. If not, the lady at TCNA will call one for you."

"Thanks. We'll clear Customs when we get back. Probably an hour. Anybody be here?" Being in a country where smugglers dominated one of the islands made Nick nervous. The bad guys could be all over Grand Turk also. He didn't know who the players were. He wanted to know the system so that, if necessary, he could get the hell out of town in a hurry. Any undercover cop must always have at least one back door.

"Our facilities are open from six A.M. until eight P.M." The Immigration official was courteous and helpful, not one of the abrasive and officious types found in the Bahamas or in the eastern Caribbean. Few tourists come to the Turks and Caicos. The islanders still retain their innate courtesy and friendliness.

As Lance and Nick walked away, Nick muttered, "I bet a doper can come through here day or night and not have to worry about Customs or Immigration or the cops or anybody else."

The two men walked through the small terminal and stopped on the sidewalk outside. Nick and Lance, as do all cops when they exit a building onto a street, looked around, checking exits and approaches and the faces of people. Lance looked over his shoulder toward the door of the terminal and noticed a large poster on the window. Across the top in bold letters was written "AIDS," and under that was the silhouette of a man and woman. Across the bottom was the caption "You're Safer with One Partner."

Lance poked at Nick with his thumb and motioned toward the poster. "How'd you like to be a tourist who comes down here for a little hell-raising, gets drunk, decides to change his luck, then, when he's leaving to go home to Mama, sees that poster?"

Nick shrugged. He held up his hand and waved at a taxi in the shade of a long line of casuarina trees off to the right. "If a guy can't keep his pants zipped, he deserves whatever he gets."

Lance widened his eyes in mock horror. "Ooooh, that scares me," he said. "I hope you ain't got no influence with the man upstairs."

Nick did not answer. He waved for the cab to hurry.

Lance continued. "I never told you this before, boss, but I know how to prevent AIDS. I have the secret."

Nick scowled.

"Simple. You avoid intersections and buy condominiums."

The cab, a blue van, stopped. "Get in," Nick said. He looked at the driver. "You know where the governor's office is?"

"Yes, it is quite near."

"How much?"

The cabdriver, a wiry bearded man in his mid-twenties, shrugged. "Three dollars."

Nick wrinkled his nose as he crawled into the van. The seats were covered with an ersatz sheepskin and the air was filled with a sweet spray. A small plastic vase filled with plastic flowers was glued to the dashboard. Behind the flowers were folders, maps, empty glasses, and numerous assorted odds and ends. The windows were tinted. A VHF radio, common on vehicles throughout the islands, was mounted overhead.

"You got air conditioning?" Nick asked.

The driver looked over his shoulder and smiled. "The sweet fresh air of Grand Turk is the best air conditioning in the world, mon. Don't you think?"

"I like air conditioning."

Lance smiled. Nick was convinced that since South Caicos was the land of drug smugglers, Grand Turk had to be the same. Nick knew in his heart that this same taxi driver had hauled drug smugglers around the island. Therefore the guy was little better than a smuggler himself.

Nick was pissed off with everything about the island. South Caicos could not be such a sanctuary for dopers, so wide open to smuggling activity, unless somebody here on Grand Turk was on the take. The daytime fueling of aircraft loaded with drugs and the involvement of local law-enforcement officials simply cannot take place without the knowledge and complicity of other government officials. Period. End of story.

The cabdriver smiled, rolled up the windows, and turned on the air conditioning. It wheezed and groaned and burped, then squeezed out a chilled breath of freon-tinted air. The blue van rolled out of the circular driveway and north toward town. The driver proceeded slowly because of numerous potholes. He could not achieve any speed because frequently he had to stop, slowly ooze down the front side of a large hole, then slowly crawl up the treacherous back slope.

Nick looked through the tinted windows. In the eyes of people walking along the road was the flat passive stare of those whose lives have been ground down by merciless unrelenting poverty. The roadsides were littered with refuse, with paper and beer bottles and boxes and piles of junk and debris that people had simply tossed or dumped there. After a few hundred yards the driver slowed. On the left was a big sign saying "Tidy the Turks. Clean the Caicos."

"Damn Brits," Nick mumbled.

Lance turned to look at him.

"Damn Brits," Nick repeated. He pointed out the window. "Look at this. A British Crown Colony. The

queen runs this place. You'd think the Brits would
take care of it. But those class-conscious bastards have
ignored these islands because people here are black. I
bet if the locals were white, you'd see paved streets,
industry, more developed tourism, a higher standard
of living. That's why England is a third-rate country. It
is led by a selfish bunch of class-conscious, inbred,
fish-faced, stuck-up assholes."

Lance found himself in the virtually unprecedented
position of being unable to speak. He had never heard
Nick express such social concerns. He knew it was not
because of any concern for the natives, but rather
animosity toward the British. The phrase "stuck-up"
was the giveaway. Anyone who believed in a class
system, who thought some people were "better" than
others, was suspect in the eyes of Nick Brown.

The taxi driver, whose eyes kept darting toward
Nick in the rearview mirror, turned around, grinned,
and said, "That be right, mon. That be right."

Lance was so surprised that all he could manage
was, "Boss?"

"There's right and there's wrong," Nick said. "The
Brits are wrong in the way they run this place. Wrong
in letting smugglers take over South Caicos, wrong in
not doing anything about the island. Look around
you. This is the capital of the country. It's a shit pile.
You don't have to see a burning bush to know the
Brits are wrong. They're just wrong."

As the van approached an intersection, Nick noticed
a long low building to the right. A sign identified it as
the police barracks.

"That the police station?" Nick asked.

The driver turned left at the intersection, looked
over his shoulder, and nodded. "Oh, yes, mon. The
fucking cops. They be there. Fucking cops. Fuck them
all." He pronounced the word as if it were spelled
with an O, and it came out "focking."

Nick plucked at his mustache. His first assessment
of the driver was right. Had to be a doper.

"Fucking cops," the driver repeated in his crisp, lilting tones.

After proceeding no more than a half-mile, the cabbie passed the end of the runway, and then, on the right, was a carefully manicured lawn surrounded by a low white wall. A huge white house sat back off the road in a grove of tall casuarina trees that stretched down to the beach.

"Waterloo," the cabbie said. He looked in the mirror and saw the questioning expressions on his passengers' faces. "The governor's office," he explained. He pointed toward the big white house. "Governor's Beach."

The cabbie turned into the gate, crossed a cattle guard, and stopped in front of a small building that both Nick and Lance thought was some sort of outbuilding, perhaps a post for security guards.

"We are here," the cabbie said. He looked over his shoulder and grinned.

"This is it?" Nick said.

Inside the open double doors was a small anteroom. The floor was covered in large squares of black and white linoleum. Two local police officers, very British in their attire, stood behind a small desk on the left. Two chairs were against a window in the rear. The window looked over a postage-stamp-size courtyard. To the left, behind the two police officers in a small office, was the receptionist, a local woman. A large open window by her desk enabled her to speak to visitors. It also enabled the two cops to lean over the railing and flirt. Between the door to the receptionist's office and the windows facing the courtyard was another door, this one leading along the edge of the courtyard toward a brown door upon which was written "H.E. the Governor."

The two police officers and the smiling receptionist looked up as Lance and Nick entered. Lance's eyes instantly took in the setup and locked on the door saying "H.E. the Governor." He turned to Nick and asked, "What does 'H.E.' mean?"

"Must mean the governor is not a woman," Nick growled.

The two Turks and Caicos cops straightened up. The receptionist's smile vanished. "Are you asking about his excellency?" one of the local cops said, carefully enunciating "his excellency" for what were obviously a couple of primitive Americans who had wandered into Waterloo. Whatever could they want?

"We're here to see the governor," Nick said. "He in?"

The receptionist gave them her professional smile. "Your names?"

Nick sighed. He did not want to give his name. But he would not get into the governor's office without doing so. "Nick Brown. This is Lance Cunningham."

"Is the governor expecting you?"

"No, but it's important that we see him."

"Please have a seat." The receptionist stood up, smoothed her cotton skirt, and walked down the edge of the courtyard. Nick and Lance looked around more closely. Outside, oleander and palm trees bent and swayed and rustled in the omnipresent easterlies that blew at about twenty miles an hour. The windows of the office were open, allowing the breeze to blow through. Without the breeze, the heat and the mosquitoes would have made the island untenable. All around the waiting room were pictures of various members of Britain's ruling family. Lance beamed and walked across the room when he saw a picture of Princess Diana. Several years earlier, when Diana had visited Fort Lauderdale, Lance had been on her local security detail. But he was abruptly removed after he went into her suite and stole the toilet seat. He had framed it and put it in his apartment. A small plaque identified the toilet seat as the temporary home of the most beautiful ass in the world. Lance told people he once had been "very close to the royal family."

On one wall of the anteroom was a picture of Princess Diana in a ball gown. A few feet away was another picture of her in casual clothes. Then there was a formal picture of her looking over the shoulder of Prince Charles. The prince was holding their firstborn son.

"That is one good-looking broad," Lance told Nick. "But look at her old man. He looks like the village idiot." Lance, like Nick, knew that no island could be as overtly corrupt as South Caicos without at least the knowledge, if not the participation, of governing officials. For all he knew, these two local cops might be on the smugglers' payroll. He would mind-fuck them a wee bit. He looked over his shoulder at Nick, pointed to Princess Diana, and said, "Boy, would I like to jump her bones." He shrugged. "But then, if she's not any better in the sack than most Englishwomen, jerking off would be more fun."

The two local cops looked at each other, then at Lance, then at each other. They were not quite sure what to do. Lance moved around the room and stopped before a picture of the dour, puffy-faced Queen Mum. "Looking at that every morning will keep your pipes clean," he said.

On other walls were pictures of obscure nieces and nephews and cousins; horsy-faced women and lean, whey-faced men whose blank expressions reflect the immutable effects of alcoholism and various sexually transmitted diseases. Royals whose pictures probably hung nowhere else in the world were in the governor's anteroom. It was a massive dose of royals, an attempt by this bone-dry ragtag collection of parched islands, this unwanted stepchild, this remote remnant of the empire, to hang on to the faraway wet green hills of England.

Lance turned when he heard the receptionist's heels clicking along the narrow walkway. He gasped when he saw the woman trailing along behind the receptionist. She was not beautiful. She was not even pretty. She was a tall, rawboned woman whose flaming red hair had been pulled back sharply and then piled atop her head. Her strides were long and confident, and twice she had to pause so as not to run over the receptionist. Her eyes were as blue as the cobalt sea and her skin appeared untouched by the semitropical sun. Her dress was so loose that it was difficult to guess at what her figure was like. But it really didn't matter because there was about her an unconscious big-boned raw animality that stunned Lance.

"That's the kind of woman you want to fuck and then shoot," he whispered to Nick. As the receptionist came through the door, she smiled and said, "Gentlemen, this is Miss Murphy, the governor's secretary. She will assist you."

Miss Murphy's level eyes took in the two men. A flicker of disapproval crossed her face when she saw Lance's T-shirt. She proffered her hand to each in turn, introduced herself, called each by name, and said, "I understand you wish to see the governor?"

"Yes, ma'am. We do," Nick said in his flat voice.

"And you don't have an appointment?" There was the merest hint of reproach in her voice, though not enough to say she had crossed the boundary of good manners and ventured into the rudeness that seemed the natural province of these ill-dressed Americans.

"No, but it's important. He will want to hear what we have to say."

Miss Murphy, a woman as tall as Lance, stared down from her lofty height at Nick, who was almost six inches shorter. She waited for Nick to finish, to tell her what he wanted to talk to the governor about. But Nick had played this game before. It was part of his job to be able to stare someone in the eye and, without blinking, wait for him to grow uncomfortable enough to talk. He had dealt with officialdom enough to know that sometime curiosity will overcome an insistence upon the perquisites of office. He was gambling that the governor of these little-known islands had so few American visitors that he would, out of curiosity, give them a few minutes.

For an interminably long time, no one spoke. There was only the noise of the strong breeze sighing through the office and rustling the trees outside. Then Miss

Murphy made a decision. "Very well. The governor is quite busy. But he will see you for a few moments." She looked at her watch as if to mark the time. Lance had the feeling that after a given number of minutes, he didn't know how many, she probably would interrupt the meeting and remind the governor he had to put on his sword and feathered hat and go officiate at some colonial ceremony.

Ian Gatty was a slight dark-haired man of about five-feet-seven who, like all British officials, no matter how hot and humid the clime, was dressed as if he were expecting the phone to ring any second with a summons to Buckingham Palace. He wore a navy suit, starched white shirt, neatly knotted tie, and—to Nick's nod of obvious approval—highly shined black shoes. He followed the British upper-class—an oxymoronic expression—affectation of allowing his straight hair to fall across his eyes; eyes that, by the way, were extremely sincere.

As Nick and Lance entered the governor's office, by force of habit their eyes quickly swept the room, noting every detail. The walls were soft blue. To the left of the door was a beautifully finished antique sideboard. A long antique desk took up much of the room. Behind the desk were two windows through which could be seen neatly trimmed oleander bushes bending in the breeze. The office was air-conditioned and was soft and cool and peaceful; a serene reflection of the calm and order of the empire, a haven of civilization here in the outback. A small picture of the queen hung on the wall between the two windows. Across the room, and very much out of character with the desk and sideboard, was a grouping of four lime-green Naugahyde chairs and a small table. It was here that the smiling Governor Gatty, arm outstretched, directed them to sit.

"Would you gentlemen care for a cup of tea?" he asked, then, after a brief pause, "Or perhaps one of your soft drinks?"

"No, thanks," Nick said.

The governor seemed unaware of the animal magnetism that, to Lance, seemed to shimmer about the shoulders of Miss Murphy like a flaming aura. He nodded and she disappeared through a side door. Through the open door, Lance could see a large room, teletype equipment, bookcases, and another secretary.

The governor crossed his legs, steepled his hands, and looked at Nick, obviously the spokesman for these two. He glanced at his watch and then said, "Very well, gentlemen. How may I be of assistance?"

Slowly, carefully, step by step, using the same dispassionate and orderly presentation he would have used in a courtroom, Nick identified himself and told the governor all he had seen on South Caicos during the past five days. He told how Lance had observed the chief minister of the island kill a smuggler and rip off a load of cocaine. He ended by emphasizing that he and Lance had been on the island in an unofficial capacity, that they were there as tourists, but that very soon the sheriff's department of Broward County, or perhaps even an agency of the federal government, might make an official request for the governor's cooperation in allowing them to mount some sort of enforcement or interdiction effort against the smugglers' aircraft flying out of South Caicos.

When Nick finished, the governor did not respond for a long moment. He placed his chin atop his steepled fingers and stared at the wall. Then, in a controlled but nevertheless stern voice, he began speaking. "First, gentlemen, I must express a certain measure of surprise that you came to these islands in such a surreptitious fashion. After all, this is a sovereign country. Under the rules that govern intercourse among civilized countries, your government should have contacted my government."

"We are not here in any official capacity," Nick repeated.

"Nevertheless, you are police officers. American police officers. And you are here gathering intelligence information."

"We thought you would want to know," Nick said.

"Let me speak to the information about the chief minister." The governor shrugged and gave Nick a wry smile. "Being from the American South, you will understand when I say we have a bit of a problem with our local ministers. We have one who is referred to as the Minister of Unnatural Practices. Then there is Lewis the Lump. Magoo. A sad lot they are. Not at all representative of her majesty's government." He paused. "But you understand these things."

Nick and Lance stared at the governor. Neither responded.

"Very well," the governor said. "Let us move on. Do you know for an absolute fact that the textile fiber you say was aboard the airplanes was, in fact, marijuana?"

Nick and Lance looked at each other in bewilderment. Textile fiber? What textile fiber? Nick spoke. "Again, we were there unofficially. It wouldn't have been smart to pull out a test set and run a field test. But in my judgment it was marijuana. The pilots said it came from Colombia. They were going to a lot of trouble and expense to bring it to Florida."

"I thought not," the governor said. It was as if Nick had not answered. "So as far as we are concerned, the only thing we can state with any degree of certitude is that these aircraft were carrying some sort of textile fiber."

The governor paused. "And the—what did you call them?—duffel bags; did you test whatever they might have been carrying?"

Lance snorted. Unable to conceal his displeasure, he stood up. "Excuse me," he said. He opened the door into the office where Miss Murphy had disappeared.

The governor's brows lowered for a moment. Why was the young officer going into the room with the secretaries? Oh, well, they would show him to the anteroom. He turned his attention back to Nick.

"No," Nick said. "I didn't test it. But the chief pilot

over there told me it was cocaine. He bragged about how many loads he was getting into Fort Lauderdale."

"Uh-huh," the governor said with satisfaction. "So what we have are two American law-enforcement officers—two *county* law-enforcement officers whose jurisdiction does not extend beyond the boundaries of their county—venturing into the sovereign territory of a foreign country and conducting an intelligence-gathering operation, an operation sanctioned neither by your government nor by mine. While conducting this unauthorized operation, you see what you think might be marijuana and cocaine being shipped through one of our islands." He emphasized the word "through," as though the marijuana and cocaine, if that's what they were, had simply whizzed through the airport.

Nick did not respond. He pulled at his mustache and stared at the supercilious bastard sitting across the small table.

The governor shrugged and flung his hands wide. He smiled patiently. "Mr. Brown"—he paused—"Officer Brown, I am not so naive as to tell you there are no drugs being transshipped in these islands. I would even say, in the privacy of this office, that drug smuggling is a bloody great wart on the end of our nose. But, Officer Brown, you will agree that, after all, it is an American problem. It is not our problem. We have American pilots flying American-registered aircraft carrying goods to American consumers. They break none of our laws. They spend a great deal of money and are of immense help to our depressed economy. The product they carry, whatever it might be, does not stop in these islands but rather continues on to your country. They simply buy gasoline here."

Again the governor shrugged. His pasted-on smile never abated. "We are only a refueling stop. Nothing more. We provide fuel to many people." He paused. "So I am afraid I can offer you no assistance. Allow me to say again, this is an American problem. It simply is not our concern."

The governor stood up and held his hand toward the door. Nick realized he was being tossed out. He stood.

The governor raised a forefinger in gentle admonishment. "You Americans do not understand these islands. We are a much-maligned mini-state. The attitude you should have toward us is not criticism, but rather sympathy and understanding."

Then his smile disappeared. "That is all we want, all we need from you."

He paused. "And that is all we will accept."

16

Lester's Diner is on State Road 84 a few blocks west of Highway 1 in the southeast corner of Fort Lauderdale. Few restaurants have the cross section of customers that come to Lester's, everything from retired people on fixed incomes to cops to hookers to dopers to tourists—all drawn by the diner's reputation for ample amounts of good food served quickly.

Nick sat in the corner of an orange Naugahyde booth and picked up the brown-banded coffee cup. It was as big as a birdbath. He looked down the table at the four people sitting there; the four people he had called together in an effort to get federal agencies involved in the battle against Cosmos Goldstein and then to determine how to get the cooperation, the vitally needed cooperation, of the governor of the Turks and Caicos Islands.

Lance sat at his right hand. There were those who thought cockroaches were the ultimate survivors, but Nick believed that if someone dropped a nuclear weapon on Fort Lauderdale and only one living thing survived, it would be Lance Cunningham. He would come crawling out of the rubble with a smile on his face and his enthusiasm undampened. It was six A.M. and there he was wearing a T-shirt that said "Forty Is Not Old If You're a Tree." Lance kept pulling on the front of the shirt and glancing at Nick, wanting to make sure that his boss saw it.

Next to Lance, back in the corner, was Mike Love.

Mike sat erect, sipping from his glass of orange juice and talking to Lance about his squirrel, Henry. Six months earlier, Mike and his wife, Mary, had adopted a baby squirrel that fell out of its nest. Mary tied a knot in the sleeve of an old sweatshirt and then cut away the remainder of the shirt except for two long strips of cloth that she tied around her waist. The squirrel rode around the house in the pouch made by the sleeve. Mike was telling Lance how he had recently noticed the size of Henry's balls. Henry, who weighed about a pound, had balls the size of pecans, enormous balls.

"I been checking around," Mike said. "Other squirrels don't have balls as big as Henry's."

"How do you do that?" Lance asked.

"Do what?"

"Check the size of squirrel balls?"

"Every time I see a squirrel on the road that's been run over, I stop and check. This morning on the way in I checked out one."

"You stop on the road to measure squirrel nuts?"

"I don't measure them. I just look. Henry's got the biggest balls of any squirrel in town."

Nick sipped at his coffee. Across the table from Mike was Ron Williamson, a senior agent from the Miami office of the DEA. Ron was to have retired seven or eight months earlier but decided to stay on one more year, something to do with an increase in his retirement pay. He had several months left. Ron, the most brilliant law-enforcement officer Nick had ever met, had done the near-impossible: he had held on to his humanity after twenty-five years as a narc. Nick hoped he could do the same. Almost every ex-cop or retired cop he knew carried around a big bag of guilt over things he had done while he was on The Job. Nick was determined never to do anything that would cause him to feel that guilt.

Ron, who stood six-three and weighed about two hundred and fifty pounds, was, like many big men, extremely gentle. His voice was so soft that people had to strain to hear him. He was talking to Kimberly McBride about her Irish name.

"My wife, Judy, is Irish," he said. "I'd heard of lace-curtain Irish—you look like lace-curtain Irish—and I've heard of shanty Irish. My wife is different. She's bicycle Irish."

Kimberly's brow wrinkled.

Ron puffed on his pipe, tilted his head back, and blew the smoke toward the ceiling. Then he grinned and said, "Bicycle Irish are professional Irishmen who are a pain in the ass."

Kimberly laughed at Ron's joke. She fingered the smoky-quartz necklace, one of the six she was wearing this morning, and said, "Sometimes I think people must believe that about me." She puffed on her long mentholated cigarette, blew out the smoke, took another deep puff, blew it out, and then a third puff. She tapped the cigarette on the ashtray she shared with Ron. Even after the ashes fell, she continued tapping. She tapped the cigarette more than a dozen times.

"You seem nervous," Ron said quietly.

"I did something so stupid this morning when I was leaving home. I just can't get it out of my mind."

"What was that?"

"I was in a hurry and I pressed the garage-door closer while I was backing out. The car stalled and the garage door came down on top of the car."

"Hurt it?"

Kimberly shrugged. "No. Not even a dent. But it was such a stupid thing to do." She smiled ruefully. "Good thing Pete wasn't there. He would have told me how stupid I am."

"Naaah. I've done things ten times worse than that. We all do."

Ron had known Kimberly since she first went to work for the DEA. She was a brilliant analyst. It was too bad that her husband had turned out to be such a jerk. When Kimberly and her husband were divorced, she had resigned. Everyone thought it was because she did not want to work where her ex-husband worked.

And then there were the stories about how she and Pete were fighting over custody of their young son.

Nick nodded in silent approval as he looked around the table. This was an unusual group. Except for Kimberly, they had known and worked with each other for years. Oftentimes federal law-enforcement agencies are looked upon with a wary eye by local cops. That is particularly true if the federal agency is the FBI, an agency that local cops all over America respect for its assets and techniques, but loathe for its glory-grabbing and back-stabbing. Whatever dealings the FBI, the DEA, or Customs has with local law enforcement are usually not an agency-to-agency relationship but rather an agent-to-agent relationship. It is an unofficial relationship but one that is based on respect and shared experiences, and bound together by the universal brotherhood of law enforcement. That was the situation with the group meeting in a back booth at Lester's Diner. Agents around the table trusted each other. They respected each other. And they liked each other. It was almost like the old days, back when Nick had first gone into law enforcement. He remembered his first drug bust. He and two other officers had taken down a doper in a parking lot. The guy was spread-eagled on the pavement. The dope was seized. But the adrenaline was still pumping. When the doper wiggled, one of the cops said, "What's that asshole doing?" The other cop accidentally popped off a round. It hit about an inch from the doper's ear and scared the hell out of both him and the cops. But no one was hurt and nothing was ever said. No reports were filed. It simply was an accident among fellow cops. Today if that happened, the cops would be fighting each other to be the first to file paperwork about an "accidental and reckless discharge of a firearm."

Yep, these were good guys. Nick was proud to work with every one of them. He and Kimberly and Lance were in the Goldstein case for the duration. But they needed help. Ron and Mike would hear what they had to say, report back to their respective agencies, and lobby for their agencies to become formally involved in the case.

Lance tapped a spoon against his glass. "Anybody want to hear the question of the week?"

"Not if it's as dirty as the last one," Nick said.

"This one's okay." Lance looked around the table. His eyes were dancing. "Does anyone know what you call a successful farmer?"

Nick, Kimberly, Mike, and Ron came back as one: "No. What do you call a successful farmer?"

People in adjoining tables looked at them.

"Outstanding in his field."

Nick, Kimberly, Mike, and Ron groaned as one. "Where do you get that stuff?" Nick asked.

"It ain't easy. But, hey, I'm a trained investigator."

"I think you been talking to some of your friends from deep space."

Lance clutched his heart. "The secret is out."

Nick cleared his throat. "Okay, people, let's talk."

Lance looked around the table in mock surprise. "How can we talk?" he asked. "The most important people of all are not here."

"Who?" Nick asked.

"The coast rats."

Mike, who was putting two quarters into the little jukebox on the wall to his right, stopped and looked at Lance. "Don't mention those assholes."

The Coast Guard was not popular with Customs pilots. Several years earlier the Coast Guard commandant, one Admiral Paul Yost, had seen the millions of dollars going to Customs to buy boats and aircraft to use in the war on drugs. He decided he wanted a big piece of the money. He was remarkably effective not only in obtaining money but also in convincing both Congress and the American people that Coasties could perform the air-interdiction role better than Customs. Just recently two Coast Guard Falcons, multimillion-dollar jet aircraft, had had a midair collision while practicing intercepts. Their jets and helicopters, both French-made, are unable to fly about fifty percent of the time because of maintenance demands. Yet their network-television commercials and massive public-relations campaign has convinced many Americans the Coast Guard is out there on the front line stopping drugs. The Air Branch, which keeps a low profile and does not have a public-relations officer, is not known to most Americans.

Nick spoke up. "Mike, we're going to have to call on the Coast Guard if this thing works. No way around it."

"We can't bust this guy without the Coasties?"

"We need them."

Mike shrugged. "We're in bad shape," he said. He pushed the quarters into the jukebox, then punched several buttons. No one was sitting near their booth, but Mike was cautious. The music would drown out their voices and prevent anyone from overhearing their conversation.

Nick nodded at Kimberly, who reluctantly put down her cigarette and pulled two sets of papers from her briefcase. One she gave to Ron; the other she passed across the table to Mike.

"You pretty much know all we found on South Caicos," Nick said. "But this report pulls it all together, plus some stuff McBride here discovered."

Ron and Mike thumbed through the report, pausing occasionally, each showing, in his own way, surprise. Ron's eyes widened and he held up the report so he could continue reading even as he tilted back his head to blow pipe smoke upward. Mike mumbled curses, fidgeted, and seemed to grow angry just sitting there.

"This is the guy we call the Lauderdale Express," he said in his controlled intense voice. "He's been beating us regularly for months. I've bounced his aircraft at least a dozen times. They always come to Lauderdale and I always lose them." He waved the report. "I had no idea he was running so many loads.

This is unbelievable. He's beating the balloons regularly if this is true. How is he doing that? And how is he beating the sensor birds? Where is he landing?"

Kimberly started to speak, but stopped when Ron leaned forward, placed the report on the table, and tapped it with his forefinger. "Kimberly, this is the most extraordinary bit of intelligence work I've ever seen. There is only one brief reference to this guy Goldstein in NADDIS. I can tell you that. And it's something you did several years ago that we never followed up on. Basically, DEA never heard of this guy. And that means that there is somebody here in Lauderdale, I would say the biggest smuggler in America, that my agency doesn't even know about." He shook his head in dismay.

"Well, now we know about him. We all know about him," Nick said. He pointed at the report in front of Ron. "McBride is coming up with some stuff in her computers." He looked at her. "You want to tell them about that?"

Kimberly took two quick puffs off her cigarette, tapped it a half-dozen times on the edge of the ashtray, and began. "Dr. Cosmos Goldstein controls what may be the most sophisticated narcotics-trafficking organization that any law-enforcement organization anywhere has ever confronted. He is symbolic of the latest trend in narcotics trafficking—the emergence of bright, college-educated smugglers, people with no criminal background, no arrest records. People unknown in the law-enforcement community."

She paused and looked around the table. "The South Caicos end—the aircraft, the logistics—is set forth here in the work done by Nick and Lance in South Caicos. And you just read some historical data, updates, and projections based on the intelligence information from South Caicos. There also is preliminary data about the financial structure of Goldstein's organization."

Kimberly took a quick puff of her cigarette and rapidly tapped the cigarette on the ashtray while she gathered her thoughts. Her mouth twisted as she bit anxiously at her lips. She was about to venture into an area that frightened her. She exhaled sharply and continued. Without realizing it, Ron and Mike leaned toward her in anticipation.

"I have spent a great many hours on the computer in the past ten days or so, and everywhere I probe—using aircraft numbers to trace their ownership, boat numbers, real-estate and tax files, motor-vehicle records, data banks, federal computer systems—it all comes out the same."

"Where?" Ron interrupted.

Kimberly involuntarily fingered several of the stones hanging around her neck. They stood out sharply against her crisp white cotton blouse and tailored beige suit. When she continued, her voice was rapid. "Before I answer that, let me say something. Usually this sort of investigation is like tracking a tiny stream that begins high in the mountains. You see a faint sheen of moisture on a rock where water has seeped out of the ground and begun oozing downhill. Then you walk through the brambles and over the rocks until you see where it joins another tiny stream. It gets bigger. Other creeks and rivulets flow into it. You hike up steep ridges, crawl over rocks, and time after time get lost in the thickets and have to back up and start over. But all the while, you know that one day—and it might take a long time—you can track that stream into a river and the river into other rivers, and finally you break out in the broad open coastal plain and there is the ocean. You have found where it all goes; you know what it all means."

"So what does it all mean?" asked Lance.

Kimberly puffed on the cigarette. "I don't know," she said. "I can't track Goldstein. The streams don't join together; they don't run downhill."

"Where do they lead?" Ron asked patiently.

"That's just it. They don't lead anywhere. They dwindle and fade away." She nervously tapped the cigarette on the ashtray.

"Is there any common element anywhere? Something you can track?" Ron probed. He sensed that Kimberly had found something that disturbed her.

She paused for so long that it appeared she was not going to answer. "Yes," she said.

"What?"

She stared at him. When she spoke, her voice was nervous. "I may be wrong. I could be wrong."

"We can talk about it. What is it?" Ron urged.

"They're all Jewish," she said softly.

There was a moment of silence around the table. "So this is Fort Lauderdale already." Lance grinned.

Kimberly shook her head. "No. I mean every aircraft ownership, every piece of real estate I trace, every motor vehicle, everything; it all ends in companies owned by Jews. According to the computer, and I checked it a dozen times, that's the only common element."

Mike was puzzled. "The guy's Jewish. It's natural to work with other Jews. It's the same with Colombian, Cuban, or Jamaican dopers. I don't understand."

Kimberly shook her head. "That's not what I mean. Some of these are the biggest and most respectable corporations in Florida, in America. Some of the biggest hotels in Miami Beach own several of these aircraft or are owners of record of land in the western part of Broward County that I believe is really owned by Goldstein."

She paused, lit another cigarette, inhaled deeply, and said, "That's not all."

Kimberly's eyes were almost defiant. "When I was in DEA, I had dealings with the CIA. I have friends there. I passed along some of the names I found; people and corporations. My friends got back to me and said whatever I was working on, to back off."

"Back off? Why?" Lance demanded.

"Some of the corporations are . . ." She paused. "Some of the corporations are fronts, government fronts. And some of the people are"—again she paused—"and some of the people are agents." She puffed on the cigarette. "Government agents."

"What government?" Ron asked quietly.

Kimberly looked at Nick. He nodded.

"Israel."

Ron was the first to speak. His voice was low and intense. "Do you mean . . . ?"

"Yes, I mean that the Israeli secret service, the Mossad, is tied to Cosmos Goldstein."

17

Ron and Mike were back to Nick in less than a week. Both men were embarrassed. It was the considered opinion of their superiors, who, after weighing the information collected by the Broward County narcs and consulting with their offices in Washington, that perhaps Nick Brown had been in the sun too long. His elevator wasn't stopping on the top floor. The cheese had slipped off his enchilada. His headlights weren't on bright. In other words, neither the DEA nor Customs was interested in Dr. Cosmos Goldstein.

Neither agency had any information on Goldstein. Oh, there was an old DEA file that mentioned him in passing. But it was all speculation. No one had paid any attention then, and no one would pay attention now.

The idea of a young dentist running what Broward County believed was the largest cocaine smuggling operation ever uncovered was ludicrous. Hilarious. Neither the DEA nor Customs believed there could be a cocaine-smuggling operation that size that they did not know about. They did not believe such an operation could be conducted from the Turks and Caicos Islands, a small country most people did not even know existed.

The DEA and Customs, in short, were not interested in assigning agents and equipment to a wild-goose chase. If there were a case, which Raymond Dumnik, special agent in charge of the Miami office of the DEA, doubted, then let Nick Brown and his band of agents handle it.

Dumnik was in a foul mood. As was his practice, he had gone to the Miami airport early that morning to have a couple of drinks. Afterward he was sleeping in a wheelchair reserved for the handicapped—surveillance, he called it—when there had been a power outage. The ensuing hubbub awakened him. In his drunken state, Dumnik thought he had gone blind. He stood up, screamed, tripped over the edge of the wheelchair, and almost broke his ankle. The lights came on while he was scurrying about on the floor moaning that he was blind.

Then he forgot where he had parked his G-car. He reported it stolen and had the Dade County cops looking everywhere. Half of the DEA agents in Miami were summoned to the airport to join the search. One of the agents found it and asked Dade County to cancel the stolen-car report. The Dade cops laughed. Dumnik's drinking was well-known in law-enforcement circles. It had been for years. Dumnik was living proof of the adage that in the Drug Enforcement Administration, when you screw up, if you screw up often enough and badly enough, you get promoted.

Dumnik was being promoted and transferred to Nassau, where he would be the narcotics attaché at the U.S. embassy and in charge of all American antismuggling activities in the Bahamas and the Turks and Caicos Islands.

Turning down Nick Brown would be one of Dumnik's last official acts in Miami, and one of the most pleasurable.

"Nick Brown and his band of unrenown," Dumnik said, smiling at the serendipitous expression that had fallen from his lips.

"If Nick Brown and his band of unrenown want to play that tune, let 'em. But they'll play it by themselves."

18

The first thing one noticed about Sheriff Hiram Turnipseed was his face. It was pitted and pockmarked and splotched and pimpled to such a degree that one could not help but wonder if, sometime in the past, his face had caught on fire and someone had flapped out the flames with a golf shoe. When he became angry, which was often, the splotches flared and the pockmarks surged and the pimples tightened until it looked as if his face was covered with a multitude of tiny volcanoes in a state of incipient eruption.

The sheriff stood up, ambled across his office, and turned his back to Nick as he looked at the pictures on the wall. There was the sheriff with Don Johnson. There was the sheriff with the governor. There was the sheriff with the president of Mexico. There was the sheriff with Geraldo Rivera. There was another picture of the sheriff with Don Johnson. There was the sheriff with Princess Diana, who, by the way, was making no effort to hide her displeasure.

The second thing one noticed about the sheriff was his weight. If the sheriff were to lose a hundred and fifty pounds, he might appear almost normal. He was so fat that his eyes virtually disappeared. And his lips, perhaps from the weight of his pimpled and pockmarked face, not only protruded, but were flappy, and, whenever he talked, tended to scatter spittle for several yards. The sheriff had the personality of most fat people—a dangerous feral meanness. Each morning when the sheriff shaved, he hated the features of the man in the mirror. He hated everything about the face he saw. And that hate was visited upon almost everyone who crossed his path.

The third thing one noticed about the sheriff, particularly when he was viewed from the rear, was how every movement, every motion, caused his voluminous balloonlike trousers to fold and crease until it appeared that about ten yards of material had imploded into his nether regions. Either that, or some invisible being was standing in front of the sheriff, clutching the crotch of his trousers and pulling upward, causing long wrinkles and deep crevasses to gouge the seat and upper legs.

"So you want to take a proactive stance and involve the press in this," the sheriff said, suddenly wheeling toward Nick.

That was the fourth thing one noticed about the sheriff—his inordinate affection for the word "proactive," which he used at every occasion. Nick was far from being an English scholar, but he knew, at some visceral intuitive level, that "proactive" was a word used only by the world's great assholes, a stupid nonword seized upon by poseurs.

Nick nodded. He had gone through this twice. "I want Cunningham to take a newspaper reporter down there, show him what's going on, and offer him whatever off-the-record help we can provide. The stories could generate enough interest that the feds will be forced to cooperate."

The sheriff raised a sausagelike forefinger. His brows lowered over his eyes like an awning over an empty porch. "And force the governor to officially invite you down to help."

Nick nodded. He noticed how the sheriff said "you" rather than "us." "We're stymied. The governor doesn't want us down there and the feds won't help. Goldstein is bringing in maybe eighteen or twenty loads of cocaine a week. We've got to break this thing loose. I think this is the best way."

The sheriff rocked back and forth, a great tottering mountain, and even though he was staring at Nick, his vision was stretching for the future, weighing every angle, measuring the possible consequences, figuring who could take the blame if anything went wrong.

The sheriff had come out of the last election, an election the Fort Lauderdale *News* predicted he would lose, with an overwhelming victory. The newspaper later said the victory was because of the highly publicized success of an undercover operation the narcotics squad had conducted in the Bahamas, an operation that ended when a C-130 with ten tons of marijuana aboard had mysteriously crashed in western Broward County, an operation that appealed to the public's growing desire for harsh justice toward drug traffickers. The sheriff did not like the newspaper's assessment. He believed his reelection was proof that Broward voters respected him as a police officer, respected him personally; he had no affection for a newspaper that printed otherwise.

Even though the sheriff believed voters supported him out of professional respect, he often wondered about the men who worked for him. One of his first acts after his reelection was to fire thirty-one men, professional cops all, who had refused to campaign for him during the election. They were not against him; they simply did not believe that professional lawmen should campaign for an incumbent, especially while wearing their uniforms. So he had gutted the department of many longtime professional officers. He would have fired Nick but for two reasons: first, he knew Nick had no ambition toward his office. Nick wanted only to be head of the narcotics squad. Second, he had suspended Nick after the Bahamas investigation and, despite numerous entreaties by the press, Nick refused to say anything except that he had deserved the suspension. Nick was loyal. The sheriff liked such a quality in his employees, even though it was a virtue he did not understand. The sheriff believed in kissing the ass of everyone above him and kicking the ass of everyone below him.

The sheriff made his decision. "Alright, Brown. Do it. But don't take a newspaper reporter. This is too good a story for those bastards. You can't trust them. If you want to be proactive, that's good, but take a TV reporter. Take Bob Sawyer. He'll do a good job."

Nick understood the sheriff's affection for television. He had been the star in one of Geraldo Rivera's so-called specials, an hour on national television about cops and drugs. The sheriff had insisted on leading a raid on a local crack house. He ordered Nick to stay far in the background. Then he went to the wrong address and kicked in the door of an innocent old man who, after he recovered from his fright at seeing black-fatigued, flak-jacketed, shotgun-armed men crashing through his door, filed a lawsuit against the sheriff. Nevertheless, the sheriff liked to tell people, "You might have seen me on one of Geraldo Rivera's shows."

Nick did not share the sheriff's affection for television. A television reporter would have to take a camera to South Caicos. No way around it. A TV reporter without a camera was like a rapist without an erection.

"Sheriff, I don't think it's safe with a TV reporter," Nick said slowly. "They need a crew. They got cameras and lights. South Caicos will be an undercover shot. It would be safer for everyone with a newspaper reporter."

The sheriff shook his head, causing even his primary chin, not to mention his jowls and dewlaps, to tremble and quiver. "No. Go with Sawyer." He fixed his small bright eyes on Nick. "You got that?"

Nick nodded. "We go with Sawyer."

Lance slammed a fist into his palm and jumped up from his seat in Nick's office. "Boss, did a tree fall on you? You know how I hate the fucking press. You're asking me to take one of those people to South Caicos? They're all slimy bastards—vultures, sneaky untrustworthy assholes. I won't do it. I won't do it."

"It's the only way this deal will work."

"There's got to be another way. I mean, it's bad enough to have to go down there with a reporter. But to go with Bob Sawyer? I've seen him on the air. I know about some of the stories he's done. He's the biggest creep who ever shit between a pair of brown shoes."

Lance paced back and forth in Nick's office, from the door to the window, back to the door, then across the office, then back to the door.

Nick waited. He pulled at his mustache and, from the corner of his eye, watched Lance. After a moment, when Lance's pacing slowed, Nick said, "The sheriff wants Sawyer. If you don't go, I'll have to send somebody else."

"Who the hell you gonna send? One of the TV cops? Somebody with a hair dryer? Somebody who hasn't been to South Caicos? He'll get everybody killed and blow the whole deal."

Nick shrugged. "You're right. And Goldstein will keep pumping coke into this county." He paused. "Cunningham, sometimes you eat the bear; sometimes the bear eats you. Buddy, this time we have been et."

Lance stopped. "Boss, you really know how to make somebody feel good."

"You want to feel good?"

"There's more. There's something else you haven't told me." Lance threw up his hands, spun around, sat down, and crossed his legs. "Okay, what is it?"

"You'll be using the Executioner."

Lance's eyes widened and he smiled in anticipation. The Executioner was the drug squad's newest boat, a ten-meter boat that had cost almost a quarter of a million dollars. Its two 650-horsepower turbo-charged engines hooked to MerCruiser surface drives would push the boat to top speeds of more than one hundred miles an hour. A group of Fort Lauderdale bankers and insurance executives, men who had saved millions of dollars because of the drug squad's skill in recovering aircraft that had been stolen by smugglers, had bought the boat for the sheriff's department. While it was being modified, Lance had gone to the Washington, North Carolina, factory and spent a week learning how to drive it. This would be the first time the Executioner had been used on a case.

Lance's smile faded. "The bad news?"

"Two parts. First, you'll be flying down with the Coast Guard. They're hauling the boat to Provo on a C-130."

Lance jumped up and resumed his pacing. "Oh, great. Wonderful. Not only do I gotta spend a week with some dirtbag reporter, but I have to get locked up with him in the back of an airplane belonging to the coast rats. Fucking ecstasy. Joy."

Nick leaned back in his chair and propped his immaculately shined cowboy boots atop his desk. He pulled at his mustache.

Lance stopped in front of Nick's desk, threw his hands wide, and said, "Boss, I am not a happy camper."

"Wanna hear the second part?"

"What?"

"Sawyer is out in the bull pen. The sheriff sent him over. Take him in your office and work this out."

Lance opened and closed his mouth, unable to speak. Then, just as he was about to launch into a tirade, Nick grinned and held up an admonishing finger. "And be nice."

"Hey, I'm serious. I am not a happy camper." Lance turned and stalked from Nick's office. He stopped in the bull pen, saw Sawyer, and with a jerk of his thumb motioned for the television reporter to follow him. Lance waited for Sawyer to enter his office. He slammed the door.

Sawyer smiled. He had a smile like the bumper on a 1956 Cadillac. But Lance noticed when they shook hands that Sawyer's hand was clammy and his grip weak. He quickly dropped the television reporter's hand.

"I'm Bob Sawyer."

"Larry Cunningham."

"I thought your name was Lance."

"My friends call me Lance. You call me Larry or Agent Cunningham."

Lance looked Sawyer straight in the eye. "Let's get one thing straight up front," he said. "I don't like you. I don't like people in your business. I don't trust you. I don't want to take you to South Caicos. I'm doing it because the sheriff ordered me to. But just because the sheriff said I have to take you, doesn't mean you get any special privileges. I'm not a fucking tour guide. This deal is dangerous. I don't want to get killed and I don't want you to do something that will get me killed. If you want to get killed, fine, go back down there on your own and be my guest. But on this trip, do exactly what I tell you or you'll find your ass swimming home. You got that?"

Sawyer, to his credit, was not noticeably disconcerted. He smiled, parked his briefcase on the desk, and shrugged his narrow shoulders. "I've been in the reporting business for a while. I know a few moves. I can take care of myself."

Lance looked Sawyer up and down. Sawyer was extraordinarily handsome. He had black hair and sharply chiseled features. On the air he looked tall and straight. But the camera only showed Sawyer from the middle of his chest upward. And Lance could see that the TV reporter was pear-shaped. He had narrow shoulders that sloped into a thick waist and then into even thicker hips and thighs. He wore a Morley Safer bush jacket, a *de rigueur* bit of clothing for every television reporter who ever ventured beyond the city limits. He took off the bush jacket and folded it neatly, smoothing the creases between his fingers, before he placed it almost reverentially across Lance's desk.

"Yeah, I bet you can," Lance said. "You probably have a pink belt in origami."

Sawyer squeezed his thin Baptist lips together. "Danger is not unknown to me. I've covered a war. I was in El Salvador. I've spent time in the ghetto with armed crack dealers." He paused and released that smile again, a wraparound smile that showed a yard of dazzling white teeth. "The sheriff said you were his star undercover narcotics agent, that you would provide complete cooperation." Sawyer's voice underlined the words "complete cooperation."

Lance shook head in dismay. How could the sheriff do this to Nick? He threw up his hands. "Hey, I gotta put up with you for a few days. But don't squirt bullshit on my windshield, okay?"

Sawyer continued smiling. "The sheriff said there was some concern about the equipment I might bring along." He pointed to the briefcase he had placed on Lance's desk. "Latest technology. Bought just for this deal. Not another station in the country has one of those."

"Is that a camera?"

Sawyer did not notice the menace in Lance's question. He nodded. "Miniaturized. Sound-activated. Circuit boards. Not a half-dozen of these things in existence. My general manager pulled some strings with the military to get it." He paused, then asked, "Want to see the tape?"

"You been taping me?" Lance was angry. He never allowed himself to be photographed. No undercover operative did. The knowledge that a TV reporter had him on videotape was frightening. He moved close to Sawyer.

"You ever tape me again, anytime, and I'm gonna shove that camera up your fat ass sideways. You better remember that. Now, give me the tape."

Sawyer shook his head. "Can't do that. Belongs to my station."

Lance picked up the briefcase and tried to open it. It was locked.

Sawyer grinned in satisfaction. "Security. Nobody can get in there."

"We'll see. I know a safecracker who can pop this thing like a grape." He turned, opened the door, and walked into the bull pen.

Sawyer followed. "That camera cost forty thousand dollars. You can't break it open."

Several TV cops in the bull pen looked up. They had recognized Sawyer and envied the fact he was in the office with Cunningham. But what would Sawyer want in the office of a man who was loony tunes?

"Okay," Sawyer said, realizing Lance was not going to return the camera. "I'll open it."

Lance looked over his shoulder. "And give me the tape."

Sawyer paused. Lance's face convinced him he had no negotiating room. "And give you the tape."

Lance threw the briefcase from halfway across the bull pen. It hit Sawyer in the chest and knocked him back a half-step.

"Open it," Lance demanded. "Now."

Sawyer pressed several buttons, releasing the coded locks, reached inside, and opened up the side of the camera. "I don't call this complete cooperation," he said defiantly.

"Let me tell you something, asshole," Lance said. He strode toward Sawyer and jabbed him in the chest with a finger. "Stop beating me over the head with the sheriff. I know what he said. Now, give me the goddamn tape."

Several TV cops shook their heads in amazement. Only Cunningham would go out of his way to antagonize a guy who could be of so much help to his career.

Sawyer passed the cassette to Lance, who broke it over his knee, then stripped the tape into a tangled wad and dropped it into a waste can.

Lance was breathing hard. He looked at Sawyer. "You come with me," he ordered.

Sawyer, whose eyes were darting about, landed on a picture of Don Johnson atop the desk of one of the narcs. He smiled at the cop. "I see you know my friend Don Johnson," he said.

The narc's eyes widened. Several other young narcs stood up and moved toward Sawyer. "He's your friend?" one asked in awe.

Sawyer smiled. "Well, I've interviewed him several times. And once we—"

"Sawyer, get your fucking fat ass in here," Lance bellowed.

Sawyer smiled at the young narc, shrugged, and walked toward Lance's office. He tried not to hurry.

19

Cosmos Goldstein leaned over the computer screen, studied it closely, then swiftly typed two commands. The Hewlett-Packard RuggedWriter, a high-speed workhorse of a printer on the table to his left, whirred and clicked, then spewed out a half-page of names and telephone numbers. Goldstein tore the page from the machine, turned off the printer and the computer, then walked across the room, sat down at a small white desk, and reached for the white telephone.

Cosmos Goldstein followed every rule to make sure his computer room was trouble-free. Room temperature never fluctuated more than two degrees. No rugs marred the surface of the pale hardwood floors; rugs collected static electricity. No vacuum cleaner had ever been in the room; the floors and desks were cleaned by hand. The telephone, which, like the vacuum cleaner, emitted an electrical field, was across the room from the computer. The printer and computer were on separate tables. A constant power unit, a collection of batteries that emitted a continuous and even flow of electricity, provided power for the computer. And even though no one but Cosmos Goldstein ever went into the small room, the computer itself could be activated only after entering a complicated access code. If anyone tried to open the door to the room without entering the proper code in the push-button lock, incendiary devices inside the computer and inside a steel box of diskettes would explode, destroying not only the forty-meg hard disk and all the information it contained, but also all backup diskettes.

Goldstein paused with the telephone in his right hand as he studied the list. It was up-to-date.

Still holding the receiver in his right hand, he used his right forefinger to punch a series of numbers.

When the ringing stopped and someone picked up the telephone on the other end, Goldstein slid the mouthpiece closer to his lips. The other person, in a neutral dispassionate voice, said, "Hello."

"Remember what we talked about yesterday?"

"Yes."

"I have the list. I want you to come over and pick it up and make some calls."

Pause. The other person was not excited about the chore that faced him. "Okay."

"It's gonna be fine. The first part is in place. The shvartzers in Liberty City and up in northwest Fort Lauderdale have their toys. They understand that in return they must talk to TV reporters. They like that." He laughed. "Chaim Yankels."

"You know what I think about this."

"It's a great idea."

"We've always stayed away from attention. You want shvartzers waving MAC-10's on television?"

"People are concerned about drugs. I want that concern to be focused on crack, Jamaican posses, and blacks with automatic weapons."

"I am not sure we agree with your thinking."

"It doesn't matter if you agree or not. As long as the money keeps coming, why should you care?"

A long pause. "I'll be there in ten minutes."

Goldstein hung up the telephone. His quiet friends simply did not understand America, especially American television and the awesome power it wielded.

Goldstein remembered the journalism course he had taken at Emory, back when he was working on his master's degree before going to dental school. It was the only course he ever took as a lark, as an indulgence. The irony was that it proved to be one of the most difficult courses he ever had. The teacher was not a member of the faculty; he was a free-lance writer, sort of a hired gun brought in once a year to teach a basic survey course in journalism, and he took his business very seriously. Students thought he was an unreasonable hard-ass. The guy made no secret of his hatred for television and what it was doing to the minds of college students. "Television turns your minds to oatmeal," he told them over and over. But he also acknowledged the indescribable power of television to mold the thinking of a people, particularly the thinking of Middle America, of "Joe Six-pack." The teacher said reality did not matter, that for most Americans, reality was whatever appeared on the screen. Nor did it matter that the reality was presented by people who, almost inevitably, were egocentric dweebs, emotional cripples whose entire identity was wrapped up in their jobs, in the few minutes each day they appeared on the screen. "Those people want, more than anything else in the world, to be on the air as often as possible," the teacher said. "Come up with story ideas, give them a story and a way to visualize it, and they become like drug addicts. They will come back to you over and over. They talk of being reporters, of being professionals. But that is only to convince themselves. They are cosmic whores, and deep down, if they have a deep down, they know it. That is why they show such awe for the printed word. Anyone who has ever written anything about television people knows how much television people respect and revere what is in print. Their work is in the wind. In a few seconds it may be seen by hundreds of thousands of viewers, most of whom are nitwits. To show their work, television reporters must carry around cassettes. Their entire life is spent traveling from one VCR to another, poking cassettes into machines, then standing back and watching as if seeing it for the first time; validating their existence through an idiot box. If a newspaper picks up one of their stories, they cut out the clipping and carry it with them forever. It sanctifies the ephemeral, tawdry nature of what they do. But never underestimate and never denigrate the power of the medium in which they perform. They unscrew the top of a world and show the great mass of people how that world works. And what they show becomes the world."

Goldstein recognized truth when he heard it. Now he was using that truth in a pragmatic fashion; to solve problems, to get along, to make his way a little less rocky. That's why he wanted to donate a half-million dollars to Emory each year. He called his former journalism teacher and said he wanted not only to endow a chair but also to provide the money to teach three or four journalism courses a year. He should not have been surprised when the teacher said journalism was not worth three or four courses a year and certainly not worth an endowed chair. The students who wanted to write would find and develop the discipline on their own. Three or four courses in journalism would do little more than seduce people into going into television. The teacher said he would not be a party to that.

Goldstein shook his head as he remembered the white-haired old guy who taught journalism. Odd that Emory, that conservative Methodist bastion and the recipient of millions of dollars in Coca-Cola money, should have been the fount from which he got his start in the drug business ("They don't call this Coke University for nothing"), and the source of knowledge for how to keep his drug business thriving.

20

The Executioner is a ten-meter V-bottomed boat powered by twin 650-horsepower Fountain turbos that has been radar-timed at speeds of one hundred and seventeen miles an hour. It is a romping, stomping, hellfire-and-brimstone sort of boat; an exotic bitch designed with a single purpose in mind—speed: mind-bending, sphincter-tightening, eye-watering, kidney-shattering speed. At ignition, when the engines clear their throats, it sounds as if the Jolly Green Giant is gargling. At eighty miles an hour the turbos scream like enraged Valkyries. At ninety the keening shriek is like that moment on Judgment Day when all the lost souls of the world discover they are consigned to eternal damnation.

Few people have either the skill or the nerve to take the boat to the edge of the performance envelope—to drive it offshore when a heavy sea is running and push it up to seventy or eighty miles an hour, getting the boat up on its hind quarters, shoving the throttle full forward when the boat is in the water and jerking the throttle back to idle when the boat is airborne; or to punch through heavy rollers, driving the bow of the 7,300-pound missile through the waves, causing water to cascade over the boat and be deflected by the black Lexan windshield. Skipping across the waves, if not performed properly, will over-rev the engines and destroy a quarter-million-dollar boat in seconds. Punching through the waves can decapitate the driver and passengers.

At rest, the weight of the Executioner's engines pulls the fine raked bow of the boat high off the surface, giving it the appearance of almost uncontrollable speed even when sitting still, and pushes the stern down in the water over the edge of the hull graphics. The graphics on the Executioner hauled to Providenciales aboard the C-130 were different from those of other ten-meter boats that come out of Reggie Fountain's fantasy factory in Washington, North Carolina. This boat was painted solid black, a flat smoky grayish black that reflected little light. The cockpit and the top of the engine housing also were black. Along the aft edge of the hull, in muted gray letters, was written the name of the boat: *Skean Dhu*—black knife.

The C-130 landed at Provo at four A.M. and was met by the chief Customs officer of the island, a man named Forbes, who was as incorruptible as Nick Brown, a man who was deeply disturbed about the effect on the Turks and Caicos Islands of drugs passing through South Caicos. He awakened the night watchman who slept in a chair in front of the fire station, oblivious of the mosquitoes, and told him this was a special aircraft allowed to land while the airport was closed. The night watchman did not think this out of the ordinary. Provo, like most islands, has its share of intrigue, of unknown boats and aircraft coming and going. The night watchman was glad when he was ordered to go inside the fire station and shut the door. It gave him official sanction for sleeping.

The Executioner, sitting on a boat trailer, was slowly winched down the ramp of the C-130 and hooked to the Customs officer's truck. Bob Sawyer, the TV reporter from Fort Lauderdale, stood to the side, watching, wiping perspiration from his face, swatting the big mosquitoes that filled the air, and muttering about the heat and humidity. He was amazed that there could be a place even hotter and more humid than south Florida. He asked Lance to delay the off-loading until daylight, when he could photograph the boat—a suggestion that caused Lance to remind him once again that the local Customs officer was risking his career in allowing a U.S. military aircraft to land without the knowledge or approval of the British governor.

"There are things we will see and hear and do on this trip that you cannot photograph, that you cannot even talk about," Lance said. "And if you never remember another word that anybody tells you for the rest of your life, you better remember that. Things are at stake here far more important than your story. You are not going to hurt good people. You will not shit in my front yard."

Sawyer smiled his patronizing smile and turned his pear-shaped body away.

The Customs officer was growing nervous at the length of time the C-130 was spending on the ground. Fortunately, the stiff wind was blowing the horrendous snarl of the four engines away from the populated part of Provo and toward the shallow ponds on the southeastern side of the island. Hills north of the airport further muffled the sound. But even so, the takeoff would be heard by islanders, who would wonder why a large aircraft was leaving in the early morning before the airport opened. The Customs officer asked Lance to have the pilot delay his takeoff for fifteen minutes, time enough for the Executioner to be towed to the water before any islanders, awakened by the sound of the takeoff, could drive toward the airport. And he said the pilot, immediately after takeoff, should stay low and make a hard right turn toward the south in order to avoid flying over the Turtle Cove area on the north shore, where the Executioner would be launched.

The Customs officer drove out the paved road from the airport, turned left at Suzi Turn, and drove over the rough coral road between the Third Turtle Inn and the Erebus Inn. At the bottom of the hill he turned right, drove a few hundred yards and turned left, crossed a small bridge, then turned right again. At the end of the road he turned left and pointed to a house near the beach. "My house," he said. He turned around and backed the trailer over a slight rise and then down the beach into the edge of the sea, where he stopped.

Lance shook hands with the Customs officer. They were of the law-enforcement brotherhood. To them, national policies come and go, depending upon whatever politician is in office. But the brotherhood would go on. They would remain brothers long after the politicians have moved to other jobs.

"Thanks, Mr. Forbes," Lance said. "You've been a big help. I know the risk you're taking and I appreciate it."

The Customs officer smiled, his white teeth flashing in the light from the instrument panel, and nodded in the courteous way of islanders. "I hope your endeavors are successful. I am here if you need me."

Lance nodded. Both knew that he would not talk with the Customs officer until it was time to leave the island. That was part of the deal.

Lance jumped out, loosed the straps holding the boat, and walked beside the trailer. He looked offshore. The sea was flat and gray; perfect camouflage for what he had in mind. A mile offshore was the dark line of the reef that protected much of the island. "Any coral offshore here?" he asked.

"Not inside the reef." The Customs officer pointed to the left. "Stay fifty yards offshore until you come to the cut, and you'll have no trouble."

"Stop for just a minute."

As the truck stopped, Lance called for Sawyer to climb aboard the boat. The TV reporter did, wheezing and grunting as he stepped aboard the trailer and then over the gunwale into the boat.

"Okay, back up a little more."

A moment later the Customs officer tapped the brakes as he felt the Executioner shrug free of the trailer and slide gracefully into the warm water.

"The trailer will be under my house. No one will see it there," the Customs officer said.

"I'll call you when we're ready to go," Lance said. The easterly wind was causing the Executioner to weathervane, to swing its stern toward the beach. Lance was anxious to be under way.

He shoved the boat into deeper water, moved toward the stern, and crawled aboard over the MerCruiser surface drives. He crabbed across the engine housing, jumped into the aft part of the cockpit, then walked quickly toward the steering wheel. His hands moved rapidly, turning knobs and flicking switches. The vital instruments, mounted on the panel in a semicircle around the top of the padded steering wheel, glowed. Lance turned a key and almost instantly there was an explosive whoosh from two of the unmuffled exhaust pipes as, with a gargle of cooling water and a seismic rumble, the left engine ignited. He would motor into the cut on one engine. He didn't want to awaken everyone on the island.

Bob Sawyer sat up in alarm. He moved forward, away from the engine, and stood by Lance, holding on to a grab bar. Lance thought of it as a sissy bar.

"My God. The sound," Sawyer said.

Lance ignored him. He looked over his shoulder, waved at the Customs officer, then wheeled the boat toward the cut that formed the entrance to Turtle Cove. It would be dawn in an hour. When the guests at the hotels along the cove and those up the hill at the Erebus Inn awakened and looked toward the ocean, they would see the black ten-meter boat anchored in the middle of the pond. They would know King Kong was in town. And late in the afternoon, about four or five P.M., he would fire up both engines, rumble out of the cove, and blast around the northern edge of the island. When he came to Leeward Going Through, the shallow cut that had only four feet of water at high tide, he would pick up a heading of one hundred and thirty-five degrees across the broad shallow flats of the Caicos Bank. It was about forty miles from Leeward Going Through to Cockburn Harbour on the lower end of South Caicos. When he arrived, the smugglers of South Caicos would be sitting by the pool at the Admiral's Arms and eating conch fritters and drinking beer. They would hear his turbos screaming and then they would see him rocketing across the flats. They would all be watching when he arrived. Then Bob Sawyer, who would be wearing a clipped brown wig and a false mustache, could park his handy-dandy little briefcase containing the new miniaturized camera on a table or in a corner of the bar and shoot footage that, when aired in Fort Lauderdale, would force the DEA and U.S. Customs to get into the drug war. That was the plan—simply to hang out, to allow Sawyer to get tape of what took place at the Admiral's Arms and around the airport. Upon his narrow shoulders depended the success of what Nick Brown could do to stop Doctor Death.

Lance had an additional agenda. Fluf was not along this time. There was no one to remind him to play by the rules, to afford smugglers the considerations decent citizens should have. So he would play by doper rules, which meant there would be no rules. He was not going to stand by and watch one cocaine-laden aircraft after another take off for Fort Lauderdale and do nothing about it. Drug smuggling, to Lance, was not an issue with two sides. He knew that civilians hated drug smugglers more than any other criminals; more, even, than child molesters. They hated and they feared drug smugglers. They were confused by drug smugglers. The hate and the fear and the confusion all were compounded by people like Cosmos Goldstein, who did not fit the stereotypical picture of smugglers. Goldstein would walk; Lance had little doubt of that. He would come out of all this with a slap on the wrist. The connection with the Mossad would never be developed. It would never be made public. Oh, a few people would learn of it, but the only impact would be to increase their confusion and their anger. And there was a lot of anger toward smugglers. People who believed in the U.S. Constitution as they believed in the Bible were talking of standing smugglers up against a wall and shooting them. Lance believed that if vigilantes ever became a concern in America, it would be because the courts—local, state, and federal, but particularly the federal—were not taking a hard enough position against dopers; not frying the bastards. People were fed up with smugglers—men who brought nothing but despair and destruction and death to countless families—walking about like minor deities, immune from the law.

Lance smiled tightly. Once Sawyer had shot the needed tape, Lance knew what he would do. As he motored slowly toward the cut, he mumbled, "I'm going to hoist the black flag and slit some fucking throats."

21

Lance sang softly. The tune was "Camptown Races."
But the words were:

> Pee, hocky, shit,
> Dooky, damn, ass, fuck.
> Do dah. Do dah.

Lance removed the dipstick from the oil inlet of
the Beechcraft Baron, shoved his handkerchief into the
dark hole, and used the dipstick to push it to the bottom.
He twisted the dipstick tightly before moving on to
a Cessna 210. He removed the heavy woolen socks
that he wore to protect his feet and ankles from mosquitoes and tamped them deep into the oil filler. Chuck-
ling to himself in barely repressed glee, he ripped his
T-shirt into two pieces and forced part of it down the
oil inlet of a Piper Saratoga and the other part into
another Cessna 210.

As is usually the case in the Turks and Caicos Islands, the moon was so bright and the air so clean
and clear that one could see for miles. It was two A.M.
and Lance was perspiring heavily. Occasionally he swung
a hand in front of his face, feeling great clouds of
mosquitoes in the air. The mosquitoes were big; swinging at them was like swinging one's hand through a
volley of BB's, and they buzzed and hummed, sounding like power surges in a distant electrical generating
facility. The mosquitoes were relentless in their at-

tacks, but Lance was having so much fun it hardly mattered. He looked around the ramp of the airport on South Caicos. Rather than returning to Provo as he and Sawyer had done for the past three nights, he had parked near the jetty on the western edge of the island—several other go-fast boats were there in the lee of the wind—and hiked a half-mile to the airport. There he had searched out aircraft whose tail numbers he recognized as belonging to Doctor Death.

Tomorrow afternoon, actually this afternoon, after the aircraft had been loaded with five hundred keys of cocaine each and had taken off for Fort Lauderdale, the pilots would have a little surprise. About a half-hour after takeoff, maybe forty-five minutes, a handkerchief or sock or piece of T-shirt would be sucked against the oil filter and block the circulation of oil. The pilot would notice the temperature creeping up, but nothing he did would help. Within a few minutes the overheated engine would seize and the smuggler would be on a final approach to somewhere. He would be flying a glider—a glider grossly overloaded with fuel and cocaine. He would be over open ocean, not yet within range of Mayaguana. And it would be better to put the aircraft in the ocean than to risk returning for a dead-stick landing on Provo, where the crash of a cocaine-laden aircraft would cause too much attention. Those four smugglers, if they survived the crash, would be swimming. The crash would cause the unsecured duffel bags of cocaine to ram the pilot against the instrument panel. If that didn't kill him, he would probably drown. Smugglers never carried life rafts or life jackets. It was part of the mystique, the machismo, part of believing big *cojones* were all one needed to fly long distances over open water. And each time five hundred keys of cocaine went to the bottom of the ocean, it would be about five million dollars that Doctor Death would never see.

Lance wasn't satisfied with the possibility of putting four of Doctor Death's single-engine aircraft into the briny deep. The blood lust was upon him. Back in

Fort Lauderdale he had to be careful; he had to remember all the restrictions placed upon cops. He had to play by the rules. But down here in South Caicos, all the frustration and anger of the past weeks had surfaced. He remembered seeing as many as five aircraft a day take off from South Caicos for Fort Lauderdale. He remembered all the times the Doctor's single-engine aircraft had beaten U.S. Customs. The dopers won, won, won. Now it was his time. The Ghost was on the move. But he was out of material to jam into the oil intakes. What else could he use?

Then he saw one of the ubiquitous turk's-head cacti for which the islands are famous. He pulled a knife from his belt. Since Nick was not there, Lance had hidden a knife—it was a six-inch black dagger he had taken from a hitchhiker who had tried to rob him—and his chrome-plated long-barreled Magnum pistol inside a panel aboard the Executioner. The big hogleg was jammed into the back of his jeans.

He kicked a cactus, breaking off the cantaloupe-size green body, and used the knife to slash off the top and slice a big chunk off each of four sides, roughly squaring it up. He walked toward a nearby Beechcraft, another single-engine aircraft whose number he recognized, and stooped down by the nose gear. He held the cactus low, then, using both hands, shoved it upward into the oil breather with all his strength. The breather pipe cored the cactus, leaving most of the hard green material lodged inside the pipe, as the remainder of the cactus fell away. Lance picked up the pieces and tossed them into the bushes. The Bonanza would overheat and seize up about a half-hour after takeoff. He used this same technique on four more aircraft, steadily working his way from the parking apron along the edge of the ramp toward the tower.

He was stooped over, hands on his knees, the knife on the ramp before him, gasping with exertion, when suddenly he noticed two sets of feet facing him. Feet shod in shiny black pointy-toed shoes. He slowly stood up and wiped the perspiration from his eyes. Facing him was the pirate he had seen on the previous trip to South Caicos—the chief minister, who had shot up a landing aircraft, killed the smuggler, and taken his load of cocaine. The chief minister and his colleague, the guy with no sense of humor. Both were holding M-16's loaded with long clips; both rifles were pointed at Lance's head.

"I do believe it is my bird-watching friend," said the chief minister in his precise accent. "And what might you be doing?"

"Fuck off," Lance said. He felt sorry for whatever son of a bitch got the drop on him, because he knew it would be for only a moment, and then it would be his time to play.

The chief minister laughed a high brittle indulgent laugh. He could afford to be indulgent. This fellow had on no shirt. His weapon, a knife, lay at his feet. They were on the southwestern edge of the ramp in the early-morning hours with no one within sight or hearing.

"Are you protecting Ollie's interests?" the chief minister mocked. He looked about in apparent curiosity, then cocked his head toward the southeast. "I hear no aircraft. Perhaps you could enlighten me, young sir. Why are you here at this hour? And what are you doing with that rather wicked knife? Is there mischief afoot?"

Lance waved a hand of dismissal toward the chief minister. His right hand came to rest on his hip as his left wiped perspiration from his face.

The chief minister's smile hardened. "Please be so kind as to kick that knife toward me," he said.

Lance shrugged and kicked the knife. As the minister leaned over to pick it up, the barrel of his M-16 dropped several inches. Like the darting head of a mongoose, Lance's left hand flicked out, grabbed the barrel of the rifle, and pulled hard, jerking the minister forward on his knees and causing him to lose balance. At the same instant, Lance's right hand reached for the chrome-plated Magnum in the back of his jeans. He pulled it out and leveled it as the minister's friend dropped into a crouch. Lance, knowing he was a half-second from being cut in half by a fusillade, squeezed off two quick shots for the man's chest—the thickest part of his body. Blam! Blam! The thunderous boom of the Magnum echoed across the flat reaches of the airport. The minister's humorless friend was thrown violently to the ground. Two bullets, so tightly grouped that their entry point over his heart could be covered by the palm of a hand, killed him instantly. Lance continued swinging the big pistol, connecting with the top of the chief minister's head, knocking him unconscious to the ramp.

He crouched and looked about, his head darting, the pistol ready. He was gasping great drafts of air, and the perspiration had increased until he felt as if he had just emerged from a hot shower. He turned, and, in a ground-eating lope, took off in an effortless run toward the southwest. Then, as he ran, he saw lights going north on the nearby road that led to the airport. He ran faster, toward the jetty where the Executioner was tied.

He was gasping and heaving as he ran across the lighted jetty, throwing his right hand upward, motioning for Sawyer to cast off the lines. Sawyer immediately complied, and as Lance jumped aboard, his weight pushed the boat out from the concrete wall. He felt something soft underfoot.

"You jumped on my bush jacket," Sawyer whined.

"Fuck your bush jacket."

Lance noticed two men sitting in a go-fast boat tied to the jetty. What the hell were they doing there at this hour of the morning?

Lance rapidly turned keys and pressed buttons. Within seconds both engines were rumbling their unmuffled chorus of brute power. He had left the trim tabs all the way down and the drives racked all the way in. This gave the boat maximum lift as he applied the throttles. The boat, without squatting down, accelerated smoothly away from the jetty.

Sawyer was beside himself in anxiety. "Those guys tried to board the boat twice," he shouted.

"What guys?"

"Those guys in that boat at the dock."

"Who are they?"

"I don't know. Local guys. They all had automatic rifles and they kept smiling. They wouldn't say anything. The first time, they didn't see me until they were right at the edge of the jetty. Then they came back. I think they were about to steal the boat."

Lance looked at the frightened TV reporter. He might be right. The guys in the go-fast boat could be part of the chief minister's crowd of rip-off artists. The Executioner would be a most appealing target. If anyone were ripped off, the complaint would wind up on the chief minister's desk before it reached the governor. That was the chain of command for internal affairs in the islands. The chief minister would see that the complaint went no higher.

Well, that worked both ways. The minister couldn't complain about one of his pirate buddies being shot on the ramp at South Caicos. Not without risking exposure himself. So whatever action the minister took would be unofficial. And Lance thought he knew what it would be. He smiled in anticipation and pulled back on the throttles, slowing the boat, looking over his shoulder.

"What are you doing?" Sawyer screamed in fright and disbelief.

"Relax, Bozo. You're about to see some shit. The Ghost is gonna mind-fuck the bad guys." Both men were shouting in order to be heard over the sound of the engines.

"They got guns," Sawyer said, his voice rising two octaves.

Lance patted the hog-leg stuck into the rear of his jeans. "So do I." He motioned toward the briefcase. "Haul out your camera."

"You're crazy. You're fucking crazy. We could be halfway to Provo by now. You're dawdling."

Lance laughed. "Dawdling? Dawdling? Never dawdled a day in my life. My mother wouldn't let me."

Sawyer's breath whistled between his teeth. The TV reporter was frightened and angry. He was used to being treated with enormous deference. But tonight three bandits had almost killed him. Now this crazy cop was playing with them.

"You don't respect what I do," Sawyer screamed irrationally. Then the attic of his mind, which, as always, was empty of all but dust motes and knick-knacks, seized on the idea suddenly thrust into view. "That's it. A goddamn superior cop who hates television people. You've made it real clear to me you hate television people. Is there any person in television you respect? Anybody?"

Lance was looking over his left shoulder at the go-fast boat on the jetty. "Sure. Two."

"Who? Tell me who."

Lance saw the lights of a speeding vehicle coming toward the jetty, bouncing rapidly across the coral road on the west side of the village. That would be the chief minister. Things were about to get interesting. "Susan Spencer and Judy Woodruff. They're the best," he said.

Sawyer was so frightened and so angry that he had momentarily forgotten about the go-fast boat. His eyes were locked on Lance. He threw his hands skyward, the superior, impatient gesture of a man speaking to someone who obviously did not know what the hell he was talking about.

"Spencer and Woodruff! Jesus! Why? Why them?"

The car stopped on the jetty; lights beamed across the water. A running figure could be seen.

"They're professionals. They know their job. They do it straight. No smart-ass raised eyebrows. No smirks. Both of them are conduits, reporters in the best sense of the word. I used to watch Betty Rollin a lot. She has more heart and more"—Lance paused: it was not a word he used often—"compassion, than anybody else on television."

He looked at Sawyer. "Everybody else, national, state, cable, local, whatever, is an asshole. Including you." He jabbed his thumb over his shoulder toward the jetty.

Sawyer looked back. "Why are those people chasing you? What happened at the airport?"

Lance flashed his pirate's grin. "I was just carrying out the president's campaign promise of a kinder, gentler America."

"What does that mean?"

"Intelligence-gathering. Undercover shit."

"This is a hell of a time for me to find out you want to ruin my story, to get me killed. You think I'm an asshole."

"I know you're an asshole. But you're not gonna get killed, Bozo. You're safe with the Ghost. You got a job to do when you get back. Get out your camera if you want some good footage. Just keep it pointed toward the rear. Point it at me and it goes overboard. Your story will change the history of drug smuggling. You got a chance to be an asshole who makes a difference."

Lance had Sawyer's full attention. "Well, we agree on one thing: my work is important. All of my stories are important. I put people on the air and show what the news is. I paint pictures with a camera. That's what I do."

Sawyer did not like having to shout to be heard. He liked to use his practiced three-ball voice; to be low, deep, and sonorous; to, as he told young reporters, "play tricks with my voice." He could not do that when he was shouting. On the other hand, shouting seemed perfectly natural to Lance. He did it without effort.

Lance was watching the jetty, waiting. It would not be long. "You're a kid playing with a lightning bolt," he said.

"What the hell does that mean? What sort of profound cop comment is that? What makes you so fucking smart?"

Lance tensed. A dark shape was knifing through the water toward them. White water was spreading out to either side. They were being chased by the go-fast boat at the dock. Lance laughed in exultation.

He turned to Sawyer. His voice was hard and authoritative. "We can outrun them. But if something happens to the boat, if they get close and start shooting, you dive over the side."

"Sharks are out there!"

Lance was waiting, left hand on the throttles, right hand on the steering wheel, eyes on the black shape speeding toward them. "I get paid for this. You don't. You go over the side when I tell you, or I'll throw your fat ass over." Then his grin tightened into a rictus of tension. "Get your camera ready. Hold on."

He slowly pushed the throttles forward. The Executioner had a Borg Warner 72C transmission with extra clutch plates. Even so, the thirteen hundred unrestrained wild horses on the stern made the transmission the weakest link of the drive train. The application of power had to be done slowly and carefully or the high-strung and finely tuned engines would self-destruct. The four-blade stainless-steel props grabbed, then cavitated. The boat wallowed for a second; then the props grabbed again. It took eight seconds for the boat to get on plane. Lance brought the trim tabs up until they were in line with the run of the bottom of the boat; then he backed off on the drives. The boat surged and almost instantly the calibrated Nordskog speedometer showed the speed had risen to fifty-five miles an hour. Lance reached for the auxiliary-fuel-pump switches. They were under a placard that said "Activate at more than 3,000 rpm." Now the Executioner was at a speed where many so-called go-fast boats were up against the limits. But the slow-accelerating Executioner, like an actress late in reaching her prime, was just reaching a plateau from which it could achieve marvelous things. It was loosened up, running as if it were on railroad tracks, as it screamed around to the north in a broad circle.

The warm air had blown away the perspiration from Lance's body. He shrugged his wiry shoulders and looked astern, a wide grin of anticipation frozen on his face. To his left, up against the gunwale, out of Lance's reach, was Bob Sawyer—rigid, hands locked on the sissy bar, afraid both that Lance would throw him overboard and that the smugglers might catch them. He never thought of taking pictures, even though the night was almost as bright as day.

"Not a bad boat," Lance shouted, motioning over his shoulder. The go-fast boat was rapidly overtaking them. He laughed. "This is more fun than a tooty patrol."

Lance looked at Sawyer. "What would Don Johnson do in a situation like this?"

"What?" Sawyer was bewildered.

"What would Don Johnson do?"

Sawyer rolled his eyes. "I don't know. I guess he'd shoot them all. Why?"

Lance nodded in satisfaction. "Then I'm doing the right thing by running."

Sawyer looked over his shoulder. "Give it more gas. Speed up. We can outrun them." His voice was imploring.

"Not yet. Where's that fancy camera? Why aren't you shooting this?"

"Not enough light."

"Bullshit! You're a candy-ass."

He led the go-fast boat loaded with pirates around the hump of South Caicos and north onto Stake Bank toward the shallow flats west of Plandon Cay and Nigger Cay. He glanced at the depth gauge. The go-fast boat had drawn closer and easily could be seen racing across the white water. Four figures were visible. Their raised guns could be seen. And then, just as Lance glanced over his shoulder, he saw blinking red dots.

"They're shooting. Duck," he shouted. Sawyer dropped to the cockpit sole, his back against the hull, careful to maintain his distance from Lance. He did not want to be tossed overboard. He felt cloth under his fingers and mumbled, "Oh, God. I've wrinkled my bush jacket."

Lance leaned over the steering wheel and added power. Okay, so the bad guys wanted to play. The Ghost was about to show them something they would remember.

He looked over his shoulder. The pirates had fallen astern. He retarded the throttles just enough to hold his distance. The speedometer settled on sixty-five miles an hour, a more-than-respectable speed for a go-fast boat. The pirates were using good equipment. Lance looked ahead. The next few minutes would demand his undivided attention. Before this trip he had spent hours studying charts of South Caicos waters, particularly the avenues available to him in the situation he now faced. He had worked out a plan in advance. But the tide was ebbing and the flats ahead of him were dry at low tide. He guessed he had two feet of water on the flats behind Plandon Cay, maybe less. If he was wrong, the Executioner was about to become a quarter of a million dollars' worth of toothpicks. The depth gauge showed five feet.

He swung farther north, more toward Sail Rock Island, then looked astern. The pirates were hanging tight, positive they were running him aground. Lance checked the trim tabs, adjusted the drives, and tightened his grip on the throttles. Still five feet on the depth gauge. Almost time.

He took a quick look beside the boat. In the brilliantly clear night the bottom could easily be seen. Nuisance Point, the southeast corner of Sail Rock Island, was ahead and to the right. He continued into the broad shallow cove on the end of the island. The muscles in his legs were quivering with tension. He gritted his teeth and looked over his shoulder. He was abeam Nuisance Point, apparently caught inside the cove with nowhere to go. Three feet on the depth gauge. Time.

"Hold on," he shouted.

Sawyer whimpered.

Lance racked the Executioner hard to the right, pointed it a few degrees away from Nuisance Point toward Sand Bore Cay. The pirates swung wide to intercept him. Lance slowly pushed the throttles forward, hard against the stop.

The boat reacted as if it suddenly had been released from a giant slingshot. The shrill scream of the turbos spooled to a mighty crescendo. Sixty-five is high speed for a boat. The difference between sixty-five and seventy-five is astronomical. It is an order of magnitude. Tears were streaming from the sides of Lance's eyes. His hair was slicked back over his head. The water beside the boat was a blur. Lance reached forward for a set of goggles he had slung on the throttles and slipped them over his head. Now he was out of the lee of the land and heading almost directly into a chop caused by the stiff easterly breeze. He felt the wind get under the boat. The speed increased. The speedometer was indicating ninety and climbing. He had moved into a universe of speed that few people ever experience in a boat. The Executioner was low, flat-out, belly-to-the-water, sizzling at ninety-five, still straight and sturdy; screaming like a scalded leopard but handling like a docile kitten. No chine walking. No bow oscillation. But she was approaching the edge. Three feet on the depth gauge. Lance looked to his right. He had foiled the pirates' attempt to cut him off, but they were behind him, still convinced he could not go through the shallows. They might be right. The depth gauge jumped. Two feet. Speed still climbing. The Executioner sounded like Judgment Day. The chop and the speed were such that only the bottom part of the deep-V hull and the props were in the water. Lance knew the boat was drawing eighteen inches; twenty max. He was at full bore and clearing the bottom by no more than four inches—probably less. If he slowed and the boat settled, he was dog meat. He pushed on the throttles, wanting every ounce of power and hoping the high-strung turbos would hold together. He sneaked a quick look astern. The pirates were approaching the area where the water shallowed to two feet. If he had planned correctly, they were about to find that shallow water could mean deep trouble. A go-fast boat such as the one they were driving drew two feet at high speed. And they had five people on board, so they were probably drawing two and a half feet.

Then it happened. The excitement of the chase caused the pirates to forget good judgment. Their boat suddenly acted as if it had run into a pool of hardening cement. In about one hundred yards the boat slowed from sixty-five miles an hour to zero. It stopped. Dead in the water. Lance knew the props had been ripped off, and unless the occupants were extremely fortunate, the bottom of the boat was destroyed. The chief minister and his cronies almost certainly had been injured when they were suddenly thrown like rag dolls toward the bow. They were in waters where boats rarely ventured. The closest islands were Sail Rock Island astern and Sand Bore Cay ahead, both uninhabited. And there were too many deep holes in the shallows—holes where sharks often were trapped by the falling tide—for any but the most foolhardy to risk walking to either island. The pirates would be lucky if they got back to South Caicos in two days.

Lance leaned forward as he rocketed through Plandon Cay Cut into the open Atlantic. He had looked astern once and seen bare sand in his wake. The speedometer was locked on one hundred and four miles an hour as he cleared the cut, eyes intense as he searched ahead for the white water that signified a reef. In seconds he crossed the danger zone and was running unfettered in blue water. A three-foot swell was rolling in from the east, but the Executioner, at a hundred and twelve miles an hour, was tracking straight and true.

Lance reached out and nudged Sawyer with his left foot. "You have been saved by the Ghost," he shouted. "Not the Holy Ghost, just *the* Ghost."

Lance held the steering wheel with both hands, wiggled his shoulders, did a quick little dance, and tilted his head to the bright sky. "Damn," he shouted, the word faint in the wind. "Sometimes it's fun being a po-liceman."

Sawyer slowly stood up until he was crouched behind the windshield, hands rigid on the sissy bar, peering ahead, eyes almost closed. Traveling in an open boat at this speed was the most frightening thing he had ever done. He was terrified. The noise of the engines, the speed, the feeling that disaster was less than a microsecond away, all were overwhelming.

"Think we can slow down?" he shouted.

"Boat's like me. Born to run hard. Born to raise hell."

But Lance realized Sawyer was right. No sense in blowing the turbos when he had outrun the pirates. He slowly retarded the throttles until the boat was indicating seventy miles an hour. It seemed they were almost drifting. He pulled the big Magnum from his belt and stashed it behind the hidden panel.

Lance leaned toward Sawyer. "We'll reach Grand Turk in a half-hour. You've got to be in the governor's house at daylight."

"What will you be doing?"

Lance laughed, a high maniacal laugh of relief that was clearly audible even over the scream of the turbos. The past few days had been fantastic. Two long, sweaty afternoons with Pearl. Tonight he had sabotaged nine smuggler aircraft, almost been killed by the chief minister's henchman, outrun a boatload of pirates, then left them grounded on a remote cay. One hell of a day. And what he had planned on Grand Turk would be even better. But there was no need to confuse Sawyer with the facts when the boy could be dazzled with bullshit. Lance leaned close and shouted in Sawyer's ear, "Undercover stuff."

22

Lance wished he had some of Nick's after-shave lotion. He was soaking wet. The clean T-shirt he had slipped on when he left the boat, the one saying "Down with Underwear," was sodden. He took it off and used it to tousle his hair. Then he stuck it in the rear pocket of his jeans and continued trudging up the hill through the predawn darkness. Water squished in his boat shoes. Mentally he went over the timetable for the next few hours. It was dicey, very dicey; just the way he liked it.

Lance had to return to the Executioner no later than eight-twenty. The boat was anchored a hundred yards offshore from Cockburn Town. At eight-thirty he would pick up Sawyer from the dock and they would return to Provo. He would make a call arranging for the Coast Guard C-130 to land about two A.M. tomorrow to pick up the Executioner and take him and Sawyer back to Fort Lauderdale.

He hoped Sawyer, who was sitting on the beach below the governor's house waiting for daylight, remembered the plan. Sawyer was to tell the governor he was pressed for time because he was catching the eight-forty flight to Provo, where he wanted to spend a few days before returning to Florida. This was a diversion. If the governor believed Sawyer was to be in the islands a few more days, he was not likely to take any immediate action toward him. He would wait. That was the way of Brits. To ponder and study something until it was too late to do anything about it.

Sawyer, above all, must let the governor think he had been on South Caicos alone; he could not let the governor know he had been there with Lance. Sawyer had complained, saying he did not want to deceive the governor, that reporters could not lie in order to get a story.

"I told you before we left, there are bigger things at stake here than your story. You tell the governor I was here and it will cause an international incident. He'll probably jail you as a material witness and you'll have to deal with him by yourself, because I'll be gone."

Sawyer nodded. "That's different." He agreed to the plan.

It was almost six A.M. when Lance reached the top of the ridge and knocked softly on the door of the small house. The house was on the northeastern corner of Grand Turk, part of the British expatriate community. It was in the edge of a grove of casuarina trees and oleander bushes and commanded a sweeping view of the sea. It was almost dawn and the gray surface of the ocean stretched eastward into the first hint of a yellow sunrise. He knocked again.

"Who is it?" came a sleepy voice.

"Lance," he said softly.

Pause. "Who?"

"Lance. We met several weeks ago in your office. We talked while my boss was talking to your boss. You gave me your address."

After a moment the small light over the door was turned on and a curtain to Lance's right was pulled aside. There was not enough light to see who stood inside.

"The Florida bobby," she said in surprise. "Why, you're not properly clothed and you're dripping wet. How ever did you arrive here?"

"Hey, I swam ashore and then a cab brought me to the foot of the hill. I walked from there." He held his arms wide, cocked his head, and grinned. "I'm a weary traveler. Aren't you going to invite me in for a cup of tea?"

Another pause. "You Americans." The curtain dropped and the light over the door was turned off. For a moment Lance thought she had gone back to bed and left him standing there in the darkness. Then the door quietly opened a few inches.

Lance pushed on the door. It swung wide.

"Come in. And shut the door," came the woman's voice. It no longer sounded sleepy. "My neighbors arise rather early."

The English accent reminded Lance of the chief minister and his gang of pirates. But there was something different. This accent was a bit softer; it had a rolling burr.

"I can't see you," Lance said as he closed the door and looked around.

She moved from the shadow and stood in the half-light from the window. Lance's eyes widened in amazement. The governor's secretary stood there, a pale nude in the soft morning light. Her red mane was no longer tied tightly atop her head, but instead tumbled in a tousled haystack around her shoulders and framed her face in shadow. She stood with her arms hanging by her sides, her weight on one leg, a knee bent forward in a pose that exaggerated the width and the curve of her hips. She was bigger, more rawboned, more feral than Lance remembered. Her breasts, firm and erect, pointed at him. Her thighs were lush and full. Then she shifted and the light moved down her body. Lance froze at the sight of the strawberry-blond hair below her flat stomach. He had never seen such a thatch of pubic hair, a giant triangle that grew high up her stomach and halfway across to her hipbones. The thatch of red hair dominated the large, big-boned, and beautifully formed body. It was as if her entire being was centered in, it seemed, at least a half-acre of pubic hair.

"I thought you might be back," she said with a pleased note of triumph.

Her voice broke the spell. Lance spun in a full circle, bent over, and bleated, "Waaaahhhh. Waaaa-hhhh."

The tall red-haired woman drew back in astonishment. Her eyes widened. "Whatever?"

Lance grinned, stepped closer, and put his hands on her waist. "Hi, Murph."

She relaxed, then twined her arms around his neck, moved forward, and slumped into him. Her eyes were level with his. "Murphy. Miss Murphy to you. I'm the secretary to the governor, you know."

"And a very proper English lady, I'm sure."

"Scottish."

She parted her lips and kissed Lance. Her arms locked around his neck and her hands came up to hold his head so she could press harder into his lips. She writhed and twisted her head, moaning softly, kissing for long moments. She thrust her hips toward him.

Lance moved his hands from her waist and cupped her large breasts. "Scottish, mmmm?" He squeezed gently. "The Highlands?"

She smiled flirtatiously. "The Paps of Jura."

His hands drifted downward and touched her. "And this?"

She pulled back and looked into his eyes. Now her smile was a challenge. "The great Whirlpool of Corryvreckan."

She reached for his hands and pulled them away from her body. She led him toward an open door. He could see the white of her bed against the wall.

"Go ahead," he whispered. "Wait for me. I want to take a shower."

"No. Now. I don't care." She held his hands, walking backward, smiling, pulling him along. In the middle of her bedroom she stopped. Her left arm coiled around his neck, and as they kissed again her right hand slid down his stomach, flicked open the snap at the top of his jeans, and continued. Her right hand held him, squeezed, pulled, squeezed, pulled. After a moment Lance decided the situation was out of control. He was more an observer than a participant. He stood still as Murph pulled back a half-step, took both hands and tossed her hair back from her face, then crouched before him, jerking at the buttons on his jeans. She reached into his shorts and freed him, then pushed his jeans and shorts around his ankles. She stood up and looked deeply into Lance's eyes.

He sank to his knees before her. But she pulled away and spoke firmly. "I don't like that."

Lance sighed and stood up. He had had the same conversation, if it could be called that, with Pearl earlier in the week. Damn, he thought, why was it that women south of Miami did not like oral sex?

Again Murph fluffed her red hair away from her shoulders. She smiled at Lance and backed toward the bed. The sun was up now; it was the time of morning photographers refer to as "magic time," those few moments when the light is soft and orange and bathes all it touches in a surrealistic glow. Her hair, touched by the sunrise, had turned into a shimmering halo. Her body was pink marble carved by a master sculptor.

Her knees touched the bed and she sat down. Then, her feet on the floor and her legs parted, she lay back on the bed. One hand slowly moved upward and became lost in the bosky red thicket. Her eyes remained locked with Lance's eyes.

Lance was embarrassed. He was standing there with his pants around his ankles and in the terminal stages of a testosterone alert. He kicked his pants away and took a step toward the bed. But Murph held up a hand to stop him. She was curled into a fetal position, one hand still lost. "I wish I had my panties on," she groaned.

"Why?"

"So you could take them off."

Lance was becoming more than a little impatient. "Hey, Murph, can I play too?"

She sighed, slowly unfolded her legs, and rolled

over on her back. "What?" she said in a strangled voice.

"Can I play too? I'd like to do something."

Her legs relaxed and fell apart as she held her arms toward him and waved her hands, beckoning him forward. The sun was higher now and blazing fresh and clean through the windows. The thick patch of hair below Murph's stomach appeared to be on fire. It glowed and glinted and sparkled with the slight jerking movement of her hips.

"So do something."

He stared. His last thought, before he moved forward and became lost in a foretaste of eternal joy, was that Nick would never believe it, but he had seen the burning bush.

23

It was almost six P.M. when Lance entered the lobby of Trade Center South. He came in from the parking-deck side and waved as he walked past the reception-ist. "Gladys, you're working late," he said.

The elderly blue-haired woman looked up and waved in return. Lance was wearing sand-streaked jeans and a T-shirt that said "I Don't Give a Shit. I Don't Take Any Shit. And I Don't Talk to Assholes."

"You're formal today," she said with her sweet smile.

Lance laughed. "Love you, Gladys. Is Fluf upstairs?"

She nodded.

As Lance stepped into the elevator, he held the door and waggled his finger at her. "Don't stop me between floors. Okay?"

Gladys continued smiling. She looked like every-body's favorite aunt.

Trade Center South, even if it was leased at exorbi-tantly high rent from one of the sheriff's campaign contributors, was in some ways the ideal location for the narc squad. Executive Airport, where the under-cover aircraft were hangared, was less than five min-utes to the west. I-95 was across the street running north and south and offering quick access to major east-west streets that crossed Broward County. Sev-eral floors in the basement were for the exclusive use of the narcs; it was where they hid the taxis, utility trucks, cable-TV vans, trucks with the names of air-

222

conditioning companies written on the sides, sports cars, and limousines that made up the squad's fleet of U/C vehicles.

But of far greater significance than the building was the little woman in the prim suit who sat there looking out through the large plate-glass doors. She appeared to be a demure little lady, perhaps retired, who was trying to make ends meet. And her job appeared to be directing visitors to various offices. In reality she was a deputy sheriff who for eight years had been the senior firearms instructor at the Federal Law Enforcement Training Center in Brunswick, Georgia. She had won national championships in the competitive firing of pistols, rifles, and shotguns during six of those years. She carried a .357 Magnum in her purse, and attached to the underside of the ledge to her right was an M-16. She could have it spewing bullets in about three seconds. Under the overhanging edge of the wooden receptionist's barrier was a row of closed-circuit television monitors. And within easy reach of her right hand were buttons enabling her to manually control the building's four elevators. To teach young agents humility, Gladys would wait until they were in the elevator zooming upward and then stop the elevator between floors. She had left agents stranded for more than a half-hour.

Lance was her favorite agent. She did not like the arrogant young TV cops. To them she was either "Granny" or a nonperson to be ignored. Lance reveled in her skill with firearms. He never clammed up and gritted his teeth in macho frustration the way TV cops did when she beat them on the firing range. And she always beat them. Every one. She was the best shot in the Broward Sheriff's Office. Lance asked her for tips and advice on shooting. She had seen him grow from being a good shot with a pistol to being an outstanding marksman. Lance always spoke to her when he came in. Sometimes he brought her flowers. Occasionally, if he was riding the elevator alone, she would stop it between floors for a few seconds. But she always checked to make sure he was not carrying his radio. Once she had stopped the elevator only to hear him on the radio a few seconds later saying that people from another planet were holding him prisoner. The sheriff, who had overheard the radio traffic, called and wanted to know what the hell was going on at the narc squad. Were people out there smoking the killer weed?

Atop Gladys' desk, hidden in an arrangement of dried flowers, was a small microphone that was hotwired to Nick Brown's secretary on the tenth floor. If someone tried to force his way past Gladys, all she had to do was raise her voice and within minutes half the cops in Broward County would be storming through the front door. But when they arrived, they probably would find that Gladys had pulled a weapon and disarmed and cuffed the would-be intruder. Either that or the bad guy would be sprawled on the floor, full of bullet holes.

Gladys was a good cop. More than once she had alerted Nick of cars that had passed the building too many times, or of vehicles parked nearby whose occupants had no apparent business in the neighborhood. The men and women in the narcotics squad had been adopted by this dangerous little old lady. She watched over them with a benign but ever-vigilant defensiveness.

Lance stepped off the elevator, turned left, and at the end of the hall again turned left. He nodded at Navarro, the white-haired lieutenant on the narc squad. "Hey, Navarro, when you going to run for sheriff? We need you."

Navarro smiled. "I think next time I take him on."

"Great." Halfway down the north hall, Lance turned right into the Organized Crime Division offices and walked past the receptionist, through the bull pen, and into Nick's office against the north wall. Nick looked up. His thick blond eyebrows lowered a millimeter, for him a startling display of emotion, and he said, "You wear that shirt in public?"

"This is a training day. I been out at the range."

Lance looked toward the small television set on the credenza and pulled a chair around the desk so he could face the screen. He smiled at Nick. "*Jefe,* comments like that are sure signs you're getting older. I can tell you're almost forty." He stared closely at Nick. "Is that gray I see in your once-blond hair?"

Nick just looked at Lance for a moment, considering what he wanted to say. "Intel people tell me there was a bunch of emergency calls from aircraft out of South Caicos the other day."

"Oh?"

"Yeah. A bunch of them ditched south of Mayaguana."

"Dopers?"

"According to the numbers they gave, they're all aircraft we've identified as being connected to Goldstein." Nick paused. "We're not absolutely certain. None of the pilots survived."

"God's in his heaven and all's right with the world. How many?"

"Four, I think."

Lance's brows lowered in concentration. "Is that all?"

"What do you mean, 'Is that all?' Four aircraft are not enough in one day? Four deaths? All dopers? All working for the same guy? You don't think Goldstein is going crazy? He lost about fifteen mil there in less than a day. He's gonna kill somebody."

"Well, I meant, I wondered what happened. How many went down?"

"You haven't asked me when it happened."

"So when did this great disaster happen?"

"The day before you left Provo to come back."

Lance paused. "Hey, wait a minute. You don't think that I . . ."

"Did you?" Nick's voice was soft.

"Hey, boss. You tell me I'm the best you got. My hang time is measured in days. You think I need to do that?"

"Did you?"

"Come on, Nick. You know better than that."

"What I think and what I can prove are two different things." Nick paused. "You know what would happen if I could prove you sabotaged those aircraft?"

Lance nodded. "Yes, sir." He and Nick both knew that "prove" was the operative word.

Lance wanted to change the subject. He looked at his watch. Two minutes before the program was to begin. "Hey, wanna hear the question of the week?"

"Do I have a choice?"

"What is it when Ray Charles and Stevie Wonder play tennis?"

Nick shrugged.

"Endless love." Lance laughed and clapped his hands. Nick stared.

"Endless love. You know . . . aaahhh, you don't know anything about tennis. Never mind." He again looked at his watch. "Turn up the volume and let's see what the big weenie has to say."

"Sometimes I wonder who's running this office," Nick said. He turned up the volume. "I think I remember telling you to come over here and see this." He leaned back and propped his black cowboy boots on the edge of his desk.

Then the handsome face of Bob Sawyer was peering out of the screen. He was leaning forward, eyes unblinking, mouth unsmiling, and very serious indeed. Behind him was a map showing the Turks and Caicos Islands, the Bahamas, and south Florida. This was the third day of his reports about South Caicos, and even Lance was impressed with the caliber of his stories.

Sawyer's briefcase camera had worked like a dream. There were sound bites of Ollie sitting out by the pool and telling how the smuggling world was put together. Lance smiled when he saw the shots of Pearl sauntering by the swimming pool with a tray of conch fritters. "Waaaaaahhh. Waaaaaahhhhhh," could be heard in the background.

"I'm trying to watch this," Nick complained.

"That's from the television."

"Can't I get away from your craziness even when I watch the news?"

Footage from the dining room showed the table filled with smugglers laughing about how easy it was to do business in paradise. Even the footage from inside the dim little bar at the Admiral's Arms was outstanding. The interview with Governor Gatty was the most devastating piece of tape on the program. He sat there saying the same thing he had told Nick—that the islands needed sympathy and understanding, that drug smuggling was an American problem, that the islands served only as a refueling stop for pilots who might be transporting textile products and an unknown white powder to Florida.

It was one of those rare stories in which the pictures and the words on the tape were strong enough to tell the story by themselves. Perhaps that's why it was so good. Sawyer simply opened and closed it. Today was the final segment, and, in many ways, the most important. The first two segments, each six minutes in length, were about South Caicos. Today was to be about Fort Lauderdale, the destination for most of the drugs coming out of South Caicos.

Nick and Lance had not told Sawyer about the Doctor and his organization. Ollie had made a few references to the Doctor but they had slid right past Sawyer. The TV man had served his purpose—he had turned the blinding bright spotlight of publicity on the flagrant wide-open drug smuggling of South Caicos— but had not given away the investigation into the Doctor's activities. He even made it look as if he had gone to South Caicos by himself and walked into the den of smugglers. There was no reference to the narc squad or the Executioner. Sawyer had made himself a daredevil hero of a reporter and probably would win a Green Eyeshade Award.

Sawyer ruffled the papers on his desk and began talking. Suddenly there was tape of a group of young black men—their hair and dress and clipped speech identified them as Jamaicans—who were sitting around a room talking. Each was holding an Uzi.

Nick and Lance looked at each other in puzzlement. What the hell did Jamaicans have to do with smuggling coke out of South Caicos? A small percentage might be changed into crack, but that wasn't the point of what was taking place on South Caicos.

Then back to Sawyer. "This is where it ends," he intoned in his deep mellifluous voice, "with hard men on mean streets; the mean streets of Fort Lauderdale, where Jamaican posses, armed with high-powered Uzi machine guns, peddle their death-dealing goods."

Sawyer moved from behind the desk, picked up a small glassine envelope, and held it toward the camera. Ever since Walter Cronkite had stood up more than fifteen years ago and moved to a map to denounce the war in Vietnam, television reporters had used the simple act of standing up as a dramatic gesture to underline whatever they were saying.

The envelope Sawyer picked up contained a pea-sized hunk of crack, a form of cocaine. "And this is what it's all about. Crack. A cheap and deadly form of cocaine whose distribution in Fort Lauderdale is controlled by violent Jamaican posses."

Sawyer paused dramatically, then lowered his head and jutted his jaw to the left while keeping his eyes locked on the camera. "Today, milkmen in Fort Lauderdale are carrying guns to protect themselves against robberies by those wanting to buy crack."

Sawyer paused again. He dropped his voice an octave. "Fort Lauderdale and Dodge City have a lot in common."

Then Sawyer pointed to the map behind his desk. "The cocaine that leaves the island of South Caicos comes to Fort Lauderdale, where it is changed into crack, and then it is sold on our street corners, in our schoolyards, playgrounds, and parks. By these men."

The image switched to the hard-faced Jamaicans waving their Uzis and working themselves into a frenzy before the camera. "Broward narcotics officers, fearless drug warriors, are working to stop this deadly flood of crack," Sawyer said.

Lance laughed. "Drug warriors," he intoned. "Drug warriors. We are the new American hero. Holy shit, in another year I'll be a cult figure. What do you think of that, *jefe?*"

Then there was an interview with Sheriff Turnipseed, who, spittle flying, took ten seconds to tell Sawyer all he knew about crack, about how his office was gearing up to become more proactive against crack.

Nick shook his head in dismay. Lance laughed aloud. "This fucking Sawyer bozo has lost it," he said. "That's why I didn't want to go down there with a reporter. They're all batshit. I mean, this guy is Joe Shit the Ragman in stolen clothes. Where does he get this stuff about Jamaicans? If all the cocaine coming out of South Caicos was turned into crack, the streets would be four feet deep in the stuff. Can't the guy do simple arithmetic?"

Nick was silent. He stared at the screen until Sawyer's report ended. He flicked an imaginary spot of dust from his boots. He was smiling.

Lance's brow wrinkled. What was there to smile about? What did Nick see that he had missed?

Nick slowly walked across the room and turned off the television. He looked at Lance and nodded. "You're right. But that story may be the best thing that could happen to us."

"How the hell can that be?"

Nick pulled at his mustache. "You'll see."

24

Nick was right.

The ultimate fear of Middle America is seeing young black men on television waving automatic weapons.

Bob Sawyer's third report scared the hell out of people.

The Fort Lauderdale and Miami newspapers, in a rare move, published stories about the television station's stories. Two congressmen and one of Florida's U.S. senators were calling the newspapers and television stations, volunteering to give interviews about how the Turks and Caicos Islands should be closed down and telling how they were pushing for federal law-enforcement agencies to assist the Broward Sheriff's Office.

Two days after Sawyer's final report, both Ron Williamson and Mike Love called Nick to say their offices were besieged with telephone calls from angry citizens. The public wanted all those wild-eyed young black men off the streets; middle-aged men called to say they didn't want their women raped and their VCR's stolen. The first step in getting crack dealers—the wild-eyed, Uzi-waving black men—off the streets was to go down and clean up that little pissant island where all the dope was coming from.

Ron and Mike said the word was coming down from Washington: close South Caicos. Stop the flow of cocaine into south Florida. Ron and Mike said their agencies would soon be calling officially on Sheriff

Turnipseed, asking if they could put together a joint operation. The governor of the Turks and Caicos, because of pressure exerted by the U.S. State Department on Whitehall, had agreed to "ask" the Americans to come down and conduct a special enforcement operation in the islands.

Three days later the regional commissioner of Customs and the special agent in charge of the Miami Drug Enforcement Administration, along with the commander of the Coast Guard in the Seventh District, came to Sheriff Hiram Turnipseed's office. And because the operation would take place within the purview of Raymond Dumnik, now the narcotics attaché of the U.S. embassy in Nassau, he was there; and he was making no effort to hide his anger at being ordered to the office of a local sheriff. The big question was what form the joint effort would take; whether it would be an ad-hoc federal-state-local group or whether it should be an Organized Crime Drug Enforcement Task Force, a federally funded strike force whose acronym is pronounced "oh-see-det." It was decided to go with the OCDETF. The expertise various federal agencies could bring to the investigation would be invaluable; local police officers, such as the Broward narcotics squad, would be deputized as U.S. marshals with the powers of federal agents. This meant Nick or Lance would have authority to operate in the Turks and Caicos. And, finally, the money available through the U.S. government to fund the OCDETF would provide virtually limitless resources.

A week after the meeting between Sheriff Turnipseed and the feds, Raymond Dumnik returned. He obviously was pleased with himself. He took a twelve-page document from his expensive briefcase and presented it to the sheriff. The federal agencies involved in "Operation Blue Lightning," a name Lance had come up with for the South Caicos operation, had picked Sheriff Hiram Turnipseed as their leader. Dumnik said this was a great honor; that, to his knowledge, no local police officer had ever been picked to lead a federal task force.

But Hiram Turnipseed had not stayed in office all these years without learning a bit about politics. He knew a limb when he saw one. And he was not going to walk out on it. Being in charge of Operation Blue Lightning meant he was responsible if anything went wrong, and a thousand things could go wrong in an international enforcement effort. Whatever mistakes were made on South Caicos or anywhere in the islands would be placed at his door. But if the operation were successful, the feds would take full credit. They always did. The sheriff saw Blue Lightning as a lose-lose proposition.

Turnipseed, his eyes so narrow they were almost closed, shook his head. His primary chin and his dewlaps quivered. "No. I'm not signing this," he said. "I regret I cannot be more proactive on this issue, but I will not take responsibility."

"Everyone involved has picked you to lead this operation," Dumnik said. He had anticipated the sheriff's reaction; in fact, he had planned on it. The feds were angry about a local sheriff's office embarrassing them and causing considerable grief to their superiors in Washington. If Turnipseed turned down leadership of the strike force, the fledgling group would die a lingering death. The feds could say they had tried, but the local guys, the ones who knew the most about South Caicos, had dropped the ball. "It was your men who uncovered this guy Goldstein and who gathered the intelligence on South Caicos. Your men know more than anyone else about it. You should be in charge."

Again Sheriff Turnipseed shook his head. He pushed the paper across the desk toward Dumnik. "This is a federal operation. You're the senior narcotics officer over there. It's your job. You sign it."

Dumnik smiled. "Sheriff, let me say again that all of the agencies involved picked you to head this effort. You sign it or it dies."

"I'm not signing."

"It's just on paper. You could appoint Nick Brown as the operational chief. Your man would be in command."

"I'm not signing."

Dumnik stood up. He could not hide his smile. He had known how this would turn out. "I'll leave the agreement here with you in case you change your mind," he said.

As Dumnik left the sheriff's office, his smile widened. It looked as if Nick Brown and his band of unrenown were going to stay in Fort Lauderdale—in the bush leagues, where they belonged.

25

Cosmos Goldstein dialed a number on his car phone and waited, both hands on the wheel, until he heard a neutral voice say hello. He tilted his head so he could speak into the fingertip-size microphone sewn into the trim above the window. "You called."

"Where are you?"

"In the car." Goldstein rarely talked business on his home telephone. That was for calling his mama and his shiksas. Business was done in person or, sometimes, on the car telephone if it could be done in an elliptical, coded fashion. That was another thing his quiet friends told him. Always assume your home telephone is bugged. Never talk business on it. The car telephone is different. A little bit. It can be bugged. But the equipment costs about forty thousand dollars; too expensive for Broward County. Besides, monitoring a Title III, the official name for a phone tap, requires more manpower than Broward could afford. As for the feds, they have to be convinced you are a major violator and must have a significant case against you before they will allocate the time and men and resources it takes to monitor every call on a car telephone. So it's okay. Still, be careful.

Ten minutes earlier he had picked up the phone in his house and heard a voice say, "Is this the doctor?"

"This is Dr. Goldstein."

"I'm a patient. I have a problem."

Goldstein recognized the voice. "Tell me more."

"Call me later."

The line went dead. Goldstein locked his house, turned on the security system, locked the front gate, and was driving east on Stirling Road when he returned the call.

"You see the television?" the voice said.

"I did."

"What you think?"

"I think it's great; people are worried about shvartzers waving machine guns."

"I hope that's all they are worried about." There was a pause before the voice continued. "A very risky thing took place. Some are questioning your judgment."

"It worked."

"Did it? They're trying to do something about the island."

"That's private. Between them and us. It won't be public. Business will go on as usual."

"The man down there is cooperating. Bringing in a visitor from back home."

"He had to do that. Uncle leaned on him."

"We are worried."

"As long as the money keeps coming, why worry?"

A slight edge crept into the other man's voice. "We worry for several reasons. For one, we understand a rather serious virus is going around. Six people recently died."

Goldstein was surprised at the depth of the man's knowledge. It was true, he had lost six aircraft in one day. Four pilots had made emergency radio calls; two had been more disciplined and simply rode the aircraft down without calling for help. "The newspapers mentioned only four," he said lamely.

"Doctor, do not underestimate your patients. We have sources of information other than your newspapers. We are concerned about this virus."

"That particular disorder was very expensive. Its etiology is being studied closely. In fact, my professional colleagues tell me a breakthrough is expected within a few days. A week at most." Goldstein paused. "Count on it."

"That brings us to the second reason for our worry. The money. It is a lot of money. We need it. We depend upon it."

"The next time you come to the house, be there early. I'll tell you about American television."

The voice paused, then, in surprise, said, "I need to know about American television?"

"I'll show you how I used television to set an agenda. To create a reality."

Again the voice paused. When it resumed, the tone was unmistakably hard-edged. "I think you are believing what is not true. The reality is that while you intended to divert interest to the shvartzers, instead you increased concern about the broader picture. It also is a reality that you are becoming well-known in your profession. You are receiving attention from people, who may take a good deal of your time. We worry you may become too busy to attend to your old patients."

Goldstein laughed. "I always have time for old patients."

"We think they might even know who your patients are. It could be embarrassing."

"A dentist's relationship with his patients is confidential. I believe very strongly in that."

There was a long pause. It was apparent that the man on the other phone was controlling himself with great difficulty. Then the man spoke. His voice was slow and intense, emphasizing each word. "We will be with you as long as possible. Your treatments enable us to do very important work. But you must understand, there may come a time when our relationship will end. All aspects of our relationship."

This time it was Goldstein who paused. "I'm retiring from my practice at the end of the year. You know that. Nothing will happen until then."

"I hope you are right." There was no good-bye, just a click, and the other person was gone.

26

Nick held up the twelve-page document and waved it toward Lance. "This is the sort of thing that makes me want to get out of this business," he said. "Why is all this necessary? We know where the dope is coming from. We know who's bringing it into Lauderdale. Why can't the sheriff just sign the paper and let us do our job?" He tossed the papers on his desk, sighed, and spun his chair around. His glistening cowboy boots banged against the chair but he didn't notice. He stood up and looked out the window of his office. "All this bureaucratic plotting and maneuvering is getting to me. I know why Dumnik did this. I know why the sheriff did this. I keep saying this, but if all we had to do was fight dopers, we could get something done. We have to fight the sheriff. We have to fight DEA. We have to kiss the Brits' asses and ask can we please do their job for them. And we have to tiptoe around the fact that Israel, our great ally, is helping Goldstein do his smuggling."

Nick turned and looked at Lance. "You just watch. If we can put the squeeze on Goldstein, the Mossad will drop him like a bad habit. They need their relationship with America more than they need money from a doper. When we catch him, they will disappear. The State Department, somebody, will put the squeeze on the sheriff and we will have to back off. It will be as if the Mossad never smuggled dope. And they'll either kill Goldstein or threaten him or someone in his family until he's too scared to talk. We'll never flip him."

He paused a moment, then continued. His voice was intense. "Cunningham, I want Goldstein. I want to prove the Mossad is helping him. They're providing that asshole with intelligence from inside our government. I know that. It's the only way he could do what he does."

Lance shrugged and looked solemn. When Nick was angry, Lance listened and nodded. Nick's usual policy was to do what he was told, to do his job no matter the obstacles. It was only recently that Nick had begun complaining about the frustrations of his job.

"Being a narc in a big city is impossible today," Nick said. "DEA sniping at us. TV cops running around unshaven and wearing pimp suits." He looked at Lance. "And I got a deputy that spends too much time looking for Central Cuban Dispatch."

Lance's smile returned. "Hey, *jefe*. Thought I had them yesterday. Two vehicles blocked the southbound lanes of the Dixie Highway. I figured CCD had to be close. Maybe one of those big warehouses over near the *führerbunker*. But I couldn't find it."

Nick ignored Lance's reference to the *führerbunker*, his name for the sheriff's office, and pointed toward the document on his desk. "The sheriff won't sign this. It's the agreement for him to be in charge of Blue Lightning. The investigation is over before it got started. We're dead in the water. South Caicos is wide open and there's not a damn thing we can do about it."

Nick pulled at his mustache. His eyes were troubled. He was almost mumbling. "I might take that job in Naples with Joe D'Alessandro. He called again. Said I would be in charge of investigations, that he would back me up all the way."

He looked at Lance, staring through him, still mumbling. "It's tempting. I want to be a cop again. I want to enforce the law. I want to put people in jail. I can't do that in Lauderdale. Too much politics. Too much bureaucracy."

"Hey, *jefe,* before you slash your wrists, give me a shot. Let the Ghost handle this. I can get His Fatness to sign that paper."

Nick's eyes narrowed. "Don't fuck with me, Cunningham. I'm not in the mood."

Lance held his hands wide. Two curse words from Nick in one conversation, a clear sign the guy was about out of control. "Hold on, Nick. I'm serious. I can get him to sign. Let me have a shot. Okay?"

Nick looked up at Lance for a long moment. Lance had the sort of excited look in his eye that people got when they picked up a telephone and were told Ed McMahon was on the line. "How?"

Lance's smile turned maniacal and his eyebrows arched. "The important thing is his signature, right?"

Nick sighed. "On second thought, don't tell me. I don't want to know."

He picked up the papers and handed them to Lance.

27

Lance looked at his watch: five-fifteen on Friday afternoon. If his intel was correct, time to move. He opened the car door and walked across the sandy parking lot into the front door of the large one-story building housing the sheriff's department: the *führerbunker*. The building was two blocks south of State Road 84, just west of U.S. 1 and near Lester's Diner in a run-down industrial part of Fort Lauderdale. The deputy on the front desk, a forty-five-year-old woman who looked sixty-five, was as vigilant as Cerberus. She glared balefully at Lance. "Put your badge out where it can be seen," she ordered.

The deputy was uglier than a pair of green espadrilles. She wore far too much lipstick, and her lips were permanently turned down at the corners, giving her the appearance of a clown whose parents had just died. Her once-blonde hair had been bleached over the years until it had the consistency of steel wool, and it fanned out from her head like a gleaming metal halo. Eva, that was her name, ate mints constantly in a futile effort to freshen her breath, a fetid blast of air almost as deadly as her stare. In fact, it was said that her stare could peel paint from the walls and her breath could then set the walls on fire. Eva's personality matched her appearance. And Lance's cavalier disregard of office procedures did not help her disposition.

Her basilisk stare was unwavering. Damn undercover guys. Walked around like they owned the universe. Thought they were exempt from all the rules. The newer cops, the young guys, were different. They followed procedures when they came to the sheriff's office.

Lance slipped the black leather wallet containing his badge and identification card over the top of his jeans so the badge was visible. Eva nodded in approval.

Lance smiled. This was not the time to tell Eva he believed her urine could etch glass. Eva pressed a button and the locked door to the right clicked open. Lance walked down the long hall. On either side were the departments that came under the sheriff's office. Only a few people were in each office and they were supervisors. Guys working late to show the sheriff how dedicated they were. Each looked up nervously as Lance walked by; not that they were afraid of him; they were afraid of anyone who came down the hall. Ever since the day after the election, when the sheriff fired more than two dozen officers, the survivors walked around like a litter of whipped puppies. Lance's smile tightened. Maybe Nick was right. Maybe it was time to get out of Broward County and go to a small jurisdiction where a cop could be a cop.

At the end of the hall, Lance paused. He looked through the door on his right and into the sheriff's outer office, where Bettina, the sheriff's personal secretary, sat. To her left was the closed door of the sheriff's office.

Bettina was the most popular person in the sheriff's office. She used a wheelchair because of an automobile accident in which she had damaged her spinal cord. She ignored her disability as did virtually everyone who knew her. And she possessed none of the bitterness or meanness of spirit sometimes manifested by those with physical disabilities. Bettina was smiling when she rolled through the door every morning and smiling when she rolled out in the afternoon. No one had ever seen her morose or heard her express sorrow over her condition.

Bettina was not pretty. But the ten years of pain she

had suffered since her injury at nineteen had given her dark brown eyes and porcelain face an aura of angelic sweetness. Sometimes when people saw her for the first time they thought she was playing a joke on them, that a woman with such a luminous face could not be in a wheelchair. Because her hips and legs had atrophied, she was inordinately proud of her breasts and wore cotton sweaters or sundresses that emphasized their size.

Lance watched as Bettina slowly cleaned off her desk, obviously waiting for something. Then the buzzer on her telephone sounded, audible even through the closed glass door separating her office from the large office outside. Lance saw a flicker of pain cross her face as she picked up the receiver. She listened, nodded once, and replaced the receiver. Her hand remained on the phone for a moment. She bit her lips as she stared at the telephone. Lance saw her take a deep breath. Then she backed her wheelchair from the desk and rolled toward the door to the sheriff's office. She paused, her smile returned, and she opened the door. It closed softly behind her.

Lance looked at his watch. Considering the sheriff's sensibilities, five minutes should be about right. He looked down the hall. No one was about; they knew the sheriff was still in the building and they were all sticking to their desks. They were afraid of the sheriff, afraid for their jobs. Cops should not be afraid for their jobs.

Lance hoped that what he was about to do would not have any effect on Bettina. He would find a way to explain to her; to tell her that no one would ever know; to tell her he understood.

He looked at his watch. Time to get this show on the road. He pulled an envelope from his back pocket, opened it, and withdrew the document. He took a fountain pen from his shirt pocket.

Lance stepped around the corner, then slowly pushed open the glass door to Bettina's office. The door made no sound. He turned right and put his hand on the door to the sheriff's office. He listened for a moment. Not a sound from inside. He hoped his intelligence information was correct; if not, he was about to be in one hell of a lot of trouble.

Lance turned the doorknob, pushed the door wide, quickly walked inside, and said, "Sheriff, I'm wondering if you will reconsider and—"

He stopped. His timing had been perfect. Sheriff Turnipseed was standing in front of his desk facing Bettina, whose back was to the door. His right hand was behind Bettina's head and his left was in her blouse. He was leaning over her, face contorted.

Sheriff Turnipseed snapped to his left and strode around the corner of his desk, his buttocks jerking to the rear and his shoulders rolling as he tried to stuff his penis back into his pants. Bettina picked up a stack of papers on the sheriff's desk and covered her exposed breasts. She furtively wiped her hand across her mouth. She glanced quickly over her shoulder, saw Lance, blushed in embarrassment, and bowed her head.

"What in the goddamn hell do you mean busting in here that way?" the sheriff said angrily. "Don't you know how to knock on a goddamned door? You got an appointment to see me?"

Lance was apologetic as he walked toward the desk, pen and papers in his hand. The sheriff knew Lance had seen what was taking place. And he knew Lance was crazy enough to make an issue of it. He should have fired the narc months ago. He would have, except the guy was too far down the ladder to be a threat, and, even more important, his undercover exploits had brought the sheriff a lot of publicity. Nevertheless, Cunningham was as good as gone. Within the next few weeks the sheriff would find a reason to fire him.

"I'm sorry, Sheriff. I didn't realize you were busy. But I was wondering if you would reconsider taking over the Blue Lightning task force the feds want to put together. The South Caicos thing."

The sheriff's eyes narrowed until they almost disappeared. Lance would have sworn he could actually hear the sheriff trying to think.

"Nick Brown put you up to this?"

"Nick?" Lance said in surprise. "Put me up to what? No, sir. He doesn't know I'm here. I just saw these papers on his desk and"—his eyes locked with those of the sheriff—"this is important. The narcotics squad really wants to take these people down. I just thought you might reconsider, sir. Nick will accept full responsibility. He will look after your interests."

The sheriff continued on around his desk toward Lance. His large hips occasionally jerked to the rear. He must have gotten caught either in his underwear or his zipper. He snatched the papers from Lance and glared malevolently at the young agent. Yep, he was going to fire him. He would find a reason. Maybe he would screw up on South Caicos. Anything he did down there, anything at all, that was not strictly by the book, could be used as justification. If the task force, this Operation Blue Lightning, did not close down South Caicos or did not result in the arrest of this Dr. Goldstein, Cunningham would be the fall guy. He had quite a reputation among police officers. And the newspapers had written about several of his exploits. He would be a high-profile sacrifice, someone to take the heat off the sheriff.

The sheriff grabbed the pen, leaned over his desk, and signed the papers. He flung the pen across his desk and thrust the papers toward Lance.

Lance looked at the signature, nodded, folded the document, and put it back into the envelope. He reached forward for his pen.

Then the sheriff spoke. His voice was an angry rasp. "I got my eye on you, boy. I got my eye on you."

Lance smiled. He glanced down at Bettina, but she was staring at the floor. Lance stepped forward a half-step until he was between Bettina and the sheriff. He dropped his right hand and quickly squeezed her shoulder, reassuring her.

"Sheriff, thanks for signing this. You won't regret it."

The sheriff flicked his round head toward the door. "Get outta here."

"Yes, sir." Lance turned. He closed the door as he walked out.

As Lance walked down the hall, he waved the envelope in the air. The sheriff was not so smart after all. In fact, you could take everything he knew, pack it in a gnat's rear end, and still have room for a Volkswagen and two caraway seeds.

Lance's eyes were dancing and his smile was broad. As he clicked open the door leading into the front office, he walked over to Eva's desk and thwacked his palm hard against the surface. She jumped and glared at him.

"Madam," he said, smiling upon her as he folded his creds and stuffed them into his rear pocket, "are you aware that a blow-job can influence the course of history?"

28

"Those guys make me feel like Joe Shit the Ragman," Lance said to Mike.

He looked at the Coast Guard pilots and crews. They were recruiting-poster sharp in pressed and creased flight suits and spit-shined boots. Over the left breast pocket on each flight suit was a name tag on which was written in clean bold letters the person's last name and first initial. The crew members had short, neatly clipped hair and they all wore military sunglasses.

Lance looked down at his own outfit—jeans, boat shoes, and a T-shirt that said "If You Snort Cocaine, You Will Catch Communism." He looked again at the Coasties and shook his head in reluctant admiration. "I like their flight suits," he said. "I got an idea about that when we go to the islands." He settled back in the chair and stretched out.

"Don't be fooled by those pretty boys," Mike said. He made no effort to lower his voice. "They're fucking barracudas."

Mike remembered all too well a Christmas party of only four years ago. Personnel at most federal agencies in the Miami area were invited. The Coast Guard pilots, who then did not fly narcotics-interdiction missions, had shunned Customs pilots. They acted as if Customs pilots were their professional and social inferiors. "You guys chase smugglers," one Coasty said in disgust. "We want to be good guys." Now the Coasties wanted the money that went with drug interdiction and it was a different story.

One of the Coast Guard pilots two seats down from Lance overheard Mike, turned, and glared indignantly. The Coast Guard continues to look on Customs the same way the State Department looks on the Drug Enforcement Administration: as a group of animals who should be kept on a leash. The Coast Guard pilot leaned over the empty seat between him and Lance and whispered, "In another year, you Customs guys will be out of the drug-interdiction business. You'll be in your little blue monkey suits checking luggage at the airport. You do that real well."

Mike leaned over and looked at the Coasty as if seeing him for the first time. "How'd you get in the Coast Guard?" he asked curiously. "You're not six feet tall."

"You don't have to be six feet to enlist in the Coast Guard."

"Yeah you do. That way, when your boat sinks, you can wade ashore. That's why they call you guys the 'Knee-Deep Navy.'"

Lance twisted his mouth in exaggerated laughter. "Hardy-har-har."

The Coasty smirked. "See if you guys are laughing when we take over the drug-interdiction business."

"Fuck you, coast rat," Mike said. He turned to Lance. "See what I mean. Barracudas."

"Want me to lay a question of the week on him?"

Mike chuckled, a rasping reluctant noise. "Do it."

Lance tugged on the creased sleeve of the Coast Guard pilot's flight suit. "Sir," he said diffidently, "what do you call an anorexic woman with a yeast infection?"

The Coast Guard pilot, brows wrinkled, looked at Lance. Who was this guy? The brows wrinkled even more. It had been years since the Coasty had worn anything as wrinkled as his brows. He was not sure he had heard the guy properly. "What?"

"A quarter-pounder with cheese."

Lance fell back into his chair, wrapped his arms around himself, pulled one knee high in the air, and said, "Hardy-har-har."

"Gentlemen, let's come to order. Hold it down back there," said the tall aloof Coast Guard captain who was conducting the meeting. He had the faintly superior air often held by career military men who, in their heart of hearts, deeply resent that they are under civilian control.

The Coast Guard pilot near Lance turned to the captain in relief. He welcomed a world he knew and understood.

"Gentlemen, as you know, the purpose of this briefing is to acquaint you with the parameters of the exercise we're about to begin," the captain said. "This exercise is to demonstrate to our guests the capabilities of the Coast Guard Falcon; specifically, that this aircraft is capable of conducting intercepts against narcotics traffickers and conducting those intercepts as well as any aircraft now engaged in that activity. Our guests and observers aboard Swordfish One are Mr. Rusche and Mr. Wilson, members of the staff of Senator Sam Nunn, who is chairman of the Senate Armed Services Committee and who is interested in Coast Guard matters."

The captain did not add that Sam Nunn had spent much of his military career, if it could be called that, playing basketball on a Coast Guard team, and that, as a result, he usually supported whatever the Coast Guard wanted. The senator's help would be invaluable in taking the drug-interdiction role away from Customs.

The captain nodded toward the two civilians in the front row. "Gentlemen, once again, on behalf of the United States Coast Guard station here at Opa Locka, welcome to Miami."

As a concession to the south Florida heat, the two civilians had removed their ties and coats. But everything about them screamed of outsiders—their pallor, their demeanor, the way they distanced themselves from others in the room, the deference they were shown. These two men were outsiders, powerful outsiders whose report of this day's activities would either grant or deny the Coast Guard permission to participate in Blue Lightning. And if the Coasties took part and did well, it was almost a foregone conclusion they would be granted an additional ten million dollars to install the same F-16 radar on their six Falcons that Customs used on the Citation. They would be in the drug-intercept business in a big way, direct competition with Customs. But it was a highly selective version of air interdiction; they only wanted to fly in the Gulf of Mexico and the Atlantic. They wanted nothing to do with the grit and dust and frustration of the Mexican border, where Customs also flew, or of the California coast, where Customs had several Air Branches.

"Mr. Love is flying the Customs Cessna 404, the aircraft that will simulate an inbound smuggler," the captain continued. "His passenger is Mr. Cunningham of the Broward County Sheriff's Department. Their call sign today is Sierra Seven Six."

The captain nodded toward the young pilot who sat two seats away from Lance. "Lieutenant Addams will command Swordfish One, the Coast Guard Falcon that will be the intercept aircraft." The captain gestured toward a group of men sitting behind Lance and Mike, almost a dozen Coast Guard officers in flight suits. "These officers will be flying various Coast Guard assets for the safety and support of the mission," he said vaguely.

Mike was puzzled. What could a dozen men be doing to support a simple intercept? Oh, well, maybe that was the way the Coasties did business. Everything about this exercise was strange. The Coasties were trying to blow smoke on the two congressional staffers, but to do that, they needed the help of Customs. And Customs was in no mood to participate in an exercise that was wired from the beginning.

The Falcon simply was not designed to be an intercept aircraft. It normally was used in long-range search-

and-rescue missions and its swept wings prevented it from flying slowly enough to intercept small general-aviation aircraft. The Coasties were search-and-rescue people who did not have the flying skills to snuggle up under a drug-smuggling aircraft close enough to read the numbers. They did not have the commitment to land and go up against armed smugglers. In fact, when Bahamian dopers had fired on the Customs Blackhawk several weeks earlier, the crew of a Coast Guard backup helicopter orbiting nearby decided to cut and run. They abandoned the Customs crew.

While the Coasties had no law-enforcement background, they did have two things: when it came to the millions of dollars being parceled out to fight the war on drugs, the Coasties had the single-mindedness of a rutting moose. And when it came to skilled public relations, the Coast Guard had a team that could teach Madison Avenue one hell of a lot.

The simulated intercept today, if successful, might signal the beginning of the end for the Customs Air Branch. The coast rat who had spoken earlier to Mike could be right: in a year Customs could be out of the air-interdiction business.

The captain paused and stared at Mike Love. "You understand the mission?" His voice was controlled, but hard. Behind the question was animosity over the days of squabbling between Coast Guard and Customs that had preceded the briefing. The Coast Guard wanted to conduct the exercise at the south end of Andros, more than two hundred miles southeast of Opa Locka. Customs objected. They wanted to run the exercise off Bimini, only fifty-five miles offshore. The only reason for flying south of Andros was to allow the Falcon to burn more gasoline, to decrease its weight and enable it to fly slower. But Coast Guard Commandant Yost was adamant. Millions of dollars were at stake for his agency and, like any other bureaucrat, he wanted the deck stacked as much as possible in his favor. Eventually the two agencies compromised and the simulated drop was scheduled for Williams Island, about a hundred and thirty miles from Miami. The final part of the exercise would take place at Orange Cay, some fifty miles northwest of Williams Island.

Mike nodded. "I've been briefed." For a moment his eyes and those of the captain were locked. Then the captain turned toward the two congressional staffers. His smile was warm enough to melt butter. "Gentlemen, to reiterate. Today a Customs aircraft will simulate an inbound flight by a narcotics trafficker. Swordfish One will detect and intercept the target. There will be three intercepts. During the first intercept, the target aircraft will be flying at one hundred and forty knots. After the successful intercept, the target will break off. We will perform another intercept, this time at one hundred and twenty knots. The third intercept will be at one hundred knots, the speed of some of the slower traffickers. No maneuvering will be performed by the target aircraft during the first two intercepts. However, on the third and final intercept, if the crew of the Customs aircraft obtains a visual sighting of the intercept aircraft, then it may maneuver as would a trafficker."

The captain's eyes swung briefly to Mike, hardened almost in warning, then returned to the congressional staffers. He looked at his watch. "Gentlemen, the pilots must discuss the radio frequencies we will be using during the exercise and then they must get into position. That will take a couple of hours. If you would care to join me, we can give you a tour of our facilities, or, if you like, visit the Officers' Club."

The two men nodded and stood up. The captain, trim and smiling, uniform creased and chest bedecked with medals, turned to escort them to the door. After several steps he turned, looked at Mike, and held up a finger in warning. "Do it by the book, mister," he said.

Mike did not answer. The reason for the Coast Guard's absurd rules was patently clear to any pilot who knew the capabilities of the Falcon. If the Falcon could slow down to the agreed-upon speeds for the first two intercepts, it would be hanging there on the edge of a stall. If the wings rocked more than five or ten degrees, the Falcon would stall. But after two intercepts and buzzing around at low altitude, the Coast Guard jet would burn enough fuel that it might—just might—be able to tilt the wings ten degrees.

As the captain exited with the civilians, Lieutenant Addams took over the briefing and assigned radio frequencies so that all aircraft involved in the exercise could talk to each other.

Something was going on here that the Coast Guard was not telling Customs. There was no need for this many pilots and crews. Not to run a simple intercept.

"What are you guys flying?" Mike casually asked one of the Coast Guard pilots.

"E-2."

"E-2," said a second.

Mike stared at him in amazement. E-2's carried a pancakelike radar dome atop the fuselage; they were radar-tracking aircraft.

"I thought this exercise was supposed to test the Falcon," Mike said.

"That is correct," the second pilot said. "We're simply flying in a support role."

"You're going to vector the Falcon to us."

"We perform the same function on regular intercepts."

"Yeah, when you're up and working with Slingshot. But you know where we'll be and at what time. This is not a test of the Falcon. It's rigged from the get-go so you guys can get the new radar."

One of the Coast Guard pilots smiled and shrugged. "I'm a worker bee. I do what I'm told."

"Shit," Mike said. He motioned for Lance to follow him and stormed out of the briefing room. Lance caught him on the flight line and the two men strode rapidly toward the blue-and-white Cessna 404. The aircraft normally was used for marine patrol and occasionally for undercover work.

The day already was blistering. It was not yet nine

A.M. but the air was hot and sticky and oppressive. Heat waves shimmered and danced from the vast expanse of concrete parking apron.

Mike was so angry he was not aware of the heat. "We spend all this time dicking around with coast rats in a rigged exercise. Those Washington guys won't know what's going on." He blew out an angry gasp of air. "We should be up chasing the Doctor."

"Nick was saying the same thing the other day. But what the hell? It's all fun. I'd rather mind-fuck a doper, but I'll settle for a Coasty." He laughed. "The Coasties aren't as bright. But we get extra points for increasing their coping skills."

"Not me. That's not what I'm here for. I want to catch dopers."

He climbed the steps at the left rear of the Cessna 404 in two leaps. Lance shut and locked the rear door, then squeezed between the seats toward the cockpit, where he took the right seat.

Mike's hands moved swiftly over the controls. In seconds he had finished the starting sequence and both propellers were turning. "The only good thing about all this is that after today it will all be over," he said. "All the bullshit will be behind us and we can go down to South Caicos and kick some smugglers' asses."

29

Williams Island is a small unpopulated island about a mile off the western tip of Andros. It is perhaps three miles in width and about a mile from top to bottom. Most of the island is marsh and scrub and trees. But in the middle, atop a narrow ridge of high ground that rises two feet above sea level, is a strip of hard ground long enough to be used as an airstrip by smugglers. The danger of this short, rough, tree-lined strip is apparent in the carcasses of aircraft that have been bent, smashed, and broken during attempted landings. Nearby, across a half-mile stretch of water, is Billy Island, an even smaller island that for years has been used as a stash point for drugs and aviation fuel. This remote corner of Andros is one of the most violent corners of the western world. It is violent in a natural sense in that violent thunderstorms and waterspouts march through with almost metronomic regularity. Local waters teem with giant man-eating sharks. The sharks here are not solitary hunters; they travel in packs. And more than one smuggler who elected to swim from Williams Island to Billy Island has disappeared while his friends watched, simply snatched from the surface in a flurry of fins and jaws. The natural violence is carried over into the manmade violence. The rampant paranoia inherent in narcotics trafficking, combined with the popularity of Williams Island and Billy Island, has caused countless groups of smugglers to engage in shoot-outs there that would make the OK Corral look like a Sunday-school picnic. Few efforts are made to hide the violence, even when it is innocent people who are killed. One Miami pilot, a weekend flier who liked to bounce around the Bahamas on Sundays, landed on Williams Island one afternoon. He had heard the stories; he had seen the wrecked aircraft. And he simply wanted to land, look around for a half-hour, then go home with a story to tell. A smuggler was on the island guarding a stash of cocaine. He shot the pilot before the guy ever got out of his little Cessna 172. The body was still in the aircraft two weeks later when a Customs helicopter landed. Then there was the helicopter chartered by a network television crew. The crew wanted a few aerials and some footage of a clandestine strip used by smugglers. The chopper was shot down by automatic-weapons fire. Everyone on board went to the bottom of the ocean. Officially, it was all a big mystery. But the story of what happened circulated among smugglers, and then among narcotics officers. Cops used the story to illustrate how innocent people can be savaged by the random violence of drug smuggling. But police weren't broken up about a network news crew being blasted out of the air. Hey, they were just newsies.

Few people, except drug smugglers, ever visit this part of the Bahamas. It is difficult to reach and there is nothing to do once one has arrived. The western edge of Andros is a marshy, low-lying, mosquito-infested, riverine area best described by its local name: the Mud. In the mouth of one of the meandering tidal creeks are a few grass shacks. It is a small native fishing village where a half-dozen Bahamians eke out a subsistence living from the sea. It is a village out of west Africa.

The day was a typical Bahamian day. Good vis. Scattered cumulus. Off in the distance, perhaps thirty or forty miles to the southeast, was a single thunderstorm; a dark, monstrous, towering cell that soared to almost sixty thousand feet and had the classic anvil-shaped top pointing in its direction of travel.

It was here, in the skies over western Andros and over Williams Island, that Customs was to simulate an inbound smuggling flight.

Mike circled over the thatched huts on western Andros. He looked at his watch. "Smugglers sometimes have tail winds," he said. "I'm going in early." He racked the wings of the Cessna 404 around in a tight circle to the north.

Lance nodded in understanding. "Smugglers are always early or late. They don't work on our schedule."

"The Coasties have their E-2's up there watching us. They'll relay our position to Swordfish One. They're gonna impress the hell out of those two congressional geeks." Mike gently pushed the wheel of the aircraft and put it into a descent. He knew that radar aboard the two Coast Guard search aircraft could, with relative ease, detect targets flying over the ground. It became more difficult over the water. If he made a high-speed run up the west side of Andros across the riverine marshy area, the combination of rapid flight over water and then marsh and then high ground and then water might confuse the radar.

"They want me to have the profile of a smuggler," Mike said. "I'll show them what a smuggler would do."

The radar altimeter of the Cessna pinged when the aircraft descended below a hundred and fifty feet.

"What was that?" Lance asked.

"Somebody had it set up for an IFR approach. I turned it off."

Now the Cessna was no more than ten feet above the sandy soil. It crossed a large estuary, then an island, an extensive marsh area, and again was over high ground. The Cessna was traveling at almost two hundred miles an hour. Below was a white and blue and green blur. Mike's long fingers held the wheel lightly. He adjusted the trim tab without moving his eyes from the blurred landscape.

"Let's move out over the water," he said.

"Hell, yes. I want to drag my feet in the ocean."

Lance loved the hazardous low-level flying. This was one of the best parts of being a narc—flat-hatting across the deck at high speeds.

"You gonna do a pop-up?" he asked. A pop-up is a very effective maneuver that frequently is used by smugglers. They approach from the south at extremely low altitudes; some of them have salt spray on the windshields. And then, when within a few miles of their drop zone, they zoom up a few hundred feet. This gives them the altitude to confirm the drop zone visually and to see if anyone else, cops or other dopers wanting to rip off the load, is within range. Pop-ups are particularly frustrating to Customs. The balloons often do not pick up the target until after the pop-up. Even if a sensor bird is trolling in the area, much of the time it does not detect a target in the wave tops. Then suddenly there it is. The scopes show a target in a tight circle—the sure sign of an air drop in progress— but usually it is all over by the time they arrive.

"Yeah. When I get just south of the island I'll pop up to a thousand feet—that's the drop altitude—and we'll see if we can do it before they bounce us."

"Do they know about the pop-up?"

Mike chuckled. "They never heard of a pop-up. They think the dopers file a flight plan and come in on schedule."

Lance laughed. "Weenies."

Mike kept his eyes out the windshield. "Maybe the E-2 is not picking us up. If his radar works the same way ours does, he is, at best, getting an intermittent target. I know how to fuck that up for them." Mike made a gradual course change to the north, held it for a few minutes, then swung in a tight circle toward the south. The giant thunderstorm to the southeast was moving across Andros toward Williams Island.

"That do any good? They know where we're supposed to be and they're waiting."

"We'll know in a few minutes."

Mike was relaxed, eyes out the window, watching.

When he was fifteen miles south of Williams Island, he reached for the throttle.

"You ready?" he asked.

"Hey, guy. Do your stuff."

Mike pulled firmly on the yoke, bringing it back toward his stomach, and zoomed upward to a thousand feet. Then he retarded the throttle. He made a second adjustment, a small one, and the indicated airspeed settled on one hundred and forty knots.

Four miles south of Williams Island, both men suddenly swung their heads hard to the right. The Coast Guard Falcon, a distinctive swept-wing jet, white with a bright orange slash across the nose, streaked past a quarter-mile away, banking hard and climbing, sharply visible against the dark wall of the thunderstorm that now was about twenty miles away.

Mike laughed in exultation. "They overshot," he said. One of the rules for the exercise was that the Coast Guard should do as Customs did—detect the smuggler, close and read the tail numbers, then break off without being seen by the simulated smuggler.

Mike picked up the microphone. "Swordfish One, Sierra Seven Six. We have a visual; showing you at our ninety degrees for less than fifteen hundred yards."

No answer.

"Swordfish One, you copy? We have the eyeball."

"Sierra Seven Six, Swordfish One," came a firm voice over the radio. It was the Coast Guard captain. "We identified you prior to your seeing us. The intercept is valid. Break off and prepare for the second intercept."

Mike paused. How could this be a righteous intercept if the Coasties overshot and never got close enough to read the tail number?

Truth was that the Falcon, even after flying from Florida at low altitude, still was too heavy to fly at one hundred and forty knots. The crew tried, but at the first sign of a stall, they poured on the coal and zoomed past. They simply couldn't perform the intercept. The

Coast Guard captain's talk was purely for the benefit of the congressional staffers who didn't know enough about aircraft to know what the hell was going on. The staffers were befuddled by the excitement of pretending to intercept smugglers out over the wilds of the western Bahamas; out where, can you believe it, real smugglers had been.

"I question the ID," Mike said. "You weren't close enough."

The Coast Guard captain, trying hard to control his impatience, came back. "We have gyro-stabilized binoculars. We visually acquired your tail numbers and then broke off before you saw us. I repeat, this was a valid intercept. Prepare for the second."

Mike looked at Lance. "Gyro-fucking-stabilized binoculars? I don't care if their assholes squirt laser beams. They didn't slow down enough to do the intercept without us seeing them. The Coasties overshot." He gritted his teeth in anger. "If I were a doper and I saw that white jet go by, I'd know I had been popped. I'd turn and run south to wait them out. And they're counting this as a successful intercept?"

"Don't worry. We'll clean their clock on the next one."

Twice, as Mike swung north in the next ten minutes, the E-2 orbiting high overhead directed him to continue south, to wait about a half-hour before returning to the drop zone. Swordfish One needed to burn off a few hundred more pounds before trying for an intercept at one hundred and twenty knots.

Then Mike swung north. This was to be a head-on intercept. The Coasties would use their superior speed to make a stern conversion and sneak up behind the Cessna. But even with the E-2 monitoring the Cessna's flight path and relaying the position to Swordfish One, the Coasties did not have enough offset when they approached the Cessna. Mike saw the jet when it streaked past his window, no more than a mile away and clearly visible. Had the Coast Guard pilot stayed five miles off and outside the avoidance zone,

Mike might not have seen him. Mike picked up the microphone.

"Swordfish One, Sierra Seven Six. We have an eyeball on you, passing through our two seven zero at about one mile."

No answer.

"Swordfish One, you copy? We ID'd you."

Again came the voice of the captain. "Sierra Seven Six, you could not have identified us at this distance. We are continuing the intercept. Maintain your heading."

Four minutes later Mike and Lance saw the Falcon when it zoomed past on the right side.

"Swordfish One, we see you breaking off."

"After a successful intercept," responded the captain. "Break off and get set up for the next intercept."

Lance looked at Mike. "How does it feel to get fucked without getting kissed?"

Mike grunted in anger and did not respond.

"No rules on the next one, right?" Lance asked. "It's a free-for-all. You can do some banking and yanking—be a smuggler?"

"Yeah, with an E-2 sitting on top of me."

Mike banked toward the southeast. The thunderstorm was about two miles away, marching fast toward the northwest. "Tighten your seat belt," Mike said. "I got an idea."

"What are you gonna do?" Lance said as the Cessna bored straight for the thunderstorm.

"Same thing I've had smugglers do when I was on their tail. Hide." Mike turned off the transponder. "I should have done that earlier," he muttered.

Lance leaned forward in the seat and looked up through the windshield of the Cessna. The walls of the roiling thunderstorm were a distinctive purplish-black. Occasional flashes of lightning could be seen within the surging and throbbing cloud. Below the cloud, in a dark gray curtain that appeared to be at least thirty miles across, was an area of extremely heavy rain.

Lance's eyes widened. For a moment his smile faltered. "Hey, my ears are going bad. I thought I heard you say you were jumping into that concrete mixer."

Mike laughed. "Buckle up tight. It's going to be rough as hell." He reached down and pressed a lever. His seat dropped to the lowest position.

"Why you sitting in a hole?"

"I don't want to be blinded by the lightning when we get inside."

Lance moaned, then began singing, "Mama said there'd be days like this."

He was about to ask Mike what hiding inside the storm would accomplish. But then the Cessna bored inside the black cloud and all conversation ended as the aircraft was tossed first on one wing tip and then the other. The altimeter pegged in the climb mode and then, after a series of bone-rattling bounces, in the descent mode. Lightning was continuous. Rain on the aircraft was a deafening fusillade. The shock-mounted instruments jumped and floated and moved so rapidly they were impossible to read. Mike and Lance were violently tossed about against the seat belts and shoulder harnesses; both knew their skin would be blackened where they had sustained heavy bruises. The compass swung wildly.

Then came a voice over the radio. "Sierra Seven Six. Osprey Four Two."

Lance looked at Mike. "Who's Osprey?" he said, teeth rattling from the force of the violent turbulence.

Mike jammed a thumb upward. "One of. The E-2's. Lost us. Wants us. Tell him. Where we are." He reached for the microphone. The aircraft was bouncing so badly it took him several attempts before his hands closed on it. "Osprey. Four Two. Go."

"Ahhh, Sierra Seven Six," came the smooth, unhurried voice of the Coast Guard pilot who was orbiting somewhere in high, calm altitudes. "Say your transponder code."

"Negative. Transponder."

"Ahhh, Sierra Seven Six. Advise you squawk company plus seven six."

"Negative. Transponder. Good day." Mike stuffed the microphone under his leg. "Assholes. Coasties think. Smugglers. Use transponders." He was shouting so Lance could hear him. "They cheated. First two. Lied. Want me. Help them. Cheat. This one. Fuck them."

After orbiting inside the storm for twenty minutes, Mike emerged into the brilliant sunlight. The change was instantaneous. One moment they were in the darkness being tossed and rocked and beaten, and the next they were in the smooth air with unlimited visibility.

But then Mike's day was ruined. The Coast Guard jet was two miles away, turning across their path of flight. If the Coasties continued circling, they would see him in about thirty seconds. "Ahh, shit," he said. He turned and once again poked into the storm.

After another ten minutes he again emerged. This time he did not see the jet. He quickly raised his seat to the normal position.

"What was that all about?" Lance asked, relieved to be out of the storm.

"We lost them." Mike's head was on a swivel, turning and twisting in all directions, searching. He pointed to a small blur on the horizon, perhaps twenty miles away.

"There it is, Orange Cay," he said. "The E-2's can't track us inside a thunderstorm. We drifted with the storm. It was going the direction we wanted to go, right toward Orange Cay. Now, if we can get to the island before the E-2 can vector the jet to our position, we'll be in business."

He dived toward the deck and leveled out only a few feet above the surface of the ocean. About ten miles from Orange Cay, he popped up to a thousand feet. Now he saw something else, a shape in the water between him and Orange Cay.

"What the hell!"

Directly ahead was a 110-foot Coast Guard cutter, radar dome twirling madly. Mike knew that the radar, through a data link aboard the E-2, had fed his speed and position to the Falcon. Swordfish One was racing toward them at high speed.

"Those guys don't miss a trick," he said reluctantly. Then his voice turned to sarcasm. "Of course they would have a cutter in position if this were a real deal. They got cutters all over the Bahamas to vector bust aircraft." He slowed to one hundred knots and set up for the simulated drop. He made a slow circling pass over the small cay. Enough time, had he been a smuggler, to complete an airdrop. He was pushing the throttles, accelerating back to cruise speed, departing toward Homestead, when the Falcon, gear and flap extended, wallowed past on the right. Even rigged for landing, the configuration at which an aircraft flies slowest, the Coast Guard jet could not slow to one hundred knots.

"Swordfish One. Sierra Seven Six. We've completed the simulated drop. RTB this time."

No answer. The Falcon continued circling to the right.

"He's circling to get on our six," Mike said in amazement. Lance watched through his window on the right. "They're coming around behind us."

"Stupid son of a bitch. He knows he can't do that. Tell me when he makes his final turn."

Lance watched, face pressed against the window. "He disappeared. Coming in behind us."

Mike waited, counting off the seconds until he figured the Falcon would be closing on his stern. Then, in one smooth coordinated motion, he twisted hard on the yoke, pressed the right rudder, and added full power. The 404 pivoted on a wing tip. Now Mike was dead astern the Coast Guard jet, locked tight. He glanced at the airspeed. A hundred and ten knots. If the Falcon banked more than five degrees at this slow speed, it would stall. The Falcon could not maneuver at such a slow airspeed; there was no way it could outfly the 404 unless it accelerated and simply ran away. Mike picked up the microphone and pressed the transmit button rapidly; over and over. In the Falcon cockpit, the radio sounded like a machine gun. It was the ultimate insult toward the Coast Guard pilot. Mike was on his six, shooting him down. And the Falcon could not maneuver without stalling.

"Break off," came the tight voice of the Coast Guard pilot.

"Swordfish One, Sierra Seven Six. I'm on your six. Guess this demonstrates you can't maneuver with a doper."

"Sierra Seven Six. Break off." This time it was the Coast Guard captain.

"Swordfish One, my props are chewing off your tail feathers."

"Sierra Seven Six, break off. That's an order. This exercise is concluded. We witnessed the simulated drop. This was a successful intercept."

"Swordfish One. The drop was completed before you arrived."

"Sierra Seven Six. You were observed by the Coast Guard. That's what the scenario called for."

Mike peeled off. "Sierra Seven Six is RTB."

"Sierra Seven Six. A letter will confirm. But you may tell your chief pilot that U.S. Senate staff members monitoring this exercise advise me they confirmed three successful intercepts."

Mike clicked the microphone in acknowledgment. Wait until Mad Dog heard about this.

A moment later the Coast Guard captain fired a parting shot. "Sierra Seven Six. We will look forward to having you work with us in Blue Lightning."

30

F-16 pilots were shooting high keys at Homestead Air
Force Base, blasting off the runway in an almost vertical climb, zooming upward until they were mere dots,
then pulling power and spiraling down to the low key
position and finally to a simulated emergency power-
off landing. During the roll-out, the pilots added power
and performed the procedure again. Over and over
they shot high keys in the nimble little F-16. And on
each takeoff the roar of the jets echoed across the
broad open expanse of Homestead Air Force Base.

The roar outside was nothing compared to the roars
from inside the Customs Air Branch, where Mad Dog,
the chief pilot, was going into a lip stall.

Until Mad Dog had become chief pilot, few people
knew, or remembered, his name was Roger Garland.
He was one of the senior pilots at the Branch who,
because of the unrelenting nature of his pursuit of
smugglers and the fact that he would quite literally do
anything to prevent a smuggler from escaping, was
known as Mad Dog. Part of his nickname came from
his size; his head sloped into powerful shoulders and a
thick chest. He had virtually no behind and was constantly pulling up his pants. And then there was his
intensity. When Mad Dog became excited, he talked
faster and faster until he wound up sputtering, pro-
nouncing only pieces of words and talking so fast it
sounded like a burst of automatic-weapons fire. Not a

single understandable word came out of his mouth.
Pilots referred to this as his lip stall.

After Mad Dog became chief pilot, his superiors in
Washington felt his nickname was not seemly for an
executive. His pilots didn't care what Washington
thought, but when people from Washington, or from
Air Castle East, the supervisory office for all of the
Customs Air Branches east of the Mississippi, were
around, the pilots shortened "Mad Dog" to the initials
M.D., and began calling their boss M.D. Garland.
This soon became "Doctor Garland," which, for some
inexplicable reason, was acceptable in Washington.
Garland was proud of his nicknames—both Mad Dog
and Doctor. Customs pilots were an irreverent lot,
and when he considered some of the nicknames they
had hung on their colleagues, he knew he had done
well, that they respected and admired him.

Mad Dog, Mike Love, and Roger Woolard, and one
or two others, were the only remnants of the old days,
back in the seventies, when Customs pilots simply
jumped into aircraft and flew offshore looking for
smugglers. They had no radar, no FLIR, and there
was no Slingshot. They simply got up and drove around
until they saw a low-flying aircraft. They shoved the
throttle forward and, if they caught the suspect, came
up alongside and looked in the windows. If they saw
what they thought might be marijuana, they put their
badges up against the window and motioned for the
guy to land. Sometimes the guy landed; sometimes
there were long chases. Mad Dog, flying solo, had had
as many as three busts in a single day. It did not
matter what maneuvers a doper went through, Garland stayed with him. "If he can do it, I can do it," he
said. "When I get on him, I got him. He's mine."
There was no such thing as a red line; no such thing as
a performance envelope. If the doper could outturn
Garland, then Garland went vertical to stay with him.
Once Garland followed a smuggler into a cloud. The
smuggler began tossing out bales of marijuana, trying
to force Garland to crash. It was out of that experi-

ence that the rule came to stay above and slightly offset from a smuggler once a Customs pilot was on a doper's tail.

One January, Garland chased a smuggler from the Bahamas to Indianapolis where he landed in a driving snowstorm. Garland was wearing cotton pants and a short-sleeved shirt. When he jumped out of the aircraft, he hit the icy runway and fell flat. But he kept his shotgun trained on the two smugglers. He jumped up and ordered one of the smugglers to take off his coat. Mad Dog put it on.

"You freeze, you son of a bitch," he said. "You're the crook."

A few weeks later he followed an aircraft into Ocean Reef, the resort island on the south end of Biscayne Bay about twenty miles from Homestead. The smugglers jumped out of their aircraft and ran. Mad Dog taxied after them. He simply roared off the runway, across a golf course, and down a road in hot pursuit, the noise of the aircraft engine sounding like a berserk lawn mower as he accelerated to cross damp grassy areas, then slowed when going down residential streets. The sight of an airplane taxiing at high speed down the staid and dignified byways of Ocean Reef unnerved more than one person. When Mad Dog was stopped by a line of trees, he jumped out, pistol in hand, and ran door to door, sweating, panting, and asking, had he not been in a full lip stall, what would have been understood as, "You seen two guys?" As it was, no one understood. They shook their heads and pointed down the street, hoping this pistol-waving madman would leave their door.

It took more than an hour, but Garland caught and arrested the smugglers.

Garland's nickname was cemented forever after he landed on a dirt road behind a smuggler. Six people, all carrying automatic rifles, were there to meet the smuggler and off-load the marijuana. It wouldn't have mattered to Garland if there had been sixty people. He was a U.S. Customs pilot and it was his job to stop dopers. That gave him a moral authority no smuggler or group of smugglers could ever match. He jumped from his aircraft and charged into the smugglers armed only with a .38-caliber pistol. The smugglers were so astounded they broke and ran. Garland followed the pilot down a road. The pilot swam across a canal and raced down a road on the other side. Every time Garland got close, the smuggler again dived into the canal and swam across. Garland was not too fast in the water and once became tangled in lily pads. Passersby heard him bellowing and called the local cops. They saw a dirty, grungy, cursing, lily-pad-covered guy waving a pistol and arrested him. Garland was so angry he went into a lip stall. After he calmed down, the local cops allowed him to show his identification, then released him. Garland commandeered a three-wheel-drive all-terrain vehicle and resumed the chase. A half-hour later he saw the smuggler pilot standing by a telephone booth. He waited, dripping black oozing mud, draped in lily fronds, hair streaked, a seething bundle of anger and frustration. When the car came to pick up the pilot, Garland jumped out of hiding and arrested not only the pilot but also four of the six men who had been at the landing site.

Mad Dog thought it was a cardinal sin for a smuggler to escape from a Customs pilot. He tried to instill this dedication and perseverance into the new guys, the ex-military pilots. They were hot sticks and could fly as well as anyone. But sometimes they were reluctant to go to the edge. They had to be taught to be fire-eaters. They had to be taught that they stayed on a smuggler's tail, no matter what the smuggler did or how long he flew. They had to be taught that they carried with them an omnipotent moral authority, that on their backs rode the reputation of the oldest agency of the U.S. government.

Garland had just been briefed by Mike Love, one of his favorite pilots, on the practice intercepts and how the Coast Guard would be participating in Blue Lightning. He did not take the news gently. Earlier in the day, while Mike was flying, Garland had finally read Kimberly McBride's intelligence report on Cosmos Goldstein. It had been on his desk for more than a week. He learned that the single-engine aircraft that had been regularly escaping from the Citation all were operated by a dentist named Cosmos Goldstein, a smuggling chieftain whose nickname in the smuggling world was "The Doctor."

That's when Mad Dog went into a lip stall. The very idea that a smuggler had the same nickname he had was too much to bear. He jerked at his pants and walked out of the operations room and across the hall to his office, where he slammed the door.

About ten minutes later he called Mike and ordered him to the office.

"You catch that son of a bitch. You hear me? We can't have him running around loose anymore," Garland said, running the sentences together until they were a blur. "He's making us look like idiots. He's beaten us I don't know how many times. And he's got my name."

"Assign one of the 'Hawks to me and put me on the evening shift full-time. I'll catch him."

"He's beaten you before."

"That was in the Citation. I got an idea. I can take him in the 'Hawk."

Mad Dog leaned across the desk and pointed a finger at Mike. Mike Love was the best pilot he had. He might be even more aggressive than Garland. Once, on Bimini, he had seen a smuggler taxiing for takeoff. He radioed for a BAT team, one of the Bahamian bust crews, but they were twenty minutes away. So Mike hovered the Blackhawk so close to the smuggler that the smuggler, in fear, stopped his aircraft. Mike put the long screaming rotors so near the smuggler's aircraft that the doper could not open the door without having his head sliced off. Mike waited there, hovering, not moving more than an inch in any direction, until the BAT team landed and seized the load. It was a brilliant bit of flying.

Mad Dog's heavy eyebrows lowered over his eyes. He shook his finger again at Mike. "Okay. You're on the four-o'clock shift until Blue Lightning begins. That's about ten days. Unless there is a done deal going down, seven zero is yours. But you catch him. You catch that doctor. You hear me? I want that son of a bitch. I want him bad. He's using my name. We can't have a bad guy called 'The Doctor.' You get him."

Mike nodded and walked out. Mad Dog was going into another lip stall.

31

"Launch the Blackhawk. Launch the Blackhawk. This is a scramble. Launch the Blackhawk." The voice of the duty officer, crisp and professional, came over the loudspeakers at the Miami Air Branch, inside the trailers, into the bull pens and offices, through the cavernous hangar and maintenance offices, and then echoed across the ramp.

Mike Love had been leaning over the desk when the red telephone connecting the Air Branch to C3I had rung. Twice tonight he had refused to launch the 'Hawk. There was a call from the Bahamas about a possible deal at West End and another from Boca Raton. But Mike had a feeling, just a gut-level intuitive feeling, the calls were to sucker the 'Hawk out of position.

The other pilots on duty that evening were wondering what was wrong with Mike; why had he not launched on the other two targets? Mike had the only game in town tonight; the other Blackhawk was down for maintenance. If Mike didn't go up, there would be no bust aircraft. But Mike knew what he was waiting for and this was it: a small single-engine aircraft, a pop-up that suddenly appeared near Nassau. The Citation had launched, pulled up under the guy, and gotten his tail number. The Citation pilot relayed the number to Slingshot. It was a hit. Radar operators there said the number was positive in the system; it had been reported several weeks earlier by two Broward County officers who had seen it loaded with cocaine on South

Caicos. Slingshot then called the Air Branch so the Blackhawk could handle the bust.

Mike raced out of the office, around the corner, down the hall, and was running out of the air-conditioned coolness into the hot, humid, and breeze-less grease-and-oil smell of the hangar by the time the announcement ended. Then, long legs pumping, he ran across the ramp toward the 'Hawk. Damn! Why did they keep the 'Hawks parked so far away? The Citations were either in the hangar or on the ramp in front of the hangar, the 404's were only a few yards from the hangar; even the Gonad, the expensive Australian mutation of an aircraft, was closer to the hangar than the 'Hawks.

As Mike threw his flight bag into the cockpit and pulled himself up and into the right seat, Fred was entering the left door. The four members of the apprehension team, led by Big Ed, were climbing into the rear. Big Ed, six-feet-four and two hundred and thirty pounds of romping, stomping certitude, was wearing, in addition to his regular regalia, a red Rambo rag around his head. That, and his drooping handlebar mustache, gave him the appearance of a very large and very mean fellow. The mere sight of Big Ed peering down the sights of a CAR-15 had made many dopers rue the day they ever decided to smuggle dope. Everyone was sweating. But in a moment, with the doors open, the warm limpid air of Miami would rush through the chopper and cool them.

Mike checked the overhead circuit breakers behind Fred's head while Fred checked those behind his head. Exterior lights were off. Generator was in position. Radios off.

He turned the APU on. The APU was the source of power for the two 1,560-horsepower turbine engines. He hit the boost and the automatic APU was up and running.

While Mike was cranking, Fred was setting up the radios and the com system on the big center console. He also was testing the stabilator. Fred punched the "test" button, then "auto," and waited as the stabilator, the broad flat horizontal stabilizer at the end of the tail, was programmed up to four degrees, then down thirty-nine degrees. If warning lights indicated a single part of the stabilator tests had failed, the flight was off. The electrically controlled, hydraulically operated stabilator was absolutely crucial to flight, and the slightest malfunction meant a no-go.

Mike checked the TGT. Below one-fifty. Good. He hit the starter switch, then moved the power to idle. After ignition, he had forty-five seconds to check the oil and transmission pressure. Rotor was turning. Everything in the green.

Backed up by the rising shriek of the engines, the honeycomb composite blades turned faster and faster until they were a screaming, whooshing blur whose power caused the chopper to shake and throb.

There is less time in the doing than in the telling of all this. From the time the crew crawled into the cockpit until Dave radioed for takeoff clearance, less than two minutes had elapsed.

The tower gave clearance and Mike eased the 'Hawk off the ground. As airspeed climbed, Fred kept his eyes on the instrument that gave the status of the stabilator. "Stabilator is programming," he said.

Marconi strips, rows of tiny light bulbs, each strip on a separate circuit, lit the instruments. If one strip failed, there still would be cockpit lighting. The panel of amber caution lights and green advisory lights was dark. Stabilator still programming.

The computers, avionics, and multiplicity of systems in the Sikorsky Blackhawk make it one of the most complicated aircraft in the world, and one of the easiest to fly. But every moment it is in the air the pilot is nagged by the knowledge that dozens and dozens of black boxes, little containers of electronic witchcraft, are packed into every nook and cranny. If one set of black boxes breaks or goes—as pilots say—tits-up, an expression they translate phonetically as "tango uniform," there is a backup; and another backup. But there are exigencies the black boxes cannot overcome. In addition to the stabilator, which occasionally goes psychotic and drives the aircraft into the ground, there is the chance, albeit remote, of a transmission failure. If the transmission fails, the five-million-dollar Blackhawk becomes a ballistic object, a brick tumbling through the air. The high-tech black boxes also are susceptible to interference from certain types of radio towers. Blackhawks flying in the proximity of radio towers have inexplicably dived out of control into the ground.

When the 'Hawk's systems are up and operating properly, it is one of the best helicopters in the world. But, as with any high-strung piece of electronic wizardry, when the black boxes fail, there is little that can be done except hold on and hope Sikorsky lives up to its reputation of building very strong machines.

Mike held the chopper low as he gained airspeed. He was trying for one hundred and sixty knots. But the helicopter was full of fuel—three hundred and sixty-two gallons in the mains and about the same in the aux tanks—almost two tons of fuel. Big Ed and his crew, plus all of their weapons and ammunition, added another thousand pounds. Survival gear added more weight. Stripped and light on fuel, the 'Hawk might reach one hundred and sixty knots. But tonight, heavily loaded and flying in hot muggy air over Biscayne Bay, Mike could not push it beyond a hundred and fifty.

That was too slow for Mike but it would be fast enough to keep up with the target inbound toward Fort Lauderdale.

"Slingshot, Omaha Seven Zero. Requesting bogey dope."

"Good evening, Seven Zero. Target bears zero four five for five six miles."

Fred looked at a sectional chart of south Florida. He measured the distance with his fingers, then pressed the intercom button. "We should swing to the west. We can't intercept him over water; he's too close. I estimate the intercept near the coast."

"Is Five Two with him?"

Fred keyed the microphone. "Slingshot, Omaha Seven Zero."

"Seven Zero, go."

"Is Five Two with the target?"

"That's affirm."

Mike nodded in approval. Omaha Five Two, the Citation, was behind the target. The sensor bird had the bad guy locked up on radar and the FLIR. Mike knew the single-engine aircraft would elude the jet. But he would be there; he would see how it was done; and he would track the doper to wherever he landed.

Minutes later he heard the Citation copilot radio that he was over Port Everglades, on the south side of Fort Lauderdale, and westbound.

Mike was coming up I-95, pushing the Blackhawk hard. Below him the lights of North Miami had merged with those of Hallandale, then Hollywood, then Dania. Fort Lauderdale was only a mile or so ahead. Out there, stretching north to the horizon, was a fifteen-mile-wide band of lights that began at the ocean on the east and stretched west to the Everglades. The only dark spots he could see were lakes, which reflected light, and airports. Odd that an airport was always the darkest place on the landscape when seen from an aircraft at night. It was only after one drew closer that the runway and taxi lights could be seen. In the middle of each dark spot was the occasional flash of a beacon, identifying it as an airport.

Then to his right was the silhouette of the Citation. Directly ahead, down low, was a flash of reflected light from the single-engine aircraft. It was a Cessna 210, banking hard toward the north. It descended until it was no more than a hundred feet above the expressway. Mike followed, but swung more to the west. He knew what was about to happen.

The Citation banked and followed the 210 north. Mike was close enough to see the 210 when it again banked hard, this time to the left, flew a few miles toward the Turnpike, then turned north again. A moment later he saw it reverse course and fly south over the Turnpike.

The Citation's radar operator lost contact. "Omaha Seven Zero, we lost him. Good luck," radioed the Citation pilot.

Mike exploded. "Goddammit," he yelled. Fred heard him over the noise of the helicopter.

Mike peered toward the smuggler. He had him in sight, but just barely. He thought the smuggler would turn west along State Road 84. But the smuggler turned early. And it appeared he had increased his speed.

Mike pulled collective, trying to nurse another few knots out of the chopper. He cut the corner trying to intercept the Cessna. "Five Two wasn't supposed to radio us," he said over the intercom. "The bad guy heard him. I don't know how, but he did. That's why he turned west early. He usually goes along an east-west road. This time he turned early."

"How could the bad guy hear the Citation?" Fred asked.

"I don't know. I don't know. But he did."

"How do you know?"

"It's the only explanation. Didn't you see the guy break west the minute Five Two called? Until then, he thought all he had on his ass was the Citation. And he can eat the Citation for breakfast." Mike was flicking his shoulders forward, trying to nudge a bit more speed out of the helicopter.

Then, in and out of the light, a flitting wraith that sometimes he thought he saw and sometimes he thought was lost, the Cessna reappeared. It was descending.

"Where the hell is he landing?" Mike asked.

Fred checked the charts. "Nothing out here. Must be a private strip that's not on the map."

"See any lights down there?"

"Nope. But he must know where he's going." Fred looked up. "Where are we?"

"Over Sunshine Ranches." Then Mike remembered. Cosmos Goldstein had several homes out here. Would the smuggler be landing at one of Goldstein's homes?

"I'm not sure we can get in front of him," Mike radioed Big Ed on the intercom. "So this will be a rear apprehension on a single-engine Cessna."

"That's affirm," Big Ed responded. He and his men checked their weapons, unplugged their headsets from the aircraft intercom system, and plugged them into the radios on their waists.

The pilot of the single-engine aircraft looked to his left and then to his right. He was lined up on his markers. He checked the altimeter. He was descending rapidly. He knew the Blackhawk was behind. But he had a few seconds; that was all he needed.

The small aircraft landed and rolled through the open doors of a barn sitting in the middle of the pasture. Even before he was inside, the doors began closing.

For Mike, it was a familiar story. One minute the doper was there; the next minute he had vanished. Disappeared.

"He's gone," Mike said in amazement.

"Did you see where he landed?" Fred asked.

Mike pointed. "I saw him dive toward that dark area. Then he disappeared. Son of a bitch."

"Think he just got down low and scooted out west over the 'Glades?"

"No. I think he landed. Somewhere right below us."

Under the rules of evidence and the rules Customs has for arresting smugglers, Mike would have been taking a big risk to land and search for the aircraft. He had reason to suspect the aircraft had originated in a foreign country, so he was okay on that angle. But while the smuggler was landing, Mike had been out of position for a few seconds and temporarily lost sight of the target. The chain had been broken. This case was too important to blow on a technicality. The safest course was to get a search warrant. But then it would be too late. Mike cursed in frustration.

"Punch in this location," he said. The helicopter circled over Sunshine Ranches, over the place Mike believed the smuggler had landed.

Fred punched several buttons on the navigation system, locking the location into memory. Later, Mike could transfer those coordinates to a map and have a precise location of where the smuggler landed.

"See anything?" he asked.

"Nothing." Fred paused. "The people down there are going to complain if we don't move out."

People in residential areas complained about the noise of the Blackhawk when it circled low. It interfered with their watching Don Johnson on television. Don Johnson was the standard for being a narc. He kicked ass without circling over citizens' homes in a noisy helicopter. So why did the U.S. government need to buzz around? Why couldn't Customs officers work days like Don Johnson?

Mike sighed. "Okay, let's go home. At least we're one step closer to knowing how he does it. And we have a location."

As the helicopter swung south, Cosmos Goldstein smiled in triumph. He was on the porch of his house. He had seen the single-engine aircraft land. It was followed several minutes later by the Blackhawk. He knew the Blackhawk had not been close enough to know precisely where the aircraft landed.

Once again he had beaten the best one-two punch the U.S. government owned. Customs would never catch him.

He laughed.

He was invincible.

32

Nick Brown stood in front of the conference room in the sheriff's department and looked out over the crowd, most of whom were military officers or federal agents. Broward County was the only local agency represented, and it was clear that various federal types did not relish the idea of a county narc's being in control of the Organized Crime Drug Enforcement Task Force called Blue Lightning. Ray Dumnik, the narcotics attaché to the U.S. embassy in Nassau, and several members of his staff sat stony-faced, staring straight ahead. Ron Williamson and several other Miami DEA agents were there. A female Marine captain was there, the C.O. of the crew of Marine radar experts who would be manning the new portable radar in the Blue Hills on the northwest corner of Providenciales. Call sign for the radar site was "Bonny Sue." The Marine's call sign was "Frisco." Mike Love, Mad Dog, and a half-dozen Customs officials were there. There was also a high-ranking Customs official; Mike referred to him as "GS God," who was from the National Narcotics Border Interdiction System—the acronym was pronounced "Nimbis"—who talked about the sound-activated sensors that had surreptitiously been installed on every airport in the islands. Nick only half-listened. He knew that Nimbis was a cover for the CIA. The spooks used Nimbis as a way to install sensors and video cameras to keep an eye and an ear on virtually every airport in the Caribbean.

The Customs call sign, when talking to Bonny Sue, would be Street Gang. Lieutenant Addams of the Coast Guard was following the silver-haired Coast Guard captain like a pilot fish hanging under the belly of a shark. The captain had wanted to hold this briefing at the Coast Guard station at Opa Locka, an effort to gain control by meeting on his own turf.

Lance, who had ripped a page from the Coast Guard book, prowled the room wearing a flight suit with "Drug Warrior" written on the name tag. The Coast Guard contingent was highly annoyed.

There were several Marine pilots who would be flying the FLIR-equipped OV-10 Bronco out of Homestead. The Marines' call sign was "Yazoo." The Navy, which would have several large vessels just off the north coast of Colombia's Guajira Peninsula, was there. Guantánamo Naval Station on Cuba's southeast corner, call sign "Almighty," would be available as an alternate landing site for Blue Lightning aircraft. Two Air Force officers were present to tell of the high-altitude reconnaissance role their TR-2 spy planes would perform. Even the Army National Guard was represented; members of the 151st. Military Intelligence Battalion, a top-secret intelligence-gathering unit based at Dobbins Air Force Base north of Atlanta. They flew the OV-1 Mohawk, a twin-engine aircraft under whose belly was mounted a sophisticated side-looking radar and powerful cameras.

Two men in civilian clothes, men who plainly did not want to be at the meeting, spoke. They made sure the doors were shut and that an armed deputy was standing out front to prevent anyone from entering. One man was from the National Security Agency, the most secretive of America's electronic intelligence-gathering agencies; and the other from SATIN, an equally secretive subagency within Customs. SATIN was so named because the Customs official who set it up had a daughter by that name. He came up with Strategic and Tactical Intercept Network as the name of the agency, SATIN for short. It was located in a small Gulf-coast town in Mississippi, with remote stations around the Southeast, and like NSA, used a combination of computers and electronic eavesdropping equipment to pluck from the air radio and telephone conversations. NSA, for purposes of Blue Lightning, would use its skills in South America, the Caribbean, and the Bahamas. SATIN would operate in the Southeast. Both agencies would provide information gleaned from electronic eavesdropping to Blue Lightning. The two civilians representing NSA and SATIN were evasive when someone asked exactly what information they could provide. And they wanted it clearly understood that the information was for intelligence purposes only. It could not, under any circumstances, be used in court, as that would mean that defense lawyers, under the rules of discovery, could dig into their agencies and discover tactics and techniques that dopers should not know.

When the NSA representative said the information could be used only for intelligence, there was a general stirring and moving about in the room. He held up his hand for quiet, and, after a pause, continued. "Ladies and gentlemen, to emphasize the inflexible nature of that rule, let me say that if it comes down to your losing this case if we don't go public with whatever information we might provide, rest assured we will have no compunction, none at all, about losing the case."

"Then why are you here?" Lance asked.

"Because we were ordered to attend," the NSA guy said. "But understand that our primary concern is national security, not drug smuggling. And we certainly have very little interest in any single smuggler, no matter how big he might be. National security is more important than smuggling. No smuggler is worth compromising the capabilities of our agency."

Lance shook his head. Why did everyone think that a violation of national security was a Backfire bomber flying five hundred knots at thirty thousand feet? Dopers violated America's national security every day. They punched through the AIDZ as if it did not exist. Rarely were they intercepted. Why couldn't terrorists in small aircraft bring in suitcase-size nuclear devices? The technology was there. If dopers could violate America's borders almost every hour, terrorists could do it. Oh, well.

Each of the military and civilian agencies gave a brief outline of his duties and responsibilities. Then Nick concluded. He spoke slowly and carefully. It was obvious that he lacked the polish of many of the federal agents. But it was also obvious that many of the federal agents lacked the integrity and devotion to law enforcement possessed by Nick Brown.

"A lot of money has been put into this special operation," he said. "A lot of thought. A lot of manpower. We have to make sure the taxpayer gets his money's worth; we have to show results. Some of you have asked why we're not going straight into South Caicos with armed officers; why are we staging out of Provo? We have to do our job but keep a low profile. The British don't want everyone to know we're down there in their country doing a job they should have done. We'll have a team on South Caicos. Team members will go in every morning and leave at dark. Their job is to seize loaded aircraft. We're putting the radar and aircraft on Provo for several reasons. The long runway there; what we think is better security; less danger. It also makes the governor down there feel a little more comfortable."

Nick looked at the young blonde Marine whose call sign was Frisco. She was a graduate of the U.S. Naval Academy and as gung-ho as any woman who elected to join the Marines. "You military types, particularly you Marines, keep a very low profile. You've been briefed. But the governor particularly emphasized that he doesn't want people in the islands to know U.S. Marines are operating a radar site on Provo. You've got a condo on the beach. Stay there when you're off duty. If anyone asks what you do, tell them you're with RCA and you're working on the cable-TV system."

He looked over the crowd again. "I think that's it. Everyone knows what he's supposed to do. Let's go do it."

Six days later every man and woman taking part in Operation Blue Lightning was in place. The Marine radar was up and operating. Frisco had to talk with the editor of a local newspaper after stories were published saying the radar was rendering islanders sterile and causing their hair to fall out. Navy ships were on station. U.S. Air Force and Army spy planes were on patrol. And Sam Nunn, Georgia's senior U.S. senator, had, probably in gratitude for their allowing him to play basketball during his military career, approved the purchase and installation of F-16 radars for the Coast Guard Falcon jets. The Coast Guard public-relations wizards now called the Falcon by the improbable name of "Night Stalker," a name that sent Customs pilots into gales of laughter. But Customs pilots knew the Coasties would get great media coverage by convincing reporters the Night Stalker was the ultimate weapon against drug traffickers.

As far as Nick Brown was concerned, there was both good news and bad news during the first week of Operation Blue Lightning. The good news was two-fold: first, Blue Lightning had been under way for only several hours when Lance arrested the chief minister of the islands. He caught him red-handed on South Caicos in the act of off-loading an aircraft filled with cocaine. The minister was shocked to realize that the man who had killed his associate, then caused his boat to run aground, was a cop, an American cop. Lance had backup officers videotape both the arrest and the field test of the cocaine. Nick, though he was composed and respectful, later took great delight in showing the tape to Governor Gatty and telling him that the field test, which would be upheld in court, demonstrated that the "white powder" was, in fact, cocaine.

The second piece of good news was that the Coast Guard had been tossed off the island. The chain of

events that led to their humiliating ejection from Blue
Lightning began when the Night Stalker was sent up
the second night to identify a target picked up by the
Marines' radar. The pilot reported he could not get
close enough to read the numbers and broke off the
chase. A Customs radar operator working with the
Marines at Bonny Sue overheard the radio conversation and scrambled the Street Gang. They nudged the
Citation up under the tail feathers of the target, identified it as a turbine Commander, and followed it to
Opa Locka, where it was popped with seven hundred
keys of cocaine aboard. It was not one of the Doctor's
aircraft.

Two things happened: Customs began referring to
the Coast Guard Falcon as the "Night Crawler," and
the Coast Guard began flying only days. The Coasties
refused to run intercepts at night. Coast Guard crews
spent their evenings in the bar at the Erebus Inn,
telling anyone who would listen that they were not
really cops, that they were there simply to build flying
time so they could get jobs with the airlines. The
Coast Guard launched on schedule every morning.
They were predictable, as their launch was timed so
the flight ended about one P.M., the time when all of
the nubile maidens at Club Med, located on the eastern end of Provo, were on the beach, many of them
topless. On the third day, the Falcon flew down the
Club Med beach at one hundred feet, causing one
woman on a para-sail to become so frightened she
released the para-sail and fell into the ocean. Club
Med officials complained to the Coast Guard lieutenant in charge. The lieutenant laughed. The next day
the Falcon came down the beach with its loud hailer
blaring out the lyrics to "Let's Get Drunk and Screw."

Governor Gatty then got into the act. He was angry
about the Americans virtually forcing him to sack the
chief minister. This was his chance for retribution. He
told the Coast Guard lieutenant that the conduct of his
men was reprehensible, that they were maintaining a

higher profile than he had envisioned, and then he gave them six hours to get off the island.

That was the good news. The bad news came when Kimberly McBride prepared a situation report in which she said there had been no discernible slowdown in Cosmos Goldstein's operation. Single-engine aircraft thought to be controlled by the Doctor simply flew to South Caicos, refueled, and returned to Lauderdale. Her report said twenty aircraft thought to belong to the Doctor had departed South Caicos the previous week. Even though the Blue Lightning team at South Caicos reported the aircraft were empty, it did not make sense to have pilots simply fly down to refuel and return. Kimberly believed, and no one could argue with her logic, that the Doctor was not sending aircraft to South Caicos just to have the pilots build flying time. They were hauling cocaine back to Fort Lauderdale. Somewhere in the Turks and Caicos Islands the Doctor's men were loading the aircraft with cocaine.

But where? And how?

33

"They're coming through West Caicos," Kimberly said to Nick. "That's how the Doctor is beating us." She handed him a folder. "It's all there."

Nick took the folder and looked at her in disbelief. He pulled on his mustache and glanced around the Provo airport terminal. Kimberly had arrived on the two-thirty Pan Am flight that came to Provo three days each week. The return flight departed at four P.M. and the airport was jammed with passengers. The tin roof of the terminal made the building a giant oven. Ceiling fans twirled slowly. Floor fans, trembling and pulsating in frustration, pushed hot air a few feet. The doors of the terminal were too few and the windows too small. The heat and humidity were stifling.

Nick was wearing jeans, cowboy boots, and a short-sleeved shirt. Kimberly, as usual, was wearing a suit and high heels. She was most uncomfortable. She toyed with the idea of going into the ladies' room and removing her panty hose.

Nick walked across the terminal and leaned over to look closely at a T-shirt displayed in the gift shop. His elbows stuck out from his body like the wings of a wet rooster. Wait until he heard the remainder of the bad news. She watched as he studied the T-shirt. It had a map of the islands on the front.

Nick stood up and again pulled at his mustache. He had refreshed his memory. West Caicos was the large uninhabited island west of Provo.

Nick motioned with his head and Kimberly followed him through the door of the terminal onto the blazing heat of the ramp. Even after both of them put on sunglasses, the glare still was such that they squinted. Sunlight in the islands is not only of equatorial intensity; its brightness is otherworldly. Nick and Kimberly walked toward the Citation parked on the edge of the ramp.

"Tell me what you found," Nick said.

She took off the coat to her suit and breathed a sigh of relief. "I called the DEA and talked to Ron. I told him about the Doctor's aircraft landing, refueling, and taking off again. He talked to somebody and they agreed to use a military satellite to check it out. His smaller single-engine aircraft, the ones with good short-field performance, are flying to South Caicos, refueling, then flying north to West Caicos, where they are loaded. Then they fly to Lauderdale. The Doctor is stashing a lot of cocaine on West Caicos. In addition to his aircraft, he has go-fast boats picking up coke on West Caicos, hauling it up to Mayaguana, and flying it out of there. Four or five boats leave West Caicos every morning at first light. We got pictures of them off the military bird. The Doctor's bigger single-engine aircraft are picking up the stuff on Mayaguana and flying to Lauderdale."

Kimberly paused and fingered one of her necklaces. She slowly shook her head. "Blue Lightning hasn't affected him at all." She looked around to make sure no one could overhear. "The people at SATIN picked up some conversations that confirmed this. The Doctor is coming through West Caicos."

She looked at Nick. "Why didn't Nimbis tell us? They're supposed to have sensors on every airport. They're supposed to know anytime an aircraft lands anywhere in the islands."

Nick pulled at her elbow and they continued walking toward the Citation. "We were told the airport was too hazardous for landing, that barrels had been placed on the runway. My guess is that the people from Nimbis flew over, looked at the field, and were afraid to land and install the sensors."

Nick paused. "Obviously somebody went over and moved the barrels." He stopped and looked at Kimberly. "Got any ideas on how the Doctor knew, how he manages to stay one step ahead?"

"He's got a source somewhere. This operation is so big and so many agencies are represented, it could be anybody. But you're right: someone is talking to him."

Nick nodded. "I'll send Lance and Mike over to West Caicos. They'll plug that hole tomorrow morning. What else?"

"Well, just as a matter of information, we now have hard facts on how the Doctor and the Colombians are tied in with the Cubans. One of the Air Force spy planes picked up a doper taking off from the Guajira yesterday. He crossed Cuba. We had a sensor bird waiting on the north side. But the bad guy saw the sensor bird and turned around. NSA picked up his conversation. He called Colombia on HF. After no more than five minutes, the Colombian contact came back and gave him Cuban radio frequencies and a name to call. NSA monitored it all. The guy called the tower at the nearest Cuban Air Force base, went in, and landed. We're sure he sneaked out later after the sensor bird went home."

Nick mumbled something that sounded suspiciously like profanity. When Kimberly looked at him, he said, "You're holding back. What's the bad news?"

Kimberly cleared her throat. "Dumnik wants the Citation and the Blackhawk at Autec the day after tomorrow at ten A.M."

Nick stopped. "What the hell for?" he growled.

"For a briefing. He says the Doctor is going to make an end run and bring nine hundred keys in over Cuba and make an airdrop on Dog Rocks."

Nick shook his head and continued walking. "Tell him no. This operation is too important."

"Nick, he's gone over your head. He got the DEA administrator to go to the attorney general."

"I thought Blue Lightning had priority over everything."

"Dumnik pulled out all the stops, said his information was righteous and the deal was certain to seize about nine hundred keys. Said he would take your assets for only one day."

Nick sighed.

"They're counting the deal day after tomorrow as part of Blue Lightning. Dumnik said you will get credit for taking down the load."

Nick squinted behind the sunglasses. "Why would he do that?"

"I don't know. Maybe it's his way of apologizing for disrupting things."

Nick smiled. Kimberly was naive. Dumnik never apologized. He enjoyed disrupting the activities of other agencies.

Kimberly continued. "Customs has been ordered to fly the Citation to Nassau and stand by to track the target tomorrow. The 'Hawk has to go. The Coast Guard is sending a C-130 down tonight to pick up the Executioner so they can put it in position. Even the Army Blackhawk in Georgetown is involved. And the other Customs Blackhawk and Citation at Homestead are being ordered to be on standby in case backups are needed."

"The Executioner belongs to Broward County. The feds can't order me where to put it."

"They've contacted the sheriff and told him that all the assets in place down here are for Blue Lightning, and everything being used by Blue Lightning is being diverted for this thing Dumnik has."

"What the hell will I be left with?"

"For that day, nothing. But all of the assets are returning the following day. It's just for this one load. Dumnik says he has a CI in the Doctor's organization. He's guaranteeing nine hundred keys. Washington is salivating over that."

"Dumnik's a bigger idiot than I thought. Too many

things can go wrong, even in a controlled delivery, for anybody to guarantee anything."

Nick turned and looked back across the ramp. The Pan Am flight was loading and a ragged line of sunburned passengers stretched across the ramp.

"You on that flight?"

"Yes."

Nick nodded. "Come on. I'll walk you through security. Their guys are working with us." He paused. "Not everybody down here is a bad guy."

"I have a couple of other things."

"More bad news?"

Kimberly smiled. "Afraid so. And I'm embarrassed to be the one who tells you. But the sheriff ordered me to tell you he is not happy with Blue Lightning. He called me in yesterday and complained for a half-hour. He says that unless he gets some results, unless you take down the Doctor in the next few days, he's shutting down the operation and recalling you and Lance."

Nick stared across the ramp for a moment. "Good to have the support of my boss," he mumbled.

"I do have one bit of good news."

Nick waited.

"You and Lance were right about Ollie, one of the Doctor's pilots. He flew to Lauderdale the other day and we grabbed him for a little talk." He rolled over. He's giving us some good solid information."

Nick looked at Kimberly with respect. "You flipped Ollie?"

She nodded.

"Put together a report as soon as you can. Anything really significant, let me know in advance." He nodded toward the Pan Am 727. "Come on. You better get aboard."

As the two strode toward the gate, Kimberly flung her suit coat over her shoulder. "Nick, I have bad feelings about this thing day after tomorrow. Real bad."

"I have bad feelings about anything Dumnik is involved in."

"I'm serious. Do you realize the strategic implications of what he's doing?"

Nick nodded. "Yep. It means every possible aircraft that can intercept a smuggler will be over on the far western edge of the Bahamas. Anybody who wants to come through here or even up through the eastern Bahamas will have an open door."

34

"Fluf told me what our little necklace-wearing, strategic-minded intel lady discovered, and said for us to get our asses over to West Caicos and shut it down," Lance said. His eyes were dancing and his maniacal smile stretched from ear to ear. "He said West Caicos was a den of iniquity. Hey, there are times when I think Nick sees himself as some kind of Old Testament guy. It's his job to clean up the world."

"He say how he wants us to do it?"

"Do what? Clean up the world?"

Mike chuckled. "No. Just West Caicos."

"Nope. Just said shut it down. When I asked him if he had any ideas, he said, 'Let the secular festivities commence.' Then he walked away. Sometimes Fluf is weird."

Mike raised his eyebrows.

Lance slowly swung his head from side to side. "Hey, I don't know what he meant by secular festivities." He paused. "But I have an idea that Fluf's as frustrated as we are. He wants the job done."

"Then let's go kick ass."

Lance held up a forefinger. "We in law enforcement like to refer to that as attitude adjustment."

Mike pulled out the aviation charts of the Turks and Caicos Islands and spread them on the table of his room at the Erebus Inn. Lance pulled out a thick book titled *Pilot's Bahamas Aviation Guide* and turned to the section on the Turks and Caicos Islands. He found the chart for West Caicos and the bleak description of the island.

West Caicos is nine square miles and runs roughly north and south with a twenty-four-hundred-foot runway that runs east and west. On the northwest point of the island, only a hundred yards off the beach, is the fabled "wall" that attracts scuba divers from around the world. Strong currents sweep the island, and big pelagic sharks come out of the dark depths to cruise close to the beach. Between West Caicos and Provo is a line of reefs that have trapped dozens of vessels over the centuries. Southwest of the island, near Molasses Reef, is the wreck of what some say is the *Pinta*, the ship of Christopher Columbus.

Lance tossed a folder onto the table. "This is McBride's report."

For a half-hour, neither man spoke. Then Lance looked up. The view from the room at the Erebus was spectacular. Lance and Mike had a room in the new wing, the one that stretched across the top of the ridge overlooking the ocean to the north. Through the wall of glass at the end of the room, one could see, at the bottom of the hill, the line of marinas and shops that ringed Turtle Cove. Then there was what local people called "The Pond," which was in reality an inlet from the ocean. It was through the narrow cut off to the left that Lance had brought the Executioner several weeks earlier. The Pond looked lovely, but it had no exit and the water was not circulated. Consequently, runoff from the hotels had caused the Pond to have such a high fecal-coliform count that it was not safe to even wade there. The beautiful water was almost toxic. Lance liked to tell people the Pond was filled with "the effluent of the affluent."

At the bottom of the hill was the hotel where Lance had stayed on that first trip. The manager had seen the Executioner and assumed Lance was a smuggler. Because the manager was far too friendly, Lance asked Mike to run the guy's name through the TECS computer. The computer lit up like a Christmas tree. So now all the members of Blue Lightning were staying at the Erebus Inn.

Across the Pond was the north shore, a sandy beach that stretched to the horizon in both directions. Beyond the shallow green water, perhaps a half-mile offshore, was the reef, and then the dark blue waters of the ocean. The surface was riffled by the omnipresent easterly breeze.

"I think we should go for the boats taking the stuff up to Mayaguana," Lance said. "They can't get out of there at night because of the reefs. They have to go in the daytime. About dawn. We can have a big impact in one day. If we put the hurt on the boats, we can shut West Caicos down in a matter of hours."

"Got any ideas?"

Lance nodded slowly. "Yeah," he said. "I got an idea that will reveal the majesty of the law to these assholes." Lance's grin was so wide that even Mike was unnerved.

"What is it?"

Lance leaned forward and began talking. After thirty seconds, he had Mike's undivided attention.

It was still dark when the 'Hawk took off, flew to the northwest corner of Provo, and then north over the ocean for about a mile. By then there was only the faintest trace of light to the east. But daylight in the islands comes quickly. There is little transition time. One moment it is dark, and the next the sun is bright and racing upward.

Mike pressed the intercom button. "Keith, this is a maintenance flight."

The young copilot to Mike's left turned and nodded in agreement.

Mike preferred to conduct this little operation without a copilot. But Customs regs decreed that two pilots fly the Blackhawk. Mike knew he could trust Keith.

Big Ed and his apprehension team were not aboard. Only Lance was in the cavernous rear of the Blackhawk.

Most of the seats and much of the floor space was taken up with tarpaulin-covered containers.

"That stuff okay?" Mike asked over the intercom.

Lance picked up the corner of one of the tarps and pushed on the edge of the container. He reached for the long cord attached to his headset, found the transmit button attached to his flight suit by an alligator clip, and pressed it. "Timing should be just about right. It's getting loose around the edges. It will fall out okay."

"There they go," Keith said. "The nose-candy express." He was looking toward the west, toward the north coast of West Caicos. "We're in good position. With the sun behind us, you can see the wakes easily."

Wending slowly through the treacherous reefs and coral heads off the north shore were five go-fast boats, one behind the other, low in the water, wallowing. Go-fast boats are not meant to poke along lazy-like; it is not their way. They are spirited, high-strung racing machines built to go fast in high seas.

"Let's wait until they clear the reef. It'll be more fun," Lance said.

"They'll scatter when they hit deep water," Mike said.

"Yeah, but they're all going to Mayaguana. That's sixty miles, about an hour for them. We're more than twice as fast as they are. Let's mind-fuck them."

Keith looked over his shoulder at Lance. It was the first time he had worked with the Broward narc. He was beginning to see why the guy had such a reputation.

It took about ten minutes for the go-fast boats to clear the reef. Then they added power and fanned out until they were about fifty yards apart. Their wakes changed from the deep froth of a wallowing slow-moving boat into the narrow trail of foam left by a boat that has little in the water but the propellers. They were on the step, gaining speed, and Mike knew the noise of their engines was ratcheting across the quiet dawn. They were taking four-foot waves on the starboard stern quarter, but all were riding confidently, unaffected by seas that would have given a hip-twitching motion to many boats twice their size.

"How many engines those guys got?" Lance asked.

Keith picked up a pair of binoculars. "Four. Four on each boat."

"Fishing boats." Lance laughed.

"Right," Mike said. "They can get out to the fishing grounds in a hurry. If they don't do any good, they can get home fast."

He turned the chopper toward the west. "I'm going to give them a chance to stop and follow us back to Provo."

"Come on, Mike. You know they won't do that. Let's get on with it."

"Not yet. I'll come out of the sun, make a low pass to let them know we're here, then come up at a forty-five-degree angle from the stern. I'll approach the lead boat on his port side. That way, I can keep an eye on him. If he stops, fine. If not, I'll get his attention another way. If that doesn't work, then we'll do it your way."

"Mike, you know what they'll do. Let's short-circuit the whole process and do it my way."

"You're probably right. But be patient."

The Blackhawk crossed the lead boat at about fifty feet. Lance leaned out the door, held only by his restraining harness, waved at the boat skipper, and shouted, "Weee'rree Heeeerrrree."

The black helicopter circled to the south and then to the east, wrapping the go-fast boats in its trailing aura of power, then came up astern, demonstrating to the smugglers that the greatest strength of a go-fast boat— its speed—was of no consequence, that the helicopter easily could round them all up like a herd of wandering sheep.

Mike dropped the sun-shield on his helmet. He came up on the left side of the lead boat, slowing until he matched its speed. Lance was leaning out the door, M-16 held at the ready. If the boat driver picked up a weapon, Lance would cut him in half.

From an altitude of perhaps twenty feet, Mike looked down into the cockpit of the speeding boat and, as the driver looked up, drew his hand sharply across his throat, indicating that the driver should stop. The driver raised his left hand, middle finger extended, then pushed hard on the throttles, trying for another few knots of speed. The boat driver knew Customs was working out of Provo, that this was a Customs chopper, and that Customs could do nothing. The helicopter carried no armament except automatic rifles. And unless the smugglers fired first, Customs would not shoot. All the boat drivers had to do was keep going toward Mayaguana, straight into Abraham's Bay, where the boat would be off-loaded for the short jaunt to the airport. If the Customs chopper hung around, the boat skippers would laze about offshore until the helicopter had to refuel. The go-fast had enough of a head start to outrun any boat sent out of Provo to intercept them. Even the Executioner. The smugglers were home free. The Doctor's load of coke was coming through, and there wasn't a damn thing the feds could do about it.

Mike was indignant when he saw the smuggler's raised finger. "You see what he did?"

"What'd you expect?" Lance asked. "A welcome wagon?" He secured the M-16.

Mike slowed the helicopter a few knots, allowing the go-fast boat to move out from under it.

He wiggled his shoulders and clasped the cyclic a bit more firmly. His mouth was a tight, determined line across his black beard. Now the lead go-fast boat was a hundred yards ahead. The driver looked over his shoulder and again tossed up an erect finger. Mike could see him laughing.

The helicopter suddenly accelerated. The stabilization-augmentation system kept the helicopter flat; it did not dip into the nose-low mode of most helicopters as they accelerate. As the speed increased, Mike adjusted the cyclic and the collective until the black helicopter was about four feet above the water. He

kept his eyes on the go-fast boat. This would be a bit
dicey. As the chopper passed low over the lead go-fast
boat, Mike lightly, ever so lightly, fed in a little aft
cyclic and dragged the tail of the chopper across the
boat. At the end of the Blackhawk's tail is a large and
very sturdy wheel. It is sturdy because when the
Blackhawk performs an assault landing, the tail is the
first thing to touch the ground. The tail wheel can
withstand eleven and a half G's.

The tail wheel raked across the cockpit of the go-
fast boat, tearing out the seat to the left of the driver,
the windshield, and part of the bow. The force of the
tail was such that the bow was dragged under a wave.
As Mike pulled away, he saw blue water pouring
across the bow, ripping out the remaining pieces of
windshield. But the driver was good. Very good. He
ducked low in the cockpit, held the wheel steady, and
pushed hard on the throttles. The bow of the go-fast
boat emerged from the wave, shook off the water, and
kept going. The driver was not intimidated. As Mike
swung off to the left and again made the slashing
motion across his throat, the driver angrily raised his
extended middle finger.

"Some guys are slow to learn," Mike said.

Again he dropped astern. The next maneuver was
one requiring great delicacy. If he misjudged, the upper part of the go-fast boat could rip into the belly of
the Blackhawk or tear off the standpipe and antennae.
Mike dropped lower. His hands were light on the
controls. His eyes never left the go-fast boat. He came
in fast off the boat's port quarter, then slowed to
match the speed of the boat. His altitude was perfect.
He nudged the antitorque pedal and the enormous
right wheel of the helicopter's main landing gear bumped
the go-fast boat. The driver wheeled sharply to the
right and recovered.

When the boat driver looked up, Mike again made a
slashing motion across his throat. The driver had learned
enough that he did not throw up a finger. But neither
did he slow down.

"Flip him, Mike," Lance said. "Flip him. Put his ass in the water."

"He doesn't give me any choice," Mike said, eyes locked on the boat.

Keith looked toward Mike in alarm. He was a young ex-Air Force pilot, a former F-16 jock, a hot stick. But even the Red Flag exercises, which were as real as one could find outside of actual combat, were not like this. He had heard other pilots talk of "bouncing" a go-fast boat, and this morning he had experienced it for the first time. He had also heard how a great pilot—not just a good pilot or an outstanding pilot, but a great pilot, one with *cojones* the size of Toyotas—could "flip" a go-fast boat. It was a dangerous technique. And it looked as if Keith was about to see how it was done.

Again Mike came up on the port side of the lead go-fast boat. The rotor wash of the Blackhawk was powerful enough to hold a twenty-thousand-pound aircraft aloft; a small tornado, an enormous downwash.

Mike held the right wheel of the chopper's landing gear over the gunwale of the go-fast boat and plunged several feet, causing the boat first to plow under the water, then to bounce high. The powerful roiling vortices of the rotor wash roared under the bow and suddenly the go-fast boat snapped over on its back. It happened so fast, the driver was in the water before he knew what had happened. In less than the blink of an eye, the boat was on its back. The boat stopped, sloshed about sluggishly, then slowly drifted under the surface, its bottom visible for almost a half-minute as it sank slowly in the clear blue waters.

"Anybody see the driver?" Mike asked.

"Yeah. He was thrown clear. He's out there paddling around."

"Any raft?"

Lance leaned out of the open door and looked astern. "No life raft or life jacket."

"I've never seen a doper with either a life jacket or a raft."

"They walk on the water," Lance said. He leaned out the door again as the chopper circled to the south. "The second boat's stopping to pick him up." Lance watched for a few seconds. "All four of them still going balls to the wall toward Mayaguana." Lance paused. "I think those fellows need a good talking-to."

"Okay, guy," Mike said. "I can't flip them all. Now we do it your way. You ready?"

Lance laughed. "I am a ready teddy. Come up astern the last boat. Let me get my aim right. Then we play with them." He pulled the tarp off the containers.

"Drop a couple in front of the boat first. Don't hit him. Give him a chance."

"Sure," Lance said. He reached for one of the containers. It was a five-gallon plastic bucket. Inside was a solid block of ice that had been frozen at the blast freezer on Provo, the one where lobsters are frozen before being shipped to the States. Twenty of the five-gallon buckets, each filled with a block of ice weighing approximately thirty pounds, were inside the chopper. A thirty-pound projectile traveling at more than one hundred miles an hour would do a lot of damage to a boat. Knock one hell of a hole in it. Even if the smugglers complained, which was unlikely (What would they say?—"There I was, smuggling a load of cocaine, and a helicopter ice-bombed me"?), who would care? And what evidence would the dopers have? The ice would melt in minutes. They weren't going to take a cup of water into court as evidence. Nope, these smugglers, who thought law enforcement had to follow certain procedures, were about to learn what it meant when the cops played by dopers' rules; they were about to gain a sudden respect for what Lance called "the majesty of the law."

Lance wiggled the bucket. The ice had melted enough around the edge that it was loose. When he turned it upside down, the block of ice would fall freely.

"He's coming up on the left side," Mike said.

"Stay about fifty feet over him. I want my bomb to have a little speed when it hits," Lance said.

"Thirty seconds."

"Thirty seconds until motivational training." Lance leaned out the door, one hand on the handle, the other cupped under the bottom of the bucket. The slipstream blew his short hair back until it was plastered against his head. Under the amber-tinted goggles his eyes were wide in anticipation.

"Ten seconds."

Then Lance saw the boat, a thirty-footer, painted red. Looked like a Cigarette. Four big outboards—probably a hundred and fifty horsepower each—on the stern. The boat was a floating Molotov cocktail; it was jammed with gasoline tanks and cocaine, and slicing across the waves at probably fifty-five, maybe sixty miles an hour.

Lance leaned out, paused, then flicked the bucket upside down. The gleaming block of ice began tumbling slowly, sparkling and glinting in the early-morning sunlight, a gently revolving glob of fire and vengeance. For a moment Lance thought he had missed, that he had dropped the ice too late. Then the forward part of the bow disappeared. It simply disappeared. About two feet of boat were obliterated by the tumbling projectile. As the chopper swung to the north, Lance saw the skipper's hands retard the throttles and the boat settled in the water, its wake widening. But the speed of the boat had been so great that when the bow was knocked off, the interior almost immediately filled with seawater. Now waves were washing over the stern into the cockpit.

"Mike, I think I missed. I hit it," Lance said over the intercom. His voice lacked contrition.

"How can you hit it if you missed?"

"Well, I was trying to drop it off the bow like you said. Just to get the guy's attention. But I didn't aim too well. Seems like I gave him a nose-job."

"A nose-job?"

"Yeah, I ripped the nose off his boat." Lance laughed.

"He's in water up to his knees," Keith reported,

looking through binoculars as the chopper again swung in astern the racing go-fast boats.

"Mike, you got one. The Ghost got one. That's two down, three to go," Lance said.

But he missed on the next two passes. The boats were weaving back and forth like berserk water bugs, crossing each other's wakes, slowing and accelerating, changing course suddenly, in their frenzied efforts to escape.

On the fourth pass, the ice bomb landed just aft of the transom and knocked off the two port-side engines on a yellow Magnum.

"Looks like you zigged when you should have zagged," Lance mumbled. "Asshole," he added as an afterthought.

He watched the crippled boat. The weight of the trailing engines immediately snapped the fuel lines. Gas was spraying all over the cockpit. The suddenly frightened doper remembered the story he had heard a year ago about a Customs chopper that had come up on a coke drop south of Bimini. The pilot sprayed fuel into the go-fast boat, then popped a flare into it and burned both the boat and millions of dollars of cocaine. The boat skipper worked frantically to cut off the fuel. The boat was difficult to control, too much power on the starboard side.

As the chopper swung around to make another pass, Keith was staring through the binoculars. "You winged him. Want to finish him off or go for the others?"

"The others," Lance said. "We can always come back to this guy. Looks to me like he's going in a circle. He might disappear up his own asshole."

"Coming up on target number four. Thirty seconds."

Lance picked up another bucket.

The driver of the go-fast boat panicked. He kept looking over his shoulder and racking the steering wheel from side to side in a frantic effort to escape the malevolent black helicopter that seemed to anticipate and match his every move.

Lance turned over another bucket and cradled the block of ice between his feet. Another bucket was in his hand. As the chopper came over the boat, he kicked and poured at the same time. The two projectiles hurtled down, each narrowly missing the bow of the boat.

The driver jerked the wheel first one way then the other. He looked up, terror etched on his face.

"I got him mind-fucked," Lance said gleefully. "Smuggling cocaine suddenly ain't so much fun for this guy. He's going through an attitude adjustment. Make another pass. If he doesn't bail out, I'll kiss your ass."

Lance was right. As the chopper came up astern, the panicked driver looked over his shoulder, then suddenly jumped to the gunwale and dived overboard. The boat continued.

"We gotta sink the *Bismarck*, boys," Mike sang over the intercom. Two ice bombs through the forward part of the deck did just that. The boat, heavily loaded with fuel and cocaine, quickly sank. Another driver was in the water. But the fifth boat, the one carrying two people, did not slow.

Five minutes later, it, too, had been sunk.

One by one, Mike hovered over the drivers while Lance tossed a rope ladder to them. As they came aboard, exhausted and panting, feeling like survivors in a bombing attack, he swiftly cuffed them. They were in the rear of the Blackhawk, near the auxiliary fuel tank, sitting on the floor, hands cuffed around the frames of the seats. Several were bleeding from wounds where ice had shattered on their boats and lacerated them.

"You guys are crazy," one of the dopers shouted over the noise of the helicopter. "Dropping ice on people. Wait till I talk to my lawyer. You fuckers will go to jail."

Lance poked the smuggler hard in the chest with an extended forefinger. Shouting over the noise of the engines, he said, "Hey, asshole, nobody made you smuggle dope. You did it on your own. Everybody knows it rains ice bombs on dope smugglers. It's an occupational hazard. You want to be in a job where it doesn't rain ice bombs, go sell insurance."

He sat in one of the aft-facing seats, watching the five soaked, bedraggled smugglers. "What we gonna do with these guys?" he asked Mike.

"I think part of the agreement down here is that the locals prosecute them. They'll go to jail down on Grand Turk."

"Think they'll flip?"

"I don't know." Lance leaned forward, closer to the smugglers, all in their early twenties, and shouted, "You guys going to jail on Grand Turk. No bond. You're gonna get fucked in the ass by some eight-foot ganja-smoking Jamaican. In two weeks your little white asses are gonna be big enough to hold go-cart races in."

One of the smugglers looked toward the others. He clearly was unnerved. "Where we going?" he demanded. He was wary of this guy in the flight suit who had "Drug Warrior" on his name tag and a weird light in his eyes. The guy smiled too much.

"I saw Elvis in a grocery store on Provo," Lance shouted. "We're taking you there so you can get his autograph." Lance backed up and looked at the smuggler as if he were a laboratory specimen. Then he leaned close and shouted, "You going to jail, asshole. That's where you're going."

Lance moved forward in the chopper, sat down, and slid the microphone tight against his lips. "I just told them what's going to happen when they go to jail."

No one spoke for a moment. The chopper was headed toward Provo and the three lawmen were feeling an adrenaline letdown. Then Keith's relieved voice came over the intercom. "I learned a lot this morning."

"You think this is what Fluf had in mind when he said we should begin the secular festivities?" Lance asked.

Mike grinned. "We won one today. Even Doctor Death can't afford to lose that much coke without feeling some pain."

"Especially since it's happened before," Lance said.

"That's right. He had some airplanes crash down here a few weeks ago." Mike had a sudden revelation. He twisted in the seat and looked over his shoulder at Lance.

Lance shrugged and grinned.

Mike laughed and shook his head.

"Problem is, Doctor Death will find a hole and bring it in somewhere else," Lance said.

"We'll plug that one."

"He'll find another hole."

"We'll plug that one."

"He'll find another one."

"We'll plug that one."

"How long will this go on?"

"As long as it takes to finish the job."

Lance grinned in approval. "You got that right. We gonna put his ass in jail. We gonna change that fucker's zip code."

35

The Atlantic Underwater Test and Evaluation Center is a secret U.S. Navy base on the southeastern side of Andros Island. Autec, as it is known, cannot be found on marine or aviation charts. However, the restricted area MY 3003, identified on aviation charts as a "missile range," hints at the presence of a military facility by forbidding pilots to fly over an area southeast of Andros that is offshore from Autec. The restricted area begins at the surface and extends up to eight thousand, five hundred feet, a very low ceiling for what is supposed to be a "missile range." Another hint that something unusual takes place here is the inordinate number of helicopters that come and go. Autec is abuzz with helicopter traffic.

This secret base, about a half-mile from an airport, is a key bargaining chip for the Bahamas when the U.S. government starts issuing ultimatums about stopping drug trafficking in the islands. Bahamian officials nod and half-listen, because they know it is all talk. The Americans simply cannot afford to push too hard. The threat of losing Autec always makes them back off. The base is too important to America's national defense for America even to think of diplomatic sanctions against the Bahamas.

The proximity of deep water makes Autec's location ideal for its secret function. Little more than a hundred yards offshore from Andros, the Tongue of the Ocean, easily seen on aviation charts, drops into the abyss. Between Andros and New Providence and thence south along the eastern edge of Andros, is a long tongue of water that is more than a mile deep. It is here that America's nuclear submarines practice firing top-secret torpedoes. And it is the job of people at Autec to recover the highly classified torpedoes after they have been fired. The Tongue of the Ocean has been electronically "wired" so that even if someone passing through on a sailboat dropped a wrench overboard, equipment at Autec could track the descent of that wrench as it fell to the bottom. It is a measure of the importance of work done there that Soviet trawlers are on permanent station in the Tongue of the Ocean, listening and tracking and occasionally trying to snatch one of the highly classified torpedoes.

Southwest of Andros, in the barren and trackless wastes that front on "The Mud," shallow-water exercises with torpedoes take place.

From the air, Autec is an innocuous place. It has two ramps, one on the north side of a large hangar, one on the south side, that can accommodate a dozen or more helicopters.

Tourists at nearby resorts have little inkling that some of the U.S. Navy's most secret research is taking place almost within rock-throwing distance of their hotels. One reason people have so little knowledge of Autec is that most personnel there wear civilian clothes. The two senior naval officers wear uniforms. Their lives are quiet and obscure, and they like it that way.

On this particular morning, the life at Autec was about to become anything but quiet. Mike Love radioed when he was ten minutes south that he was landing. A puzzled radio operator knew from the Omaha call sign that it was a U.S. Customs aircraft on a tactical mission calling for landing clearance. A moment later an Army Blackhawk called. Then two Coast Guard choppers were inbound. Autec was humming, and the Navy commander in charge didn't like it.

When the Customs Blackhawk landed, the commander, bent over in anger, came steaming across the

ramp. He waited impatiently for the turbines to cool
before the engines were shut down, and then he stared
in amazement at those who dismounted. The pilot
stepped out of the chopper as if he owned the island.
He was a tall bearded guy in blue jeans, loafers with
no socks, and wearing a pistol in a shoulder holster.
He wore military sunglasses. His copilot, a short, stocky
guy with long hair, wore jeans, tennis shoes, and carried a sawed-off shotgun slung over his shoulder. Out
of the back crawled the grungiest bunch of brigands
the commander had ever seen. One guy was grinning
like a psycho. He wore a flight suit with "Drug Warrior" stitched on the name tag, and he had a chrome-
plated Magnum strapped on his hip. The sleeves of the
flight suit were rolled up above the elbow, and the legs
were rolled up above the guy's knees. The guy next to
him, who appeared to be the biggest man God ever
made, wore a red bandanna around his head, had a
droopy mustache, a knife on his hip that appeared to
be the size of Excalibur, and an automatic rifle cradled
in his arm. Extra clips of ammo were jammed in his
belt. Behind him were two more men, though not as
big. All told, the men on the helicopter looked like a
scruffy bunch of Mexican bandits.

"Who the hell are you people?" the Navy officer
demanded, hands on hips, chin jutting out. "And what
the hell are you doing on my ramp?"

Mike looked down at him in annoyance. Another
bureaucrat with his Jockeys in a wad.

"U.S. Customs."

"Why the hell are you on my ramp? I don't know
anything about this." The commander was almost
shouting.

Mike sighed. Another screwup. All he wanted to do
was chase dopers. Why did the U.S. government, the
leader of the free world, have so many assholes in
positions of authority? "We were told to be here, that
it had been cleared. We have a briefing with DEA."
He pointed his finger at the officer. "We need fuel for
the Blackhawk."

"You need advance clearance to get in here, that's what you need. This is a top-secret base. You can't just pop in here and tell me you're having a briefing."

"I told you we were ordered to be here," Mike said. His voice sharpened. "This is a DEA deal. We represent a special government strike force. So if you got a problem, take it up with the DEA."

Mike stepped closer to the officer. "And stop raising your fucking voice at me."

The officer opened his mouth and started to say something. But these guys were carrying too many weapons and they looked capable of using them. Besides, American narcs working the Bahamas were crazy. They had to be to chase dopers through the islands. The squid—the Navy guy—changed his mind about chewing out the pilot.

"Well, leave your weapons here. You can't come inside like that."

"No way."

"What?"

"I said no way. We can't leave these weapons on the aircraft out in the middle of the ramp. We got enough stuff here to start a war. We'll take our weapons with us."

Again the officer started to speak. But by then the Army Blackhawk was landing. And behind it were two Coast Guard helicopters. The Navy officer hiked back inside to get on the radio and find out what was going on.

"Not many people are perfect. But that guy is a perfect asshole," Mike said.

"Yeah, but just think of Cay Sal," Lance said. "We'll get down there early. Nobody ever goes down there. The waters are filled with lobster. We can get a few lobsters and catch some sun. Then, if this DEA guy is right, we'll get a big load of dope. You might even get to bounce the 'Hawk up and down on the bow of a go-fast boat. I hope they run for it. We'll make a bunch of arrests. We'll have lobster, dope, and bodies. It will be great."

Big Ed nodded after the Navy officer. "Mike, you want me to do some attitude adjusting?"

Mike laughed. "Naaah."

"Down, boy! Down!" Lance said. He liked flying with Customs. For purposes of Blue Lightning, he had been made a member of Big Ed's apprehension team. These were his kind of people. A little tightly wrapped, maybe. But, for feds, they had a lot of promise.

Mike watched the Coast Guard and Army crews saunter inside the hangar. Dumnik, who crawled off the Army chopper, was wearing tiger-striped fatigues that were bloused over jungle boots.

"Guess we should get inside and see who's in charge of this goat-roping," Mike said.

Inside a small air-conditioned building near the hangar were four rows of chairs facing a lectern. Dumnik stood in a corner talking to the Navy commander. Whatever Dumnik said appeared to mollify the officer. He sat on the back row, arms folded, glowering. Dumnik walked to the lectern, then turned and pinned a chart to the wall.

As Mike and his crew of sweaty, heavily armed men ambled in, they passed the Coast Guard contingent, all neatly pressed in beautifully tailored clean flight suits. They looked as if they had been hauled out of a modeling agency to pose for pictures of what the quintessential Coast Guard pilot looked like. None was armed, and when they saw the weapons carried by Customs, there was a collective intake of breath and an unconscious moving away from the Customs crowd.

"Good God. Did you see all the guns?" one whispered.

"Yeah," another said. "Ridiculous. The Customs guys been taking their macho pills."

Mike stopped in front of two Coast Guard pilots. "I see the coast rats are here," he said. "You guys still driving the Night Crawler?"

"Night Stalker," one Coasty said. Mike had desecrated the altar.

"That's what I said. Night Crawler." Mike sauntered away.

"Gentlemen, let's be seated," Dumnik said.

He stood, hands on hips, waiting. His fatigues were unbuttoned down to the waist, revealing his half-dozen gold chains and his bellies, one layer cantilevered above another. His face had become tanned since his transfer to the Bahamas. The tan hid the red of his nose, the sign of his long affection for the bottle, and his newly grown mustache gave him a dashing air. He would be a handsome guy at an embassy party in Nassau; quite the urbane narcotics officer. Today he was doing his leader-of-men routine. He waited until everyone was seated and then paused until all conversation ceased. He looked at them like a schoolmaster chastening a group of mischievous boys.

"Gentlemen, here's the drill," he said.

"We have an aircraft inbound from Colombia via Cuba that is going to air-drop nine hundred kilos of cocaine to two go-fast boats waiting at the Anguilla Cays. This is a controlled delivery. DEA has a CI aboard. The drop is scheduled for about four P.M. Our assets are as follows: we have a Customs Blackhawk, an Army Blackhawk, and two Coast Guard helicopters. The Coast Guard has a hundred-and-ten-foot cutter north of Dog Rocks, and a high-speed hovercraft in the Damas Cays. Broward County also has a high-speed boat in the Damas Cays."

Dumnik turned and pointed to the aviation chart he had pinned to the wall. "The four helicopters will fly to Cay Sal." He pointed to the small island about forty miles north of Cuba. "Once there, one of the Coast Guard choppers will keep the APU going in order to power his radios. Customs has a sensor bird that will let us know when the bad guy crosses Cuba. An Air Force E-3 is following him up from Colombia and will radio us when he penetrates the Cuban ADIZ on the south side. We will stay on Cay Sal until the drop is in progress. The bad guys will have two go-fast boats to pick up the load. Customs"—he pointed to Mike—"will take one of the go-fast boats. The Coast Guard chopper"— he pointed to the Coast Guard pilot—"will take the other. The second Coast Guard chopper will pick up the dope. Once the go-fast boats are secured, members of the Customs apprehension teams will board and take them into Key West. When the bad guys are apprehended, they will be put aboard the Army helicopter and transported to Miami. Meanwhile, the sensor bird will be tracking the drop plane. One of the choppers, probably the Customs Blackhawk, will later follow."

He looked over the crowd of men. "Gentlemen, as I said, this is a DEA-controlled delivery. It is locked down tight and is expected to come off smoothly. Any questions?"

Mike, like most Customs pilots, was extremely skeptical of DEA's controlled deliveries. These were loads of cocaine brought in by DEA informants. The drugs sometimes were bought with DEA, that is, taxpayers', funds. Usually the CI also was paid by smugglers. Oftentimes a DEA undercover aircraft was used. This meant that a DEA informant, flying a DEA aircraft, was buying drugs with DEA money. Sometimes the controlled deliveries were not so controlled; there had been several instances when loads of cocaine got on the street. The idea was to let the load get through so DEA could take it down later without placing suspicion on their CI. When Customs knew of a controlled delivery, they started tracking it as far to the south as possible. There had been numerous instances when a CI told his DEA handlers that he was bringing in five hundred keys of coke when actually he was bringing in seven hundred keys. He would air-drop two hundred keys to his accomplices, then come in and land, load the coke on a truck, and see it taken down by DEA agents. The DEA agents thought everything had gone smoothly. They did not know their CI's were smuggling under the protection of DEA. Sometimes DEA ordered Customs not to bust a controlled delivery until the entire crew had had time to flee the airport. Everyone got away. There were no bad guys. For a while, DEA had tried to bring in controlled deliveries without notifying Customs. But Customs popped several loads and jailed a few pilots who said they were DEA informants. As a result, DEA usually, but not always, notified Customs when it was bringing in a controlled delivery. Great tension built up between the two agencies over the issue.

If the Coast Guard assumed a great role in air interdiction, their inexperience meant DEA would run wild with controlled deliveries. The Coasties would be party to a highly suspect activity and wouldn't even know it. And if one day the shit hit the fan, as it surely would, the DEA would cut and run, leaving the Coasties to explain a situation they didn't understand. The Coasties were going to find themselves, as the president liked to say, "in deep doodoo."

Mike wanted to learn more about this delivery that was so locked down. He held up his hand. "What can you tell us about the doper's aircraft?"

"It's a converted Navajo."

"That thing will do two hundred knots. No way the 'Hawk will even get close."

Dumnik smiled a patronizing smile. "Correct. But it's coming out of Colombia and will be slowed for maximum range. He'll be flying at a hundred and fifty knots. Same speed as the 'Hawk. You'll be able to keep up with him."

"Where's he going after the drop?"

"We think Bimini."

"Is the CI flying?"

Dumnik looked away. "Yes." He impatiently looked over the crowd, then at his watch. "If there are no further questions, then—"

"I have another question," Mike continued. "It's about forty-five miles from Cay Sal to Anguilla Cays. It will take us about twenty minutes to get there once we launch. He'll be long gone. Can't we launch when he's inbound?"

Dumnik shook his head. "Negative. He might see us. I don't want to blow the deal. We wait until the drop is in progress." He looked at his watch again, then slapped his hands together in dismissal. "Okay, that's—"

"Wait a minute," Mike said. Even the Coast Guard crews were incredulous that Dumnik had omitted what, to pilots, was the single most important part of an operation like this. "What about frequencies?"

"Frequencies?"

"Yeah, you got helicopters from three different agencies out there, plus boats. Plus a sensor bird. If we're going to talk to each other, we need some common freqs to work."

Dumnik waved a hand in dismissal. "You flight crews work that out." He again looked at his watch. "It is thirteen-twenty-two. We take off at thirteen-forty." He walked from the room.

Mike shook his head. "Can you believe that? He was going to send us out with no common frequencies. It would have been a real cluster fuck. Where does DEA find these people?"

Lance clapped him on the shoulder. "Hey, don't sweat the small stuff. Go talk some aviation talk to the Coasties and let's get out of here. We're gonna get some lobsters, some dope, and some bodies."

The three helicopters climbed as they crossed Andros on a southwestern heading, then flew across the shallow Hurricane Flats toward Cay Sal. It was cold at five thousand feet. The three helicopters, fanned out in fingertip formation, were flying high to avoid being heard by the crews of go-fast boats that might already be waiting at the Anguilla Cays. Actually, the Blackhawk is so noisy it can be heard—on a quiet night—from eight miles away. Unless there was a three-foot sea running and creating a lot of ambient noise by slapping against the hulls of whatever boats might be waiting, this subterfuge would fail.

Mike scanned the horizon. He was looking for the small scout airplanes that dopers often send out an hour or so before a deal goes down. The scout aircraft pokes around looking for boats and to see if law-enforcement aircraft have landed on nearby runways.

Dumnik, who was riding in the Customs helicopter, reached out and shut the door on the right side of the Blackhawk. Guys who drink as often and as much as Dumnik have little tolerance for cold. He shivered once, then sat there stoically, staring straight ahead. Lance noticed he had a tic in his face, an uncontrollable jerking at the corner of his mouth. He had seen that often in DEA agents.

There was little conversation during the flight. Dumnik came up on the intercom every five minutes and asked Mike to call Slingshot or Panther—the DEA radio station in the U.S. embassy in Nassau—to determine the status of the doper flight. It was uncomfortable in the Blackhawk. Straps of the personal flotation devices cut into shoulders and armpits. Seat belts and harnesses rubbed stomachs and shoulders raw. Headsets, after a half-hour, caused ears to be surrounded by a burning ring of pain. To lift a headset even for a second's relief was to be assaulted by the painful scream of the two jet engines and the thwacking of the long rotors. After a half-hour in the Blackhawk, passengers experienced nothing but misery. They lolled into half-sleep, simply enduring until they landed.

Then the Blackhawk crossed Dog Rocks. To the left were the Damas Cays. Farther south were the Anguilla Cays, where the drop was to take place. The land area of all the Cay Sal Bank, from the Anguilla Cays, through Damas Cays and Dog Rocks, then west through the Muertos Cays and Water Cays and Elbow Cay and then back south to Cay Sal, comprised about two square miles of land.

When the chopper began descending, the crew knew that at last they were approaching Cay Sal, the most southwesterly and most remote island in the Bahamas. The island is difficult to locate but easy to identify. It is the only island on the Cay Sal Bank surrounded by a white sandy beach. The sandy runway is on the northern side of the island and runs from the beach to the large lake that in turn extends to the southern shore of the half-mile-long island. The two-thousand-foot runway has numerous sand pits and is partially overgrown with vegetation. It is extremely hazardous. Even so, many smuggling deals have gone down on the island. And the small remote island has such a reputation for violence that it is avoided by many mariners.

Lance loosened his seat belt and opened the door as the Blackhawk swung wide and approached from the north. His face was gleeful as he looked into the pellucid waters a few feet below the helicopter and muttered, "Today we're gonna get some lobsters, some dope, and some bodies." He looked over his shoulder to make sure his small flight bag was there. It contained his bathing suit and snorkeling gear.

Then the helicopter was flying along the pitted landing strip. Bushes and trees and vegetation along the edges bent and swayed in the powerful downwash of the blades. Mike found a relatively smooth spot and gently set the chopper down. Everyone was impatient, waiting for the turbines to cool enough that the engines could be shut down and people could dismount.

Lance was the first to see them. He was looking out the door at a path disappearing into the woods, wondering if it went to the beach, when he saw a movement. There was a man with an automatic rifle. For a second Lance was amazed that here, in the outermost reaches of the islands, there was another person. Then, in that second, four more men appeared. They too held automatic rifles. And all of them were pointed toward the helicopter.

36

One of the quiet men slipped on a pair of black cotton gloves as he walked across the ramp at Tamiami Airport south of Miami. He made sure the big heavyset man in the middle did not notice.

"Why do we have to do this in the middle of the night?" the heavyset man asked.

"We can't afford to be seen," one of the men said patiently. "This is a very busy airport."

"Yeah, but I could have told you boychiks what you need to know over the telephone."

"We need to see for ourselves. Much is at stake. You know that."

The three men continued down the long row of aircraft on one of the back ramps. The heavyset man noticed that the other two men never tripped over the cables stretched under the aircraft as tie-down points. They were no strangers to airports. He stopped and pointed toward a yellow Bonanza. "There it is. You want to load it through the front or through the cargo door?"

"The front is customary, is it not?"

The heavyset man nodded. "Yeah, easier to control the CG that way." He burped. He had been drinking beer all afternoon and evening. Whatever these guys wanted to do was okay with him. The Doctor had called him in the bar in Coconut Grove and told him to meet these guys at the airport. They wanted to see if a Bonanza with full fuel could carry seven hundred and fifty keys rather than the usual five hundred. So sixteen hundred and fifty pounds of fertilizer were going to be loaded on the Bonanza, and then he would show them he could fly anything with wings on it. He would take off, then come around for a landing, and that would be that.

"Go get the truck," one of the quiet men ordered. "Back it up to the wing."

The heavyset man nodded agreeably and turned toward the parking lot. As he turned, one of the men raised a stiffened hand, fingers extended into a taut straight line, and chopped hard on his neck just below his right ear. The heavyset man fell unconscious to the dark parking apron.

"Hurry," said one of the quiet men. He reached into the heavyset man's pockets, searched, then tossed a key toward the other.

The man wearing black cotton gloves caught the key and walked quickly around the wing of the Bonanza. He crawled into the cockpit, checked to be sure the brakes were locked, then turned the key to "Both," pushed the fuel to full rich, then turned the key all the way to the right. The engine coughed once and caught. The man in the left seat waited a moment; he wanted to make sure the engine was running smoothly. Then he crawled swiftly from the seat onto the wing and jumped to the ground.

The other man had pulled the unconscious heavyset man into a sitting position. "He is very heavy," he said.

The two men picked up the unconscious man—one of them under each arm—and carried him toward the Bonanza. They were standing a few feet from the whirling propeller. They never flinched, but slowly, ever so slowly, moved forward another step. They looked at one another. One man began nodding. On the third nod, the two pushed the unconscious man forward, backed up a step, then turned and quickly walked away.

For a second, for a few rpm's, the noise of the

engine deepened. Then the man's body, or what was left of it, slumped to the pavement, where, after a moment, it fell forward into the propeller. The noise of the engine again deepened, then coughed, then regained speed and turned over smoothly.

37

"Guys with guns. Two o'clock," Lance said over the intercom.

Mike and Big Ed's apprehension team reacted instantly: Mike was on the radio, voice urgent, alerting the incoming helicopters, and Big Ed's team reached for their weapons and clicked off the safeties. Every head in the 'Hawk instantly looked a few degrees right of the nose. The men in the bushes were half-crouched, automatic rifles pointed toward the helicopter.

"Hold on," Dumnik said to Big Ed. "I know them." He unhooked his seat belt, waddled to the door, waved, and jumped to the ground. He was smiling and both hands were waving.

The men in the bushes stared. The leader recognized Dumnik and spoke to his men. They rested their gun butts on the ground. Reluctantly. They watched warily as Dumnik approached. He and the leader of the riflemen talked for a few moments. Then Dumnik returned to the helicopter.

"Bahamian Defense Force," he said. "They live here."

"You knew that?" Lance asked.

"Yes."

"Would have been nice if you told us. I thought we were about to get shot," Lance said.

Dumnik shrugged. "Forgot. You guys stand by until I get everything squared away." He turned and walked north on the airstrip, holding his arms up in a V shape and guiding the Coast Guard helicopters, showing them where to land. The second chopper, the one that had landed about halfway down the runway, kept the APU going after its blades stopped. Dumnik was there, a headset on, talking into a microphone, for about ten minutes.

Lance was impatient. "I want some lobsters," he said to Mike. "You know how few people ever come here? This is the ass end of the universe. Lobsters out there are begging to be put into a cooler. They want to go to Florida. They told me so."

Mike laughed. "You'll get 'em. Hang on."

Then Dumnik was marching up the runway, shined boots pressing clumps of grass. His unbuttoned cammie shirt revealed long rivulets of perspiration running down his chest and over the cascading layers of stomach. The perspiration dripped from one little roll of fat onto a plateau of rounded skin, slid to the edge, hovered, dropped to the next layer, and on down his stomach like a slow-moving stream easing over cataracts.

"The deal's moving faster than I thought," he said. "The doper's crossing Cuba. He's early. As soon as the sensor bird says he's descending for the drop, we crank up. Stay close and stand by to take off on short notice."

Dumnik ran back down the runway, this time back to the Coast Guard helicopter, where he again put on the radio headset.

The crews sat on the runway, sweating, swatting at the large mosquitoes massing in squadrons from the nearby lake. Their clothes were stuck to their skin, and great welts covered their bodies. Lance groused that he had to sit in the chopper when he could be out catching lobsters.

Only the Coast Guard thought it unusual that the doper was coming across Cuba. The Customs crew knew that allowing drug smugglers to cross the island apparently was an official policy in Cuba. All too often they had tracked aircraft from the south up to the Cuban

ADIZ, where they had to break off the chase. The dopers always continued. One Customs pilot continued the chase until his back-seater saw a target appear on the radar, a target that zoomed to five thousand feet in about twenty seconds, a target whose airspeed was climbing through four hundred knots before the back-seater realized what was happening.

"Hooooly shit!" he said over the intercom. "We got trouble. Time to go to warp six, guys."

About the same time, Guantánamo naval base radioed, "Omaha Five Two. Almighty. You're getting heat. Bug out. Now."

The Citation turned, dived for the deck, and fled to safety outside Cuban airspace.

Dopers cross Cuba daily. And if a doper is intercepted in the Bahamas and turns and flees for Cuba, as often happens, Customs must break off the chase at the ADIZ.

Dopers crossing Cuba are predictable. Sometimes they use the airway on the east, from Simones to Punta Alegre, but, more often, the route is from Cayo Largo to Varadero. Varedero is a large resort about eighty miles east of Havana. Apparently it was built for visiting Russians. Most of the time it is empty. Marinas with no boats and hotels with no guests. When smugglers are intercepted in the Bahamas and flee for sanctuary in the south, Varadero is where they often land.

Twenty minutes later Dumnik returned to the Customs helicopter. "They're approaching Anguilla Cays," he said. "The sensor bird has them. Fire it up. We'll listen on your radio."

The smuggler circled Anguilla Cays, then departed on a northwesterly course. Dave, who was flying the sensor bird, radioed, "No joy at Baker one six. He appears to be headed for Baker one zero."

Mike translated. "He didn't drop at Anguilla Cays. He's going to Dog Rocks." Mike was the only pilot in the Air Branch who memorized the new code books each week. He could read them twice and fix in his mind the sector names, the overall phonetic titles for each group of islands. The numbers for the individual islands in each group then fell into place.

The Blackhawk's engines were going and the rotors turning. Grass around the chopper was flattened and, again, the bushes were jumping and tossing and flailing about from the powerful downwash.

Tension aboard the chopper was palpable.

"Shouldn't we go?" Mike asked Dumnik.

"Not yet. Not until he begins the drop."

A few moments later Dave radioed from the sensor bird. "No joy at Baker one zero. No boats in the water. New course appears to be for Delta one."

"He's headed for Orange Cay," Mike said. He looked over his shoulder at Dumnik. If the bad guy was already north of Dog Rocks and headed for Orange Cay, it was time to get this show on the road. They would never catch the doper if they didn't move out.

Dumnik's tic was more exaggerated. He chewed his lips. Perspiration rolled down his face and neck and stomach. The shaking of the helicopter caused occasional droplets of sweat to jump from his body. "I don't understand. You sure he didn't drop at Dog Rocks?"

"Sensor bird says no."

"What about go-fast boats? Were they there?"

"Negative. I think we should go."

"Ask the sensor-bird pilot if he's sure that's a Navajo conversion he's following."

After a hurried conversation, Mike was back on the intercom. "Panther told him to stay back to avoid being spotted. He's not sure. He thinks it's a Navajo conversion."

Mike stared at Dumnik. Panther was the radio room at the embassy in Nassau, and this guy Dumnik controlled the radio room. If radio operators there had told Dave to stay back, it had to be on orders from Dumnik. What was going on here?

"Affirm on that," Dumnik said. "Tell him to hang

back. I don't want the doper to see him. Okay. We'll take off. Advise the Army chopper to stay here as backup. The sensor bird may not be following the correct aircraft. Tell the two Coast Guard choppers to follow us. Call your Air Branch and ask them to scramble another sensor bird. I need it down here patrolling off the Cuban ADIZ so it can pick up the doper in case we're not following the right one."

Then the chopper was off, staying low over the water, quickly building up airspeed. It soon was at a hundred and fifty knots and shaking and throbbing as if it would fall apart.

Dave was back on the radio. "Negative on Delta one. He's taken up a course toward Zulu one."

"San Andros. Northernmost strip on Andros," Mike said. He listened for a moment on the radio. "Sensor-bird pilot wants to know if he can move in and get a positive ID on this guy?"

"Not yet. Tell him to stay back. He might drop on San Andros."

The two Coast Guard helicopters, far slower than the Blackhawk, soon announced they would be landing on Andros for fuel. They were out of the race. The Blackhawk pounded on into the middle of the afternoon, throbbing, bouncing. Already the excitement of the chase had settled into discomfort. For ten minutes no one spoke. Then Mike was on the intercom. "Sling-shot says they have information a bad guy is aboard the Navajo. Says an alert is out on him, that he's wanted for murder and for a half-dozen smuggling charges."

Dumnik did not respond.

"Did you know that?" Mike insisted.

"Yes," Dumnik said defiantly.

"Our people need to know that. We're chasing this guy. We're going to take him down."

What Dumnik had done was unforgivable. He had withheld information that could have resulted in the death of a Customs pilot. Pig Pen, the copilot, looked at Mike. He half-expected Mike to go nuclear. But Mike pressed his lips together and said nothing.

About half an hour later, Dave called. "Negative at Zulu one. New heading is toward Foxtrot two."

Mike snorted. The doper would not land at Nassau. "Omaha Five Two. Negative on that. Expect him to turn north. My guess is he's landing at Juliet."

"What's this all about?" Dumnik demanded. "Keep me updated."

"I told the sensor bird the doper would not land at Nassau, to expect him to turn north and land at Mores Island."

"Why Mores Island? Why did you tell him that?"

"These guys like to land at dusk. That's in about two hours. I don't think the doper will go to Eluthera. Airport there is too busy. Same with the Abacos. Mores Island has a coral strip. It's remote. No cops there. No hotels. And if the doper maintains his present airspeed, he will arrive there about dark. It's logical. He's going to Mores Island."

"Okay, have the sensor bird move in and ID this guy. Make sure it's the right aircraft. But tell him not to be seen."

"Yessir. I think we can manage that."

A few minutes later Mike called Dave and asked if Slingshot had any information about radio traffic from the doper. Was the bad guy talking to anybody?

"Slingshot advises negative."

Mike shrugged. Once, every doper coming up from the south was a Chatty Cathy, on the radio constantly. But now too many of them knew about NSA. Some even knew of SATIN. The good smugglers never talked to anyone. They just sat there and flew their aircraft.

Ten minutes later Dave called. It was a Navajo conversion he had been chasing. A gray one. He gave the numbers. "That's it," Dumnik said. "Belongs to Goldstein. Has nine hundred keys of cocaine aboard."

Lance rolled his eyes. He was beginning to wonder about Dumnik.

As Mike had predicted, the doper swung north when approaching Nassau. He passed the Berry Islands. Mores Island was straight ahead. The helicopter pushed on into the late afternoon. All the men aboard were bone-weary. They were drenched in stale odoriferous sweat. Their ears were burning in pain from the pressure of the headsets. The noise, even through the headsets, had induced a numbing fatigue. Straps from the flotation devices had chafed their armpits raw.

From radio conversations with the sensor bird, Mike knew the doper was maintaining his speed of about a hundred and fifty knots. Mike was slowly gaining. In cold weather the Blackhawk can reach about a hundred and sixty, maybe a hundred and sixty-five knots. But in this heat, a hundred and fifty was all Mike had been able to get without ignoring the temperature restrictions. For the past hour, that's what he had been doing. He was flying the 'Hawk's guts out. He grabbed an extra five knots, held it for ten or fifteen minutes until the temperature climbed into the red. He backed off until the temp dropped, then eased it back up. When this flight was over, he would tell the mechanics at Homestead to give the bird a thorough check.

Mike was now only fifteen minutes behind the smuggler. But night was coming on. "Here I am sucking the hind one in a tail chase. I hate this," Mike muttered.

The banshee wail of the Blackhawk's two jet engines and the staccato thumping of its blades echoed and pounded across the limpid Bahamian waters. It was almost dusk and the smuggler was holding his course for Mores Island. The runway there was too short for the sensor bird to land. It was up to the Blackhawk to seize the load. The helicopter had reached a hundred and fifty-seven knots and was vibrating and pulsating and threatening to fall apart. The noise, even with headsets on, was deafening. The vibration was bone-rattling. The chopper was still eight minutes behind the smuggler.

"Let's wait until after they land and get cleared out

before we land," Dumnik said. "I've got a CI on the ground who will lead me to the dope. I don't want to burn him. This will not be an enforcement stop."

Mike's voice was hard over the intercom. "I didn't chase this asshole all day to let the dope get away. I'm making an enforcement stop. Big Ed, get ready."

Dumnik knew from Mike's tone that the pilot was not to be dissuaded. The DEA agent started to say something, then stopped. He glowered and sat back, lips tight, sweat cascading.

"Got it," Big Ed said. He made sure the doors were full open and locked. Lance did the same. They would be coming out fast.

The apprehension-team members checked their weapons. Cocked and locked.

Goggles down.

Pigtails from the radio headsets plugged into the radios on their waists.

Shoulder straps removed.

Now all they had to do was flick the seat belts open and jump out.

The sensor-bird crew watched the FLIR in impotent frustration as the Navajo slowed and lined up to make a straight-in approach to the twenty-six-hundred-foot runway. The runway was surrounded by trees. On the west end, a road led south for a few hundred yards and then into a small fishing village on the beach.

Now the compression factor would give Mike a few minutes' advantage. While the doper was slowing and lining up to land, Mike was still coming in full bore.

"We're pedaling as fast as we can," Pig Pen said over the intercom to no one in particular.

"He's landed. He's landed," Dave radioed. "There are three, no four"—Dave paused—"eight vehicles there to meet it. Lots of people. I estimate thirty people. Forty people."

Mike looked at the readout on his Omega VLF, the long-range navigation system manufactured by Tracor that is aboard the 'Hawk. "Two minutes out," he said. The chopper was crossing an offshore reef. It was low, no more than ten feet above the water, hugging the surface to muffle as much as possible the horrendous wail of the engines.

"Are you the only bust aircraft?" radioed Dave. There was concern in his voice. Nine hundred kilos of cocaine, even at a rock-bottom wholesale price of ten thousand dollars a key, was worth nine million dollars. After the dope had been stepped on, the street value was ten times that amount. There were forty people down there who wanted all the good things the cocaine would bring them. They weren't going to surrender the load without a fight. Big Ed's boys were outnumbered ten to one.

"Affirm," Mike said in his calm, almost lazy voice.

"Be advised there are a lot of people down there. They're taking boxes, containers of some sort, out of the Navajo and loading them into vehicles."

"One minute out."

"They're at the west end of the field. When you pop over the trees you'll be on top of them."

"Thirty seconds out."

"We have you on the FLIR." On the green screen, the Blackhawk's blades whirred almost in slow motion. The sensor-bird crew, orbiting at about three thousand feet, beyond the hearing of those on the ground, watched as the Blackhawk thundered across the last hundred yards of ocean, popped up over the trees, and then suddenly was over the end of the runway. In the last lingering traces of dusk, the people on the runway and the aircraft were silhouettes.

In the split second that the thunder of the Blackhawk overrode the noise of the off-loading crew, the people on the ground were caught in a frozen tableau. Pig Pen switched on the nine-million-candlepower Night Sun, the powerful searchlight on the belly of the chopper, and dusk suddenly was turned to high noon.

The 'Hawk pounced.

Mike reared the chopper almost vertical to bleed off airspeed, then plunged into the middle of the off-loading in what Customs pilots call an enforcement stop. The long tail of the 'Hawk reached for the ground, probing like a scorpion's stinger, touched, bounced once, touched and held firm. Mike plopped the nose down. The rotor-wash kicked up a sandstorm and flung it toward the fleeing crowd. Big Ed and his crew along with Dumnik jumped from the helicopter in hot pursuit.

"Go get 'em. Go get 'em," Mike said.

The Bahamians around the Navajo scattered like a covey of frightened quail. Some took off on foot. The blinking of taillights could be seen on the road as drivers tried not to run over each other.

"They're running. They're running," came Dave's relieved voice. He was watching on the FLIR as a movie unfolded in real time.

The Blackhawk leapt into the air and scurried back and forth over the small island, dodging power lines and a radio tower, seeking to stop the fleeing cars and trucks. But it was too late. The off-loaders had found sanctuary. The chopper returned to the airstrip and landed. Mike and Pig Pen stood on opposite sides of the Blackhawk, shotguns at the ready.

The Blackhawk is the most feared aircraft in the Bahamas. It materializes out of nowhere and discharges armed men. More than one Blackhawk has been fired upon. The Bahamians would miss no chance to sabotage one of the machines.

A half-hour later Dumnik and the apprehension team, sweaty, covered with mosquito bites, tired, thirsty, were back at the chopper. The cocaine was gone. They did not find a single kilo.

Mike wiped the blood of a crushed mosquito from his arm and looked at Dumnik. He was angry. "Your CI fucked you. He put nine hundred keys on the street."

Dumnik bowed up and moved close to Mike. "I don't appreciate that."

"I don't give a fuck whether you appreciate it or not. This was your deal. You said it was righteous. The dope is gone. Your CI fucked you."

Dumnik looked around to make sure none of the Bahamians could hear him. "Just for your information, there was no cocaine. I talked to the CI. They dropped the load short of Anguilla Cays. Just outside the Cuban ADIZ. We'll go down there in the morning and pick it up."

"You find any dope down there and I'll kiss your ass."

Their conversation was interrupted by a call from Dave in the sensor bird. His radar had picked up the Army Blackhawk. It was about ten miles out, inbound. After waiting for an hour on Cay Sal, it had joined the chase.

"What's going on down there?" Dave radioed. "We're watching you on the FLIR."

Mike keyed his hand-held radio. "I was just telling DEA what his CI had done to him tonight."

Over the radio came the sound of Dave's rueful laugh. "Stuck it to him royally. That's what he did."

Dumnik grabbed the radio from Mike's hand and keyed it. "I don't appreciate that," he said.

Mike reached out and snatched the radio back. "You said that once. Face it, guy. You lost nine hundred fucking keys of cocaine. And that's what our records will show."

"My records will show the cocaine was dropped outside the Cuban ADIZ."

"Piss on this guy," Lance said. "Let's get out of here."

As the Customs crew walked toward the Blackhawk, Lance shook his head. "I heard that guy was a drunk and terminally stupid. But I never heard he was bent. You think he's bent?"

"I don't know."

Lance did not speak for a moment. Then, his voice quiet, almost disappointed, he said, "Doctor Death beat us again." He sighed. "McBride was right. He's a smart son of a bitch. But we'll get him. He won another battle, but the war is going to be ours."

Lance stopped beside the 'Hawk. "This has not been a good day. No lobster. No dope. No bodies." He swung his arm in the darkness. "What the hell's the name of this town, anyway?"

Mike did not have to look at the chart. Angry and frustrated, he chuckled at the day's final irony.

"Hard Bargain," he said.

38

Kimberly knocked once, and without waiting for an answer, strode into Nick's office and asked, "Did you see the story in the paper?" Her eyes were wide and she was controlling herself with a great deal of effort. Nick was expecting her. He stood up and moved from behind the desk, careful not to scuff his boots on the chair.

"I saw it." He motioned for Kimberly to sit down. A quick look at her face caused him to walk across the room and shut the door, something he rarely did when female cops were in his office. He sat next to Kimberly, waited a moment, then said, "Don't blame yourself."

Kimberly shook her head. She bit her lips to keep from crying. Her eyes darted toward Nick. She pulled a package of cigarettes from her pocket and, with a shaky hand, lit one and took a deep lung-filling breath. Her hand trembled when she tossed the match into the wastebasket.

"But I do. I do. It's my fault."

"Nobody made him talk to you."

"I made him." Her voice was filled with pain. "It was so important for me to do a good job. I intimidated him. I threatened him. I hammered him."

Nick would have smiled had Kimberly not been so serious. The idea of this patrician woman "hammering" a career drug smuggler was almost comical. She had just hit him at the right time with the right logic. Nick had found that many smugglers were racked with guilt, just waiting to talk to someone, anyone. Kimberly had simply given the guy an opportunity to do what he wanted to do.

She took two long drags off the cigarette and continued talking, smoke pouring through her nose and mouth. "Now he's dead." She shook her head and fingered the crystals strung around her neck. "My God, what a horrible way to die."

"He was a smuggler. He's been a smuggler ever since he got out of the military. You're a cop. You flipped him. You did your job."

"Look what happened." She hugged herself with her left arm and took another drag off the cigarette. She stared out the window.

"He was drunk. Homicide said the medical examiner found a high amount of alcohol in what was left . . . in his body. He could have walked into the prop." Nick's voice was not very convincing.

Kimberly snapped her head toward Nick. "You don't believe that for a minute."

Nick stared at her. "No, I don't." He pulled at his mustache. "But remember that he was a smuggler. He brought tons of cocaine into Florida. As Cunningham likes to point out, nobody forces smugglers to get into the business. They do it because they want to. He knew the risks. If he wanted a low-risk job, there are plenty of them out there."

"I know he was a smuggler. But he was still a man. A person. He had an ex-wife. A daughter."

"They hadn't seen him in years. His ex-wife knew he was a smuggler and wouldn't allow him around the house. She kept him away from their daughter. He liked being a smuggler better than he liked visiting his daughter."

"But, Nick, he was still a person."

"Dope smugglers are not people, Kimberly. I knew this guy. His life should be measured by the misery he brought to other people. How do you think his daughter felt about him? He was not worth your concern."

Kimberly looked at Nick for a long moment. "I am

not sure enough of what I do to say that. I'm not that tough. You may be correct. I don't know. However, I do know that he did not deserve to die because of me, because of anything I did."

Kimberly jabbed the cigarette butt into an ashtray. She rubbed the bent and twisted butt around the ashtray, round and round, tamping, stirring.

"You want a day or so off?"

She shook her head, exhaled a long breath, and stood up. "No. Goldstein is still out there."

"Kimberly, we deal with bad people. Sometimes when we do our job, these things happen. But if his dying will prevent the death of a child, or prevent a family's life from being turned to an endless ocean of pain, or prevent a cop from being killed in a shoot-out with coke traffickers, then it's better that he died."

Kimberly wiped at her nose. She sniffed. "Intellectually, I can't argue with you. It's just the idea that I contributed to the death of a fellow human being. I've heard agents joke about dopers and say they're slime. And they are. I know that. If I caught one trying to sell drugs to my little boy, I'd kill him. I would. It's just that . . ." Her voice trailed away and she shook her head.

She exhaled again and looked at Nick. "I'm going back to work."

Nick nodded. He waited until she walked out, then picked up the telephone and dialed.

"Boiler room," said the voice on the other end.

Nick pulled the phone from his ear and looked at it in consternation. He again placed the phone against his ear. "Who is this?" he demanded.

Lance laughed. *"Jefe."*

"Answer the telephone like you're supposed to. The sheriff calls out here and you answer the phone like that, he'll put a uniform on you and have you working midnight shift at the airport."

"Hey, it was a call on my extension, not on an outside line. Had to be somebody in the office."

"I want you to talk to McBride. Take her downstairs for a cup of coffee."

"What's the matter? She okay?"

"You see the morning paper?"

"You know I don't read that shit sheet."

"That doper we met on South Caicos—Ollie, the guy she flipped?"

"Yeah?"

"His body was found on the ramp at Tamiami this morning. He walked into a propeller."

"Sounds like Goldstein's friends in the Mossad found out Ollie was talking."

"Yep."

"That bothers her?"

"Yeah. Buy her a cup of coffee. Cheer her up."

"I'll ask her the question of the week. What's green and white and red all over?"

"I don't—"

"A frog in a blender."

Nick sighed. "Cunningham, considering what happened to her CI, I don't think you should tell her that one."

39

The Bahia Cabana is a small caravansary on the part
of A1A known as Seabreeze Boulevard. It is across
the street from the Yankee Clipper Hotel near the
corner where A1A swings west as the Seventeenth
Street Causeway. The bar at the Bahia Cabana is the
quintessential Fort Lauderdale watering hole: a spectacular collection of rough, unpainted wood tables and
benches on three levels with the highest level being at
the entrance and the lowest level overhanging a half-
dozen slips in the Intracoastal Waterway. The Bahia
Cabana hotel and restaurant are modest, but the bar is
known far and wide. When one enters the bar from
the courtyard, past the Jacuzzi stuck out in front of the
rest rooms, the bar is on the right. Even from the
doorway, one is struck by the view across the sparkling waters of the Intracoastal Waterway and the
procession of expensive yachts, go-fast boats, and
double-decked tourist boats that lumber back and forth.

Suspended from the ceiling behind the tall chairs
that surround the bar is a row of three-quarter-inch
ropes, each with a loop in the end. They hang there
like the straps in a commuter train, and it is the habit
of local people, once they begin to wonder if they
have had enough to drink, to poke a wrist through a
loop and hold on. It is not uncommon to see people,
one hand through the loop, feet planted, rotating and
lurching as they gaze with bleary eyes over the never-
ending procession of suntanned young men and women.

The bar is open on two sides and therefore is not air-conditioned. Tourists usually take the seats over the water. They want to watch the go-fast boats tied in the slips below. But these seats are exposed to the blazing south Florida sun and to the frequent intense rain showers that drench Fort Lauderdale, particularly in the summer months. Regulars, the bronzed goddesses in shorts and blouses and the young men in khaki shorts, boat shoes, and colorful T-shirts, sit at tables toward the rear of the bar. DEA agents use the bar as a meeting place or to set up undercover deals, and they always sit in the rear and along the sides with their backs to the wall, thinking they are the coolest dudes in town. What gives them away as cops is their clothing. They all look alike. They sit there in one-hundred-percent-cotton ensembles, hair tousled, sunglasses, stubbled faces, making like Don Johnson clones. The only thing they lack is a sign emblazoned across their foreheads: "DEA."

Kimberly entered the bar late one afternoon. She looked around and realized that, as usual, she was the first to arrive. She bit her lip in a quick flash of anger at her compulsion always to arrive early, then sat at a table where she could watch the entrance. She wore a trim black suit, a white blouse with a high collar, and black pumps. She reached for a bowl of peanuts and began eating.

She was morose. The sheriff had recalled Nick and Lance from Provo. Blue Lightning was over. Dumnik said the only effective part of the operation was the Mores Island deal. There was talk that he would receive the Attorney General's Award, the highest award DEA gives its agents, for the Mores Island deal. Once again the DEA was about to reward and honor a man who should have been prosecuted for criminal negligence. Dumnik never found the cocaine he said had been dropped just north of the Cuban ADIZ, but he said it was there, that he had stopped nine hundred keys. And he wrote a report about Blue Lightning saying that although a number of aircraft had been seized on South Caicos, all had belonged to nickel-and-dimers; that the Doctor, the objective of Blue Lightning, had not been affected; that he was bringing in about twenty or twenty-one loads of cocaine a week.

Neither the Customs Air Branch in Miami nor the Customs official in Washington who had responsibility for the Air Branch would grant interviews about Blue Lightning. This created a publicity vacuum that the Coast Guard was all too anxious to fill. The Coast Guard used information received in intelligence briefings to take credit for every interdiction and every seizure that had taken place. Even though the Coast Guard had been tossed out of Provo, almost all of the publicity about Blue Lightning revolved around them. Their stats looked great, and Senator Sam Nunn was boasting about the great job his boys in the Coast Guard were doing out there on the front lines of the drug war.

The sheriff could not stop a federal agency from tooting its own horn, but he was bitter because he believed he should receive credit for the aircraft and boats that had been seized. It was the Coast Guard publicity, more than the lack of progress in stopping the Doctor, that was gnawing at the sheriff. He sat in the *führerbunker* a few blocks from the Bahia Cabana, stewing, trying to figure how to come out of Blue Lightning with some glory. If there were no glory for him, if Dumnik were telling Washington that Blue Lightning had been a failure, then someone's head was going to roll. He would need a sacrificial lamb to appease the blood lust of the press. Since Nick Brown had been in charge of Blue Lightning, it would be Brown. Brown and Cunningham. Mustn't forget that psycho Cunningham; not after he had barged into the office and virtually blackmailed the sheriff into signing the authorization papers for Blue Lightning.

Nick knew this. He knew how Hiram Turnipseed thought and he was waiting for the shoe to fall. The irony, to Kimberly, was that she might have come up with at least part of Goldstein's secret. She was on the edge of having the answer. That was why everyone was meeting today: to thresh things out; to see what had been overlooked; to figure out what could be done in the next three days. Even though the sheriff had recalled everyone in Blue Lightning, technically the operation remained alive for three more days. There might yet be a way to catch the Doctor, to bring the sheriff his glory and save Nick's job. Like Lance, Kimberly felt protective toward Nick. He was a good and idealistic man in a profession that tended to rob people of their goodness and their idealism.

Kimberly smiled and waved as Nick and Lance came through the door. Nick was solemn and unsmiling, all business. Lance, as usual, had a wide smile pasted on his face. He was wearing a T-shirt with a detailed color picture of a cockroach that covered his chest. Under the roach was the legend "Fort Lauderdale Night Life."

A few moments later Ron entered. He was the only man in the place wearing a tie. He hustled across the floor, sat down, and lit his pipe. He tilted his head back and blew the smoke skyward.

Then Mike entered. He stopped at the door and looked around, mentally cataloging everyone in the bar. A quick scowl crossed his face when he saw several young men, beepers at their waists, whom he recognized as suspects in ongoing investigations. He strolled over to the table, sat down, and said, "Hi, guys."

"Welcome to vespers," Lance said.

By unspoken agreement, business was deferred until drinks and munchies came. Ron ordered Scotch, single malt on the rocks. Kimberly ordered a white wine, Nick and Lance had beer, and Mike wanted tonic water. They shared a basket of chicken sticks and a basket of boiled shrimp.

"So what went wrong?" Nick said, as usual getting right to the point.

For a moment no one spoke. Then Ron put his pipe on the table and cleared his throat. He looked down at his glass of Scotch, slowly turning it on the table. "Ya know, I been on The Job twenty-six years. I've seen dozens of these goat-ropings. This was one of the best-organized, best-thought-out operations I've ever been involved in. Nothing went wrong. Everything went wrong."

Mike looked up from eating a chicken wing. "What do you mean?"

Ron sipped at his Scotch. He shook his head in frustration. He opened his mouth and looked away, gathering his thoughts. "We did our jobs," he said. "But we put up a Potemkin defense."

Kimberly stared at him, waiting.

Lance rubbed the cockroach on his chest, leaned back, and said, "What the fuck is a Potemkin defense? You feds are too smart for me."

Nick glanced sharply at Lance. Such profanity should not be used in front of Kimberly.

"It's a shell, a facade; it lacks substance," Ron said. "There's nothing there."

"Nothing where?" Lance asked.

"The war on drugs. It's not working. It never has worked. It never will work. Not until there is no demand for drugs." Ron turned to Mike. "Last fall, when George Bush was campaigning, he said trafficking could be stopped by interdiction alone. You've been flying for Customs for what? Fifteen years?"

"About that."

"You think interdiction alone can stop smugglers?"

Mike snorted in disgust. "We're not stopping them. They're beating the balloons. They're beating the Citations. They're beating the 'Hawks."

Ron puffed on his pipe and blew the smoke toward the ceiling. "The source countries won't do anything. Colombia is an outlaw nation, completely taken over by drug smugglers. That country is in a state of anarchy. And look at the Turks and Caicos. A remote collection of islands that, in an accident of geography, just happened to be placed halfway between Colombia and Florida, the perfect refueling location, the perfect stash point. The governor there has his head firmly up his nether regions. Here in south Florida, everyone is worried about Jamaicans and crack, afraid some black guy will break into their house, steal their TV set, and knock them in the head. They've forgotten the great numbers of white people out there putting stuff up their noses. A hell of a lot more white people are using cocaine than there are black people using crack."

Lance's attention was diverted when he saw two tall, slender, strikingly attractive young women enter the bar. One was a redhead, the other a blond. Their makeup was a little too noticeable and their clothes a little too revealing. As they walked around the bar, Lance watched the muscles in their rear ends bunch and knot under too-tight skirts. He thought their asses were hard until he saw their eyes. Hookers. High-priced hookers working tourists. Either that or looking to party on a doper's boat. Nevertheless, attractive in a mean, gritty, get-down fashion; the sort of women that, if a man hates himself, he likes to bed.

Lance leaned over the table. A low, guttural "Waa-aaahhhhhhhh" came from his lips.

Ron stopped talking and looked at him in bewilderment.

"Testosterone alert. Testosterone alert."

Nick flicked Lance's shoulder with the back of his hand. "Cut that out," he ordered. He turned to Ron. "Go ahead."

Lance cupped his hands around his mouth and, in stentorian tones, as if speaking through a bullhorn, said, "Recall the tooty patrol. Recall the tooty patrol."

Ron ignored Lance. "I've read all the reports about this operation," he said. "I've talked to a lot of the people involved. About the only time we win big is when we step outside the pale."

Lance sneaked a glance at Ron. Did he know about the shooting on South Caicos? About sabotaging the aircraft? About the ice bombing of the go-fast boats?

"Or when there is some sort of divine intervention," Ron continued. "Not only is everything we do of doubt-ful significance, we are so busy sniping at each other that our efforts are diluted. The Coast Guard snipes at Customs. We snipe at the FBI." He pointed at Nick. "Inside your own department, you have more to worry about from the sheriff than you do from dopers."

Nick pulled at his mustache. "So what are you saying? That we should give up?"

"Yeah," Lance said. "Or should we do to the drug kingpins what we did to Qaddafi? Should we launch the F-111's against doper headquarters?"

Ron nodded toward Lance. "That's not a bad idea. After all, we attacked Qaddafi because he was behind the bombing of a bar in Germany where an American soldier was killed. But how many people have been killed by drugs? And what bigger threat to our national security could there be than these dope planes that bust the borders with impunity day after day? The dopers have declared war on America and we worry about communism."

Ron turned back to Nick. "To answer your question: no, it doesn't mean we should give up. Not at all. We've got to keep on keeping on; doing what we're doing. My point is that smuggling is like racism: it can't be stopped in a year or ten years. It can't be stopped until several generations have seen their lives disappear up their noses."

"That's happy stuff," Lance said. "We always like to hear we're doing great. Makes us happy campers. Yes, sir, sleep well tonight. Your friendly narcs are . . . what the hell are we doing?"

Ron held up a hand. "One more thing. I gotta say this. It really bothers me. I got a lot of black friends. Agents. They tell me that when there is a crime of some sort, the first thing a black person thinks is, 'Oh, God, please let it not be a black person who did it.' It's the same with Jews. A lot of Jews in America came here after fleeing from Hitler or from oppression in dozens of countries. Name one. Generally, they contribute more to society and have a lower crime rate than almost any other ethnic group you can name. Now we're after a guy named Goldstein. When we get him, and we will get him, every Jewish person who reads the newspaper or watches television will cringe. Goldstein has poisoned the well for Jews all over America. And if for no other reason, I want to"—he looked at Kimberly—"cover your ears"—he turned back to Nick—"step on his dick."

Kimberly was exasperated. She leaned across the table. "Ron, why all this concern about my not hearing profanity? You and Nick!" She snorted in exasperation. "Have you two forgotten I was married to a DEA agent? That I'm old enough to have heard every word you could ever come up with?"

"But you're a lady," Nick said, as if that were all the explanation necessary.

Kimberly sighed and sat back in her chair.

Nick looked at Ron and continued. "I understand that. All the other stuff I don't understand. What you say may be true. But I can't afford to look at it that way. I don't have time. I get paid to put dopers in jail. That's my job."

"It's mine too," Ron said.

"I haven't put the Doctor in jail. He's still out there bringing in poison every day. Ruining people's lives. The sheriff is about to can me because Goldstein hasn't been apprehended. Now we've got three days to do something. We're here to figure out what."

Ron leaned toward Mike. "We're on the same side. We want the same thing. I'm about to retire and I tend to look back over my career and try to figure out what it has all meant. Sometimes I think not much. Sometimes I think we did a lot. But you're right. The point is to nab that son of a bitch." He looked at Kimberly. "So what have we got?"

Kimberly clasped her hands and leaned over the table. She was about to speak when Lance suddenly pointed a finger at her. "You're not smoking," he exclaimed. "I just noticed. You quit?"

She smiled, a quick diffident smile. "I'm trying to."

"Hey, that's great. You can do it."

Kimberly was surprised. She looked at Lance as if

to make sure he was sincere. Unconsciously, her left hand moved to one of the crystals said to increase one's mental powers. She took a deep breath, looked at Nick, then said, "Mike and I talked about his last intercept of one of Goldstein's aircraft. It was apparent the pilot, somehow, overheard the conversations of both C3I and the Customs aircraft. I determined from a CI that he was right. Goldstein is using something called a blue box."

Mike leaned forward in quick interest.

"I would have called you, but I only confirmed it today," she said. "The blue boxes are about the size of a large purse. They detect all forms of RF energy, whether it's UHF, low freq, VHF, HF, or FM. The pilot simply plugs the blue box into the aircraft's electrical system, pops up a little antenna, and he's in business."

Her voice lowered. "Through the blue box, which acts more or less like a scanner, except that it is tuned to all of the appropriate law-enforcement or military frequencies, the bad guys can hear every radio conversation they need to hear. If an inbound smuggler hears C3I vectoring an aircraft, the smuggler goes on alert." She nodded toward Mike. "If he hears Mike say, 'I have a judy,' he knows the Citation is locked on. Once you come up and ID him, he hears the description and the tail number when you call Slingshot. He knows when the Citation and the Blackhawk are working together and what each aircraft is doing."

Mike grunted in anger. "I knew it. I knew they were hearing us. But I didn't know how. Where do they get these blue boxes?"

"They're made here in Fort Lauderdale. The manufacturer—it's one man—is making a fortune selling them to dopers."

"What can we bust him on?" Lance asked.

Nick shook his head. "Nothing. It's not against the law to make scanners."

"There's more to it than this blue box," Mike said. Everyone turned to him. "Goldstein knows the capabilities of our radar—what it can do, what it can't. He has to. I think that's why he uses single-engine aircraft. They can bank and yank better than the Citation. They can be slowed down over an expressway, down below the notch on the radar. I think the guy knows more about the capabilities of the FLIR and radar than I do."

No one spoke for a moment.

"Can you bust him?" Nick asked.

Mike nodded. "Yeah, I can bust him. I almost had him a couple of weeks ago. The 'Hawk is the way to do it. But what I can't figure out is how the aircraft disappear so quickly. They just land and disappear. It's like they drive into a big cave and the door slams shut. They're swallowed. They just disappear."

Mike leaned back in the chair, his big hands clasped around his glass of tonic water.

Kimberly stared at him. "What did you say?"

"I said they disappear."

"I know that. But how? You said it's like a big cave, and a door slams shut."

Mike shrugged. "Well, I tracked only one to a landing. That was right before we went to Provo. I was in the 'Hawk and managed to stay with him until he dropped toward a pasture out in Sunshine Ranches. One minute he was landing, and the next minute he disappeared."

Kimberly was rummaging through her purse. She found what she was looking for and held it up triumphantly.

"What's that?" Mike asked.

"A garage-door opener."

Silence. Nick and Lance and Ron and Mike stared at her, their faces frozen in astonishment and revelation. Mike nodded slowly in the sure and certain knowledge Kimberly was right.

"That could be it," he said. "The guy lands. He's in a single-engine aircraft. Landing speed loaded, say, seventy or eighty knots. He hits the brakes hard and presses his garage-door opener. The door to the barn . . ." He turned to Kimberly. "Does every one of Goldstein's houses out there have a barn or big building on the property?"

"Yes."

"Okay, even before he's inside, he presses the garage-door control again. I do that coming up the driveway. Runs my wife crazy. She thinks the door will hit us. He rolls inside and the door shuts behind him."

Mike was as excited as Lance had ever seen him. He looked at Kimberly. "You were right. Goldstein is one smart son of a bitch. Something as simple as a garage-door opener. The simple way is always the best way. The aircraft rolls in and disappears. Minimum exposure. He knows we have to keep the load in sight in order to pop it."

He looked at Kimberly with respect. "We know Goldstein's aircraft are losing us somewhere over either I-95 or the Turnpike. The one I followed in the 'Hawk went west and landed at Sunshine Ranches. So I think we can assume that's the technique for all his aircraft. It's all we have to go on."

Nick nodded in agreement. He pulled at his mustache. "Kimberly, how many houses does Goldstein own in Broward County? Or in western Broward County?"

"I know of five. He owns, directly or through shell corporations, or is allowed to use, a total of five houses out there. Four in Sunshine Ranches. One slightly north."

"How far apart are they?"

Kimberly thought for a moment. "It's about eight miles from the northernmost to the southernmost house."

"Less than three minutes in the 'Hawk," Mike said. "We can take him. But it will have to be just us. Just the people around this table. I'll vouch for my crew and I'll brief them at the last minute. Nobody else should know. Somebody is feeding Goldstein information—either to him directly or to his buddies in the Mossad, who are relaying it to him."

"If you bust him, the Mossad will cut him loose," Ron said.

"What do you mean, 'cut him loose'?" Lance asked.

"They will deny any knowledge of him. They will walk away from him. That game will be over. The Jews don't want the world to think they are involved in cocaine smuggling. You bust Goldstein and the Mossad will drop him like a hot rock."

Nick nodded in agreement. "And the Mossad will walk away. We'll never be able to do them." He leaned over the table. "Kimberly, good work. You did a fine job."

Lance grabbed Nick's arm. "Hey, *jefe*. How'd you like to have Goldstein's ass for your fortieth birthday?" He looked around the table. "We can do that, can't we? Kimberly did her part. Now let's get out there and do ours."

Kimberly bit her lip, looked down at the table, and blinked back quick scalding tears. She could take abuse. She had learned how to do that when she was married. But it was difficult for her to accept such open, heartfelt praise. It somehow did not seem legitimate.

"That would make me forget how old I am," Nick said. "I'd like that." He looked around the table. "We got three days." He leaned forward. "Here's how we'll do it."

40

"Slingshot, Omaha Five Two. The bogey is feet dry. He's now westbound along state road eight four. Was Home Plate able to launch the Blackhawk?"

"Negative, Five Two. Maintenance problems. Home Plate advises you should track the bogey and determine his landing site."

After a long pause came the weary and disgusted voice of the Citation pilot: "Roger. Five Two."

Mike nodded in approval. The target had crossed the beach and was about to go into a predictable routine of banking and yanking over I-95 and the Turnpike, after which he would continue westbound to land in Sunshine Ranches. If the bad guy had been monitoring Customs on his blue box, he knew the sensor bird was on his tail. But he now believed the Blackhawk was unable to launch from Homestead; he thought he was home free with another load of cocaine.

"Don't let him get away, Mike. This is our last chance." Nick's voice was a low growl in the intercom.

"Don't worry," Mike said as he began ignition sequence on the Blackhawk. The blacked-out helicopter was two miles northwest of Sunshine Ranches, perched atop the only high ground in western Broward County—the county landfill—where it waited like a wise and experienced bird of prey for its victim to come closer before striking. Three times during the previous two nights the Doctor's single-engine aircraft had eluded Mike. Last night, two had escaped. But each time,

Mike had narrowed the gap before they disappeared. Last night he had been over the end of the pasture when he saw the huge barn door sliding shut over a Beechcraft Bonanza. McBride was right. They were doing it with a garage-door opener, popping open the door on roll-out and then dropping it as they rolled inside the barn. Simple. Inexpensive. Reliable. And highly effective.

The plan to catch one of Goldstein's aircraft was refined and fine-tuned and adjusted each night, and each time with a growing sense of desperation. Tonight was the last chance. Operation Blue Lightning was over at midnight. Tonight the 'Hawk would not assist the Citation in the chase. It would wait. And the radio transmissions from the Citation to Slingshot actually were status reports to Mike. But he would not respond. He would not use the radio until the bust went down. He was operating in the black. It was the only way to beat the blue box.

Tonight had almost been a disaster. It had almost ended before it began. The Coast Guard, which had wrested control of the radar balloons away from Customs, had picked up an intermittent target over Eleuthera. The Coast Guard Falcon launched and was vectored to the target. But the doper, a single-engine aircraft, was flying below one hundred feet. To read the tail numbers, the Coast Guard pilot would have had to descend to about forty feet over the ocean, then come up under and behind the target. The Falcon pilot would not do that. "I'll follow him," the pilot radioed.

John Stevenson, a Customs radar operator at C3I, exploded. "Swordfish One Six, Slingshot. I want an ID," he radioed in clear biting tones. "If I wanted somebody to follow him, I'd call the Red Cross."

But the Coast Guard refused to drop down low enough to identify the target, so Customs launched a sensor bird out of Homestead. John Boy, the gung-ho former Marine, was driving the Citation. J.T., the back-seater, quickly brought him in astern the Falcon.

John Boy was grinning in glory. The Corps was about to show the Knee-Deep Navy how it was done. He picked up the microphone, paused a moment, then said, "Swordfish One Six, Omaha Five Two. Break off." He paused and then added, "You can take the Night Crawler home, son. The first string is in."

"I'm reporting you for improper radio procedure," the Falcon pilot sputtered.

"Semper Fi, Coasty." John Boy changed freqs, dropped down to forty feet, and said, "Awright, J.T., put me up his ass."

J.T. laughed and leaned forward over the green symbology on the radar screen. The FLIR was up and working well. "Target bears three five five for two miles." He leaned closer. "Looks like a Bonanza. Straight tail."

After that, the intercept was a textbook classic. John Boy was locked on the doper's tail, tracking him straight toward the Florida Power and Light stacks at Port Everglades. Mike, who was monitoring the conversation on his radio, nodded in approval.

Now it all was coming toward the end of the funnel. This was Mike's last good chance to pop one of the Doctor's aircraft; the last chance to bust the ass of a man who, for months, had made a laughingstock of the air wing. For Nick and Lance the stakes were even higher. The sheriff was going to announce tomorrow morning that he was firing the head of the narcotics squad. If Doctor Death was not busted tonight, Nick would be out of a job.

Then came John Boy's slow laconic voice. "Slingshot, Omaha Five Two. Target turned north at I-95."

"Roger, Five Two. Stay with him."

"Five Two."

Mike nodded. "He'll go north until he mixes with the traffic at Executive, then turn south." His eyes flew over the instruments.

Pig Pen, his copilot, gave him a thumbs-up and said over the intercom, "Parking brake off. Tail wheel locked. We think we know what we're doing."

Mike nodded. "When he breaks west, we'll be waiting." He half-turned to the rear. "You guys ready?"

Nick looked at Lance. When Lance nodded, Nick pressed the transmit switch on the intercom and said, "Ready." They were the apprehension team, the only people in the rear of the 'Hawk. What they planned called for fast movers—a Mr. Inside and a Mr. Outside. A four-man apprehension team would be too big for tonight's work.

Since the two were flying aboard a Customs aircraft as part of Operation Blue Lightning, in fact the last time Blue Lightning could strike, since the strike force's life ended at midnight, they were wearing green flight suits. Lance had provided a suit for Nick. Nick never noticed that his name tag said "Prayer Warrior"; he simply assumed it was the same as Lance's "Drug Warrior."

Lance and Nick checked the long clips in their M-16's. Both men wore their personal sidearms: Nick a Browning nine-millimeter and Lance his chrome-plated Magnum hog-leg.

"You remember the drill?" Nick asked over the intercom.

"Just like we planned, *jefe*. I hit the ground running and you cover me."

"What if there are people inside waiting?"

"They blink and they're dead."

"Be careful."

Lance laughed. "Hey, *jefe*. What say we get this done and get out of here early tonight? I want to look for CCD. Think I got them pegged for sure this time."

"Just be careful."

Lance puffed up his chest and pounded it with a fist. "You looking at the bionic man. I'm going to stick a fist down that doper's throat, grab his balls, and yo-yo his brains out."

Nick was not used to riding in the Blackhawk. It was more uncomfortable than he had realized. It shook and vibrated too much for him. But the worst thing of all was the abundance of braces and bolts and protuberances. His boots were scuffed and scratched so badly it would take hours to clean and polish them. He held on to the M-16 and looked out the open door into the warm south Florida evening. The smell of burning jet fuel was rich and heavy in his nostrils.

"Slingshot, Omaha Five Two. Target turned west at Commercial Boulevard. Lotta traffic. Still holding him."

"Roger, Five Two. Keep us advised."

John Boy made no effort to stay on the tail of the Bonanza. He climbed to five hundred feet and slowed in anticipation of the smuggler's banking-and-yanking maneuvers east of Executive Airport. J.T. turned the notch down on the radar so it would track targets traveling slower than ninety knots. Even so, the radar would not hold the target over the expressway. His fingertips caressed the trackball as he rolled the FLIR's sensors, keeping the target in the middle of the screen. It was a video game with a five-million-dollar load of cocaine as the prize.

If J.T. had not been briefed on what to expect, he would have lost the smuggler over the intersection of Commercial Boulevard and the Turnpike. The smuggler, who was at two hundred feet and eighty knots, turned north over the Turnpike, then did a one-eighty. J.T. had anticipated the maneuver and stayed with him on the FLIR.

"Bad guy is southbound," J.T. told John Boy on the intercom.

John Boy picked up the microphone and looked at his copilot. The copilot was studying a code sheet. "We lost him," he said.

"Slingshot, Omaha Five Two. We lost the target over the Turnpike."

Mike nodded and gave the instruments a final check. "That means the bad guy has turned south. We launch in thirty seconds."

Now the timing was crucial. The Doctor's four houses in Sunshine Ranches had been given code numbers. If John Boy was able to stay with the doper and broadcast the landing site in time for the 'Hawk to launch, there would be a slight chance of catching the doper before the barn door shut. But even if everything worked to perfection, the timing was critical.

"Slingshot, Omaha Five Two. Searching. No joy."

"He turned west," Mike said. "Let's go." He pulled on the collective with his left hand and wiggled the cyclic with his right. The 'Hawk rose slowly from the landfill, a black bird rising from a garbage dump, hovering, then moving ever so slowly toward the southeast. "Stay alert, guys," Mike said. "Things are about to start happening fast."

"You get us there," Nick said. "We'll do the rest."

"I'm going to put down as close to the barn as I can. It will be a rear apprehension. When we hit the ground, run straight off the nose and don't step on our wheels. We may be rolling."

"Affirm," Nick growled. He checked his M-16 again.

"Hook up the pigtails. They're rigged with a hot mike. No more transmissions until we're on the ground."

Nick and Lance hooked up the pigtails from their headsets into the radios strapped on their waists. Both checked their seat belts. A flick of the wrists and they would be free.

"Slingshot, Omaha Five Two. Three more orbits and I'm breaking off the search."

That was the signal. House number three. The 'Hawk surged forward in a burst of speed. Pig Pen picked up a drawing with a numeral three written across the top. It was an aerial photograph of the pasture where the doper was landing. "Field runs northwest-southeast," Pig Pen said. "He'll swing south and land to the northwest."

Mike nodded in agreement. He would fly south for about a mile, then swing in behind the doper. If all went as planned, the doper would be too tired after the flight from South Caicos, and too busy with his landing procedures, to notice a blacked-out helicopter to his left. He would have heard no transmissions from the chopper, and it appeared the Citation was breaking off the chase. His attention would be on the landing—landing at night in a field with no lights. Even so, Mike would stay as low as possible to minimize the chance of the doper catching sight of him as he crossed a road or a lighted area.

"Slingshot, Omaha Five Two. RTB this time."

"He's landing," Mike said to Pig Pen. He bent the chopper around in a tight circle to the east. The whump-whump of the rotors lowered toward a deep and anxious bass note. Pig Pen was leaning forward. He looked at the drawing on his lap, then looked up and pointed. "There's the house." He searched the sky. "You got the aircraft?"

Mike did not answer. He was looking. The 'Hawk was light on fuel, had a small crew aboard, and was handling like her namesake—nimble, fast, aggressive. "Got him," Mike said triumphantly. He changed course slightly to be a bit above and behind the Bonanza. He had to be careful. If he pulled in too close, the Bonanza pilot would hear him. The Blackhawk had a distinctive sound, and it was loud enough that it could be heard by the pilot being pursued even over the sound of his own aircraft. But if Mike lagged too far behind, the barn door would shut and the chain of evidence would be broken. The next few seconds would take every bit of skill he possessed.

The doper crossed a road adjacent to the pasture where he was landing, and for a fraction of a second was silhouetted. Mike adjusted the power and began to close in. Then he saw a narrow beam of light as the big garage door in the middle of the pasture began to open. The beam widened. The barn door was waist-high and climbing. The Bonanza was fifty yards from the barn.

Then the 'Hawk reared, nose high, slowed, and the tail probed for the ground.

The Bonanza was inside the barn and the door was dropping. The beam of light inside was narrowing. The Bonanza pilot heard the helicopter but it was too late. He was inside and could not turn the Bonanza.

He could not flee. He was penned with the 'Hawk blocking his exit. The smuggler was willing the door to close faster. The beam of light was narrowing. It was waist-high and closing.

Lance was on the ground, M-16 at port arms, running fast toward the door. Nick ran to the front of the chopper and stopped, M-16 at waist level, turning rapidly from left to right and back again, searching as he covered Lance. Mike and Pig Pen, listening on the FM radio, heard Nick's rapid breathing through the hot mike.

Mike and Pig Pen sat in the chopper, eyes locked on the falling door, wondering, hoping, mentally urging Lance to run faster.

The door was about knee-high when Lance dived sideways and rolled, then came up inside the barn, M-16 at the ready, as the door slammed shut with a loud clunk. The pilot, a tall darkly handsome man whom Lance had met on South Caicos, was stepping out of the cockpit onto the wing of the Bonanza. He froze, one foot inside, one on the wing, as he and Lance stared at each other.

Lance was an apparition. The goggles, headset, green flight suit, chrome-plated sidearm, and the M-16, especially the M-16, made him an intimidating presence. And it was all capped off by that unnerving gleeful maniacal grin. The doper knew by the look in the eyes behind the goggles that his life had never dangled by such a slender thread. One sudden move, one misstep, and he would be sliced in half by a burst from the M-16.

Then Nick and Mike and Pig Pen heard the transmission they were waiting for. "Okay, asshole, step off the wing," Lance shouted over the noise of the chopper. "Quick. Quick. On your face. In the dirt, asshole. Quick. Now. Or I'll blow your fucking head off. Down. Hands behind your back. Now. Behind your back."

Lance was following accepted law-enforcement procedures. Overwhelm a perpetrator with noise, authority, and firepower. The public often does not understand that this is the safest way to conduct an arrest. Do it quickly. Take control of the situation before the perpetrator tries to be a hero.

Lance snapped the cuffs on the smuggler. "Don't move, shit maggot," he shouted. "Keep your nose in the dirt. You twitch and I'll blow your fucking head off."

Lance quickly looked around the barn. No one else in sight. "Where's the garage-door opener, asshole? Where is it?"

"In the right seat," came the mumbled frightened response.

Lance jumped on the wing, eyes darting overhead and around the barn, never resting, finger on the trigger of the M-16. A quick glance in the rear of the Bonanza caused his eyebrows to jump upward. Duffel bags packed with what he knew was cocaine jammed the cabin of the aircraft.

The narcs had done it.

Blue Lightning had struck.

He found the door opener, squeezed it, and jumped to the ground as the door began rising.

Nick, M-16 at the ready, stooped over and entered the barn. Lance was standing there with one foot on the doper's back, M-16 held in his right hand, and his left hand held over his stomach. His head was up and a smile of victory creased his face.

"Do I look like the great drug warrior?" he asked. "Do I look like America's next cult figure? Am I America's sweetheart?"

Nick turned toward the chopper. "All secure," he said. "Shut it down."

"I'll radio the ground units and we'll join you," Mike said.

Then came the laconic voice of John Boy circling in the Citation. "You guys are movie stars," he said.

"You got it all on the FLIR?" Mike asked.

"That I did, good buddy. Stand up in any court in the land."

He paused. When he came back, there was a note of deep satisfaction in his voice. "Semper Fi."

Mike chuckled, reached forward, and began turning the switches that would shut down the engines of the Blackhawk.

Doctor Death was history.

Epilogue

Kimberly walked into the bar at the Bahia Cabana and looked around. Her lips tightened in exasperation as she realized that, again, she was the first to arrive. Then a finger poked her in the back and a voice whispered in her ear, "You don't look like a cop to me."

Kimberly looked up and smiled at Lance.

"As a matter of fact, you look good enough to cause a testosterone alert."

Kimberly pointed across the room. "There's a table."

The two sat at the table and waited. Lance put the small paper sack he was carrying on the floor and ordered a beer. Kimberly ordered a glass of white wine. Her attention was drawn to a couple at the bar. The girl, who appeared to be in her mid-twenties, wore a filmy red blouse with spaghetti straps. Jeans, cut off very high, were tight on her hips and showed off tanned legs. She had long dark hair that kept falling over her eyes. Her friend wore khaki pants and a black shirt. He had a mustache and his black hair was thick and long. He held eye contact as he made a big production out of kissing her on the shoulder. The girl watched, her lips parted and arching. She watched his mouth rather than his eyes. She shrugged and smiled as one of the spaghetti straps fell down her arm. She looked at the strap, then looked at her friend's mouth. Her eyes were smoky. As her friend leaned forward, she parted her lips even more, put her hand on his leg, and they kissed deeply and passionately.

Kimberly sighed.

"They're going to have to move out of here and find a bedroom," Lance said.

Kimberly clasped one of the crystals on her necklace, took a sip of wine, and looked out over the water.

"Hello, people," Nick said. He pulled out a chair and sat down.

"Seen Mike?" Lance asked.

Nick jabbed a thumb over his shoulder. "He and Ron are parking. Saw them as I came in." He caught the waitress's eye, pointed to Lance's beer, and held up a forefinger. Then he sat back in his chair and eyed Lance's T-shirt. It had a picture of Lance and the legend "Young Stud" across the front.

"Modest," he said dryly.

"I got you one that goes with it."

Nick did not respond.

"How's everybody?" Ron said as he and Mike sat down.

Lance was reaching for the paper bag. "I was just telling Nick I bought him a T-shirt. Sort of a birthday present."

Ron laughed, rolled his eyes, and reached for his pipe. Mike almost smiled. He ordered a mineral water and Ron ordered Scotch. Single malt. On the rocks.

Lance unfolded the T-shirt and held it up. On the front was a picture of Nick and the legend "Old Dud."

"Since Nick and I work together, I thought we should have appropriate T-shirts. The young stud and the old dud." Lance pulled the shirt aside and leaned over the table. "You all realize he turned forty yesterday."

"Happy birthday," Ron said, holding up his Scotch.

Nick looked at Lance and shook his head. "You the craziest sumbitch I ever saw," he said.

"Happy birthday, *jefe*," Lance said. He looked

around the table. "Want the waitresses to come over and sing 'Happy Birthday'?"

"Try it and I'll bust you back to uniform," Nick said. He was alarmed. The last thing he wanted was waitresses standing over him singing.

"I wanted to buy everybody a drink and to thank you for all your good work," he said.

"I want a medal," Lance said.

Ron laughed.

"The Doctor made bond," Nick said. "He'll go to trial. We got the goods on him. Unless we get an absolutely screwed-up jury, he'll be convicted on trafficking charges. We can't prove the homicides, so he won't get much time and he'll probably spend it in one of those country-club minimum-security prisons." Nick looked at Ron. "What will happen on the seizures?"

Ron blew a stream of smoke toward the ceiling, pursed his lips, and did not answer for a moment. "The evidence is clear and overwhelming that those houses in western Broward were used to further his smuggling activities. They will be seized by the government and sold at public auction."

He looked around. No one appeared to be listening. When Ron began talking again, he did not move his lips. Sound was coming out but his lips were not moving—the sure mark of a man who has worked undercover many times. "The IRS is looking into his offshore bank accounts, trying to identify them. He's got money in the Turks and Caicos Islands, Bahamas, Panama, and Liechtenstein. They think he might have accounts in Switzerland too. They're trying to find them."

He took another puff from his pipe. "I think the Doctor is going to wind up with a lot less money. He will be under close surveillance for years. He jaywalks, and somebody's gonna bag him. He's marked."

Mike grunted in satisfaction. "What about his buddies?"

Ron nodded. "As I understand it . . ." He paused and looked at Kimberly. "Your contacts there are better than mine, so help me out. I'm told they cut him loose, just as you predicted, Nick. Denied knowing him. Denied any knowledge of his activities or of assisting him in any fashion."

Kimberly nodded. "We gave hard data to DOJ and they passed it along to State. You know how that is. State ignored it. Said our close and special relationship with Israel is too valuable to jeopardize over a deal that, even if it were true, is now over, and its leader going to jail."

"There are times when I wish for the old days," Lance said. "Back when some guy like the Doctor would disappear. Just disappear." He looked at Nick. "I personally don't know of any situations like that; I've just heard of them," he explained.

"I don't think society wants us to be a bunch of Dirty Harrys," Nick said.

Lance shook his head in disagreement. "People are so fed up with drugs and what drugs are doing to their homes and schools and communities, they don't care what you do as long as you get the scumbags off the streets. Everybody but fuzzy-thinking federal judges and wimpy editorial writers wants to shoot the bastards out of the sky."

"I don't believe that. And I won't allow any of my people to behave that way."

Lance held up his hands in surrender. "Hey, *jefe.* Nobody's doing that. I'm just telling you how I think people feel today."

Nick was silent for a moment. After the load of cocaine had been seized at one of the Doctor's houses, the sheriff was contacted. He came out and personally arrested the Doctor. Trailing along for the arrest were a half-dozen reporters. The next day the sheriff was on the front page of the Fort Lauderdale *News.* He was the lead story on the six-o'clock news at both Fort Lauderdale and Miami television stations. The sheriff was astounded at the telephone calls and telegrams from local citizens who congratulated him on being the brains behind the arrest of the most successful cocaine

smuggler in America. Not since the end of the Bimini
case a year earlier had the sheriff seen such a universally favorable outpouring of support and approval.
He knew Nick was responsible. And he decided not to
fire the head of the narcotics squad. He hadn't made
up his mind about Cunningham. He would have fired
him, but in his heart of hearts he was a bit afraid of
the wacky young narc.

Nick knew how close he had been to being axed. To
him, a professional cop's job should not be so precari-
ous. All he wanted to do was catch dopers. And he
wanted to do it without having to worry that a gun-shy
and treacherous boss might fire him in a capricious
moment. He wanted support from his boss. He wanted
somebody who would stand behind him all the way.
Because the sheriff would never do that, Nick had
made up his mind about a decision he had been wres-
tling with for weeks.

Nick looked slowly around the table. He had been
through a lot with these people. Now it all was changing. A quick and unexpected flash of sadness washed
over him. He shrugged. Such emotions made him uncomfortable. He looked at Mike. The tall, quiet, shy
man was the most aggressive pilot at the Air Branch.
He had received a promotion and was being transferred
up to Jacksonville. It was a good time to leave. The
Air Branch was going to hell. A minimum-security
prison was being installed at Homestead Air Force
Base adjacent to the Air Branch. About sixty percent
of the inmates would be there on drug charges. They
would be roaming around the base and could get on a
pay phone every time they saw a Customs aircraft
taxiing for a launch.

And Ron. Good old Ron. The wise old man. His
best contact at DEA. The wizard. The guy who knew
as much about people as he knew about high-tech
goodies. Now Ron was retiring. His time was up.
After twenty-five years on The Job, Ron was becoming a security consultant.

Kimberly had stopped smoking and had a new look

of confidence in her eyes. Nick had noticed that she no longer wore the multiple necklaces of crystals every day. This morning Nick had overheard her on the telephone talking with her ex-husband. There was, for the first time, no defensiveness in her voice. She went head-to-head against Pete. Finally she told him, in a voice that was full and strong and confident, "I don't need your criticisms. You're wrong. You're trying to assuage your guilt by criticizing me, and I'm tired of it. I won't put up with it anymore. Don't call me again. If you have any questions about Jonathan, write me a letter." She paused and then in exasperation at whatever it was Pete said in response, said, "That's ridiculous. All you were in our marriage was a . . . a . . . sperm donor."

She slammed down the phone and looked up to see Nick smiling at her.

"I can't believe I did that," she said. Her voice trembled. She looked at the telephone as if expecting it to react in some way. Then she looked back at Nick, laughed, and shook her head.

Nick nodded in approval. "You did it," he said.

Kimberly was going to be okay. She was a brilliant intelligence analyst. She deserved, more than any other person, most of the credit for arresting the Doctor.

And Lance. Fruitcake city. Loony tunes. Rarely had a serious thought unless it was about dopers. But the guy was fearless. More brass than an Army band. Loyal. And the best undercover narc who ever walked.

Nick took a deep breath and looked down at the table. "I decided to take the job in Naples," he said. "I'm leaving the BSO. Turned in my resignation a half-hour ago."

For a moment there was stunned silence as everyone at the table stared at Nick.

"Why?" Kimberly asked in a voice of painful disbelief.

"Simple. I want to be a police officer. I want to put people in jail without having to worry that I might get fired any day. I want to work with real cops, not TV cops."

No one spoke. Then Lance said, "They got a lot of bad guys over in Naples?"

"Enough to go around."

"Need any help?"

"A lot."

"Okay," Lance said. "You're too old to go over there by yourself. I'll come along to help you cross the street and to do all the real work." He leaned across the table toward Nick, sniffed loudly, and laughed. "It's that shaving lotion, you handsome devil. Keep wearing it and I'll follow you anywhere."

"One day I'm going to sign papers and have you sent away."

"As long as you come with me."

Nick turned to Ron. "Can I call on you, Ron?"

Lance leaned back and waved his hands. In mock seriousness he said, "Nick, the guy's a secular humanist."

Nick's eyes widened momentarily. Then he looked at Lance and said, "Why don't you wait outside?"

Lance laughed.

A very serious Ron shook Nick's hand. "Anytime. All you have to do is call."

"Mike, you'll be up in Jax. I'm sure we'll be working together again."

"Better believe it, guy." He reached across the table to shake hands. "Good luck over there."

Nick turned to Kimberly. "You'll be okay. You're good at your job. Very good." He paused. "And you got a job with me if you ever want it."

Kimberly was surprised. "The county has intel positions?"

"It's my office. I need an analyst. You're the best. The job is yours if you want it. I'll pay you more money than you're making here."

"My blood-sugar level is up from all this," Lance said. "I don't know if I'm going to get diabetes or throw up." He held up his empty beer can for the waitress to see, spun his forefinger around signifying another round, then turned to Nick. "Okay, *jefe*," he said. "We jailed Doctor Death. Who's next? Who do America's new cult heroes take down next?"

"Ever hear of Everglades City?"

"Little fishing village in the Ten Thousand Islands. Sure. Rough bunch of people over there."

Nick stared at Lance and did not continue.

Lance's eyes danced and his grin broadened in anticipation. "You mean the first thing you're going to do is take on a town? The meanest bunch of fishermen in Florida?" Lance contorted his face and shook his hands in mock fear. "An entire town?"

Nick nodded. "The whole town."

Acknowledgments

Several people at U.S. Customs deserve special thanks. At Air Ops East, my longtime friend Jim Dingfelder not only allowed me to fly in the Citation for several weeks, but somehow got me aboard a Blackhawk helicopter for a drug bust in the Bahamas. Harry Betz was indefatigable in his assistance. Bill Perry, Robby Viator, Larry Karson, and John Stevenson made my research much easier with their cooperation. The one-and-only Mad Dog told me of the good old days. Most of all, I want to thank the pilots and crews with whom I flew.

Up at the Broward County Sheriff's Office, Dale Owens provided a helicopter tour of the county. Nigel "Houdini" Fullick, the greatest undercover narc ever, straightened his tie and told me how it was on the street. Pete Charette, assistant special agent in charge of the Miami office of the U.S. Drug Enforcement Administration, explained how the south Florida drug world is put together. Various officials of Her Majesty's Government in the Turks and Caicos Islands were most helpful; however, as is customary among British civil servants, they do not wish to be identified. Paul Mann, Washington Bureau Chief of *Aviation Week and Space Technology*, dug through back issues of that splendid magazine to provide stories about Customs aircraft.

Nathalie DuPree demonstrated the selflessness that has made her the den mother of Atlanta writers. At

Jackie and Lee Walburn's cabin on the Oostanaula River, and at James and Shirley Blankenship's cabin on Lake George, I began putting all of this together. Finally, thanks to The Muffin, who continues to hold it all together.

ABOUT THE AUTHOR

ROBERT CORAM has written about drug smuggling for more than a decade. He was twice nominated for the Pulitzer Prize while a reporter for *The Atlanta Constitution*. His articles have appeared in many national magazines, including *The New Yorker*. For the past eight years, Coram has been a part-time journalism instructor at Emory University. He lives in Atlanta.